THE LIVES OF

*This book is for all the Ettas
I have known:*

*my mother, Geri, Karen, Denny,
Barbara and Betty*

and for my father.

1

*Life is not so mathematically
idiotic as only to permit the
big to eat the small. . . .*

—*Strindberg*

•

THE FIRST INTERVIEW
WITH RILEY CHANCE

OCTOBER 25, 1980

3:00 P.M.

I swear to God I didn't kill that black woman. I know she was in my arms when she died, and I had no business taking her out of that place—but she was probably going to die anyway. You know what sort of shape she was in. She looked nearly eighty, and she wasn't even fifty yet. How long could she have lasted? She might have died at exactly the same time without me moving her. And that's all I did. I moved her. So while I had her she died.

You may wonder about my intent—why I carried her out, got her in the cab. I don't know if I can tell you that. I don't have any secret pathological motives or anything—it's just that I'm not sure you'll believe me, and if you don't believe me, then you'll be thinking I must be trying to hide something. That's all I need. Then I look guilty of something, and when it gets to trial, I'm a murderer. You see why I'm so afraid.

The cab driver will probably testify. I was pretty scared when I got in the cab, and he said, "What's wrong with her?" He had one of those caps on that cabbies wear in all the movies—you never expect to see them in real life (at least not in Champaign, Illinois). And his nose was flat, with tiny slits for nostrils. I wondered how he could breathe, but then I figured at least everything was pretty well filtered for him. His eyes looked like olives. He watched me put her on the back seat, and then he said, "What's wrong with her?" He'll testify, all right.

I told him there was nothing wrong with her. I pushed her legs up a bit, and sat at her feet.

"Where're you going?" he said. I could tell he was nervous.

"I don't really know, yet," I said. It was cold outside, and I wanted to get her to some place warm and comfortable. I couldn't take her home right away. I just wanted to get her out of that hospital. It was a horrible place. Just horrible. Especially for a woman in her condition.

The cabbie put his arm up on the seat and turned his nose around to look at her. "Is she alive?" he said. You should have heard his voice. He sounded like he was talking with a tiny vibrator in his mouth.

"Of course she's alive," I said. I put my hand on her arm, felt her move slightly. "I don't want her to die," I told him, and I felt my eyes beginning to burn.

"Well, you've got to go somewhere," the cab driver said.

"Can't we just drive around?"

"You got money?"

"A little."

"You'll need quite a lot to just ride around." His nostrils opened slightly, and I thought of time-lapse photography and Venus flytraps.

"I could take her to my parents' house," I said, but I was only talking to myself. I heard the cabbie let out a slight but high whimper. "It's all right," I told him. "She's somebody I used to know. I'm trying to help her."

"Where do your parents live?"

"On Green Street."

"Near the college?"

"Near there, yes." She moved slightly, let out a soft moan. That's probably why the cabbie thought I was choking her.

"Why don't you go to a hospital?" he said, leaning back in the seat and adjusting his position. You'd have thought he was sitting on thorns or something.

"She was just in a hospital," I said.

He shook his head, and put the car in gear. "She was in a drunk tank."

"Same thing."

We pulled out into the lights. I sat back and looked at her. I could not believe it was really *her* when I first saw her. But looking at her in the cab I knew it was. It was her. My father used to say,

"Such are the ironies of life." He said that whenever anything happened he couldn't explain to me. And I always thought I knew what he meant until that night in the cab.

There really is a design, you know. It isn't random at all. Earth has plot, and it's a long story. I think it's a pretty sad story too. I suppose that's why we try to think of it as a series of events with causes and effects and all that—a random series of events that are connected by things we like to think of as causes. But even those, if you go back far enough, ultimately seem random. They *seem* that way, but they're not. I'm not talking about God, either.

Maybe when I get out of here I should take a class in philosophy at the college or something. I know more about life than anyone. More than you. More than anyone. That's part of my story. It's also the part I'm not sure I can tell yet.

I guess I could tell it to you, and if you don't believe me we could decide on some other defense. But I think it's one of those "ironies" my father talked about—if you don't believe me and I have to make up something.

I hate this city. I hate Illinois. Even this time of year. Look out that window. Ever see a sky more empty of color in your life? And it's not even November yet. I don't know if I can tell you everything with a sky like that. It makes me think of the horrible times. The horrible times.

I guess this is a horrible time, isn't it? Look at my hand. See that? See how smooth the skin is there, how normal. See how it covers every knuckle? Once I got this hand caught on fire, and all the skin was burned black. It peeled off like the outer skin of a dried onion.

I know, there's no scar. That's because it didn't happen to this hand. It didn't happen to the other one either.

This is going to be harder than I thought.

I can't tell you about her unless you let me start at the beginning. I have to go back further than you can imagine to get it all told. If you'll just have a little patience and bear with me. . . .

ROBERT BAUSCH

I've been here before. I mean way before. I never knew it until a few years ago—when I was fifteen. I had no idea until that time. We lived in Chicago, and I just believed I was like everyone else —except I did worry about things my mother thought were rather odd. For a reason I wasn't aware of, I hated black and white photographs—I used to get sick to my stomach if I saw one—and I didn't like anybody to mention the word "cancer" when I was around. My mother used to talk about getting some help for me, but she never did. I went along being her "odd child" until I realized everything—that I'd been here before and all. It was a sort of a shock. I got real sick for a while.

But that's not the beginning. I have to start at the beginning.

The first time I was here I lived in Pennsylvania with a man named Benjamin Ezra and his wife. I never have been able to remember her name, so I just made one up after a while. You can probably tell what I remember of her by the name I gave her: I call her Ogra.

If you want, I won't tell you all of this. I really don't feel like it, you know. But you said I should tell you the truth, that I should tell you everything. I should start at the beginning, right? I didn't kill that old woman, and I'm not in any way responsible for her death either. She just happened to die while I had her. That's all. And the only way I can explain what she was doing with me is to tell you everything.

The world tells you to look at it a certain way, and that's the way you see it. Sure. I expected that. Isn't surprising. Everybody sees it that way. But you go to Wilkes-Barre and see if you can't find the Demon Match Company. Find out if there wasn't an employee named Benjamin Ezra who worked there from 1886 to 1905. See if he didn't have a wife and two children, and if he didn't get his brains knocked out in a union riot in 1905. Go ahead. And remember the name of the man who killed him. When you get back, I'll tell you his name and I'll describe him for you, because I saw him do it.

Maybe I need to tell someone about this, get it out of my head. Maybe that's a part of it. So what do I do? You want me to make something up? I need time for that, I don't think that well on my feet. But I thought you wanted to know. I thought you said I should tell you only the truth. It might do you good to hear it.

This is a gray, sort of end of the line, everything in its place and already discovered world. There's nothing new, right? Isn't that what you think? I've lived through the end of one century and I know. Everybody thinks the end is coming, or that there isn't anything new or valuable anymore and the end *ought* to come. People get bored, go to science fairs and Back to Nature camps, get carried away by their own ailments and their own private crimes. Everybody looking for something new, something completely new. Believe me, the end of a century is a terrible thing. I wonder why people think anything as big as the world has to end on an even number? I know, I know. We've incurred the wrath of God and this thing has got to go in all its tortured beauty. But think about it for a minute. What would He replace it with? What could possibly be more interesting? Man was created in the image of God according to the Bible. And I've never met a man who could take his TV out into the back yard and destroy the son of a bitch. The world is like a TV: it's the only thing God has for entertainment. And it doesn't really matter how awful we get.

We're running out of a lot of things, but that's a sign of change —not necessarily a sign of the end. A man doesn't necessarily die because he loses the use of his legs. Right? Things change for him, sure, and it's hard to get used to. But does he die?

I was paralyzed once. I couldn't move any part of my body but the mouth. And I lasted a long time. An eternity. Believe me, I have a better idea what eternity is than you, or anyone else. It's a terrible thing too. Being paralyzed was a temporary eternity. Think of that.

If you want the truth you'll just have to listen. Even if what I tell you isn't true, you might enjoy the story. It might entertain you at least.

I don't remember much of my early childhood in Pennsylvania. I had an older sister named Sara, who had red hair and freckles, and who couldn't make it home without somebody throwing something at her, or laughing about her tall thin body and great red freckles. She took care of me—held me whenever I felt afraid or whenever I hurt myself, and she pinched my cheeks when she wanted to make a point, or get my attention.

We lived in the "factory yard." I think that's what they called it. My father worked the splint making machine in the factory, and my mother worked in the laundry. The factory owned everything. Or I should say, Mr. Silver owned everything, because he owned the factory. My father hated Silver, and so did everybody else who lived in the cabins along our street. I don't remember the first time I saw old man Silver, but I got to know him pretty well later on. He was a fat sloppy man who wore clothing one or two sizes too large —as if he could hide the great bulges in his flesh with loose, dangling cloth. He looked like a circus animal that poked its head through the top of the tent and ran away with it. On Sundays he would walk around among the cabins, smiling and nodding his pear-shaped head at everybody: "How are you this morning, Mrs. Harrison?" "Great day for the children, eh, Mrs. Yerbich?" He pronounced it "cheeldreen," as if his face was too crowded with cheeks to get words out with any air in them. He wore a black bowler hat to cover his bare skull—a skull that looked like a map of South America had been hand painted on it—and he carried a cane that he tapped along the dusty ground as he went. The ladies smiled at him, and when he had passed they talked in whispers about what would be the most satisfactory way for him to die. They all wanted him to perish in some sort of violent stillness—a death like the death of a tree, perhaps. They all agreed it should take a long time, and that he should feel it in every layer, every leaf and limb.

My father worked in the factory six days a week and half a day on Sunday. Ogra did the same thing in the laundry—people who made matches back then got awful dirty with phosporous, and Ogra had to clean just about everybody's clothing every day. Back then, you had to wreck your life in order to make a living.

I guess the first thing I remember clearly is Sara, my sister, coming in the front door one day, her socks around her ankles, her hair blown by the wind across her face, and tears in her eyes.

I guess I was eight or nine, and she was near thirteen. I was born in 1895, and this was 1903 or 1904. I still don't have all this clear in my memory.

"Where you been?" my father said. I don't think he really cared, though. He just sort of hung around the place. Ogra was the beast in the tiny little unkept rooms of that house. But there was something about the old man that made him an enemy too. I never truly hated him that much, actually—but Sara did. Sara hated him as completely as human beings do anything, and although I think I know why now, I didn't really understand it then.

On that day he said, "Where you been?" Sara looked shocked that he said something to her. She said, "Walking." She cried so silently all the time you had to be looking at her to know she was doing it. I went over to her.

"Leave me alone." Her voice was all broken, and quiet like a cat when it dreams. She crossed the floor and went into her room. I followed along. She tried to close the door on me, but I went through too fast. She stood there holding the door, looking at me with those green eyes. Her front teeth were too large, and I guess she really was sort of ugly.

"Please, Kenny," she said. That was my name. Kenny Ezra.

"What's the matter?" I said.

"I hate myself." She closed the door.

"Why?"

"I just do." She cried, sat on the bed.

"I don't hate you," I said.

She put her arms around me. She smelled of tar and ice—an odd combination of odors that made me love her and want to be held by her. I told her again that I didn't hate her.

"I'm ugly," she said.

"Don't cry."

"I'm ugly."

"So am I. I'm not crying." But, in truth, I was. I couldn't help it. Sara was the only person in that house who knew how important it was for me to be held by somebody—and she seemed to know when I needed it too.

"They all pick on me." She pulled my head against her breast. I knew who "they" were: the factory boys—the ones her age and older who worked with my father.

"Tell Daddy," I said.

She looked at me. "No." Sometimes her eyes could freeze in her face like knots in wood.

"I hate them," I said. I got really angry, and I think I got my first taste of helplessness. I recognized it then, I guess.

Sara lay on the bed and sobbed. I remember the way her socks wrapped around her ankles, and the tiny hairs in the calves of her legs.

My father came in. "What's the matter with her?" He came and put his big hard-boned hands on her, pulled her up. "What's got into you?"

"Don't," she said.

"Tell me."

I thought he might do something if she would only tell him. I went over and rested my head on his hip, thinking maybe he really was going to make everything all right. He put his hand on my head.

"I wish I was dead," Sara said.

He took his hand from my head and in one motion swatted Sara over her right ear. She went back on the bed as if she were a blanket he'd just thrown there.

"Don't you ever say that," he said.

"Daddy," she cried. She wept into her hands, her ankles crossed neatly over the edge of the bed. My father pulled me out, still against his hip. I felt like I'd hit her too. I saw her ear sticking out of her red hair, her thumbs twitching as she cried.

"We'll leave her to cry," the old man said. *We'd* hit her all right. He made me a part of it, and I didn't have the courage to let go of him and go to her. I wish I had. Even now it bothers me that I went out with him and left her there.

So that's sort of the beginning. It's the first thing I remember that has any sort of chronology. Maybe I should remember it as my first betrayal, because it was always Sara and me against Ogra and the old man.

Sara. Sweet Sara. She had this quiet way of looking at everything. She was as lonesome as anyone I've ever known, but she
lived each day as if something miraculous might happen; as if she
might suddenly fly up out of the world into some blue cloud. I
could never get into that mind of hers, find out what went on
there. I never understood how she came to know the things she
knew, or what made her value the things she loved. She never told
me anything secret about her life—except the time she told me she
hated herself. I remember going out of that room with my father,
feeling like a part of his body, as if I had slapped her too. There
was an old cedar chest under the front window, and I went and
sat there, watched my father get a bottle out of a metal locker he
had by the kitchen basin. He went to the table, which sat in the
middle of the room, lit a lamp, and set to drinking. Ogra was in
the next room, their room, with the door closed. She may have
been asleep, or drinking. I never knew when she closed that door.
Sometimes she stayed in there through supper, and Sara would fix
something for me and the old man to eat. My father never said
a word until he was finished eating. Then he would get up, take
another drink, and go into the room with Ogra. They'd sometimes
get to laughing behind that door, and Sara and I'd stand there in
puzzlement. We couldn't understand what either one of them
might find amusing.

Anyway, my father took to the bottle that night, and I sat on
the cedar chest feeling awful for betraying Sara.

"What's the matter with you?" my father said.

He looked dead in the half light from the kerosene lamp. A head
shaped like a potato, and skin the same texture.

"You gonna cry too?"

"No."

"Well, what's wrong?"

"You hit her."

"She's a bitch. They're all bitches." He swallowed a gulp of the
whiskey.

"She's sad," I said.

"So am I. Everybody's sad."

I wanted to ask him why, but he stared at his glass. I heard Sara whimpering behind the door. Outside the wind began to push things. I watched the white sky—a sky much like that one out there right now—and wished I was something else.

"Work tomorrow," the old man said.

"I'm hungry."

He picked up the bottle and came over to me. "Here, have some of this." He had a round face, with black hairs on it. A thin irregular pattern of black hair on the top of his head. I remember his belly, the way it hung over the brown belt of his trousers, and the cracking noise his ankles made when he moved.

"No," I said.

"It's probably all you're going to get tonight." He sat next to me, letting out a growl. "My goddamned knees."

"Why does Sara hate herself?"

"What?"

"Sara hates herself."

"She's just going into woman problems, that's all."

"What are those?"

"They bleed."

"They do?"

"Not so you can see it." He raised the bottle, made a loud gulp. I saw his throat open and close. "She'll get over it. Then she'll plague every male that knows her."

"Even me?"

"Even you."

"Why?"

"Because you *don't* bleed. They never get over that."

We sat there for a while and I watched him drink. The whiskey looked like kerosene. Then Sara came out of her room and went into the kitchen, and he sort of straightened up. He looked around the room and sighed, shook his head. "Work tomorrow," he said. Then he got up and went into the room where Ogra was. Just before he closed the door he hollered back to Sara, "I don't think I want anything to eat tonight, honey." Sara didn't answer him.

I think I went into the kitchen, found it too dark in there, and then I came back into the room, saw Sara standing in the dark, staring out a white window at the moon. And I said, "What are you looking at?"

"Nothing."

"The moon, huh."

"Nothing."

"I'm sorry," I said.

"For what?" She turned around, but I couldn't see her face.

"I hate Dad for hitting you."

"So do I," she whispered.

"Are you bleeding?"

"He didn't hit me that hard."

"No. I mean the other thing."

"What?"

"Are you bleeding because of the other thing?"

"What?"

"You know."

"Not now. I'm not bleeding now."

"But do you?"

"Yes."

"Does it hurt?"

"I hate it. But it doesn't hurt."

"I hate it too, then."

"It won't happen to you."

She was wrong about that. I bled, all right. I bled for her too.

"I bleed here," she said, pointing at herself. "Once a month."

"And it doesn't hurt?"

"No." She glanced out the window, as if she were looking for someone to contradict her. We moved back into the room toward the table with the lamp. The coal stove made a clicking noise, and I thought of the stories Ogra told us about little children being burned black in coal stoves for misbehaving.

Sara asked me if I was hungry, and I told her I was. She smiled then, a look in her eyes that seemed to vibrate the orange light in the room.

"I'll make you some bread and jam?"

"OK."

I watched her thin legs as she moved with the lamp toward the kitchen. I saw the light move the shadows on the walls, and got up to follow her.

"Do you bleed very much?"

"It's just a little."

"And Ogra? She bleeds?"

"Yes." She cut a piece of bread and went to the cupboard for the jam. "Only women bleed regularly."

"Is that why the boys make fun of you?"

She spread the jam on the bread without answering me.

"I'm sorry," I said.

She came to me, put her arms around me and squeezed my neck.

"I hate everyone but you," I said.

"Don't, now," she whispered. "Don't do that." She cried so silently.

When I finished eating, I told her I had to go to the privy. She walked out there with me, holding my hand. The privies were in front of the cabins, half dug into the dirt there. We descended three wooden steps to get to them. Each privy was made of block and felt cooler inside because of the sweating stone. There was one privy for every five cabins, so sometimes you had to wait a considerable time before you could use one. That night Sara and I stood outside, in the near dark, watching the other cabins send streams of white smoke in lazy columns toward the rising moon.

When I was coming out of the privy, Sara said, "I don't want to stay here anymore."

"I'm done," I said.

"No, I mean here. In this place."

I wondered then if anybody really loved the world. It all seemed such a lasting ache. We went back into the dimly lit kitchen, stood by the window there watching the sky outside as if we were waiting for a tornado to touch down and change everything for us.

"It will be winter soon," Sara said.

"I know."

"I hate it when it's cold." She put her hand on my shoulder and then blew out the kerosene lamp. "Let's go to bed."

"Can I sleep with you?"

"OK."

She went to the coal stove, opened the black door. "Think there's enough in here for tomorrow morning?"

"It might go out."

"It's too warm for this thing." She closed the door. I wanted her to put more coal in it. It was her job, and this time of year, she never seemed to get it right. Either she put too much in and got the cabin so hot everybody's nose burned, or she didn't put in enough and the fire went out, leaving Ogra without any cooking surface in the morning. She got in the most trouble when the fire went out, and the fire she showed me that night seemed far too weak and yellow to last the time to morning. I didn't ever want her to be hurt and cry again, especially if I was there to see it.

"Put some more in," I said.

"No. Now let's go to bed."

I went in her room, slept next to her that night. Near morning, I went out and put more coal in the stove. Or I tried to anyway. As I was placing a piece of it into the back of the burner, my sleeve caught fire. That's how I burned my hand. I screamed, ran to my sister's room. Ogra came out of the other room, her hands clutching the front of her nightdress as if there were a mound of flesh there.

"What's going on?"

Sara screamed. She wrapped the corner of her blanket around my hand and the fire went out. It still seemed to be burning inside my hand, but the flame disappeared with the blanket.

Ogra said something to Sara, pulled me away. I couldn't hear very well because I was crying so loud. Ogra looked at my blackened hand, then dropped it as if the sight of it sickened her.

"What were you doing?" I heard that. She screamed it.

"Putting coal on the fire," I said.

She looked at Sara, and I knew I had betrayed my sister again.

"Putting coal on the fire," Ogra said. She never took her eyes off Sara.

"It was too warm last night," Sara pleaded.

"Look what you've done," Ogra said. She grabbed my arm, raised my hand up waving it in front of Sara's eyes. I saw tears there, and I hated myself.

"You little beast," Ogra screamed. Then she slapped Sara across the face.

"Don't!" I said.

She pushed me away. "Get out of here." She led me out and closed the door. I sat outside the door, crying, holding my hand, the same hand that Sara had held, and listened to Ogra giving it to her. And that is my first memory of that life, and of Sara. I never was much good for her.

•

THE SECOND INTERVIEW

OCTOBER 27, 1980

1:00 P.M.

That year I burned my hand was a bad one. The winter came in like an unexpected train, and even the smoke from the houses seemed to freeze when the wind hit it. Sara forgave me the transgression with the coal, and she and I began to gang up on the old man and Ogra. Sara was pretty smart about tactics—a sort of unorthodox field commander in the family war. She wouldn't hit and run—she'd hit and *stay*—sometimes taking the most extraordinary risks. "I want to see the fun," she'd say. Ogra and Daddy didn't know what to make of it. They blamed her for some of the mishaps she engineered, but most of the time they didn't think she'd hang around if she caused the mess, so they'd look elsewhere. You'd think they might blame me, I know. But they didn't. I hung around too. My father began to think the house was haunted.

I remember Sara's first maneuver was in the privy. She had me watch for Ogra and the old man while she caught one of the yard cats. Then she placed it down in the muck of the privy, without so much as a smile.

"Will he live?" I asked.

"Long enough," Sara said. "Daddy'll get him out, once he finds him there."

We were huddled by the door, late in the afternoon, watching steam rise up out of the privy. It was cold out there, but neither one of us made a move to go inside. I had my hand wrapped in yellow cloth.

"I wish we could be right here when he finds it," Sara said.

The cat started to cry.

"We gotta give him something to keep him quiet," Sara whispered. "Get some of that salted ham."

I went in the kitchen and cut a piece of the ham my father won playing horseshoes the week before. If he'd known I was taking some of it he would've found some way for me not to ever forget it. He probably would have referred me to Ogra. Like I said, she was the one we had to watch out for.

Sara put the piece of ham down in there, and the cat got quiet after a while. I guess he figured he might as well eat. There was no way he was going to get out of there without help.

We watched a while longer, until the wind started to slap us around. We went inside as if we were going to murder somebody.

Then we sort of forgot about the cat. Or at least I did.

About an hour later, one of my father's friends came strolling by. His name was Bailey, I think. Something like that. He had no family, lived by himself near the end of the first row of cabins in the yard. He was as wide as the breast of a cow, and I think he was older than my father, although he acted like most of the company boys. He didn't seem to have a neck, and I remember the way hair rose up out of the back of his shirt, as if it started somewhere in the middle of his back. Anyway, he came walking up to the door whistling a tune.

"Your daddy home?" he said, when Sara opened the door.

"He's in the bedroom with Momma."

Bailey came on in, breathing out a little sigh to let us know he wasn't nervous or anxious about just walking in like that. When the old man came out he looked as if he'd been sleeping.

"Thought I'd drink some of your whiskey," Bailey said.

"You mean you dreamed it."

Bailey laughed. Then he cleared his throat and said, "You going to the meeting tonight?"

Daddy sat at the table and rubbed the top of his head. "I don't know. I don't know."

"I'm going." Bailey moved to the table and sat down too. The old man looked at the two of us children standing by the door watching them. "Go on, get out of here," he said.

We went into Sara's room and closed the door. But when we leaned against it we could still hear them talking. I didn't really care, though. I just wanted to hear if one of them got up to use the privy. I think we were hoping it would be the old man, even though, if we'd thought about it, any one of the people from any of the five cabins sharing our privy might get there before the old man or Ogra. I guess we were optimists, since we believed, for sure, one of them would get there before anybody else and we had the gall to hope it would be the old man.

At the time, I could not have said why he was the enemy, although he did hit Sara that time, and he'd belted me a few times too. I think the problem was that he was never really there. At least that's what bothered me. Even when he occupied space in the room, he wasn't there. He didn't offset Ogra enough. He probably hated her as much as we did, and I bet he was just as afraid of her. But he never made a move to join us, and when she went on one of her rampages, he just sat there and watched—as if he were at a cockfight or something. More than once I caught him laughing. Sometimes I wonder, even now, what he was proud of. I guess the idea of a union got him excited—he went to enough of those meetings before the trouble started. Maybe Sara got me thinking of him as the enemy. Like I said, she really hated him. And she had to stand there whenever he wanted to put his hands on her. He touched her far more than he did me. Sometimes, when Ogra screamed at him, he'd get up and go over to Sara and put his arms around her. To this day I can't get the look on Sara's face out of my mind, nor the sound of my father's voice as he held her. "There's one woman in this house," he'd say. And Ogra'd push him aside and let Sara have it.

I wish I could see a picture of them now, just to see if they really were as I remember them. I guess I want to see a picture of me too. Maybe a family portrait, the four of us staring blankly out of that black and white place. Except, you see, it would *have* to be a black and white photograph, and like I told you, I can't stand to look at those. I guess that qualifies as another one of those ironies.

Anyway, after Bailey came, we forgot about the cat again. We listened to Bailey drinking and talking about Mr. Silver. Bailey did most of the talking at first, trying to convince my father that Silver needed to be "taught a lesson." I didn't know what he was talking about first. Then I heard my father say, "He might listen to reason." This made Bailey mad. He yelled so loud I wasn't sure I heard him right. He said something about a union, then something about "rights," and then he said the word "blood." I heard my father say, "Organization takes time," and then Bailey laughed. He laughed very loud and called my father a coward.

"We got to wait," the old man said. Then I heard his chair move.

"I'm sick of all these secret meetings where nothing happens," Bailey yelled.

"We got to wait," the old man said again. His voice was getting distant.

"He's going for it," I said to Sara.

She came off the bed, where she had been making mountains out of the blankets, and put her head against the door. That frozen look came into her eyes again. We heard the door open and close.

"I hope the cat doesn't make any noise until he sits down," Sara whispered.

"How do you know he's going to sit down?" I said.

"I hope he does that too."

"Maybe he—" I started, but then we heard a scream outside. It was a high sort of last resort scream. I couldn't tell for sure if it was my father or the cat.

Sara said, "Sit on the bed, and I'll tell you a story." She didn't even laugh. And she should have. She was extremely lucky in her first strike—the cat jumped at just the right time and tried to grab onto what, for him, must have looked like something to play with, if not his salvation. My father said he thought a snake got him.

For a month after the cat episode, Sara washed the old man's drawers in salt water. I don't know if it made any impression on him although he did scratch himself a little more than usual during that time. The only thing we didn't like about getting him that way was that we *didn't* get Ogra, and Ogra laughed. She got a lot of pleasure out of it, and we didn't want her to have any of that.

Sara followed her around, trying to think of her next foray, I suppose. Ogra was not easy to get. She was not the sort of person who got involved in very much, and you can't really break cover against someone who lies in bed all the time. But Sara stalked her in the late afternoons and Sunday evenings. I knew she'd come up with something.

One day she came to me all excited and asked me to do her a favor.

"What?"

She held out a bottle of perfume, half empty, and said, "Pee in this for me."

"How'd you get that?"

"I crept into her room while she was sleeping." Sara said this with absolute triumph, as if she had made it through the lines and brought the boys back.

I had a sailor's hat that my father got for himself and never wore. I went and got it and gave it to Sara.

"Put this on," I said.

"Why?"

"Put it on."

She rested it on the top of her head, looking up at it as if a bird had landed there. I went to my chest and pulled out my secret policeman's badge—a piece of scrap metal I found in the yard—and I stuck it in the brim of the white hat, stepped back and saluted her.

"Victory," I said.

She bowed, and the piece of metal fell to the floor. She picked it up and handed me the bottle. "Pee," she said. I think there was a smile struggling for a soft spot around her mouth.

"I don't know," I said. It began to hit me what she was planning. I was beginning not to like this war. "Can't we do something else? It's a great victory that you got that bottle. Let's hide it from her."

"Pee in it."

"Why?"

"She dabs it behind her ears every morning."

"I'm scared."

"There's still perfume in it," Sara said. "Here, smell it."

It smelled like a hatband to me.

"She'll never notice it."

"Why don't *you* pee in it?"

She looked at me, frowning.

"Oh," I said.

"Come on, now. Do it for me." She looked at her hands, and I remembered the way her thumbs twitched when she was crying on the bed after my father hit her, and I remembered how I had betrayed her.

"OK," I said, taking the bottle. I started fooling with the buttons on my pants.

"Not here," she said. "Do it in the privy."

"What if they catch me?"

"Nobody's going to catch you." She took off the sailor hat and put it on my head. "Be a brave little soldier," she said.

I just wanted to get it over with. I took the top off the bottle. "That hole looks awful small."

"That's why you should do it in the privy. You'll have some left over, you know." She took the bottle and put the top back on it, then she put it in my pocket.

"It bulges," I said.

"They won't notice it. Put your hand over it."

"Do we have to do this?"

"It will be a triumph. Don't be afraid. I've got to put the damn thing back in her room when you're done. Think of that."

I went ahead and did it. It was a mess too. I couldn't hit the hole right, and I got it all over myself. I started to cry, but gradually the bottle filled. When I gave it to Sara, she went back out and poured some of it back into the privy, then she shook the bottle and mixed it up real good.

"She'll never know the difference," Sara said.

"Then why do it?"

"I'll know. So will you. And probably so will anyone brave

enough to get close to her." I think I did see a smile then; just a slight one broke through, perhaps. "We're going to need a miracle to get this back in her room."

"I'm not going to do it," I said.

She took the hat off my head. "Put this away somewhere. You're going to need it a lot in the next few days."

That night, Sara slipped a hot piece of coal into the lard bucket that sat next to the stove. I don't know how she did it without burning her hand, but it worked. Within minutes the whole cabin was full of black smoke, and Ogra came running out of her room as if a fox had rousted her. My father got heroic and tried to carry us out, but Sara eluded him and disappeared into the smoke. When she came outside with the rest of us, my father calling her frantically in the darkness, as if he couldn't bear the idea of losing one of his own in a dark fire—a fire that didn't give off any light —there was finally, finally a great wide smile on her face. I knew it was another triumph.

So the war went on. Ogra continued using her perfume, and my father thanked his lucky stars that the great fire was only a smoking lard bucket. (He told everyone it was a "ghost's" fire, that the souls of all the victims of Silver's match factory were crying out for retribution and justice.) For the rest of that year, in between more than one major defeat, Sara moved stealthily through the house, making sorties. She put a thumbtack in the bottom of my father's boot; drowned a ladybug in my mother's hot coffee, put kerosene in the old man's whiskey. She caught a chicken and put it in the bathing tub—it made a mess even the cat couldn't stand the smell of (Ogra made a pet of the cat after the privy episode; I guess she figured anything that got its claws that deep into my father ought to be rewarded)—and Sara continued to stand around and watch the result of each stroke, as if she wore the uniform of the enemy and had no fear of being captured. And of course, even in spite of her triumphs, she got slapped around whenever Ogra got bored, or whenever my father decided to make the comparison between his daughter and his wife. The old man called Sara a "real woman" more than a few times that year, and Ogra's hand swelled up and turned red from smacking Sara's hard, thin bones.

"I'm winning," Sara said one night, holding her cheeks with trembling hands. She knelt on the bed, pounded her fist into the mattress. "I'm winning, damn it. I'm winning."

By that time, I wished more than anything that she would just surrender her sword.

•

THE THIRD INTERVIEW

OCTOBER 28, 1980

11:00 A.M.

I asked my father one day soon after that conversation with Bailey what a union was. He told me it was a holy headache that wouldn't go away. But by the time I asked him that, he was really in it. There were pieces of paper all over the cabin that said: "Workers unite. Stop exploitation and injustice." Nobody really understood what a union was then. I don't think they did, anyway. I think a lot of people went along with it because they knew Mr. Silver was against it, and because it was born with several various phrases all beginning with the word "STOP." Everybody wanted to stop something. Stop the use of phosophorous. Stop the long hours and low pay. Stop child labor.

The use of phosphorous was the big issue. That's what my father talked about most. Phosphorous caused a disease named "phossy jaw," and just about everybody who worked in the factory got it eventually. So many people died in what my father called "bare toothed agony," since the disease rotted the lower jaw until it simply fell away. I remember seeing one old man who had phossy jaw, and I thought then that he'd been chewed by a bear or something. It was awful.

I think the union wouldn't have gotten hold of anyone if it weren't for phossy jaw. My father believed that, anyway. He made speeches in broad daylight near the end, when the union was out in the open and the factory found itself, ironically, ready to ignite. In the beginning, though, there were only the pieces of paper in the house, and a curious change in my father's behavior. He started taking all of us to church. Sara and I hated church. We thought it was a permanent change, and Sara knew she would have to go to work in the factory that summer, which would limit her time to fight the war; once she was in the factory, her only time for striking blows would be Sunday mornings, and she didn't want to have to spend that time walking behind the old man to church, watching everybody nod as we passed.

There were some things about church that I didn't mind, if I were to be honest. I liked the singing and the music. I'd sit next to my father smelling the only clean shirt I ever saw him wear (even when they buried him, my father was wearing a cigar-colored jersey he'd worn to work all those days he was alive). There was something peaceful and normal about those tolerable moments in church—as if there was at least one thing you didn't have to struggle for. So I suppose I only hated church because Sara did. I have to admit I never minded it once I got there. But Sara used to wear herself out just twitching like a snake on the other side of the old man. The preacher kept calling God "the father," and that really must have set her teeth. When we came out of church those Sunday mornings, Sara looked as if she'd been swimming in her clothes, and I couldn't get her to make a sound, utter a single syllable. She walked next to me as if she were a shadow, or a soul; something that escaped from my body to watch over me. It was eerie.

And the old man nodded at everybody on the way home. By then, he was getting fairly popular, since he was one of the earliest union organizers, and a lot of those pieces of paper had his name on them.

I guess the worst thing about a union was all the people who came to our cabin to talk to my father. That's how Sara met Walker Adams, and eventually, how I came to know Mr. Silver.

I was ten or eleven years old, and Sara was nearing fifteen. Walker Adams was one of the factory boys who made fun of Sara all the time—even after he started coming to the house. Those people who came always came late, and Adams was usually among the first. He was young, probably not much older than twenty, and he had a hard angular face, a face with corners in it. His skin was as smooth as a postman's visor, and nearly as dark. He had black hair all over the top of his head, and green eyes that seemed incapable of blinking. The first time I saw him, I thought he was dead.

"I came to see Benjamin," he said. Only his mouth moved. Sara came up behind me and closed the door in his face.

"Who's that?" I said. I heard him knock on the door again.

"Go away," Sara said.

I started to go, but then she said it again, louder, and I realized she was talking to him.

Daddy came out of Ogra's room, and Sara retreated to the window next to the door.

"Open the door," Daddy said.

Adams came in, looked at Sara and said, "What's the matter, Skinny?"

Sara looked at her feet. I thought she would be so beautiful if she would just hold her head up more. She left the window and moved off into her room. She wore a long blue dress, so I couldn't see her feet, and she walked so quietly it looked as if she might have been on rollers. So now I hated Walker Adams too.

He never said much to me, but he wouldn't let Sara alone. One night, after my father had gone out front to smoke with some of the men from the factory, Adams came into the cabin and went to Sara's room. I followed him in there, stood behind him while he talked.

I think he tried to be nice at first. He said something like "How come you're hiding those eyes in here?"

Sara didn't answer him.

He put his hands on his hips, tilted his head. "What's wrong with a little girl doesn't want to be social?"

Sara moved to the other side of the bed.

"When are you going to get some titties?" Adams whispered.

"Get out of here." Sara was loud, a slight tremble in her voice.

I grabbed his arm, tried to pull him away, but he only laughed at me. "I was a little brother once too," he said. Then he knelt down and looked at me with those eyes. "When's your mean, big sister going to get some titties, eh?" He smelled like my father.

It went on like that. Whenever he could get Sara alone, he'd say something to make her mad or get her crying. I started watching the back of his neck, thinking that the power of the hate in my eyes would cut through flesh. About two weeks after that night he followed Sara into her room, if I'd had a knife I *would* have cut him. I came upon him in Sara's room again, only this time he had her lying back on the bed, crying—her eyes so wide she looked like a trapped fawn—and he was pulling her underwear aside and looking between her legs.

"Lay still," he said. He didn't know I was behind him. He breathed as if he'd run a great distance. Sara tried to sit up, and he pushed her back, his hand on her throat. "Now lay there and don't move."

I leaped on his back, pulled him off her. He threw me against the wall, stood up over me like a bear. "You little son of a bitch." He ran the back of his hand over his mouth, looked at Sara on the bed. "Remember what I'll do to that little bastard if you tell anybody," he said, pointing at me.

Sara only cried.

Adams made this short little laugh, then he walked out of the room.

I went to Sara, helped her fix her dress. She kept crying, although she tried to smile at me. I felt so sorry for her I started crying too. I knew there was no way I could give her back what Walker Adams had taken from her; that something private had been stolen, and she'd feel its loss every day.

"I hate him," I said.

She shuddered, shook water out of her eyes like a cat or a bird. Then she said, "Daddy does that to me."

"What?"

She tried to smile again, tears running on either side of her nose. "I want to die, Kenny."

"Please," I said.

"They won't leave me alone." She hugged me, sobbed on my small shoulder as if I was someone who could protect her.

I think my father liked Walker Adams. He was always glad to have the union people there, because it probably made him feel like he was doing something; and Adams followed him around, calling him Mr. Ezra and all. And both of them had made Sara cry. I understood, for the first time, why Sara hated my father so. From that moment on, I tried to hate him too. He was very ugly after that—a sort of upright wild animal. But events got in the way of my budding hatred.

I began to notice another change in my father's behavior shortly after the meetings started. He drank more than usual and didn't seem to notice it when people were near him. He stared into space a lot of the time, and it was hard to tell sometimes if he was listening, or if he could hear at all. At meals he'd chew as if there was something caught in his throat, and his hands shook. Ogra'd be moving around slapping plates down and he'd barely notice it. He seemed to be listening to something inside his head. I probably wouldn't have paid any attention to it, but then one night, instead of a big meeting Bailey came to the cabin alone, and he never took his eyes off my old man from the time he came in the door until he left. He stared at my father as if he was waiting for him to burst into flames or something. I knew there was something really wrong.

You see, I wasn't a worrier or anything, but every now and then I got to wondering what would happen to me, and then I'd get sort of nervous. I don't know how to explain it, except to say that sometimes a person gets a picture of the world when they aren't going to be in it anymore, and it isn't going to matter one way or the other to anyone that they aren't and so it may as well be so that they never *were* here to begin with. Do you know what I mean? Let's say you get sick one day, and it really hurts. You go on bearing the pain, standing up to how it feels. That's an effort, right? It takes expending energy, strength. What for? It can't be so you'll get to feeling better, since you were only feeling better before you got sick, and that wasn't anything that had any lasting value or you wouldn't have got sick in the first place. It doesn't do any good to get well, since you'll only get sick again. So when you are sick, *why* are you sick? And *why* should you stand for it? Why should you try to get any better?

Even now, I can get to worrying about these things. I think I

have explained, as accurately as memory will allow, the anxiety
I felt sometimes back there in Pennsylvania. In any event, that
night Bailey came over, I felt the same kind of fear, because he said
to my father, "You seen the doctor yet?" And my father had gone
white.

"I don't need to," my father said. He nearly whispered this. I
was sitting on the cedar chest under the front window, watching
the sun sink behind the smoke from the factory. I don't know
where Sara was. I think she was in her room, or maybe she was
working out back. Ogra always had her doing wash or cleaning
up the yard.

"You ain't worried about it?" Bailey said.

I turned around and looked at them. They leaned over the table
by the coal stove, neither paying any attention to me, though they
continued to whisper.

"It's only a toothache," the old man said.

"Toothache, hell."

"Now don't try to scare me," Daddy said. His voice was barely
a whimper. I realized he was scared to death, and of course, that
widened my eyes too. Even when you hate your old man, he's a
powerful figure. You never expect to see him afraid of anything.

"I'm trying to scare some sense into you," Bailey said.

"What good's a doctor going to do me if I got it?"

"Well—"

"If I don't have it, I don't need a doctor. And if I *do* have it
—hell, I don't need no doctor then, either."

"Don't you want to know?" Bailey slapped the table at this, his
voice a note higher, although he was still whispering.

I knew what they were talking about, finally—and when it hit
me I felt cold and sick to my stomach all at once. They were
talking about phossy jaw.

"It's just a toothache," Daddy said. "I'm more worried about
my knees."

"It can start there," said Bailey. "It's your bones. Your bones."

"I can't worry about it."

"What about these children?"

Neither my father nor Bailey looked at me, but I had the feeling that somehow they were watching me anyway.

"Leave it, will you?" Daddy's voice was louder.

I didn't want to move. I was afraid they'd see me and stop talking—and I was also afraid I'd feel the pain of phossy jaw beginning in me.

"Remember Old Man Yerbich?" said Bailey.

I didn't remember Mrs. Yerbich ever having a husband, so I listened closely. I don't know how I held so still, as scared and sick as I was getting. But I think there must have been something else going on in me then—another thing besides fear of phossy jaw running in my heart. I've tried to identify what else troubled me then; every time I think about that time it bothers me that something else upset me that I've never been able to explain, or even give a name. If Mrs. Yerbich's husband had phossy jaw, I may have *wanted* my father to have it. Mrs. Yerbich's husband was gone: some secret gristle in me may have wanted the old man to be gone too. And yet, I was so afraid that he *might* be gone. I did not know what it was like not to have a father (I didn't know I would find out). For all I knew it might be worse. I had to keep from imagining me and Sara alone with Ogra. It was like this: every now and then my father would trap a groundhog for dinner. When he was ready to cook it he'd hit it over the head to stun it before he killed and skinned it. For sure the groundhog didn't like being trapped in a cage; he probably wasn't too happy about being hit over the head either. But if he knew what was coming so soon after that, he might not mind the cage so much. I felt sort of like the groundhog.

"Remember Yerbich," Bailey was saying. "He didn't have a lower jaw. If you tried to hit him in the chin you'd cut your hand on his upper teeth."

"I remember."

"It was awful."

"Yerbich lived longer than most."

"And Mrs. Yerbich has it too, now."

"They both worked dipping the splints. I don't do that."

"You're in there. We're all in there."

They weren't whispering any more now. It didn't seem to matter that I was in the room.

"Yeah," my father said. "We're all in there." He leaned back in the chair. "God."

"You scared?" said Bailey.

The old man started to shake his head, but gradually it turned into a sort of desperate nod.

"Shit, let's do it now."

My father sat back up close to the table. Bailey grabbed his arm. "Let's do it now," he said.

Daddy closed his eyes, shook his perspiring head. "No, no," he whispered. "This summer. This summer."

Bailey got up to leave, so I shot across the room to Sara's door. Neither of them said anything to me as I went out.

Sara held a book against her chest, leaned against the wall staring at something on the ceiling.

"What are you looking at?" I asked.

"I'm dreaming. Not looking."

"I think we're in trouble," I said.

"They found the mice?"

"What?"

"Tell me the trouble."

"What mice?"

"Tell me what trouble."

"Daddy's got phossy jaw."

Her eyes widened a bit, but she didn't lose any breath or make the slightest sound. She looked at me like that, for a few moments, then she said in a quiet sort of subdued voice, "How do you know?"

"I heard him and Bailey." Then I think I must have been near tears, because she pulled me over to her and put her hands on my face.

"Don't be afraid, little Kenny. Don't be afraid." She was fairly singing.

I found out a little later that Sara put a dead mouse in Ogra's bed. She told me she put it under the pillow. She also put one in my father's shirt pocket—she claimed to have done this while Ogra folded the wash right next to her. The mice were not discovered at the same time, however—since my father sometimes took weeks to claim a clean shirt. The one in Ogra's bed hadn't gotten stiff yet, although it was dead long enough to freshen up the bed where it was found. Ogra actually screamed, came running out of the room holding the thing by its tail.

Daddy called it the wrath of the dead.

Ogra threw it out the front door, then she told my father to shut up.

When my father found his, he screamed too. The mouse was stiff as glass, and had almost no hair by the time the old man fished it up out of his pocket.

Sara was standing right there, staring into Daddy's eyes. "It's the wrath of the dead, Father," she said confidentially.

I asked Sara later how she caught the mice and she told me she didn't—that the cat did. She described how the cat played with the mice, batted each of them around before ministering the fatal bite. She described the sound of the skull of the first mouse, how it crackled like a peanut shell when the cat bit into it. She was fascinated by it, seemed almost to have discovered it first; as if she was the only person in the world who yet knew about it. It was our secret.

All I could think about was this awful design—this theatrical design where everything eats everything else so that everything can go on eating everything else.

Later that same day, Sara and I decided to venture out into the factory yard. She wanted to go somewhere secret, that's how she got me to go. I thought she was going to surprise me with some hard candy or something, but instead she walked down behind the cabins and into the woods that occupied the entire world as far as I could see in that direction—I think it was west of the factory;

ROBERT BAUSCH

I can't remember if I watched the sun go behind those trees, or come from there in the morning. Anyway we walked into those woods and I started whimpering.

"Stop it," she said. She held my hand tightly.

"Where're we going?"

"Just for a walk. I want to show you something."

We went along a thinly worn path, up a rise in the trees, and then down along a high green hedge. The leaves whispered faintly, and Sara hummed a tune. To the right of us were the great thick trees that rose up behind the cabins, and to our left was the hedge. The path began to take on the character of a road.

"Here," said Sara. We stopped by another road, a thinner one, which took off into the hedge on our left.

"What is it?"

"You'll see."

We walked up the thinner path, came to a place where the hedge opened up, and there, on the top of a gradually rising and smooth green hill, was an enormous white house. It was almost as big as the factory. There were columns in front, a black hanging lamp, great red doors. I still dream about that place.

"That's Mr. Silver's house," said Sara.

"God," I said.

"Isn't it wonderful?"

"God."

"Come on." She took my hand.

"No."

"Come on. He likes children."

"How do you know."

"I've talked to him."

"You have?"

"Yes." There was triumph in the word. It was the same tone of voice she had when she told me of any of her victories.

"To him?"

"To Silver. The boss."

"Why?"

"He likes me. I came walking back here one day and there he

was, standing in the path with his cane." She pointed to the house.
"I've been in there."

"God."

"Stop saying God and come on." I walked with her a ways.
Then I thought about seeing Silver close up, about perhaps being
in the house and somehow carrying away some taint of the place;
some evidence that Ogra would recognize and know.

"Sara," I said.

"What."

I pulled my hand away, stopped. She looked at me with a face
that betrayed nothing, a face that might have been asleep except
for the open and unblinking eyes.

"What have you been talking to Silver about?"

"You know."

"Tell me."

"What do you think?"

"You've told him about Daddy?"

"And Walker Adams, and Bailey. All of them."

"Why?" I was really disappointed. I couldn't have said why—
at least not right away. It was a different kind of war now. When
it was only Sara and me it seemed important. But this was an
alliance; an alliance with the hated Silver who was everyone's
enemy.

Sara smiled then, when I cried "Why?"

She said, "Because I'm going to win."

I was ashamed of her.

"Why are you looking at me like that?" The smile left her.

"I want to go home."

"Don't you want to see the house?"

"No."

I started to leave, but then I heard a shout, a deep voice shout-
ing "Halloo." It was Silver, coming down the path with his cane,
trying to make funny noises for us children.

"Stay and meet Mr. Silver," said my big sister.

ROBERT BAUSCH

Mr. Silver had the kind of voice you never forget, even if you've died twice in between remembering it. He came down that path with a handful of hard candy, and spoke slow and deliberate words of friendship and admiration—sweet and fat words like "buster," and "buddy" and "fellow" and "youngster." He rubbed the top of my head, told me I should have a talk with my "daddy."

"Your papa is not being very nice to Mr. Silver," he said. He called himself Mr. Silver a lot. He leaned over me, smiled so broadly I could see his tongue bathed next to his bottom teeth. "And you," he said his voice as sweet and high as a woman's, "You ought to come and see old Mr. Silver more often. Why— maybe we could go fishing in my pond over yonder."

"He ain't ever been fishing," Sara said.

"He *has* never been fishing."

"That's right," I said. "I ain't."

"You haven't." He was leaning over me and smiling again. His cheeks sagged like a bedspread.

"I don't want to, either," I said.

"Suit yourself. Maybe Mrs. Silver made some cupcakes. Want some cupcakes?"

"My daddy has phossy jaw," I said.

"No, I don't believe it." His face seemed to close up.

"He doesn't know for sure," Sara said. Silver reached over and put his hand on the top of her head, then down behind it onto her neck.

"A lot of people get the disease," he said. "I hope your daddy isn't one of them."

"He got it working in the factory," I said. I don't know what got into me. I guess I realized what true hatred is, and that I was only *angry* at my father most of the time. I guess I didn't really hate the old man after all. I hated Silver. I hated him because he had such a big house; because he had a long green hedge, a great wide county fair sort of lawn, and a black hanging lamp on his front porch the size of our coal stove; because he owned the factory, and because he touched Sara with affection and she seemed to like it.

"No one knows how a person gets phossy jaw," Silver said.

"Daddy says you get it from the phosphorous fumes."

"Maybe."

I felt like I wanted to cry—as if I'd lost something soft and wonderful and was only going to have to do without it for the rest of my life. I remember the way the wind moved the tiny leaves of the hedge, and how swiftly Sara's eyes searched behind me while Silver talked. She was watching for witnesses. As if she wanted to get caught talking to the big man—the enemy.

"Let's go, Sara," I said. I felt as if I'd swallowed an ice cube.

"Don't you want something sweet, buddy?" Silver said. "Why don't you kids run up to the house and see if Mrs. Silver has anything sweet for you."

"We've got to go," I said.

Sara smiled up at him. "We'll be back," she said.

THE FOURTH INTERVIEW

OCTOBER 29, 1980

12:30 P.M.

I couldn't understand Sara wanting to be with Silver like that. It was the beginning of a period which to this day I don't like to think about—although it's the most vivid memory I have of that time. Sara moved farther and farther away from me, and I found myself more completely alone than I had ever been.

My father's jaw turned the color of a gun barrel by the summer of that year, and he couldn't say words with b's or p's in them unless those letters came at the end or in the middle somewhere. He sounded as if he had a wooden tongue. And in late August, something happened that changed the way I felt not only about Sara but Ogra too. My father had really begun to suffer by then, and I saw Ogra finally defeat him—drive him so thoroughly out of the house that I didn't think I would ever see him again. It was only later, that fall, when we were all in tents and Silver had closed the factory that I saw him—and that was the day he died.

But I'm getting ahead of myself.

Sara and I had made frequent visits to Old Man Silver's house by that August. We'd eaten sweet cakes, hard candy, and even corn bread, while Silver told us what good "urchins" we were, and how he'd like to have such well behaved and swell children. "Cheeldreen." God. Silver said he was sure sorry my father had gotten sick and couldn't make his full day at work anymore. And Sara even told him about some of her forays. She told Silver about the time she lowered one of Daddy's cigars, tied to a string, down into the privy—soaked it there almost a whole afternoon—then dried the thing in the sun of the tin roof, and placed it back where she found it. Silver really laughed at that, although he took the cigar he was smoking out of his mouth and rested it between his knuckles for the rest of the time we were there. Sara had stolen it for him. The thing that gets me is he knew she hated Daddy.

He knew that about us, and we didn't know anything about him at all. Oh, his wife told us one day that he wet the bed until he was almost twelve. But that's not much. I felt like we knew something about his body, but not anything about his feelings. So he wet the bed. That was like her telling us he was fat.

I wish I could tell you why I went back to that place. I sensed the alliance dying—Sara had found a more powerful ally—and I didn't want to just let it happen. I felt like I ought to be able to do something about it. Maybe show up Silver—make him look foolish. But Sara probably didn't like him, anyway. I didn't know how to make him look less powerful than I was. And it was his power that attracted Sara. So I got sort of dragged along, you know? I could not give up Sara, although I hated the idea of her and Silver in the same army. I would not betray her. But I didn't really feel like betraying my father either. I really was on his side. On his side, and Sara's side. The only thing is, they were enemies. If I had to choose between the two of them I'd have taken Sara every time. What's that called, anyway? When you can't make up your mind, so you just go along and watch everything and don't have anything to do with any of it. Talk about being powerless. There's nothing more helpless than a person who can't make up his mind.

But who could in a situation like that?

Anyway, I was going to tell you about my father's defeat. The thing that sticks in my mind about it is not so much that he was beaten, but that Ogra celebrated with a bottle of gin. And Sara joined her. Oddly enough, the fight began over the very bottle that Ogra opened after Daddy retreated.

She'd been sitting at the table by the stove, skinning some carrots, I think, or something like that. She was doing something with her hands, and he came over and asked her where the bottle was, and she got up, took the bottle out of the cupboard and put it next to her on the table and told him to get lost.

"I want some gin," he said.

"So you can give that disease to me?" She laughed.

"You don't catch it that way."

"Drink your own gin."

"That *is* my gin."

"Sure it is."

He moved closer to her. "Come on."

"Big union leader needs a drink, eh?"

He looked sad. I may have felt sorry for him.

"Big lover boy," Ogra said.

"Christ! Ogra," he whined. "I'm gonna die."

"Not today."

"I'm dying!" He tried to yell, but his voice didn't have the strings anymore.

"Well, then you'll be joining me. I died a long time ago."

He grabbed the bottle and headed for the door.

She got up and from behind, slapped him on the ear. I heard him cry out as I moved to Sara's room. When I opened the door, she was standing there, looking at me, a smile on her face. I turned and saw my father grab Ogra around the neck and pull her down on the floor.

"Hit her," Sara screamed.

He sat on top of Ogra, his eyes bulging out of his skull, and she held both his arms and laughed in his face—a bald and roaring circus laugh. He pulled his arms free, got up and cradled the bottle of gin, moving toward the door. Ogra was on him before he got to it, both of them tumbling to the floor like the collapse of some enduring thing in nature; something forged by thousands of years of dripping water and the changing seasons. My father laughed and screamed at the same time. He crawled toward the door with Ogra on him, pounding his back. He managed to get out, minus the bottle of gin. Ogra sat by the door frame, breathing heavily, laughing, drinking the gin as if it provided air.

"Big union leader," she said.

Neither Sara nor I moved. I think we must have stayed that way for some time—Ogra on the floor by the front door, and Sara and I standing next to each other in front of the sanctuary of her room. I don't know what we were waiting for. It had rained most of that day, and outside the window next the door, I could see huge black crows playing in one of the yellow puddles in the yard.

Finally, Ogra got up and moved to the table. She was an enormously fat woman, with ankles that looked like smudge pots and little tiny pig eyes under stretched and rubber lids. I'm sorry I haven't described her as completely as I probably should. It's just that I do not have any memories of her that a normal person might call fond. Only Mr. Silver was fatter. And he was probably meaner too. But not by much. When I was ten years old, a mother was a huge beast who, when disturbed, smashed through rooms leaving blue marks on everybody. She was immense in the same way a tornado or an explosion is immense. The thing was, you could not predict how she would be. Her best days she left us alone. And after my father got involved in correcting the injustices at Mr. Silver's match factory, she didn't have too many of those days. And we couldn't avoid her. Although Sara had a room, and I had a room, and Ogra and Daddy had a room, it was a very small cabin.

That day she beat up my father, Ogra went over to the table and sat down, holding the bottle of gin in front of her, and Sara went over and sat across from her. When Sara went over there, I was so afraid I couldn't focus on them; they leaned toward one another, the bottle of gin between them like a glass figurine.

"What do you think of your big daddy now?" Ogra said.

"I want some gin," Sara said in a voice so steady I began to think I was dreaming. The two of them stared at each other. Sara's hands were folded in front of her, almost as if she were praying. There was only a white light from the windows in the room.

"You're not old enough," Ogra said.

"I go to work in the factory. This year."

"Hah," Ogra laughed. "Your big daddy will fix that."

"Why do you hate me so much?" Sara asked. I noticed her voice was beginning to lose its strength.

"I don't hate you any more than I hate anybody else."

Sara bowed her head again. "You hate everybody."

ROBERT BAUSCH

"It's a rotten world. A sour place. No fun in it." She took another drink. "I don't hate you. I want you to be tough. I want you to be ready for it."

"You hate me."

"I want you to grow up hard, like me."

I went over to the coal stove, behind Sara. I couldn't believe Ogra was actually talking to her, and I had this feeling something was about to happen. I wanted to be near Sara so I could protect her. I was still trying to make up for the times I had betrayed her. She seemed so alone and small there at the table across from Ogra.

"What would you do if I died?" Sara asked her.

"You going to die now too?"

"What would you do?"

"I'd have one less brat to worry about."

Sara started to cry. I saw her shoulders tremble.

"Don't start slobbering all over the place," Ogra said. Her voice was louder. "What'd you want me to say? 'Oh please, baby. Don't die.' You just told me I hate you. That's what you believe. Besides, you'd be doing yourself a favor if you died. Dying's probably the good part."

"Why don't *you* die, then?"

Ogra sat forward, took the bottle in her hands, studied the liquid in it. "Heh," she said. "Since I was your age, I thought I might do just that. But I figure if you can't make yourself get born, you ought not to try and make yourself die." She took another drink. "So I won't be eating matches or playing with pistols late at night. I'm going to stick around and see what happens."

Ogra actually smiled then, as if she were remembering something pleasant. I walked up and put my arm around Sara.

"You look just like your father," Ogra said. She put a fat hand up and patted her hair. "Once—" she smiled again, seemed to chew on a word, taste it, then swallow it. "Aaah hell," she said. "It's been such a disappointment."

Sara and I were both looking at her now. It was a sort of peace conference.

"Life's not fair to some folks. Things happen to a person. If

you're around ugliness enough, you get ugly." She raised the
bottle, rinsed her teeth with the gin. Then she was yelling at us:
"You always just *end up* in this world. You end up alone, or
pregnant, or crippled, or fat, or old—or dead. That's what happens to you. You *end up.*"

Sara reached for the bottle of gin, and Ogra slapped her hand.
"I want some," Sara said.

"*Want, want, want,*" Ogra bellowed. "That's the trouble with
brats. They always want something. The only thing either one of
you ever gave me was a sore tit, a headache, and a pot full of shit.
Every now and then you throw up. The rest of the time you only
want something."

"I don't want any gin," I said.

"Good for you."

"But can Sara have some?"

"Both of you get out of here," she said, waving her bulging arm.
I started to move, but Sara pulled my hand. Ogra frowned over
the bottle. "You," she said, "look like your old man. And Sara lets
him—I hate you both." She smiled when she said this.

Sara started to cry loudly now, a wail rising in tone like the saws
in the factory that cut poplar and pine into blocks for the splint
maker. I pulled Sara's arm, tried to get her body out of the chair.
She never took her eyes off Ogra, who drank her gin now with
peculiar violence—as if each turn of the bottle extracted a tooth.

"What's the matter?" I begged, looking at both of them. Sara
wailed, and Ogra drank.

"Come on, Sara," I said.

Ogra leaned over, put a hand on my chest and pushed me away.
"Get the fuck out of here."

Now I was crying. I did not want to go back to the table, but
I had to help Sara. She wouldn't look at me.

"Sara," I yelled. "Let's go."

I heard the cat whine at Sara's door.

"Go let the cat out," Ogra said.

Sara took in a breath, held the scream in now, as if she was just
beginning to remember it, discover it in the room.

"Here," Ogra said to her. "You little bitch. Have some gin."
She pushed the bottle across the table. Sara took it in her hands
as if it were a weapon, and put it to her lips. I went in and kicked
the cat and told it to shut up.

You can imagine how I felt. Daddy out of the house—staying
happily with Bailey—and Sara drinking regularly with Ogra. I
thought I might just leave; walk on down the road until I came
to some other place. In one way, though, I wanted to hang around.
I needed to see how it was all going to end up.

The next time Sara and I visited Silver, he knew about my
father's new living arrangements.

"A family should stay together," he said.

Sara offered him one of my father's cigars, and he said, "No,
thank you." His cheek twitched a bit around his mouth—a brief
convulsion which made me think he was about to laugh.

"Daddy's going to die anyway," Sara said.

Silver frowned. "Nowwwww," he said. "Don't be talking like
that."

He was sitting in one of the largest chairs I have ever seen. It
was burgundy in color, thick around all the edges, and made of
material that seemed to be woven from spider's webs or something. It was smooth and slick and soft. He couldn't cross his legs,
so he had one foot resting on top of the other, like a sort of fat
Christ—except he had on a baggy black suit and shoes that looked
like they were made of black satin. Sara and I were sitting on the
thick carpeted floor in front of him. I suppose it was like a close
warm family circle. I might have found a way to enjoy it, except
I knew what Silver really meant to all of us—to Sara, Daddy, and
even Ogra. He had the money, and the property, and because of
that, he also had the hours. He controlled my days—everybody's
days. Any one of us might have been a trinket under his Christmas
tree.

I don't know what he derived from our visits. He talked about
everything—books, the theater, death. He was big on death.

Sometimes he'd read to us out of the Bible. Stories about suffering servants and a fellow named Lot; he liked Job. He said my father was like Job in a way.

"I understand turmoil," he said that day we sat in front of him. The windows behind him were as big as a fireplace, and light from the afternoon sun washed all over us, made tiny points of light on the tips of his shoes. "Turmoil is absolutely necessary."

I looked out the window. There was a vague odor in the room; a sort of perfume, perhaps, that smelled like the inside of a rose.

"In a way," he went on, "I'm thankful for your dad."

"Thankful," said Sara.

"Yes. Thankful."

"Why?" I asked. I really wanted to know.

"Because he provides me with the thing that all human beings need in order to live fully—conflict."

"He does?" I said.

He looked at Sara. "Everything you've told me about him—all the plans he's making secretly—well," he smiled here, put his hands up and inside his suspenders. "Well, I'll be ready for him. I've been able to anticipate, you see. Conflict provides the necessity for such things, and of course, your days get pretty full making preparations."

"What sort of preparations?" I said.

"Tents."

"Tents?"

"I own all the houses. When the work stops, you have to live somewhere. I can't have good little children like you out in the cold, can I?"

"We're going to be kicked out," I said to Sara.

"It wouldn't be Christian of me to let you people get cold."

"How come you own everything?" I said.

"I don't own everything," he smiled.

"You have a lot of money," Sara said. She was staring at the rug, making patterns with her index finger.

"Look," Silver said. "The earth is a huge place—it doesn't get run by itself. Now you've got opposites everywhere; conflicts.

Night and day. Hot and cold. Good and bad. Rich and poor. If everybody were rich, then nobody'd be rich. See what I mean?"

"I think so," said Sara.

"If everything were cold, all the time, exactly the same temperature—why, you'd not even know what hot meant, would you?"

"I guess not."

"Some people have to watch over things."

"Matches," I said.

"That's what my family has done since the first colony."

"What's the opposite of matches?"

"You don't understand. For me, the opposite of matches is no matches at all." He shifted in the throne—put his feet out flat, one right next to the other. "Your daddy needs to work so he can have a livelihood; all the other people need to work. I need to work and to have income too. And folks need matches to light their coal stoves, their cigars and so on. Everything fits very naturally."

"Except you've got all the money," I said.

"I'm an opposite," he smiled again, looked directly into my eyes. "I'm the opposite of poor, and I'll fight to stay that way. Your daddy will fight to get a piece of my pie, of course. He's an opposite too."

"What are we?" Sara asked.

"You're in the middle," he said.

Boy, were we in the middle. I can't begin to count, even now, how many things I was in the middle of. I was between Sara and Daddy, Sara and Mr. Silver, Sara and Ogra, Mr. Silver and my father, my father and Ogra. I'd been on the earth for a little over ten years and if you sat down and tried to make a map of the people and things I was in the middle of you'd end up with something that looked like a tree in the wintertime. I had branches everywhere. There didn't seem to be anything in my life I was definitely on the side of except the cat—and I had kicked that only two days before when Sara took her first drink of gin from Ogra.

Anyway, while we were sitting there, somebody knocked on the door. We'd been there before when Silver had visitors—people I'd never seen before, dressed like other rich people—so we didn't think anything of it. But when Silver opened the door to the "drawing room" where we were sitting, and listened to the maid whispering about who was at the door, I started to get the feeling that something was going to happen.

Silver came back and said, "That was a man named Bailey at the door."

My capillaries emptied.

"Your father and his union have just walked off the job," Silver said. It was as if he'd just won a lottery or something.

"I told you," Sara said.

"How did you know?" I asked. "How—"

"I had a long talk with Mr. Walker Adams," she said.

"Sara."

She looked at me, and there was something fixed behind her eyes that, once I recognized it, I didn't think it would ever change. It was a different Sara who peered out of the green crystal.

"You children will have to go home now."

I got up, tried not to look at Sara. I didn't know if I would ever be able to look at her again.

"Even Walker Adams," I said.

You know, I understand more now than I did then the magnitude of Sara's hatred. She knew how to love well. She loved me mightily. And I guess because of this, she knew also how to hate. When I was that ten-year-old boy, I had no idea what she had to do for Walker Adams to get from him when the strike was to begin. I only knew she had talked to him, and that was evil enough. I don't know what I would have done if I'd known about the other evils of the world—if I'd known about the other impulses that lead to conflict as Mr. Silver so aptly put it. As it was, I went out of Silver's castle, and without looking back—without knowing if Sara was behind me or not—I began the fierce walk back to the cabin, searching along the way for some sort of weapon. I was going to kill Walker Adams.

———————————

Have you ever thought about killing a man? I don't mean making him hurt or anything like that—although of course that's a part of it. I mean forcing him to stop breathing. I wonder if

anything innocent ever dies in a man. You ever thought about
that? What part of a living, breathing human being—what part of
Walker Adams did I hate? Want to kill? You know you have to
kill the whole person: the part of him that betrayed my father and
talked to Sara, and the part of him that liked the way the sky looks
after a rain.

I didn't think about much of this while I was hunting for
Walker Adams. I pictured him dead. I thought a lot of people
would see me do it, and they would talk about me afterward, and
I didn't care. In fact, I may have liked the idea. I would be famous.
A ten-year-old murderer. The trouble was, Walker Adams was a
big man, and I was less than five feet tall. I couldn't figure out how
I was going to do it.

Sara ignored me the rest of that day, and all of the next. She
could tell how I felt. When Mr. Silver came to the cabin and asked
us to kindly leave, she didn't even look at me.

Silver had deputies—I don't know where he got them. Maybe
from the town. But he personally went to each cabin and asked
the families to get out. When he came to ours, Ogra didn't bat an
eye.

"I ain't leaving," she said. "I'm still working."

"Mrs. Ezra," Silver said. "Nobody's working. The factory is
closed until further notice."

"I'm not with the rest of them."

"Here," one of the deputies said. He handed her a sheet of
paper. "We're putting up a tent village across from the print shop.
This will get you in."

"Look here," Ogra said.

The deputy frowned. He had a wide mouth, like a goat's, and
a dirty cap pulled down over his brow. "When Mr. Silver begins
to hire again, he'll be glad to talk to you."

Silver made a short nod of his head, then pointed his finger at
Ogra. "You be good to those kids," he said.

They turned to leave, then stopped. "By the way," the goat said.
"If you're not out of the cabin by tomorrow, we'll have to—well,
be out by then, OK?"

Ogra slammed the door.

"That son of a bitch," she said.

I started to hunt for Walker Adams again. I did this from the front window. But Ogra was really angry, and she yelled into my ears until I had to look at her. "See what your father got us into now?"

I nodded.

Sara sat at the table, drinking a glass of what I wanted to be water. But I knew it wasn't.

"See?" Ogra said. "Now none of us will have jobs."

If I'd had any courage I might have defended him. I can truthfully say that, even at that age, I was against the things my father was against. I wanted him to win. But what could I say to Ogra? She was wrong. But she was always wrong. So I only nodded, and I'm sure she thought I was agreeing with her.

So we packed our things and moved across the yard to the tent city erected by Silver's deputies. This was near the end of September. Ogra behaved in the tent the way slugs do when you pour salt on them. She was miserable. She cursed my father, yelled at Sara and me. I still didn't say anything to Sara. She said only what was necessary—things like "move over," and "want some?"

Ogra shriveled in the corner of the tent, drinking and moaning, and Sara tried to make the place private—tacking the front flap of the tent closed, even in broad daylight. She acted as if she didn't even know I was mad at her.

Tent city was almost as large and populous as Wilkes-Barre. Silver bought Civil War Army surplus. The fabric was white, so the whole landscape looked like a storage bin for sailor's caps. I never saw so many little white dwellings in one place. Trash started to accumulate right away, and Silver wouldn't let any of us use the privy houses, so some of the men dug a trench behind the field of white tents, and it was there that I ran into Walker Adams and took my revenge.

I wasn't looking for him on that day. I guess it was about a week after we moved into the tents, and I was looking for my father.

ROBERT BAUSCH

I had heard from one of the women in tent city that the old man was going to be arrested, and I was trying to warn him. (I had also heard that he died of the phossy jaw—a lean woman who worked with Mrs. Yerbich came to the tent and told us that—but none of us believed it. Funny how sometimes you just know when a thing is true. I knew my father was still alive. I sensed it somehow —perhaps the way a spider knows something's disturbed its web. Sara and Ogra seemed the same way. We didn't say anything, and the woman just shrugged her shoulders and walked away.) But I believed it when I heard he was going to be arrested. He was the leader. They all went out because he said to go. No matter how Sara felt, I could not help but be proud of him. So I needed to help in some way. Maybe even tell him how I felt. The thing is, once I decided to find him and warn him, I realized how good it feels to finally decide what you're going to do and go ahead and do it. I wanted to kill Walker Adams out of anger—it was not something I decided. Here, finally, I felt as if I was coming down on the side of something and taking some sort of action.

You may get the wrong impression, but it was the first time I ever went looking for my old man without fear. I was warm, and full of blood, and felt as if I was actually growing a few inches as I walked. I could feel the child in me dying. And I sensed something else trying to come to life.

I walked among the tents, imagining people saying, "There goes his son," as they pointed secretively at me, and I discovered a sense of power I had not experienced before. It mattered what I did and where I went. I was the son of Benjamin Ezra. A hard man, to be sure. But a leader. Silver's enemy.

I figured the best place to find Dad was at the trench, since even heroes eventually had to visit there. The odor of the place wasn't too bad yet, if you stayed a few feet from the actual edge of the trench, so I took a seat in the wild grass near the back of the last tent in the city and waited. A few yards down toward the end of the trench was a sort of wall made of two poles, some tight wire, and one of the tents thrown over the wire, and I remember thinking that it must be for the women (it never occurred to me that a man might want to hide his hind quarters too), and as I was staring at it, imagining I would find a way to see what went on on the other side of it if a woman went down in there, I saw Walker Adams come out from behind one of the tents and start toward the makeshift wall.

He looked at me, said, "What're you doing here?"

"Nothing," I said.

He stopped, his back slightly turned to me, peering at me over his left shoulder.

"Where's your sister?"

"Not here."

He let out this short one-syllable laugh. "Oddball kid," he said.

I was looking for a weapon.

He walked up to the tent wall, stepped between the two poles. The sun was right overhead, so his shadow went in there with him. I couldn't tell any more if he was there.

Near the edge of the trench I saw a piece of block—blue cinder block—the same stuff they used to build the privies. I picked up what turned out to be half a cinder block—the heavy end of it had been hidden in the tall grass—and I lugged it over to the makeshift tent wall, trying not to breathe. I still couldn't hear anything. The odor of the trench was stronger near the tent wall, and I felt myself beginning to choke. I made a noise, and Adams said, "Being used."

The tent was just draped over the wire, so I pulled it back as quietly as I could and saw Walker Adams, squatting over the edge of the trench like an ostrich laying an egg, and he looked up, saw my face and let out a small, timid, shy sort of whimper of a sound. I hit him square on the top of his head with the block. His head seemed to sink in, like the top of a hot pie if you touch it too soon, then he put his hand up there, rubbed it, never taking his eyes off me.

"For shit's sake, man," he said. Then he toppled over backward and rolled down the side of the hill into the trench.

———————

ROBERT BAUSCH

On the second day of my fugitive life in the back of our tent, it rained. The rain came in with the moon the night before and stayed through all of the next day. Of course the floor of the tent was the bare ground, so by morning, by the time the moon disappeared again, we were all soaking wet.

I didn't tell anyone what I had done. I didn't know whether Walker Adams was dead or not. No one said anything about it, so I felt that he might be alive. But I truly didn't know. At first, I didn't care. I spent the whole evening and all of the next day after I hit him laughing at the sound he made when he first saw me with the cinder block. I think he knew what I was there for. I mean, how would you feel if you were in that position, doing what he was doing, only half finished with the job, and you looked up and saw a ten-year old with a cinder block in his hands and murder in his eyes?

The thing is, I started thinking about how *I* would feel. That did the trick. I started hoping right then that he wasn't dead. Which created guess what? If he *was* alive, he would kill me. It wouldn't be good for him to be alive. I couldn't stand for him to be dead. I couldn't stand the idea that I killed him, and especially that I killed him in one of his most private moments. So there I was, once again, in the middle of something.

I was awake when the rain started, listening for footsteps in the darkness, and I thought that the first sounds of the water on the top of the tent were the tappings of Walker's soul.

I didn't have any sort of religious convictions then. Nothing to tell me I had done something wrong. But I felt the most terrible sense of guilt. I can't describe it.

I may be arguing for a sense of right and wrong as a part of the natural makeup of human beings—something we're all equipped with no matter what. Where else would I get the feeling of remorse I felt that morning after the rain? This is what I want to study some day, when I get out of this mess; when I convince you or somebody that I didn't murder that old black woman in the taxi.

I remember huddling in the back of our tent, near tears for most of that day, and Ogra stared at me as if I were a lizard or something. It occurred to me that maybe she knew about it. Maybe she had been told Walker was dead and that someone had seen me do it. She kept staring at me, fixing her dress around her fat knees, sipping her gin.

I was afraid to go outside. If Adams was alive, he would be wanting to see me out in the open somewhere. If he was dead, I might see him and go all to pieces. I tried to dream about what I wished would be my fate: my father and I would go to the gallows, heroes to everyone. Sara would stand at the foot of the stairs, crying. "Daddy, I *did* love you," she'd say. And my father, while they were placing the noose around his neck, looked at me, smiled, and said, "I'm proud of you, my son." Then he looked at Sara, told her he loved her, but she was never the match for me as a child. And just as the noose tightened around my neck, I cried out, "She loved me mightily, father. Oh, Sara!" And then I went into darkness. Of course, once I was there, I had a comfortable seat somewhere, a seat like Silver's maybe, and I watched Sara weep uncontrollably for me. I think I ate a banana while this was going on. I remember thinking the darkness was really rather pleasant.

But then I'd open my eyes, and there I'd be in that tent, with Ogra's prosperous knees staring me in the face, and the ground wet and cold.

Sara came and went like a waitress. She carried the dirty linen, the fruit rinds and bones, a porcelain pail full of Ogra's perfume among other things. Since we were out in the open like that, where everyone could see us, Ogra seemed helpless. She needed Sara to do everything for her. But she didn't yell at us anymore. It was a curious transformation. Ogra drank, cursed my father and Silver and his deputies; every now and then she let out a moan. There was defeat in her movements, as if she were a prisoner and waited only to find out what would happen to her.

She was, like the rest of us, truly alone.

So it wasn't a matter of *us* against *her* in the end. The war settled into a sort of desperate peace. The only thing Ogra said to us, and she did this pretty regularly, was, "This is where we end up. We end up in this place, children."

On that day it rained, when I was just beginning to feel the guilt for having murdered a man, Silver came to tent city with one of his deputies and asked everyone to step out for a moment. The deputy with him was the one with the goat's mouth. They stood side by side, in front of the first row of tents, and blinked their eyes in the gray rain. I had crawled to the front flap of our tent, which was on a little rise in the third row, and I could see between Ogra's broad legs, down the slight incline to where Silver and his deputy twitched in the rain. If I had had a gun I could have shot both of them before anybody finished a sentence. I may have hated Silver enough that, even in my guilt over Walker Adams, I was capable of dreaming Silver's murder. I don't know if I could have done it, though.

"I have an announcement," Silver yelled. He had on his bowler hat and a long black coat. The rain made a steady rhythm on the tents and splashed in the brim of Silver's hat.

Ogra shifted her weight. Her calves looked like Indian pottery.

"There is a fugitive among you," Silver went on. The word "fugitive" seemed louder than the rest—I heard it in the marrow of my bones. "A fugitive from the law who must be punished, who must be turned over to me and this deputy at once." Silver seemed to be chewing on something. His eyes were little gray stones.

I put my head in the crook of my elbow, tried to hide behind my arms.

"You all know who I'm talking about," Silver said.

So Ogra did know. They all knew. I couldn't breathe.

"He is already guilty of inciting to riot."

I didn't do that. I never did anything like that.

"He preached revolution and the overthrow of authority."

Nope. Definitely not me. Maybe they didn't know. Maybe they were talking about some other crime. I lifted my head, felt my breath returning.

"This fugitive committed the barbarous act of murder only two days ago in this very camp."

Me.

"In this very camp," Silver said, for emphasis. The crowd let out a sort of unified gasp. The rain pelted the top of the tents, made little puddles in footprints and wheel tracks. It was suddenly very quiet except for the rain.

"Silver," Ogra said, finally. He looked up at her. "Who got murdered?"

"The man our fugitive murdered was a fellow conspirator; even a friend. Only God knows what caused—"

"Who?" Ogra hollered.

Silver ignored her. "Lord knows what caused the final break between them. But a man is dead, and Benjamin Ezra is free to walk among you. Perhaps to kill again—"

Ogra shook her head.

My heart didn't beat for a minute.

I laid there listening to Silver, and I knew I wasn't ever any good for anybody—least of all myself. What could I do now? I didn't have to hide anymore, so I got up, swallowed something that seemed to leak out of my teeth, and walked out of the tent. I stood next to Ogra, tried not to think about anything at all. Silver went on and described the way Adams's body was found, how it was lying in the trench with a crushed skull, all twisted. How he must have died in the most embarrassing and helpless of circumstances. I tried to listen, but all I could see was my little dream oddly reversed, with Daddy on the scaffold and me at the bottom of the stairs trying to convince anybody—anybody at all—that it was me. It was me.

THE FIFTH INTERVIEW

OCTOBER 30, 1980

9:30 A.M.

You see the irony here, don't you? Here I am trying to convince you that I didn't kill that old woman in the taxi—and back there, in Wilkes-Barre, around the turn of the century, I was trying to convince anybody who'd listen that I killed Walker Adams.

So I *have* killed a person. I don't think I did it on purpose, though. I went after him, I admit that. And I hated him enough to kill him, but I didn't think I could really do it. And when he made that sound, rubbed the top of his head like that, I knew I had done something truly evil. No one needed to tell me anything about it—about morality, or goodness, or the difference between right and wrong, or any of that. I knew the way you know your foot itches. I had done evil.

Nobody'd listen to me. They all thought I was trying to protect my father. I told anyone who'd listen that I was guilty. I was the murderer. Who would believe that a ten-year-old boy could kill a man the size of Walker Adams? Even Sara wouldn't believe me. I told her as soon as I figured it out. I grabbed her arm and pulled her back into the tent just as the deputies were starting their search for my father (Silver told them to empty every tent).

"What's the matter with you?" She could tell I was sick.

"Daddy didn't kill Walker Adams."

"How do you know?"

"Because—" I looked to see if Ogra was listening. "Because, I did it."

"*You?*"

"Yes."

"I don't believe you."

"I did."

"How?"

"I hit him with a cinder block."

"Where'd you get it?"

"I found it in the grass."

She blinked, ran her tongue over her lower lip. "I still don't believe you."

"I did do it."

"Shut up."

I couldn't tell how she felt about it. "Are you glad he's dead?"

She looked at me, an expression on her face that reminded me of Ogra: sort of flat, and mean and dead looking. "I don't care," she said.

"Sara," I said. "I'm telling you the truth."

She looked out the front flap, at the rain and the dying afternoon.

"I hit him with a cinder block." I was getting a little angry. I thought she'd really appreciate what I had done. I thought she'd see how much I loved her, and—well, you know what I mean. I figured I'd pretty much wrecked my life for her.

"Why?" she said.

"What?"

"Why'd you kill him?"

"Because he—" I didn't quite know how to put it. To tell the truth, I didn't really know why I did it. He betrayed my father— but Sara had done that, and I didn't want to kill her. He'd talked to Sara, she'd been nice to him in ways I couldn't quite understand, but I knew it had something to do with her not being Sara anymore—and he'd been so mean to her before, so terribly cruel.

Maybe he was just the end result of too much accumulated anger—at Ogra, Mr. Silver, my father (half the time). When he wasn't a hero, my father was a pretty miserable person. He'd been the enemy for so long.

"Well?" Sara said.

"I don't know."

"You don't know?"

"I thought it was because he was so mean to you."

"Walker Adams?"

"He was so, he—" I started to cry. For the first time since we started visiting Mr. Silver regularly, Sara put her arms around my shoulders and hugged me.

"You don't have to take the blame for anybody," she said. She stroked the top of my head.

"Oh, Sara," I said. "What's happened to you?"

"I'm grown up now, Kenny," she said. She set me back away from her and looked into my eyes. "I'm a woman, now."

"What about me?"

"You're a little boy."

"I killed a man," I said, fighting back tears.

"No, you didn't."

"Why won't you believe me?"

"Because you're ten years old."

"Will you believe me when I'm eleven?"

"Stop it."

She got up and went outside to start the dinner fire. When the deputies got there, I was sitting alone in the back of the tent.

By the time the deputies got there, the rain had stopped, numerous fires crackled in the camp, and smoke curled toward the white sky like thin strips of black ribbon. I remember thinking it might be the way a soul winds toward heaven. By that hour, I was praying a lot.

One of the deputies put his head into the tent and said, "You'll have to come out of there."

I crawled out and stood by the fire, watched as two deputies searched through all the rags, dirty clothes, pots, and accumulated lanterns, bottles, plates and bowls. When they were done, the tent was leaning to one side like a ship about to roll over in the water, and all our belongings were strewn about the fire. One of the deputies walked over to Ogra and said, "Silver wants you all out of here by noon tomorrow. We will be rounding up the tents then."

"Where are we supposed to go?" Ogra said.

He shrugged. "It's a big country." His face had the texture of an orange peel and he looked tired and impatient, his eyes drooping under a brown, wide-brimmed hat. He touched the brim of the hat with his finger and started to leave. Without thinking, I stood in front of him, looked up into his nostrils and said, "I want to confess."

He looked at Ogra, then back to me. "Confess what?"

"I'm the man who killed Walker Adams."

His eyes got narrow, and he leaned down, real close to my face and said, "You ain't no man at all, you little son of a bitch." He straightened up and spit green tobacco juice next to my foot. "Now get out of here," he said. "And if you see your daddy, tell him I'm looking forward to meeting him."

When the deputies had gone, Ogra said, "Wherever we're going, it'll be on foot."

Sara poked at the fire. It was nearly dark by then, so the fire's light seemed brighter. I wondered where my father was, and what would happen to all of us. It was like a sickness coming over me; I felt hot and shaky at the center of myself, like something overripe and soft inside, beginning to decay.

"I guess we should pack," Ogra said in this funny sort of almost timid voice. Then she said, "Ohhh." Like that. And began to cry. She cried loud and high like an owl, and for the first time I felt sorry for her. I looked at Sara, saw that she too was starting to cry.

I knew the whole thing was my fault. Everything was ruined because of me.

"Don't cry," I said to the fire.

"We got to pack," Ogra said. She started moving around the fire, like a huge bear, moaning and rooting through the clothing and the cups and the tin cans. "We got to pack," she kept saying. Sara got up and started putting things into a sack.

"Don't cry," I said again.

Ogra stood up, spit into the fire (which made a sizzling sort of pop). "We're going to steal the tent," she said.

"The tent?" Sara watched her, seemed to be truly an ally now. It's funny what happens to enemies when the earth crushes them both.

"Where are we going?" I said.

"Away from here," Ogra said.

"But where?"

"There's other factories in this world. We'll go to Maryland."

"Maryland," I said. "How far's that?"

"We'll go to Baltimore. I've never been to Baltimore." Ogra wasn't crying anymore. She looked at me. "We'll pack everything, then get some sleep."

"OK," I said.

"We'll leave real early in the morning, so we can take this tent."

Sara was putting something into the fire, leaning over the light as if it were a pool in which she could see her reflection.

"What's that?" I said.

She looked at Ogra, then back to me. "It's something private," she said. "Something very private." It was a piece of paper with writing on it.

"Are you going with her?" I said, nodding my head toward Ogra.

"Sure," she said.

"What about Silver?" I was whispering, but I probably didn't have to. Ogra was moving farther and farther away, talking to herself about Baltimore.

"What about him?"

"And Daddy?"

"We've got no place to stay," she said. I heard Ogra cough. "Daddy's going to be hanged."

And then I knew I would have to go have a talk with Silver. I would tell him about my crime and beg him to forgive my father. Perhaps things would be the way they had been, I thought. Perhaps I could fix things for everybody. Silver would believe me.

"Everything's going to be all right," I said. I wanted Ogra to hear me too. I wanted her to know what I was about to do for her; what I was about to do for all of them. "Everything's going to be all right, Sara," I said. "You'll see."

She turned over a light gray delicate ash.

"What are you doing out so late?" Silver said when he saw me. I was standing next to his maid, feeling cold and like a shadow, and Silver sat in the same big chair, smoking a cigar. I had crawled past the deputies he had stationed in front of his property, gone through the hedge, in fact, and run across that wide green pasture in front of his house. He was very surprised to see me.

"I had to talk to you," I said.

He closed his eyes and opened then, slowly, like a chicken, and I thought he might be falling asleep. "What do you want?" he said.

"I have to say something to you."

"Well, say it."

"I want you to know I'm telling the honest truth."

He puffed on his cigar, studied my face from behind the cigar as if he were sighting a pistol. "You know you shouldn't be here at all, don't you?"

"Yes," I said.

"Yes, sir."

"Yes, sir."

"So why should I believe you're telling me the truth if you sneak around here like—well, like a nocturnal thing."

"What's that?"

"What?"

"Nocturnal."

He sighed. "What do you want?"

"I know you'll believe me," I said.

"Good."

"It's about Walker Adams."

His eyes seemed to change focus. "I know, I know. You saw somebody else do it and your Daddy's—"

"No."

"What then."

"I went down to the trench to find my father and—"

"Did you see your father do it?"

"No. I went to find him and he wasn't there, so I waited."

"Go on."

"I hated Walker Adams."

"Why?"

"I don't know." I was angry when I said this because I really did not know why.

"You need a reason to hate a man."

"It's got to do with my sister."

"Oh." Silver said that as if he knew more than I did.

"I wanted to hurt him." Something chimed in the hall, a quiet and rhythmic metallic noise that came from a device I would never know. It tempted me; left me feeling small and like a pet. It also touched a nerve somewhere in my head, and I heard myself saying, "I killed Walker Adams. I hit him with a cinder block, and he said, 'For shit's sake, man' and fell into the trench. I wanted to kill him and felt very happy when I saw him go into the trench."

Silver didn't move. Smoke curled around his head, the cigar held tightly in his fat little fingers. I looked at the floor, at his shoes that looked like satin, his striped pants. The cigar smelled like the inside of a shoe. It was absolutely quiet.

Finally, I said, "So my daddy is innocent." I couldn't tell if Silver was still looking at me. I wanted him to believe me, but I think at that moment I was frightened in every pore that he would.

"I killed him," I said, again. I nearly whispered it. Then I looked up, and Silver was staring at me through the smoke. His eyes were tiny, like watermelon seeds, and they didn't seem to be alive.

"I wanted you to know," I whispered.

"You know what you're doing, don't you?" he said finally.

"Yes."

"Do you really know?"

"I'm telling you the truth."

"How old are you?"

He knew that. "I'm ten, almost eleven."

"And look at you. You can't weigh more than seventy pounds."

He was preparing the ground for not believing me, and I was amazed that a part of me was superbly pleased. Still, the part of me that came to that room persisted. I had to save it somehow, since I was reasonably sure that he had been close to believing me.

"Look," I said. "I held the cinder block up over my head like this," I held my hands up. "Adams was squatting over the trench, his head was right in front of me. And I let the block down as hard as I could."

I demonstrated. Silver blinked.

"I felt the top of his head give in."

"Good God," Silver said.

"See?"

"I see."

"You believe—"

"I want you to go home."

"Everything—"

"You go home and don't come back here." He got up from the chair, put his hand on my shoulder.

"I don't really have a home," I said, as he moved me toward the door.

"Wherever you sleep," he said. He bit the cigar, seemed afraid of something, and angry too.

"I only wanted to straighten everything out," I begged.

The maid came to the door. "You see what happens?" Silver said to her. "See what happens when you try to be kind to them?"

"Wait," I said. He moved me out the door, into the arms of the maid. She was a small, fruity-smelling woman.

"Take him out of here," Silver said.

"What about my father?"

He stopped, looked at me. "I don't know where your father is, and I don't care. It's not my problem."

"He's innocent." I said.

"I'm not after your father."

"Who should I tell?"

"Tell the sheriff."

"I tried to tell a deputy; he wouldn't believe me."

Silver looked at the maid, put the cigar up to his mouth. "Get him out of here."

She pulled me out, put me on the front porch under the lamp

that hung above me like somebody's coffin. A deputy stood there, leaning against a white column. "Mr. Silver wants this boy removed," the maid said.

The deputy took me out to the road by the hedge and told me to beat it. I stood there, looking at the glow of fires from tent city, which was on the other side of the factory, and the dark, almost sinister clouds that hovered over my head. I hadn't fixed anything. I'd only made Silver nervous; hell, I made the bastard sick.

I decided to walk down the road. I needed to think. I went away from the fires, away from the factory and Silver's magnificent house. I walked toward what I hoped would be the edge of the earth; I needed space to hurl my body into, and lose it. Maybe it was death I hunted that night. I wouldn't have tried anything—don't get me wrong. I wasn't going to kill myself. But if I should die? If death found me in my solitary walk? I wouldn't have minded so much.

This was one of the worst times for me. As I walked down that dark, tree-lined road, I made a list of the things that happened to the people who had the misfortune of knowing me: My sister would be driven from the town, homeless and fatherless. She carried bruises on her soul from the number of times I had got her in trouble; she'd have been better off if I'd been a man-eating plant. Ogra, my mother—in my heart, this was no pity—would also be driven out, without work and with no place to go. She would take Sara with her, and me too if I wasn't killed on this night. Lord knows what I would bring them to. My father would be hunted, accused of a crime I committed. If he didn't die of phossy jaw—which I had nothing to do with—he'd be hanged. Walker Adams died. He rubbed his head, mumbled, "For shit's sake, man," then rolled back into the ditch. He probably didn't know the blow would kill him. And just a few minutes before I began the walk in the dark under the moon, I made Silver sick. He got physically ill at the sight of me. He told the maid to get me *out* of there. I thought the world would be better off if I was just a pile of bones somewhere.

I was walking along, under the black clouds and the white moon, thinking about all my victims, when I heard what I thought might be whispering. It could have been the leaves on the trees, but I stopped anyway, held my breath.

I felt a breeze brush my back. There was no more sound. I took a few more steps, thinking this would be the death I was looking for, and I heard the sound again—voices, whispering in the bushes off the road to my left. I stopped again, decided to wait for it; wait for whatever it was that would remove me from this world and save countless future victims. But it only got quiet again, and I found myself listening to my heart. I was suddenly very frightened. I couldn't even court death without botching the job. Even when you want to die, you're afraid of death.

I hollered as loud as I could, "*I killed a man!*"

It was so quiet, my voice seemed to linger in the leaves of the trees. I could hear the fluid moving in the canals in my head.

"*I'm a killer!*" I screamed.

I felt an arm go around my neck, and a hand covered my mouth.

"What's the matter, little boy," a voice said. "You touched?"

I tried to turn around, but he forced me into the underbrush. I thought, "This is *it.*" We went back along a path to a little clearing in the woods. There was a small fire there, and an old man sitting in front of it like a fisherman leaning over the side of a boat. He had a beard that seemed yellow in the light of the fire, and he poked the coals with a long twig, didn't seem to notice me at all. The man who had ahold of me deposited me in front of the fire and sat down next to me.

"So who'd you kill?" he said.

I looked at his face in the firelight and realized it was Bailey.

"Bailey," I said.

He looked at me. "I'll be damned."

The old man said, "Know each other?"

"This is Ben's kid," Bailey said.

"You don't say."

"What are you doing out here?" Bailey said.

"Have you seen my father?"

The old man poked at the fire. Bailey put his hands together in front of his knees, stared across at the old man.

"I'm looking for my father."

"He's not here," Bailey said. There was a vibration in his voice —as if his words might shatter the strings in his throat.

"Do you know where—"

"Your father is a stubborn man," Bailey said.

"Where is he?"

"He just left us."

"Is he—"

"He ain't coming back this way, though," the old man said.

Bailey frowned at the fire, said, "Shut up."

A breeze moved the fire back and forth, made a sound like running water in the leaves overhead.

"Where'd he go?" I said.

"He went—" Bailey paused, put his hand on my shoulder. "He and the rest of them went to have it out with Silver."

"Not at his house—I just came from there."

"They cut through the woods there," he pointed across the road. "They're going to the factory."

I stood up.

"Don't go looking now. They're probably already there."

"May as well stay here with us cowards," said the old man.

"Shut up," Bailey said.

"I've got to go," I told them, moving back away from the fire.

"There's nothing you can do." Bailey was crying. "It's all over."

I ran back out to the road, ran with tears on my face toward my father and what I knew would be the end of something.

I already told you what happened. There was a riot, and I saw my father get killed. A deputy named Bradford Taylor—the one with the goat's mouth—hit my father on the side of the head with a billy club. It made a sound like a wooden bucket dropped into a deep well. The old man went down right in front of me and I saw his eyes roll. He twitched like a moth, and I just stood there, screaming.

No. He wasn't the enemy after all. Not even the things he did to Sara could make him an enemy after I watched him die. If only Sara could have been there to see it. Maybe it would have affected her the way it did me. I thought my father was a sort of hero.

Just before the riot started, I came running up behind the strikers. There couldn't have been more than twenty or thirty of them. A paltry number from a factory that employed at least 200 people. I screamed for the old man, and the strikers stepped aside, let me through. When I got to the front, there was my father, kneeling in the moonlight, waiting for me. Beyond him, I saw the road leading to the factory and Silver's house, and lined up across the road were the deputies. All of them. They knew what was going to happen. They all knew about it. There must have been fifty of them, and they all had billy clubs and guns and knives.

My father actually smiled when he saw me. "Well, you're a bit young for this, son." Everybody laughed. I think even the deputies laughed.

I stood in front of my father, trying to catch my breath.

He put his large hand on my shoulder. "Your mother got my note?"

"What note?"

"What are you doing here?"

"What note?" I remembered the piece of paper I saw Sara burning, and I felt something in my spine give way, as if a bone slipped out and left me trembling in the center.

"What's the difference? You didn't get it."

"Did you say anything about tonight?" I tried to whisper this to him.

One of the deputies hollered to disperse.

My father stood up. "You go on then. Go back."

"What did the note say?" Everyone heard me.

He looked at the line of deputies, sighed. "I thought everybody'd be here."

"Was it about tonight?" I was crying.

One of the men next to the old man said, "We should have known she wouldn't help."

"Who?" I said.

My father leaned down. His eyes were dull brown, his face white in the darkness. I could see the blue patches of his jaw, the thick hair over his long ears. He smelled of whiskey and tobacco. He looked into my eyes and said, "We weren't really expecting anyone. I'm thankful you came, though."

"Was it—"

"Go on," he whispered. "Before this gets going."

Then he turned, raised his arm, and walked toward that billy club.

When it was over, he was settled in the dirt at my feet, and everybody was running down the road behind me, screaming and howling in pain, or fear, or both. The deputies made almost as much noise, and they too were now behind me, chasing the last of the strikers. It got quiet gradually—so quiet, I thought I could hear the blood dripping out of my old man. There were one or two others lying around us, but they weren't making any noise either. I might as well have been a toe in somebody's boot. The whole thing lasted a few minutes, and although I got knocked down once or twice, I found myself standing there when the fighting stopped and the running began.

When I couldn't bear the sight of my father's body any more, I left him there in the road, and walked back toward the tents.

———————

Whatever he might have done, my father would have been one of Silver's victims. Either he died fighting Silver, or he died of the phossy jaw the way most of the others did. I knew, even at my age, that Silver would go on.

Perhaps my father was the enemy. He was never the kind of man who took a kid up into his arms and got his face wet. He didn't tell me any stories, take me hunting or fishing—or offer me a pat on the head when I had a toothache. I remember I got a boil on my ass once, and he took a whiskey bottle, put it up against the boil, and hit the bottom of the bottle as hard as he could. The boil burst into the bottle, and I nearly went into the bottle with it. Pain has a way of making you very small. He laughed at that. And I went into the next day dreaming of his death. Wishing it.

It was only in the end there, when he fell down so helpless in the road, and his eyes rolled back like the eyes of a frightened horse; only then did he seem fully human. My father, dead before me.

I wanted to talk to Sara. I was as close to hating her as I ever got. I wanted to find out what was in the note; if she had shared it with Silver; if perhaps, because of her, the strike was broken. I wanted to know if she had been responsible for the death of her most hated enemy.

I guess I wanted to yell at her too. Wail into her face that he wasn't such a bad man after all. Maybe a bad father, but not such a bad man. I wanted to tell her he was a hero.

But the tent, all our belongings, Ogra, and Sara were all gone when I got back. Only the cat remained, sitting in the mud where the tent had been, licking her front paw as if she'd just eaten the rest of my family and all the little things we owned.

•

THE SIXTH INTERVIEW

NOVEMBER 2, 1980

9:00 A.M.

I never saw Sara again. Never even found out what happened to her. She may have gone to Baltimore with Ogra, or perhaps she went to some other place on her own. I figured Ogra made her leave me behind. I didn't really feel betrayed. I was just lonely. Me and the cat.

I felt like the last person on earth. Everybody I knew was either gone or dead or sick at the sight of me. And Sara wasn't going to be around to hold me up any more.

I always hoped Sara would find a place where she wouldn't have to make sorties and night raids. Maybe she found it. Maybe she found peace before she died. I came to think of her as a victim, like my father. Like me.

So there I was, standing where the tent used to be, so completely alone I might as well have been a soul. Not even the cat noticed me.

I never did convince anyone, except possibly Silver, that I killed Walker Adams. It bothered me that I couldn't tell my father about it before he was killed. I kept going over it again and again in my mind, trying to listen to what he said, and to what I said—trying to see if there wasn't an opening in there for me to tell him it was me. I should have told him. At least he should have known that before he died.

I never got over the guilt, either. It hunted me; followed me around like an odor. I came to think of it as an injury—as if murder had created a permanent wound in my brain. I kept seeing the look on Adams's face, kept hearing the sound of his voice when he said, "Being used," or "For shit's sake, man." Imagine those being your last words.

Murder has a way of following you around. Oh, I know some people can kill a person and light a cigarette afterward. I know men have laughed like children while they barbecued some poor black or Indian. I've read things in the newspaper, heard all the horror stories of this century, believe me. But it still seems hard to understand that such things are possible, knowing what I know about murder.

What is it behind a man's eyes, anyway? You look into a man's eyes and you know something's there—something private and important. When my father died, his eyes were still the same color, still bathed in fluid; but he wasn't there anymore and you could see it. His eyes only reflected light.

You would think, with what I've been through, I would know something about all this—that I'd have some answers about what the thing behind a man's eyes is, and where it goes when he dies, and what death really is.

Well, I'll tell you: I know what it feels like to die. I've done it twice. But I don't know what it feels like to be dead. You know what I mean?

Believe me, there is no good way to die. It hurts. It hurts worse than all the pain you ever felt. And I don't mean all the pain leading up to it either—I'm not talking about the kind of pain you have when you get real sick and die. You've got the pain of being sick—that's one thing. But then you've also got the pain of dying. It's always separate. And you haven't felt anything even close to it.

My father probably felt the pain when his skull fell in; but, you see: dying is all by itself and after. He had to endure that too.

The worst thing about dying is you can't move. Not even an eyelash. And inside, right under the skin, almost at the base of each hair, you've got this raging struggle. Noise so loud you hear it twice, and an odor as foul as any sour or rotten thing you can remember. It's as if somebody stretched your skin over a ferocious dogfight. It's just awful. And it all starts *after* the flash of light and the feeling of euphoria.

But once it's over? Dying is a different thing than death—the same as birth is a different thing from life. I can't explain what being dead is like because I don't remember it—any more than I remember being born.

ROBERT BAUSCH

I know one thing: being dead is not like when you're asleep. I've heard people hoping it was so, but it isn't. It's about as close to sleeping as getting born is to waking up in the morning. When you're dead you just are not any more, you know what I mean? Like before you were born. Remember that?

———————

After the riot, Silver had the deputies go to tent city and drive everybody out. He was like a mad preacher, screaming out names and curses, waving his cane in the smoky air. The deputies went through the white tents like a cavalry troop.

I was so afraid and alone I couldn't cry. I just stood there watching the little tents fold and listening to all the hollering and wailing. Nobody put up a fight, but the women cried and cursed Silver.

I was pretty much in a daze around then. I remember somehow ending up with Mrs. Yerbich, standing next to her watching two deputies bury my father. They put him in a white pine box, said a few prayers over him and lowered him into a brown ditch. Mrs. Yerbich cried. There were a few people there.

When it was over, Mrs. Yerbich picked up her belongings and moved on down the road. She looked like a pack animal, carrying two sacks over her shoulders. She was all hunched over, and I felt sorry for her. I followed her into Wilkes-Barre.

She didn't seem to notice me. She rented a room above a laundry and went to work there pressing clothes and folding linens. I thought she'd ask me to live with her, so when she first rented the room, I went up the stairs after her, crying all the time, but she looked at me and said, "I'm going to die soon. I've got the phossy jaw. You find somebody else to help you."

So I slept outdoors.

Wilkes-Barre was a one road town back then, and it was a dirt road at that. I remember there were still wooden sidewalks that you could crawl under. The houses were all white, and they sat right on the street. There were white picket fences, and wrought iron stair railings everywhere. You couldn't find a billboard or a telephone pole. The shops had signs you could read, and not a single store had a sign that lit up. At night, you couldn't find your way around the town.

Remembering that place now makes it seem like a small village on a south sea island. A place warm and orderly and clean, you know? Everybody seemed to do what he was supposed to do, and only troublemakers like my father got into any real pain. And, of course, I was a troublemaker nobody knew about—except Mr. Silver. But he didn't care about me. Nobody cared about me. I was like the cat.

It's funny about the cat. He went to the funeral, walked behind Mrs. Yerbich and me for a good mile or so—you know, he slunk along real casually, stopping every now and then to let us get a little further ahead, as if he wanted to escape or something and thought we might try to stop him—and then he just wasn't there anymore. I turned around and he was gone. I remember thinking, hell, why not? It wasn't any percentage in staying with me.

I figured that some day I would save somebody's life and make up for Walker Adams. I guess I was thinking I ought to save my own life as well. It was going to get cold soon, and I was sleeping under sidewalks. The best place was in front of the hardware store that sat across from an open lot where men pitched horseshoes on Saturday afternoons. The store was called simply HARDWARE —which was the way people identified places of business back then. Catchy names didn't come until later. Maybe Sears or J. C. Penney started that sort of stuff.

The ground under the sidewalk in front of the hardware store was soft, and the bricks near the front door were warm, so that's where I started sleeping at night. I stayed on my own for most of that fall. The hardest thing was getting food. I ate a lot of grain and raw carrots and potatoes—things people leave lying around in stables or that they take their time harvesting. Every now and then Mrs. Yerbich would give me some soup. It was really hard to eat anything around her, though, no matter how hungry I was. She looked like a skull somebody started to put skin on and didn't finish the job. Her lower jaw looked like a wounded foot.

"How're you making it?" she'd say.

"I'm doing OK." I'd be looking at the soup—it was usually potato soup, yellow with milk and butter. I guess it was good for me.

"Find a place to stay?"

"Yes." I always lied to her. I didn't want her to feel bad about me.

"Good." She'd try to smile, and her lower lip would crack, like a piece of hard candy. I knew she was going to die soon, and I didn't want her to worry about me. I really wasn't doing so bad —I wanted to get some money, though. Try to get to Baltimore and find Sara. I may even have wanted to find Ogra. It was hard not having anybody.

The man who owned the hardware store was named Boone. That's all anybody ever called him. He was as lean as a walking stick, with a short white beard and no mustache. He wore wire glasses and had the longest, most pointed nose I've ever seen. He came and went at exactly the same time every work day. He was never where he was not expected, and I don't think he ever did anything he didn't know he was going to do a day in advance. He had a set pattern of existence, like a wasp or a cicada, and he went about it with a deliberate and mechanical motion—as if his joints had ground glass between them and it hurt him to move.

One day, not long after it started to get cold at night, I got to my resting place too early, and there was Boone locking the store.

"Evening," I said. I stood there in the street with my hands in my pockets, staring at the wood floor of the sidewalk. I must have looked like a rodent of some kind: I hadn't been washed in at least a month, and I'd been sleeping in the dirt.

"Who are you?" he said. There was a slight tremor in his voice.

"I'm nobody," I said. I believed it.

"Everybody's somebody. Even dirty little boys like you." He took the key from the lock, placed it in a tiny pocket of his black vest, and came over to where I was standing. "What are you doing here at this time?"

"At this time?" I didn't know what he meant.

"Not going to buy something, I take it?"

"What?"

"No. I don't think so." He nodded his head. I didn't understand what he was talking about.

"I beg your pardon, sir?" I said, after a pause.

"You got something on your mind?" he said.

"No."

"Well, what are you doing in front of my store?"

"Oh," I said. "No, I'm not going to rob you or anything."

He laughed. "How old are you?"

"I'll be eleven in December."

"What's your name?"

I told him.

"Do you have parents?" He leaned over me, put his hands on my shoulders. He smelled of fresh cut wood, and pine oil.

"My father's dead."

"Oh."

"He got killed in the riot." I was proud of that, and I guess it showed.

"I'm sorry," Boone said.

"My mother got driven out."

"And you're alone?"

"My sister went with her," I said, and then I realized I was crying.

"And you've got no one," Boone said. "Well, you come with me."

Boy, was I glad I started crying. I followed along after him and joined his routine. I began what was, for him, the longest robbery in the history of the world.

It was a long robbery because it lasted seven years. I took money, watches, and jewelry from Boone—gradually trying to build enough funds to go to Baltimore and find Sara. I didn't know how much it would take, so I kept collecting it, a little here, a little there. I sometimes went months without counting it. When I did count it, I had to estimate because I didn't know what a lot of the jewelry was worth. I never had confidence in my guesses, and maybe that's why I was always going to go next year. He must have known I was stealing from him, although at the time I didn't think he suspected me.

He was a very strange man. Almost a preacher, except he owned a hardware store and expected me to work there all the hours he did. At night he put me through my "schooling."

These are the things he taught me:

That the world is a round ball which, by some force none of us understands, spins around the eye of God. The sun makes light for the world because God is not blind. Since man is blind to God, the sun only makes light for the world half the time. The other half, we are in our darkness and must suffer our own tattered hours without God.

God is not in woman.

He is not in any animal, except man.

A woman is on earth to serve man by day and tempt him at night—thereby confirming the dual nature of the sun, and night and day.

The only way to avoid the temptations of woman—he always said it singularly like that, as if he had one particular woman in mind—the only way to avoid her temptations was to avoid her services during the day. You could not have contact with a woman at night if you didn't have anything to do with them during the day.

Since women were evil, marriage was only a weak compromise with the dark angel—a sort of agreement with evil for one's own comfort.

Since the race could not go on without such compromises, all life is merely the stubborn refusal of evil to quit. God is in all men because man is the only product of evil that is good and it is good because God has chosen to be in man. God has chosen to be in man to free the world from evil. All men do not accept God, but when they do, procreation will stop, and when that happens, evil will simply "wither away." So, of course, will man.

He also taught me that money was the sacrament of a good

man, and the weapon of a bad one. (This made me feel good about my stealing. All I was doing was receiving the sacrament of our little private religion.)

He taught me that begetting children was the greatest evil a man could do—since he was directly counteracting the grand design. As long as new men were being produced, withering away could not be taking place.

He said that murder was also an evil thing, because you never knew if you were killing a man who had God in him and accepted Him—hence you could not know if you hadn't killed a disciple of the great design.

I asked him if it was OK to kill a man who you knew was not part of anything grand. His answer was, you can't ever really know that. I didn't want to argue with him.

He said love was a feeling created by the evil one to make us want to copulate. Familial love too was bad because it made us dependent on one another, and made it impossible for us to accept the principle of withering away.

I asked him about hate, and he said it didn't really exist. "Hate," he said, "is merely the zealous absence of love."

"Do you hate me?"

"I don't love you."

"Why did you take me in?"

"I needed help in the store, of course."

"And I was free."

"Ah, yes." He didn't look at me.

So went many of our lessons. He taught me mathematics and the proper uses of the English language and even some history.

But most of our lessons eventually turned on his grand design ideas and withering away. I heard those two words so often I began to think I was losing weight.

And, of course, I felt less and less like a thief.

Poor Boone. He worked so hard trying to make me believe his theories, and I bet there wasn't even another human being aware of them. He needed me in the store so he'd have somebody to tell these theories to.

ROBERT BAUSCH

I asked him one time what happened to his mother and father, and he looked at me as if I'd cut him or something.

"I shan't talk about it."

He was leaning by a stand of rakes and shovels, dusting off the blades and talking to himself when I asked him about it. He went back to doing whatever he was doing there, and I went around the counter and stood next to him.

"Why not?"

"I don't think about them."

"But why?"

"You have work to do."

I was nearly fifteen by then—had grown to a good height, six feet at least, almost as tall as Boone—and he had me cleaning the pistols and rifles he held behind the counter. But I wanted to know about his parents. I'd been thinking about mine, and didn't think his experience could be any worse. Besides, I wondered why he felt the way he did about the world—why he went about everything as if he'd been mechanically programmed to do it. He lived as if the movement of a clock sent signals to his brain.

"My father was a hero, but he wasn't—"

"I said I don't want to talk about it," Boone said. He put down his cloth, went over to the seed barrel and picked up a broom lying there.

"They were pretty bad, huh?" I said.

He put both hands on top of the broom handle, leaned on the hands with his head down. "Terrible things happened to them," he said.

"What?"

"There was a panic. They lost all their money."

"Oh."

"My mother was very kind."

I wasn't really interested any more. I went back to where the pistols needed polishing.

"She had to do something to help my father."

I picked up a Colt, wiped the barrel a second time.

"My father was not a man of God. He couldn't handle the loss of his fortune."

I put the Colt on the blue cloth that Boone thought attracted the attention of his customers.

"My mother sold herself."

"What's that mean?" I said.

"She let men have her for a price. She was a whore."

There was a slight tremor in his voice, as if there was something caught in his throat.

I didn't have the heart to tell him that women were merely agents of the devil anyway.

I wanted to ask him if his father was religious or anything. Maybe I wanted to find a cause for a man to be so sure of everything. I might have believed his system at first—maybe I really believed the universe was arranged the way he said. But when I was sixteen, I saw a woman naked for the first time, and I knew that no matter what Boone thought, such a thing just couldn't be evil.

We lived in a boarding house near the stables at the opposite end of the town from the hardware store—Boone thought you should have a long walk before work in the morning. I had an upstairs room next to Boone, and one night I crawled out my window onto the front porch—actually onto the roof of the front porch. Above where I was lying, I could see three other windows, all lit up and yellow in the dark. I remember thinking no one in any of those rooms could see me, even if they looked directly out because the light in those rooms was so bright. I was going to play pool in town—I didn't only steal from Boone, you see—and as I was making my way to the edge of the front porch roof, I looked up and saw, in the window to the left of mine, a young woman pulling a white slip up over her head. She must have been somebody's guest, because I'd never seen her before. When she was naked, I couldn't escape her window; I was trapped in its frame, breathing through each pore, my eyes burning as if I had soap in them. It could have been the first time I actually beheld beauty. Oh, I'd seen pink sunsets and yellow dawns, and cloud formations like soft white folds of satin cloth; I'd felt the texture of a rose or followed the way a leaf moves slightly in the breeze. But I'd never seen real beauty—the kind that made you feel like you didn't have any bones and like breathing was a completely new experience.

I waited there, like a lizard in a spotlight, until she disappeared from sight. She just sank from view; I could tell she lay down on the bed in there. A movement that nearly paralyzed me forever. If I was going to live, I knew I had to get back to my window and into the house. I was not going to make it to any pool room on that night. I went slowly up the roof to my window. I thought of sneaking over to her window to see what she might be doing on that bed—but I was afraid by then, having gotten some control of myself, and I could feel my heart beating so fast and hard I thought everyone must be able to hear it.

Once inside, I sat on my bed and considered the future. I was not going to Baltimore. I would not be able to get to know the woman next door, because Boone would disapprove. I would live the rest of my life trapped in a yellow window frame, unable to move, watching beautiful things move away from me. My life was only thinning smoke; a sort of unnoticed evaporation.

Right then I knew I had to get away from Boone. End the robbery.

But when I lay down on the bed and began making plans in the dark, I thought of the poor, long-nosed fanatic's life without me —I wondered who he would tell his theories to and who would help him in the store—especially in the spring when the seed orders came in. I saw him, making his way through the routine days, like a busy insect, alone; and I was so suddenly sorry for him I felt my heart skip a beat.

How could I leave him?

I still puzzle over all this. I'm sure I didn't love the old robot. I thought he was crazy—especially after I beheld beauty. But I could not leave him alone. He fed me, clothed me, and gave me something to do every day including weekends. He tried to teach me about the world, and he trusted me. (I couldn't have stolen nearly so much if he hadn't.)

Maybe I knew that leaving him alone would be another sort of betrayal. In my mind, something wasn't complete yet. I needed him to catch me stealing—I wanted him to find me sitting on a pile of his stolen merchandise. Whatever he meant to do to me, I would accept—and he could have his precious jewelry, and money, and even hardware back. All of it. Maybe then, I'd be free to leave—if I was still alive. And yet, it was so much fun trying not to get caught. I couldn't just let it happen. I needed him to find me while I was trying my hardest not to get caught. It had to be a fair exchange. I would not simply let him grab me.

I guess I couldn't leave him because I didn't want to be alone either. I've thought of that. I swear, I lay on that bed and cried when I thought of Boone going through his miserable schedule without me. Isn't that the damnedest thing?

The next morning I got up and went downstairs early, hoping to behold beauty again.

Boone and I didn't eat breakfast in the house; he liked to eat at a place called Pinky's near the store, and we'd start out at seven each morning no matter what was being cooked in the house. Some mornings I smelled hash browns and fried eggs when I came downstairs, and I nearly fainted from hunger. I'd have killed for a cup of coffee; but Boone would come down and put his hat on, take his walking stick, and out we'd go into the freezing cold.

This one morning, though, I came down at 6:30 and I snuck into the kitchen and paid for a cup of coffee.

I sat at the table in the dining room—a large room more like a hotel lobby than a room in a normal house—sipped my coffee, saying private little prayers that the woman would come down and sit across from me, or at least walk in front of me on her way someplace. I wanted to look at her so bad I didn't even taste the coffee.

But guess who came down?

Boone.

There I was, with my nose inhaling hot steam from the cup in front of me, and Boone says, "What are you doing here?"

I swallowed what I had in my mouth. "I couldn't sleep."

"You know we don't eat here."

"It's just a cup of coffee," I said.

"I see." He went in front of me and passed into the kitchen. It was just he and I and the cook awake in the house. I sat in front of a kerosene lamp and waited for him. I wasn't thinking of the woman any more, because it hit me that it wasn't seven o'clock yet. Boone had broken his routine for some reason.

When he came back, he had a cup in his hand.

"You having coffee, too?" I said.

He sat across from me. "I want to talk to you," he said.

"OK." I thought maybe he'd seen me stealing something, or perhaps he saw me on the roof last night.

"I've gotten a letter."

"A letter?"

"It's from—" He paused, looked into his cup. Then, he reached into his coat pocket and withdrew a white envelope.

"Who?" Maybe Silver told him I was a murderer. I was really beginning to lose my appetite. Boone looked as if he'd lost a limb and was watching the wound bleed.

"It's from your mother," he said.

Naturally he wouldn't listen to me when I told him I didn't have a mother. He insisted on reading it to me, his voice trembling all the way through it, and my only response was anger. Ogra said she was alone—I felt relieved for Sara, then; but I knew what would follow from that little piece of information: Ogra needed me.

"She wants you to come home," Boone said.

"Where's that?" I said. "The last time I saw her it was a pup tent."

"She's in Pittsburgh."

I hoped she was working in the mines.

"How'd she know where I was?" I said.

"I don't know."

It had to be Silver. Mrs. Yerbich was dead nearly six years, and I didn't know anyone in Wilkes-Barre that really knew who I was, or where Ogra might be. Silver, though, was still in his factory—

only three miles down the road, and I figured he knew where I was. He may have even seen me, although I never ever saw him.

"I'm not going," I said.

"You've got to."

"Why?"

"Because you belong to her."

"I'm almost eighteen."

"All she has to do is write the sheriff."

"I don't believe this," I said. It never occurred to me that I might be forced to leave Boone.

He folded the letter and placed it back into his pocket. I drank the last of my coffee, staring at him. Neither of us said anything for a while. Then he raised his cup, took a loud sip of his coffee. "I can't believe you have to go and live with a woman," he said.

"She's not a woman."

"Whatever," he said.

"She's a orangutan," I said. I wasn't sure I'd pronounced it right.

He lowered his cup, said, "Nevertheless."

"You could just ignore the letter."

"No."

"She'd never come here."

"I don't want any trouble." He checked his watch. "It's nearly seven," he said.

"I thought your watch could let you know that without you having to look at it," I said.

"What?"

"Nothing."

"You needn't get angry with me," he said. "I do right as I see it and abide by the law as you should, and everyone should."

"I'm going to stay here," I said.

"It's time for us to go," he said. He got up, moved toward the door.

"I will not go and live with an agent of the devil," I said.

He smiled. "You're a good boy."

"If I've got God in me, you can't let me go to that woman."

"You don't have God in you."

"How do you know? You said we can't know that."

"You've been stealing from me."

The coffee started to boil in my stomach. "How'd you know that?"

"I'm not a stupid man," he said. There was no anger in his voice at all.

"Why didn't you—"

"Stop you?"

"Yes."

"I cannot."

"You cannot what?"

"I cannot stop a man from doing what men do."

"I don't understand."

"You, like all men who have not got God in them, are evil."

"OK."

"We live here to further the withering away process. Nothing more. I preach my message. If you listen, if you foster no children, that is enough." He put his hat on. "I cannot stop evil because life is evil—all life, in every form. If I stopped you from stealing, it would have the same impact as taking a teaspoon of water out of the ocean."

He opened the door, put his hand up into his vest pocket.

"Wait," I said.

He stood there in the door with the white sky behind him, a slight smile in the corners of his face.

"Did she mention anything about someone named Sara?"

"No."

"Nothing about a sister?"

"Nothing." He held the door, casting a long shadow into the room.

"One more thing," I said.

He bowed toward me, smiling.

"You were kind to me," I said. "I thank you."

"You're welcome." He tipped his hat.

"I guess this is good bye?"

"I'm responsible for you," he said. His voice was different; it was as if he was addressing one of his customers. "I can't deliver you personally to your mother. But I can put you on proper transportation to Pittsburgh."

"Why? It'll cost you money."

"Nevertheless." He started to go out.

"Just give *me* the money, and I'll go myself."

"Heh," he said. "Heh, heh." He went out, closed the door as if it were a coffin.

"Well," I said out loud to the whole room. "If you *really* wanted to put me on a train, you shouldn't have left me here by myself."

I was on my way to his room to get as much money and other valuables as I could carry, when I ran into the young woman whose body I had seen the night before.

She seemed afraid of me. She leaned against the wall to let me pass, and I stopped in front of her, tried to think of something to say.

She looked at my feet.

"I'm Ken Ezra," I said. "I've got to leave town."

She didn't say anything. I couldn't get her to look at me. I figured if she was going to live in Wilkes-Barre, then so would I. I'd hide from Boone—sleep under porches and sidewalks again—if only I could see this woman once in a while, standing in front of her window without any clothes on. There was no way I was going to Pittsburgh. She stood there in the hall in front of me, breathing, and I realized she smelled like fresh cucumbers.

"Are you alone?" I leaned down, tried to see her eyes.

"Oh," she said. It was like somebody squeezed her; she lost air through her throat and it made that sound.

"I'm not going to hurt you or anything," I said.

She screamed.

It scared me. I jumped back, tried to put myself somewhere else in that hall. I heard doors opening.

"What's the matter with you?" I whispered.

"Get away from me."

ROBERT BAUSCH

"I'm not a murderer," I said. Then I realized how inaccurate that was. I was not only a murderer, I was a thief.

Down the hall a man stepped out. He was only a shadow, but a large shadow, and I knew I would not get to talk to the little panting victim in front of me.

"I'm really sorry," I said. "I just wanted to say hello."

"What's going on?" the man said, as he approached us.

"I was just going to my room, and I must have scared her."

She went toward the stairs, having done her worst.

When the man got to me, I saw he had a dimple in his chin, eyes like a sad bear, and a razor in his left hand.

"Christ," I said. "She just got scared. I didn't do a thing."

"That's my sister," the man said.

"I felt that way about my sister too." I started past him, toward my room. He took my arm, turned me around.

"You son of a bitch," he said.

"Honest," I said. "It was just a mistake."

He put the razor up under my chin. "I ought to kill you right here," he said.

"Look. I'm not even eighteen yet."

"You look big enough to me." He pressed the razor against my skin.

"Don't kill me."

"You get out of here," he said into my face. He smelled like a wet dog. I noticed a bead of sweat in the dimple on his chin.

"OK," I said. "OK." When he let go of me I had this sudden urge to ask him how he shaved the hair out of that dimple.

––––––––––––––

When I got back to my room, I took my shirt off and wiped the water from my chest and arms. I felt sick to my stomach, as if I'd swallowed something wet and hot. I knew I had to pack whatever I could carry and get the hell out of there. But I just sat for a while on the bed and tried to add up all the possibilities: I could commit suicide. I could challenge the big dimple to a duel and die in the street. I could put all my loot into a pillowcase and walk out of

THE LIVES OF RILEY CHANCE

town to some other place—some place west. Maybe I could go to Texas and find oil. Sure. I saw myself at the train station, dragging a sack of stolen goods, asking for a ticket to the far west.

In the end, I left everything but the money. I had about seventy-five dollars, give or take a few pennies, and the clothing on my back. I left everything else in the room for Boone to find. I gave it all back except the money. It didn't seem worth having all his things once he knew about it. There was nothing to catch me at.

If anybody'd been out on the street that morning, they would have seen me walking alone up the road. I didn't know where I was going; just away from Wilkes-Barre, and Silver's factory, and Boone. I didn't know it, but I had about six months to live.

THE SEVENTH INTERVIEW

NOVEMBER 4, 1980

11:30 A.M.

I ended up in a place called Gravel Falls. It wasn't far down the road, but what the hell, I was tired of walking. I got a room in an old hotel called the Peterson, and I crawled into a rickety old mahogany bed and slept for two days.

I had this endless dream that I was watching my father and Walker Adams shooting pool on a large kitchen table—not a billiard table, mind you—and they talked and laughed in high priestlike voices, shooting little red and white balls back and forth. I watched, tried to stop the balls from rolling off, but none of them came close. They'd roll toward the edge as fast as a field mouse, and just as I'd lose my balance leaning over to save them, they'd stop. My father laughed, and Adams chalked his cue.

I couldn't wake up until all the balls were gone; until the last ball disappeared from the table. I never saw any of them evaporate or anything; I looked at my father and then back to the table and one or two of them would be gone. I studied the floor, began looking in the spittoons that lined the walls, trying to find one of them. It was the most important thing to me. I had to find just one of those balls.

And then I remember my father saying, "What are you looking for?"

Adams laughed. It was the same sort of laugh he made when he asked me when my sister was going to get some titties. I started hating him again.

"What are you looking for?"

I looked at my father, and there was blood leaking out of the corner of his mouth.

I woke up feeling as if I'd fallen backward a great distance. I was short of breath, and I wasn't sure who I was. No, it was worse than that. It wasn't that I didn't know who I was, I didn't know *what* I was. You ever have that experience? You wake up when

it's gray outside, and you've just opened your eyes, and you have
no sense of body, or organ, or anything solid. You can't picture
yourself, figure out what you are. You're just beast; simply a sort
of consciousness resting in a pillow, and you might be anything,
anything at all. And you have to think for a minute and remember,
"Oh, yes, I'm human. Yes, that's right, I'm a person, a person.
This is the world. Yes, the world and I'm a person, and my name
is . . . " Then you get it and you feel OK, except your heart's
beating like an engine with a part missing, and you realize there
is something in you that can think and is *not* you.

That's how I felt when I came out of that dream. It took another
few minutes to figure out where I was, and what I was doing there.

I realized my immediate problem: I was eighteen years old, or
close to it. I didn't know how to do anything but stack shovels,
shine guns, and sweep floors. I also had killed a man, so I guess
I knew how to do that too. I couldn't read or write as well as
anybody I knew; not even Mrs. Yerbich, who'd never been to
school, and who certainly had not benefited from seven years of
teaching from Boone. I could just barely spell my name, to tell the
truth, although I could add and subtract fairly well. I knew I
didn't want to work in a factory as my father had.

I lay there, staring out the white, curtainless windows, thinking
of my father and Walker Adams. And Sara. I really missed her
right then. She seemed so long ago—I knew it wouldn't bother me
half as bad if I wasn't alone again. Still, the thought of her made
me cry; and so there I was, a grown man—grown because there
wasn't anything else I could be and survive—and I was whimpering into my pillow like a widow on her first night after the funeral.

I never did find work. I lay around that room until the money
started to thin out. The room cost me forty-five cents a day, and
it didn't include meals. So I was spending a dollar every two days,
whether or not I ate. I had to do something.

I joined the army.

To be in the army you don't need brains. All you really need
are bones, and a little flesh to cover them, some ligaments and
cartilage, a few tendons, some sort of food processing mechanism,

and enough motor function to be able to use your arms and legs.
That's about it. They like it if you can dress yourself, but in case
you can't they make everybody take lessons when they first join.
That's what you spend the first few weeks of training doing:
learning how to dress. You have to do it just right, and you have
to do it with clothing that looks as if it was just manufactured. It
doesn't matter how old it is, it should look as if it just came off
the loom. They give you your clothes, but you have to keep them
clean. In fact, you have to keep everything clean, even the rags you
use to clean things with. They yell at you if they find anything
dirty, and since you can't clean something without getting something else dirty—dirt has to go somewhere—you get yelled at a
lot.

All armies are the same, I guess.

They sent me to North Carolina for my training; I was there
eight weeks, getting yelled at, and being told where to put my
body, and when to put it there and even sometimes how to do it.
I was used to being yelled at, though, so I did OK. Then they sent
me to New Jersey—a place called Walker or Wheeler or something like that. It was an air field—a relatively new thing. I went
there on a train with sixty-five other men. I wanted to go to
Baltimore, but I knew that would be too good. That would mean
something happening in my favor; the shock would have been too
much for me.

The country was getting ready to stay out of the war in Europe
back then. So they were building planes and collecting lighter than
air ships—and training people, only lucky people, how to fly them.

When I got to the town—I'll call it Wheeler, I really don't
remember. You can look it up, though. Anyway, when I got there,
I was greeted by a short, balding man with a fine looking pair of
red lips who talked backward a lot of the time. He didn't really
talk backward, he'd just reverse the first letter or two in everything
—but doing that made him nearly impossible to understand. I was
getting off this train with the other men behind me, and this man
with the red lips stood in front of us and said, "Sipe that whit
eating frin off gour yace!" He said it real loud, and fast. We all filed

out and got in line. Nobody said a word. I think they were all trying to figure out what he said.

He walked along the line, his hands on his hips, his head bobbing from side to side. His uniform looked as if it were made of light brown aluminum, and I never saw shinier boots.

"I'm Sergeant Chase," he said. "I balk tackward mometimes, sen."

I didn't know any of the sixty-five men I was detraining with, but the man next to me whispered, "Jesus." And I felt all sixty-five recruits shake as if somebody let the air out of their boots.

"Themember rat," Sergeant Chase said.

"Good Jesus," the man next to me said.

"Yeah," I said.

"I'm the chan in marge," Sergeant Chase said.

"What?" said the man next to me. I turned my head slightly, looked over at him. He had a look on his face like a man who'd just seen a horse jump rope or something. He was a tall, yellow-haired boy from someplace out west, and he'd never seen anything like Sergeant Chase.

"You treard me, hooper," Chase yelled.

"My name ain't Hooper, sir," he said. His voice was soft and kind of sad.

"Shou yuttup!"

"Oh, my God," somebody said.

"Rilence in the sanks." Chase locked his red lips after this. He looked as if he wanted to kiss one of us. He might have worn lipstick. Then, he let this sort of chimpanzeelike grin crawl across his face, and he said, "Sen I whay yump, jou jump."

"Yes, sir!" everybody yelled.

"Mollow fe," Chase said.

We mollowed him onto the air field where he showed us what we'd be doing for the next two years. We were what they called, "ground-crewmen." That meant we stayed on the ground. What we did was wash the lighter than air ships, wind and fold the lines and ropes, adjust the wheel blocks, and keep the air field clean.

We hauled sandbags, secured landing ropes. But mostly we watched the ships rise and dreamed about being in them. At least I did.

I wanted to be in one of those ships so bad it made me ache with hate and bitterness—like somebody's victim—every time I saw one rise up over a white cloud. I wanted to be so high. I just wanted to go *up*. No one I ever knew had seen the world from up there. You know? Up.

I got my wish.

But it was also the last thing Kenny Ezra ever got to see.

At first, when I told Sergeant Chase I wanted to go up in one of the ships, he only laughed at me.

"You're a shumb dit," he said.

"Have you ever ridden in one?"

"Wan masn't fupposed to sly."

By the time we had this conversation, I understood him fairly well. In fact, I found myself sometimes lapsing into balking tackward, as he called it. It's funny, isn't it, how you'll start "balking" like the people around you? I'd be strolling down the sidewalk in town, and I'd see a kid playing around somebody's new Ford, and I'd say, "Thop stat."

Anyway, when he said man wasn't supposed to fly, I told him it wasn't flying. "It's floating, only you're not floating on water, you're floating on air."

"Shit."

"It ain't flying," I said again. "Riding in a boat ain't swimming, is it?"

He frowned.

"I don't want to fly," I said. "I want to float."

Like I said. I got my wish.

The army gave a demonstration, so they invited everybody from town and promised an "air show to end all air shows." The first event was the dirigible *Robert E. Lee,* rising up over the countryside, almost without a sound.

Me and about sixty other men were assigned to hold onto the guide rope just before takeoff. Once the gas got going, we were supposed to let go and the ship would rise. But something went wrong, and the ship started to go up before any of us let go.

Now, they got this on film. Maybe you've seen it.

Anyway, the ship went up and so did we. Somebody screamed, "Hey." I think it was somebody further down the line from me. I was second from the top. There had to be fifty men on the line. Some might have jumped off as the ship started to rise, but most held on. When I looked down all I saw was bare heads below me. Almost nobody looked up. They were all holding on and staring at the ground. And the ground was going away.

"Pull us up!" the guy above me screamed.

"Hey." Somebody else yelled again. What a surprise it was to suddenly be up there like that. I was holding on real tight, thinking they would guide the ship back down to the ground, when the first man fell from the rope and screamed. He screamed all the way down. I watched his body get smaller and smaller and smaller, and when he hit he bounced. That scared me and *I* screamed.

I could see a crowd beginning to gather around the man who fell. Then another one let go, screamed like the first and the crowd dispersed like ants under a falling cinder.

The ship stopped its rise, seemed to settle in one place above the world. It was cold, the air smelled like ice.

I looked up, saw people in the cabin of the ship, staring down at me.

"Pull us up," I yelled.

The man above me slipped, grabbed the rope again with weakened fingers, his haunches falling on my hands.

"Don't fall," I said. I almost whispered it.

"My hands," he said.

"I can't hold *you* up too."

"We're so high."

Another one fell. Another.

"Jesus, they're bouncing," the man above me said. I didn't know him, felt suddenly that I ought to.

"Don't say that," I said. The wind started to rise. I felt the man shiver. "What's your name?" I asked him.

"Nichols."

"Where are you from?" I felt my hands starting to tremble.

"We're going to die."

"Could you scoot up a bit?"

"I can't hold on much longer."

I shouted, for everyone to hear, "DO SOMETHING!"

The ship started to move horizontally, as if the show was going to go on, no matter what.

"What's your name?" Nichols said.

"Ken Ezra," I told him. "You're sitting on my hands."

"It was nice knowing you," he said, and then he just went by me like a sandbag dropped out of the ship. I couldn't believe how fast he went by me. He didn't scream, and I didn't want to see him hit.

I tried to climb up the rope, but it had to be a hundred feet or more to the ship, and I'd already weakened my grip holding on for so long. I knew I wouldn't make it. But what else could I do? I'd been holding on for almost twenty minutes, and my fingers felt like they were turning to wood. I don't know how long I pulled myself up that rope. I gained inches at a time, and each time I pulled myself up just a little bit, I felt my fingers getting longer. When I finally looked up to see if I'd gotten any closer to the ship, it seemed farther away, although I could hear the people in the cabin now, yelling at me to "hold on." I remember thinking it was pretty obvious that was what I ought to do.

I looked down and noticed the ground moving under me, the tiny green trees and blue buildings cluttered in square corners below me. There were only two men left on the line besides me, but I remember being surprised they were still there, since the rope started to swing with every pull I made on it, and I assumed that meant I was the last one on the line.

I started pulling again, heard another scream.

I looked down, saw, dangling about forty feet below, the last man on the rope besides me. It was Sergeant Chase. I didn't even know he was up there with me until then.

"Fit," he said, looking at me as if I'd lowered him into a well or something. "I'm shucked." Then he let go. I saw his bald head tumble and disappear and get smaller until it hit into the top of a tree.

I don't know if it had anything to do with seeing Chase fall like that, but I started crying.

I looked up at my fingers, watched them begin to slip down the rope. "H-hold on," I whispered. I was talking to my hands.

I started breathing heavy. I think my lungs were getting ready to be crushed and finished. They used up such columns of air in the last moments up there. Maybe my whole body was getting ready for death. I felt a drop of perspiration run down from under my arm—it went its ticklish way down the side of my chest.

By now I had a whole crowd cheering me on.

I remember thinking, "This is going to be embarrassing," and as I thought the word "embarrassing" my hands let go.

I was not ready for them to do that. It came as a complete surprise.

I tried to run on the air, all the way down.

2

The law and ordinance of nature under which all men are born . . . forbids nothing but what no one wishes or is able to do, and is not opposed to strife, hatred, anger, treachery, or, in general, anything that appetite suggests.

—Spinoza

Earth is the place for expiation of old and forgotten sins.

—Hindu saying

•

THE EIGHTH INTERVIEW

NOVEMBER 4, 1980

3:00 P.M.

I told you before what it feels like to die. But the fall, that long fall: you should feel *that*. I couldn't breathe on the way down. Couldn't make my lungs work—they just kept expanding. I think my eyes must have gotten larger too, watching the ground come. I landed on my feet and just sort of went into myself. There was a violent pause while everything stopped spinning and twirling, then a loud, deep, throaty sort of crack. After the crack I was lying there, feeling the pain of hitting subside, watching the bright light, the tunnel of light, feeling just wonderful—giddy and full of relief and a kind of open-ended, permanent sort of joy that lasted maybe forty or fifty seconds. Then death started. It came as suddenly and finally as a wave of nausea or a dizzy spell—it lasts only a short time, but it seems as if it will go on forever and for all things. Just thinking of it now makes my skin quiver.

I wish I didn't remember it.

I know that's what that old black woman felt while I was holding her in my arms in the taxi. She made a gurgling sound in her throat; it sounded as if I was choking her. The driver turned his nostrils around and glared at me. He knew she was dying too, I guess. But he didn't know what she was going through.

"You know what's happening to her?" I said. We were parked in front of the assembly hall, on Neill Street, and she was going into death.

He turned back around. "I think so."

"No," I said. "I mean do you *really* know?"

He watched the pine trees around the entrance to the hall. You could hear some loud band playing in there. "Is she dying?"

"That's right."

"Shouldn't we go to a hospital?"

"Once dying starts," I said, "nobody can stop it."

It was probably when I said that that the driver panicked and drove me to the police station.

He didn't understand what I meant. And by the time we got to the station, she was dead, and I was sitting in the back seat of that cab, crying just like a child.

But I'm getting ahead of myself. Ken Ezra was killed when he hit. That's what the papers said. Died instantly. I'll tell you how instantly it was—go get a pack of matches and light your eyes, let them burn for a minute, or a minute and a half. Somewhere in that range. They'll start to drip before you can put out the fire, and you'll put out the fire at least a year before the time it takes to die. That's what it seems like. I guess that's the other bad news I have to tell everyone. There's no such thing as instant death. You lose consciousness instantly, or your heart stops and your brain quits. That might happen instantly. Death takes a long time.

I've got to get off this subject. I'm sorry. Having more than one life sounds like a good idea to everyone, but what they forget is you also have more than one death in such cases. Think of that. That's what I do. All the time.

I know, if I'm going to explain how that old woman died, I should get on with it. You've been good to listen this long. I can't thank you enough for coming back here for all this, and for giving me the time to tell you the whole story. I'm sure you won't regret it. But if you do, it won't be my fault. I'm trying to be as honest as I can.

Let's see. There are some things I think you should know about how I came into this life again. I really don't know what sort of web I was on while I was dead, or how it felt when it got disturbed and I came into being again. But I do know some things about the man who caused me to get life again. His name was Robert Pitt, and he was near sixty when he touched his young wife, Etta, for the first time, and created the ripple that would be me. Etta was eighteen.

This was 1919—the year of the red scare and the big flu epidemic. Either one may have conspired to kill my father, since he was a socialist and an old man. But he died, about four days before I was born, of a heart attack. Etta told me, when I was a little boy and wanted to know about my father, that his aorta burst. I didn't know what that was when she told me, but it sounded big and messy, and like it must have everything in the body connected to it in some way. I was real glad I wasn't born yet to see it.

Of course, I don't remember any of the stuff about getting born, or even the first five or six years. And I *never* realized I'd been here before. I was just a normal kid, I guess.

We lived in Washington, D.C. My father left us a lot of old clothes, boots and such, and a pair of vise grips when he died. That was about it. He didn't own anything. Insurance was a relatively new idea then, and Etta didn't have any of that, so she had to work.

She went to one of those glass-walled offices in the navy yard every day—dressed as neatly as any of the ladies who walked the streets of Georgetown on Sunday afternoons. I never did know what her job was, but I knew it didn't pay very much, because we were as poor as anybody we knew.

We lived in an apartment near the river. The floors were tile in that place, so the whole time I was growing up I felt as if I was in somebody's bathroom. We didn't have enough money to buy rugs or anything. Etta's pride and joy was a pair of orange curtains she hung over the only window in the apartment. She was paying Montgomery Ward for those on the installment plan.

I don't know where to start or what to tell you first about that life in Washington, D.C. It's not that I don't remember it or anything, it's that I'm not sure what you will find significant, and in a lot of ways, this part of my story is the most important.

Perhaps I should start with Etta—a woman who knew how to love and was willing to devote considerable time to the effort. I couldn't have compared her to Sara, since at that time I never even knew I'd been alive before. I know I keep saying it, but you've got to understand that the little boy who grew up in Washington didn't know he had been on the earth before. He never knew it. Never even had the slightest suspicion of it. Like I said, he couldn't compare Etta to Sara. But I can, now, and I can truthfully say that Etta was the one person in all of my times who knew what it meant to love another person and who gave me, without expecting anything in return, the one true happy period of time I ever got anywhere.

She'd come home from work in the evenings, pick me up in Mrs. Proudy's apartment—which was on the first floor and was where I spent all my days until I started school, and a good many of them after, since Etta had to work, and Mrs. Proudy owned the building and didn't have to go anywhere—she'd pick me up and say "so long and thanks" to Mrs. Proudy, and run up the stairs, carrying me at first, then when I was too big skipping steps behind me, and she'd tell me all about her day before we got to our apartment on the third floor. She did this as long as we were together. My memory includes her voice, from the very beginning. She always talked to me, and I always listened. When I had something to say, she'd look right at me the whole time—even if I lost track and ended up saying nothing at all.

Sometimes I felt like I could talk to her even when she wasn't there and she would hear me.

At night she'd let me lie with my head on her breast, and I'd listen to her breathing—the soft rising and falling, inhaling and exhaling—the wonderful woman's breathing that we all recognize if we've ever been held by a woman, and I'd think peaceful things. Like sailboats, or pink azaleas, or moist grass on a spring morning just before it rains. She'd stroke my neck and the side of my face and sing to me. It was all just too fine to be only part of a life, you know? If we had that kind of warmth all the time, it might be worth going through what you have to go through in this world. I've often thought that. We don't hold each other enough. That's our problem when you get right down to thinking about it. We all spend our time alone in our own skulls, inside our own eyes—and the world's a foreign place.

Mrs. Proudy was like an aunt, although she wasn't really anything but the landlord. She was a kind old woman, and I guess Etta and I both depended on her. I spent a lot of time with her since Etta worked six days a week and she didn't like for me to be home alone. Mrs. Proudy had been my babysitter when I was little, so there was no reason not to spend my afternoons there until Etta got home. I never did develop much affection for Mrs. Proudy, though. She was round—circular, and she smelled of garlic all the time. She wore these blue print dresses, real light ones, that hung down off her like water over a boulder, and she walked around talking to herself about "reds" and "anarchists." She hated all foreigners and especially a fellow named Bruno Hauptmann, who she said was a "barbarous child murderer." But that was late in her career—I guess I was near fourteen when Hauptmann took the Lindbergh baby and set Mrs. Proudy off.

It seemed to confirm for me, though, everything she'd told me about foreigners. I remember being fairly afraid most of the time back then. But I'm getting ahead of myself.

When Mrs. Proudy sat with me, in the early days before I started school, she'd hold me too, occasionally, and tell me stories —weird, scary things about "hoodoos" and "wooshes." She seemed afraid of everything, and when it rained and thunder shattered the clouds above our building, she'd hold me against herself and tremble like something with an engine in it. She'd say things like "don't be afraid" and all, but it was her that was wild with fear. I guess I loved her too, but I couldn't stand her to hold me like that, since she smelled like a Greek sandwich all the time and it made me sick.

Isn't that something? I just said we don't hold each other enough, and then I say I got sick when Mrs. Proudy held me. I guess you could say garlic gets in the way of a hell of a lot of crucial things, couldn't you. It really was bad though. Like somebody's feet, you know?

The human body is such a nasty thing, if you think about it. Nothing comes out of it—nothing at all, not air, not fluid, not anything—that smells pleasant. The only thing tolerable is blood. Maybe that's why we dump so much of that all over the earth.

Mrs. Proudy's favorite stories never really scared me very much, but they did make me curious. She told me one about a little boy who wanted to catch a "hoodoo" and put it in a watering can. A hoodoo wasn't anything like a ghost, or a white night shadow, or anything traditional like that. A hoodoo was a tiny man who whacked grandmothers over the head with raw celery until they cried. He only whacked grandmothers, for some reason I was never clear on, and he whacked them until they cried. He wore green shoes, and a green hat, and that was how you knew who he was.

The little boy wanted to catch a hoodoo because he hated his grandmother. She was always forcing him to eat—guess what? Celery.

That's how the stories went.

A "woosh" was a mean breeze that liked to blow clothing off lines and pots off windowsills. Wooshes weren't nearly so bad as hoodoos. When Mrs. Proudy was in a good mood, she'd tell me stories with wooshes in them. When she was afraid or feeling mean, I'd hear about the tiny man with the celery.

Etta did good things with me. She told me stories too, but I loved her for the other things. Or I loved her more for them. She'd take me outside at night and explain the stars to me. Every other kid my age would be in bed, and there I'd be, with Etta, watching the sky. We spent a lot of time on the roof when I was a little boy, and I don't remember wanting any of those times to end. I was never bored with her.

Once, after a heavy storm, she took me out to watch something I haven't ever seen since. We saw silent lightning stitching its way around huge white clouds. There wasn't even a rumble. Nobody believes me when I tell them this, but it's true. Silent lightning.

"Etta," I said—I always called her Etta, and she called me Jack although my name was John. "Etta, where's the thunder?"

"I don't know." She watched the sky. I remember the lovely line of her jaw, the way her nose pointed up. I don't know if she was a beautiful woman or not. I can't really tell you that. Who can about his mother? But I thought she was beautiful. She was small, like a green stem she was so thin—but she wasn't bony or anything. Delicate. She was sort of like a fragile thing that had been polished, so that it looked as if you could walk inside it. Like a glass bowl or something. Her eyes looked back at you, and when she was angry they'd freeze you in place. She had this habit of throwing her head back, as if she were casting water out of her hair or something, and when she did that you knew she was determined and you might as well do what she wanted you to do. She didn't have to scold me too often. We were friends, really. Good and true friends. I didn't want to let her down for anything, and she always let me know I could count on her. She only failed me once. But that was enough.

I don't want to talk about when she failed me, though. It wasn't her fault, and there's a lot I want to tell you first.

That night she took me out to watch the quiet lightning, I was about seven or eight, and I didn't really understand how amazing such a sight was. I knew when there was lightning, there was also thunder, so I knew something was missing. But I didn't have the feeling there was anything stupendous going on. Etta wouldn't look away from it, though.

"Is the thunder far away?" I said.

She pursed her lips, made this noise, then said, "That's the strangest thing."

"What?"

"There really is no thunder."

The sky lit up again. I could see lightning forking its way down toward the river. I felt like I'd lost my hearing.

"See those?" Etta said. She pointed to monstrous white clouds which rose up over the hazy city; they looked like vertical columns, and you had to stare at them for a long time to notice them moving. They seemed to grow, like a plant, and there didn't seem to be a limit as to how high they could get. They made the sky look smaller. Lightning ran behind them, made them look flat and artificial.

"I love thick white clouds," I said.

"Those are thunderheads," said Etta.

"Well, how come there's no thunder?"

ROBERT BAUSCH

She laughed. "Thunderheads don't have thunder in them," she said. "But there ought to be thunder with the lightning."

"I'm scared," I said.

"No," she said, kneeling down next to me. "You're afraid when there *is* thunder."

"I guess so."

"I'm supposed to be afraid when there isn't."

"How come?"

She smiled, put her hand on my cheek. "Oh, that was just a bad joke."

Lightning lit the sky above us. Etta stood up, put her hand on my shoulder. The lightning was so frequent then, still without the thunder, that it looked as if the sun were burning out.

"You know," Etta said, "if your father were here, he'd explain a lot of this to you."

She didn't talk about my father very often, so I pressed her. I asked her what every boy probably asks his mother when the old man isn't living—I asked her what he was like. And she said what probably every mother says, "He was a good man."

"What *is* a good man?" I really wanted to know.

She squeezed my shoulder. "A good man is like you."

"I'm not a man yet," I said.

"Your father was very kind."

Her face lit up momentarily and I saw her eyes were fixed toward the river, toward the great cemetery where my father was buried.

"Is he in heaven?"

"Sure." She looked at me. "Just about everybody goes to heaven."

"Even criminals?"

"Even criminals."

"What's the point of being good?"

She laughed. "OK, maybe *not* criminals."

"Daddy wasn't a criminal, was he?"

"No. Of course not."

"I hate him for dying," I said.

"You shouldn't say that," Etta said. Her voice was different. "You shouldn't ever say that."

"OK."

"Your father couldn't help what happened to him."

"OK."

"Nobody can help it when they have to die."

"I'm not going to die," I said. I knew for sure that was true. The sky lit up all at once, then got dark again. Etta took my arm, knelt beside me again. "I hate to tell you this," she said. Her voice was still a different tone, as if she were speaking to me through a telephone or something. "I hate to tell you this, I really do, but your life will be just like that flash of lightning. It comes and goes. And it's usually short, difficult, and painful."

I didn't say anything.

"You understand?" Her face was in front of me, waiting.

"I don't want to die," I said.

She made this sound, and her face changed. It was as if she suddenly felt this pain. "You're not going to die, son," she said. Her voice was back to normal, although I swear she was about to cry. "I'm sorry. You're not going to die."

"I know," I said.

"I don't know what got into me." She hugged me. I smelled the sweet, green, plantlike odor of her hair. "I'm sorry."

I didn't know what the hell she was so sorry for.

––––––––––––

When I was eleven years old I tossed a football in our apartment, trying to hit it into the clothes hamper, and I knocked over a row of Etta's white candles. Etta loved candles, and she got these five long white ones from my father around the time of his death. So they were special to her. She kept them in an imitation gold candelabrum which had an honored place on the shelf between the kitchen and the living room. The football hit them square—I couldn't have done better if I'd been in a carnival and I was trying to knock them off. It broke all five of them.

I picked them up and set them back on the counter. Since a wick went through each one of them, it was real easy to pick them up. All the pieces hung in a row. I set them next to each other on the counter with only a slight bend in each one, so Etta'd know right away they were broken. I don't think I was very afraid about how she would react, either. I think I was just sorry, a little. I went on with the rest of my day, to tell you the truth.

When Etta came home that night, she cried. She took one look at the candles and then cried. I was standing right next to the counter where the candles were laid out, and she was in front of me, holding a bag with lettuce sticking out of the top of it. She looked at me, then at the candles, then back to me again. Her coat was a little wet, and I remember thinking if it wasn't for the rain I wouldn't have been throwing a football in the apartment.

She put the bag down, cried silently while she stood there touching each white candle as if it were the broken limb of a child.

"I'm sorry," I said.

"What were you doing?" Her voice sounded high and squeaky, so I knew I wasn't in trouble. She was too sad to yell at me.

"I was throwing the football." I whispered this.

She didn't say anything. Now I really *was* sorry. I expected her to yell at me, punish me or something. She always let me know when she was angry.

"Can't you glue them?" I said.

"No." She was still staring at them.

Just now, I can see that small room—its high ceilings, with yellow paint peeling in the corners, the four hardback chairs which lined the wall by the door, Etta's soft lounger which rested next to her only true antique, a four-legged shaky little square table that sat under the only window in the place. There was a cold, black and white tile floor in the living room; a broad piece of furniture that looked like the back of somebody's bed and had a flat eight-inch board nailed to the top of it served as the divider between the kitchen and the living room, and it was on this little counter, as I called it, that the candles were all laid out. I can see Etta standing there, her eyes getting blurry, and I swear even now I can feel sad about it.

"I wish I hadn't done it," I said.

She didn't say anything. She put her hand on my head—she almost had to reach up to do this, because I was just beginning to grow and she was not very tall. But she didn't look at me. I wanted her to see how sorry I was.

"I'm so sorry, Etta."

Right in the middle of her silent crying, she smiled, rubbed my head. "Don't throw the football in the house," she said. Then she wiped her nose, let out a short little laugh. "They're only wax and some white string. Nothing to mourn over." With that she picked them up and threw them into the trash can in the kitchen. I watched her do this with a feeling in my throat like I'd swallowed a hot piece of coal.

"Don't throw them away."

"They won't stand up anymore. They're no good." She smiled.

I hate a woman's smile after she's cried. You know? When the tears still line her eyes, and you just know there's still two or three ounces of good crying left in her, and she just stops, wipes her nose, and then she smiles? I hate that. It kills me. It killed me back then, too, when Etta did it. It's a way women have of making your heart remember what a true son of a bitch you've been.

So I was staring at the trash can, trying not to see her teary smile, and she said, "Jack."

"What?"

"Your father gave those to me. I thought of him when I saw them all broken."

"I'm sorry." I said it again. It's never enough, though. There ought to be some other pair of words, some other combination that has impact. Words like "He's alive." Or "He's going to live." Words like that have impact. You say them, and you see something change in the person you say them to. "I'm sorry" must be the weakest two words in the language. Just about everybody says, "It's OK," after you say them. Either that, or they say, "That's not enough." In both cases, the words haven't changed anything.

When I said I was sorry, Etta only smiled again. "And don't throw the football in the house."

She called that place a house. I swear I loved her.

She went off into the bedroom to change.

The next day I went out right after school and looked for five white candles. They couldn't be just any candles either. They had to be as long as the other ones, and not yet lit by anybody.

Now consider my problem. I was eleven years old, in 1930, and I didn't have any money. But neither, as far as I could tell, did any one else I knew. I needed to find five long, white candles, which had not been burned at all. Where would you go?

I went to St. Michael's.

St. Michael's was the church that Etta took me to on religious holidays, unrainy and uncold Sundays, and at Christmas time no matter what the weather was. We were Catholic, Etta and I. That was as much a disadvantage as anything else in those days. If you don't know, Catholics see things, all things, in three basic categories: good (they call this Grace); moderately bad (they call this venial sin), and just horrible (they call this mortal sin).

I wasn't sure what sort of sin I had committed. I didn't really think it was a mortal one, since I couldn't imagine losing your soul for breaking a few candles accidentally. But if I were to rank my sins according to how bad they made me feel, I had been pretty sinful. Maybe the one act of breaking Etta's candles was good for more than one venial sin. Like twenty venial sins. And maybe if you get enough venial sins, you end up with a mortal one? I didn't know. I guess I still don't. If I were Catholic now, I would want to ask somebody. But now it doesn't seem so important.

I was taught that a mortal sin takes your soul and puts a huge black mark on it. Your soul is as white as the front of a nun's habit —that's what the sisters were always pointing out to us kids in school. One, Sister Mary Theresa, spilled india ink on the front of her habit to show us what our souls looked like if we committed a mortal sin. It made an awful mess. And she said, "See? See what sin does to your pure soul?"

One of the boys in the back of the room said, "You better go to confession and get that cleaned, Sister."

Everybody laughed, even Mary Theresa.

Anyway, I was walking down the street that day after school, feeling like my soul must be at least a fairly dark shade of brown, when it hit me where I could get five white candles. So I went to the church and walked up the front steps, like anybody stopping for a short prayer.

When I got to the huge wide oak double doors, when I had my hand on the molded brass handles, it hit me: how was I going to get the candles? I couldn't ask for them. I'd have to tell whoever I asked what I needed them for, and that would be too embarrassing. Besides, why should they give me their pure candles to make up for my venial sin—if that's what it was. After all, Etta cried. I may have had a soul as black as a top hat. (I guess I was really pissed that you couldn't see your soul—so you had no way of knowing what sort of sins you'd committed unless you memorized them all, and who can do that without becoming a priest?)

The door opened while I was standing there, and an old man walked out, looked down at me as if I were an umbrella stand and he just remembered that he didn't bring his umbrella, and then he struggled down the steps. His head was shaking as he went. I remember thinking if I was his age, I'd be in church every day. You never know what shape your soul is in after all that time being alive.

I let go of the door and went and sat at the top of the stairs, considering my problem.

I knew I couldn't ask for the candles. That was sure. I couldn't even pretend that I just wanted to buy them for a gift, because that would be a lie. I might even end up lying to a priest. Imagine that. Then you'd have to go to confession the next week and *tell* him you lied to him. Boy, I bet nobody ever lies to a priest he knows he'll see again.

St. Michael's was on P Street. You could look out over the red brick buildings across the street, since the church was at the top of a green hill. I could almost see the river from where I sat. The steps were gray stone, and they reminded me of the tombstone Etta borrowed so much money for to buy for my father. (It cost sixty dollars and said, "With great love, we remember thee." That's all she could afford, apparently. I never asked her about it. It didn't have anything else on it, just that phrase. It didn't even have my father's name on it.)

ROBERT BAUSCH

Above the houses across the street, I saw clouds beginning to shift and separate in front of what looked like a pure blue glass. It was fall, I think, when this happened. I'm not sure of the time of year, but I remember those clouds, and I remember that they reminded me of the lightning without sound Etta and I saw that night so many years before that time. And I remembered Etta's breathing, her holding me and all. I knew I couldn't really give a damn about my own soul. I had to make it up to Etta. That's who counted.

So I got up, walked into the church, and headed for what turned out to be the first of many small crimes I was to commit in order to make up for the sins of that life.

There was no one in the church. My feet echoed on the wood floor. It sounded like I was wearing wooden shoes. In front there was a rack of candles on either side of the altar, but these were small stumpy little things in red glasses, and they'd all been lit before. In fact some of them were burning when I came in. Probably the old man lit one before he left. A little prayer of a candle to relieve some of the fear over the color of his soul.

If I was going to find long, white candles, I knew I'd have to go up on the altar. It took a long time to get down the center aisle of that church, and the whole way down, all the way to the little wooden gate in front of the altar, I didn't know if I'd have the nerve to go up there where the gold tabernacle sat on white sheets like a great artillery shell, and where a wooden Christ dangled over it as if he were being lowered from the dome overhead to steal it. The last light from the afternoon leaked in through huge triangular shaped stained glass windows that made the top of the dome look like a sliced pie. And I felt as if I had trespassed into heaven; a perverted sort of Jack and the beanstalk. To the left of the altar, resting on a white ledge, was a gold candelabrum with eight, long, white, unlit candles.

I walked through several slices of light, went into the shade by the ledge, and picked the middle five candles. I left two on the left and one on the right. Then I took the one on the right, too, in case I broke one on the way home.

I had them in my hands and was just sneaking through the little wooden gate, when I heard a door creak open in back of the church. I looked up. In front of me was the long aisle, light gleaming in the middle of it from the sun shining through the open door I had just come through; to the right of the door, next to the poor box, was a small cluster of little doors, three in all, which led to the confessionals. Probably within the week I'd have to kneel in one of those little booths and tell one of the priests about this little theft. If I wasn't caught first. It's really hard being a Catholic, you know?

Anyway, I stood there, watching the light gleaming down the aisle, and waited to hear the sound again. It was so quiet, I felt like I could hear my fingernails growing. I took a few more steps, got more confident when I didn't hear the creaking noise again, and walked briskly right into the shaft of light, down the aisle, counting the pews as I went. Then I heard the sound again—it was very definitely a door opening up. I was just passing pew number sixteen. I know that, because that's where I put the candles. Most of them, anyway. One of them, the extra one, dropped and rolled a few pews in front of me. I went for it, bent to pick it up, just as a tall man came out of the confessional. He came out of the center door, so I knew he was a priest. He was about fifteen feet away from me.

"Hi," I said, my voice too loud.

"You—are you waiting for confession?"

"No."

"Can I help you?"

"I brought you this," I said, holding up the candle.

He came down the aisle toward me. In the sunlight, he was only a shadow. I couldn't tell which priest he was. I didn't know any of them, but I knew there was a young one and an older one. The older one was very soft-spoken and never yelled at the audience during his sermons. The young one, I think his name was Father Burns, was noisier. He seemed angry over sin all the time. Etta told me once that when a person gets real angry and yells at everyone about sin that that person probably has committed the most sins and that's why he yells.

He stopped in front of me, and I knew it was Father Burns.

"What have you got there?" he said.

"A white candle."

"Where'd you get it?"

"I found it outside."

"Well, we have plenty of candles," he said. He smiled at me. He didn't seem all that ferocious.

"I thought you might like another one," I said, adding another venial sin to the multitude I was collecting that day.

"That's very kind of you," Father Burns said. He took it from me. "I'll put this on the altar."

"No, don't do that," I said.

"What?"

"Would you put it in the sancristy?"

"The sacristy?"

"Yes, that's the place."

"Why?"

"So you can light it when you're getting dressed." I couldn't believe I said that.

"While I'm getting dressed?"

"When you put your robe on."

"Oh."

I smiled.

"Do you want to be a priest?" he asked. He was bald and had a permanent sort of dark shadow on either side of his face.

"Someday," I lied. I was going to need an adding machine to get this day confessed.

He smiled, started to lean toward me, then made a soft ticking noise behind his teeth and walked up the aisle and into the sacristy. I retrieved the five white candles I'd thrown into the sixteenth pew and walked casually out of St. Michael's. I was so proud of myself, I was sure just the way I felt was another sin.

———

When I got back to the apartment the sun had sunk behind the Capitol, and the sky was as white as the sheet on the altar. I carried the candles like they were baby kittens, cradled in my arms, up the stairs and into our apartment. Etta was in the kitchen, her back to me. I didn't think she'd be home yet.

"Don't turn around," I said.

"OK." She put her hands on the counter, leaned on them. I knew there was a smile on her face. I felt like I was just about to open a huge gift.

I went to the counter, which rested between us, lifted the candelabrum as quietly as possible, and placed the candles in each socket as if they were somebody's fingers and I might cause them pain. I didn't want to mar the wax on any of them. I wanted them to be perfect, long and white.

When I had them set about even, I put the candelabrum back in its place of honor, and said, "Turn around."

She turned, smiled as if she expected to notice something different about me. "Well?"

I didn't say anything. I didn't even look at the candelabrum.

"What's my surprise?" Her hand went up, touched her lower lip.

I smiled at her.

She looked at the candelabrum then. Her eyes got real small, seemed to go sort of limp. If I'd died right then, I would have seen enough to make that life worthwhile.

"Oh, darling," she said. She didn't pick up the candles and look at them, she picked me up. "You sweetheart," she said. She kissed me. "You sweet son." She was crying, holding me, walking back and forth with me. I was afraid she would fall. I was almost as tall as she was, and she was hauling me around that room, that little room. I hugged her neck.

She put me down finally, her tears wet on my own cheeks. "I love you, Jack."

She kept saying that, in a quiet whisper. I swear she was a good woman. She didn't deserve one half of what happened to her.

THE NINTH INTERVIEW

NOVEMBER 7, 1980

2:30 P.M.

Etta was so proud of me getting her the candles, she invited Father Burns over to tell him about it. She sent me to the market to buy some butter, and when I came back, there was Father Burns sitting on a stool by the room divider where the candles rested in the candelabrum. The candles sort of rose up over his left shoulder, and I felt something small and prickly change places in my heart.

"Hello," he said.

I tried to say "hi," but I swallowed it. He was dressed in that black suit, with the little white slot at the throat, and his blackened jaws spread wide by a knowing grin. I felt sick.

Etta came around the divider out of the kitchen. "Did you get the butter?"

"Yes, ma'am," I said. I tried to whisper, but my throat was trembling like a raw egg.

"Real butter?" Father Burns said.

"Nothing but the best," Etta said. Then she looked at me. "For my little hero."

Father Burns laughed.

"Is this when I get it?" I asked.

"Get what?" he said.

I heard Etta moving dishes in the kitchen, saw Father Burns lean back on the room divider. He was watching me, as if he expected me to sink into the floor or something. I couldn't look at him.

"Get what?" he said again. Etta was right behind him, working on the dinner, her head slightly tilted. I couldn't tell if he'd said anything to her yet or not.

"Are you staying to dinner?" I asked.

"Yes." His mouth closed, spread into a line from one end of his face to the other.

I almost said, "Bless me, Father, for I have sinned." But he put his black shoe up on a lower ring of the stool and crossed his hands in front of him and said, "Still think you might want to be a priest someday?"

I couldn't tell if he was trying to make me lie again. I didn't know if priests tried to drum up business by inciting people to sin or not. I figured they might, since they talked about sin so much, and since they insisted that you could be forgiven if you just went and told them about all of them. I'd like a job like that, actually. I guess I wouldn't want to go through all the other stuff, and I don't think I'd want to give up what priests give up—or claim to give up, anyway. But it might be nice to hear other people tell you their sins all the time.

Imagine listening to a woman's sins. I think I'd like that.

I realize this is serious business. But think about listening to the sins of women all the time, and you can't even touch one—ever. That's probably a kind of torture too.

Anyway, Father Burns was looking at me, and I was trying to figure out if I should lie again or not. I said, "Maybe." That wasn't really a lie, since I might be shanghaied later and forced to go through the seminary and become a priest. You never know in life.

He said, "You have to atone for your sins then."

I didn't think he would get to that. I was just beginning to think that he wasn't going to say anything, and then he says that about atonement. I saw Etta turn around in the kitchen. She leaned on the room divider behind Burns, stared lovingly at the candles, then at me.

My only way out of it would be to act like I didn't understand sin. I knew that would be easy, since it was the truth.

"What is sin?"

Burns smiled. "Stealing is a sin." His voice seemed louder than normal.

I couldn't say anything.

"You know what sin is," Etta said. I think she was embarrassed. The way she leaned over the counter and smiled at me, I knew she didn't know anything yet. He hadn't told her.

"What happens when you commit sin accidentally?" I asked. I don't know where my voice came from.

"You can't do that," Father Burns said.

"You can't?" Etta and I said at the same time.

"No." Father Burns put his hands in his pockets, leaned forward as if he were going to spit something on the floor. "Sin is a choice, a conscious act."

"But what if you don't know you're doing it?" I said.

"Then it's not a sin."

My head filled with explanations about the candles. All of them were for Etta. I wasn't trying to save myself; at least I don't think I was.

"Are all sins bad?" I said.

"Yes, but some are worse than others."

"Some are venial and some are mortal."

"Right." He smiled, looked at Etta.

"Is eating meat on Friday a mortal sin or a venial one?"

"It is a mortal one." His voice was low and serious. I remember thinking, just as he said that, how large his ears were.

"And not going to mass on a holy day?"

"Mortal."

"And missing Easter duty?"

"Mortal."

Etta was looking at me now. Her face looked red from the light through the orange curtains. "Jack," she said. I think she thought I was being rude. All I was really trying to do was keep him from talking about the candles.

"And murder?"

"Mortal again."

"What's a venial sin?"

"Stealing."

I got him right back to that again.

"Lying," he said.

Etta stopped him. "Did you say eating meat on Friday was a mortal sin, Father?"

"Yes, it is." He turned and looked at her.

"Mortal?" she said again. She couldn't believe it.

"Indeed." Father Burns reached up and touched the white slot at his throat.

"If I went downstairs and choked Mrs. Proudy to death—if I beat her to death with this candelabrum," she pointed to the candles and I missed a breath.

Father Burns leaned back on the chair so he could see her better.

"If I killed Mrs. Proudy, it's the same in God's eyes as eating a piece of deviled ham on Friday?"

"It's not the outcome of the sin that counts," Father Burns said. His voice was a note higher. I thought he might have swallowed something.

"Why not?" Etta seemed to be scolding him.

"It just isn't. Sin is based on the wishes of the Lord."

"How does anybody know that?"

"We *have* the word of God, Mrs. Pitt."

"*You* have it."

Father Burns blinked, touched the sides of his legs. I thought he might get up and walk out. But he said, "It's available to anyone."

"And it's written somewhere that eating meat on Friday and axe murder are equal sins?"

"They are equal in their offensiveness to the Lord, not in their offensiveness to us." He was trying to stay on the stool, but he leaned over so far backward he was really standing up with just his upper thigh touching the stool. I saw his jaw ripple when he stopped talking. He might have been getting mad. He stared at Etta as if he were afraid she might strike him with something.

Etta stared at the counter.

"I don't think I want to be a priest," I said.

Etta laughed, nervously. The priest smiled at her, then looked at me.

"All sins are forgivable," he said in the most tender and sadly trembling voice. He might have been trying to tell me something. I looked away from him then.

He never did tell Etta about the candles. The dinner was actually sort of pleasant. He told jokes about Irish policemen and Catholic priests, doing the accents very well, and I remember thinking he was probably a good man. I felt bad for lying to him, I guess. I figured I'd have to spend the rest of my life avoiding him.

The thing was, Etta took me to confession whenever she thought I had piled up enough sins to spend some time in the booth. And you never could tell which priest was hearing confessions when you went in there. I couldn't wait around and hope to get the old one.

It's just awful being a Catholic, especially if you steal from the church. You just have to go back there, crawl into one of those dark, carpeted, wheat-smelling booths and *tell* them you're the one who stole their stuff. "Bless me, father, for I have sinned— against you." The thought of it just made my stomach cold.

I had no idea that I'd be back in the church within the month, and I'd be trying to steal a hell of a lot more than five long, white candles.

———

The first time Etta brought Wicker home, I thought she'd been kidnaped by an undertaker or something. He wore black. He had this pale white face that looked like the front of Sister Theresa's habit, with little tiny mortal sins sticking in it. He had long white fingers, and his voice sounded smooth and silky—as if he'd come back from the dead and didn't want to disturb the universe.

"This is Mr. Wicker," Etta said.

I was standing in the middle of the tile floor, in a ridiculous pose of welcome and come hug me that I always put on for Etta when I heard her on the stairs. I put my arms down and looked into his little black eyes.

"Are you a preacher?" I said.

"No." He laughed, but his face didn't change. I thought there might be a little man hiding behind his teeth.

"I didn't mean to be funny," I said.

"Mr. Wicker lives down the hall," Etta said. I knew he lived in the building; I'd seen him leaning in the halls on late afternoons. I thought he was a drunk. He never seemed to be able to stand up straight. I couldn't figure out what Etta brought him home for.

"What's he doing here?" I said.

Etta took off her scarf, removed her coat.

"Huh?" I said.

"Jack." Etta had a way of looking at you, a way of making long speeches with one word. The tone of her voice told me to be polite, to stop asking pointed questions that might put our guest in an uncomfortable state of mind, and please understand I should behave myself.

Wicker looked at her. He seemed so sad all of a sudden; as if he, too, could understand Etta's one word speech.

"It's OK if you're here," I told him.

He took off his coat, smiled finally. His mouth looked like a blue vein in somebody's arm. Underneath the coat, he wore a white shirt, rolled up to the elbow. The collar was ratty and looked as if somebody had burned it around the edges. You could tell he was poor.

"You don't have to be polite," he said. "If you weren't expecting me."

"Heh." He really was uncomfortable.

"Jack's rude today," Etta said. She went into the kitchen.

"I suppose you're going to stay to supper too?" I said.

"Ja-ack," Etta said. She stood at the divider behind Wicker. "We had Father Burns over for supper last week."

"Oh." Wicker sat on the same stool Father Burns sat on.

"What *are* you doing here?" I said.

He looked at Etta.

"He's having a meal with us," she said.

He touched his ear with long white fingers. It was like he was afraid of me.

"And you, my little—" Etta started. Then she coughed, a short internal burst that gathered force, got going like an engine. Wicker and I waited for her to finish.

"Whew," she said finally, when she got her breath. "I don't know where that came from."

Wicker's coat slipped from the stool where he had draped it. I went to pick it up, but he leaned over, took it into his hands as if it were something newborn. "This is an old coat," he said. He set it back on the stool, patted it. His fingers looked skeletal on the black fabric. I was closer to him, and I smelled whiskey, a stale, metal cologne. He coughed, as if he wanted to make Etta feel less nervous about her own spell.

We stood there, the three of us, watching the coat.

"Well," Etta said, finally. "Let's have supper."

I guess Wicker was about fifty or so. He ate very politely—he left a hand in his lap at all times, and when he ate his green beans he didn't stab them the way I like to. I could tell he was mighty hungry, though. When Etta offered him seconds, he acted like he'd been waiting for a long time for her to do it—like he was in a starting block, waiting for the race to begin. He didn't talk much, but when he did, he talked about his children.

"I've got good boys," he said.

I smiled. I wondered what he thought a good boy was, though.

"Like you," he looked at me.

Etta said, "You're very lucky."

"Yes, indeed."

"How come you don't live with them?" I stabbed a green bean. He made this face, like he felt a pain or something.

"I'm sorry," I said.

"No," he said. He raised his hand. It looked like it was made of white glass. "No, no. That's fine."

"I didn't mean—"

"That's fine. I can't live with them, now." He blinked, put his hand next to his napkin. "I came to Washington to find work."

"What kind of work do you do?" Etta asked.

"I'm a carpenter."

"Where do your children live?"

He and Etta both said, "Indiana."

"God," I said. I couldn't imagine living that far away from Etta.

Wicker looked at me as if something had fallen out of my nose or something.

"Don't take the Lord's name in vain," Etta said.

She'd never said that to me before. I figured Wicker was pretty religious. "I'm sorry."

"Boy says he's sorry a lot," Wicker said.

Etta smiled. "He really is a good boy."

"I'm not *that* good," I said.

When dinner was over, Wicker went right for his coat. He was nervous about what to talk about, I guess. He stood at the door and smiled a white smile. He was the palest man I've ever seen. He almost glowed. I said "Bye," and he nodded his head and went out the door. He never said anything. I always thought people who left rooms or hung up telephones without saying anything were fairly peculiar. When he was gone, I said to Etta, "Is he sick?"

"He's poor," she said.

"He's as white as a soul."

"A what?"

"A soul."

"How do you know a soul is white?"

I told her about Sister Theresa.

"Your soul's not really white," Etta said. Then, "Did she really pour ink on her dress?"

"Yes."

"Good God."

"She said it's white."

"A soul," Etta said slowly, "is not white."

I thought of all my venial sins. "*My* soul isn't. But some souls are."

"OK. If you want to believe that. I can't stop you."

"I bet *your* soul is white."

She came around the divider, where she'd been putting up the dishes, and stood in front of me. "Why isn't your soul white?"

"What?" I didn't expect her to ask me that.

"You said your soul isn't white. Why isn't it?"

I didn't know what to say.

"Jack. Who told you your soul isn't white?"

"Nobody."

"Why isn't your soul white?"

"*You* said a soul's not white," I said.

She smiled. "You know, as long as I have you, I'll survive." She put her arms around me, held me. I smelled something sweet, like a rose petal. I buried my face in the crook of her shoulder, closed my eyes.

Did I lie to her? I ask you. Was it a lie to say what I said about her telling me a soul's not white—when it seemed the truth was that I'd stolen from the church and I'd lied about it to everyone I knew? It was true also that she did say that about souls in general not being white. So what I said was true. But I lied? You see what was going through my head while she hugged me? She could have held me like that until the windows went dark. I wouldn't have minded. I couldn't possibly have done anything evil as long as I was in her arms. Her breathing was the softest sound I ever heard.

That night, I couldn't sleep. Etta seemed worried about something, and I had to find out what it was.

The only thing I didn't like about Etta was she kept things from me when she didn't want me to worry. Of course, this made me worry all the time, because I never knew *when* there was nothing to worry about. It got pretty complex and confusing sometimes: in the middle of doing something, when she didn't know I was watching her, Etta'd frown slightly. I'd think she was hiding a great calamity from me. She'd see me worrying and she'd tell me not to worry, and that would make me think she was trying to keep me from worrying because there really *was* something to worry about, and then I'd *really* worry. The harder she tried to convince me, the more I'd worry. If she ignored me, pretended she didn't notice I was nervous about the fact that there was a calamity about to befall us, I knew right away there was something to worry about. I was afraid most of the time.

That night after Wicker left, I knew there was something up. I listened for Etta—tried to hear her breathing and figure if she was sleeping or not. Finally, I got out of bed and went into her room.

She was sitting up in bed, reading. "What are you doing up?" She had a small white lamp by her bed, with a cracked shade, which made the light reflect a frozen electrical storm on the far wall. It was really silent lightning, a suggestion Etta herself made shortly after that night when we watched the thunderless storm in the white clouds above the building.

"I can't sleep."

"Why?" I could tell she was trying to remain calm and act like nothing was going on.

"Something's going to happen." I stood at the foot of the bed.

"What?"

I went over to her. She was wearing a blue nightdress, smooth and shiny in the lamplight. "I was hoping you would tell me."

She reached up and put her hand on my face. "Nothing's going to happen."

"What are you worried about?"

She frowned, stroked the hair above my ear.

"Well?"

"A lot of things. Nothing you can help." She took her hand away.

"What?"

"The times."

"What about them?"

"I feel sorry for people like Mr. Wicker."

"Me too."

"He's got a family. He's a father, and he's here trying to find, trying to—" She looked away, out the dark window.

"Don't be sad," I said.

She pulled me over to her. I lay my head on her breast, listened to her breathing. "Mr. Wicker is out of money," she said. "He begged me to help him today."

"How?"

"He asked me for a loan." She put her hand on the back of my neck. "Just so he can stay in the building."

"Oh."

"I gave him two dollars," she said. Then I felt her breathing get hurried, and I realized she was crying. "I couldn't give him any more than that. We have to survive too."

"Don't cry," I said.

"Mrs. Proudy has let him stay in that room for over three months without paying."

"Don't cry."

"Oh," she cried. "I'm sorry." She sat up, took a white handkerchief out of her pillowcase. She wiped her nose. I thought she looked like a little girl there in the light from the white lamp with the cracked shade. When she was finished, she looked at me, said, "You always know. Just like your father."

I didn't have the heart to tell her that I *always* thought something was wrong, and that it was only the sheer weight of scatter gun luck that I'd hit one right. I remember thinking, too, that my father must have been a worrier as well, and maybe that's where I inherited the habit.

"What's Mr. Wicker going to do?"

"He's going to go out into the street," Etta sobbed again. I was really glad she cried like that in front of me. I felt grown up, like a man. Then, I felt bad for being glad she cried. But feeling like a man, I knew I would have to do something to fix it for Mr. Wicker.

"He's going to get thrown out," Etta went on. "Mrs. Proudy's going to have to ask him to leave."

"Mrs. Proudy?"

"She has to survive too."

I was already thinking, "I'll take care of everything. Don't worry. I'll take care of it."

I knew then that I was going back to church.

In those days, churches didn't lock their doors. They did lock their poor boxes, though, and I was mildly disappointed to find that out, the next day when I walked bravely into the colored light and tried the door on the brass box next to the font of holy water. I blessed myself first, dipping my fingers in the cold water and touching my forehead, my chest, and each shoulder. When I was finished making the sign of the cross, my fingers were usually dry. I always tried to get just enough water so that there'd be nothing left after I touched my right shoulder.

No one was there, so I didn't have to pretend to be doing anything. I just reached up and tried the little door.

In a way, I was glad it was locked. I didn't think it was too smart to leave money around like that, and I knew that if they locked it, and if my journeys were infrequent enough, there'd always be money there for the taking. Only when I needed it, mind you. I needed it for a poor person, and I didn't think it could be too big a sin to take a direct part in seeing that it got to where everybody intended it should go. It was a poor box, and I was going to give the money to a poor person.

I still had the problem of getting the box unlocked, though. The keyhole on the little door was large, and I knew if I could find a long thin piece of metal, I could probably get the box open.

You ever looked for a long piece of metal in church?

I walked up and down every pew, thinking I'd find something: a hatpin, or a barrette, or a pipe tamp, or something. I was afraid God could see me, and He was trying to keep me from stealing from Him. I felt sort of guilty when I thought of God. He'd been so nice to all of us in the world, and here I was trying to break into His poor box. But I told myself I was trying to do something good, something wonderful. He must have wanted me to do it. What was the poor box for? And why was it the first thing I thought of when I knew what Mr. Wicker's trouble was? So I stood there in the sixteenth pew, the pew in which I had hidden the five white candles of that earlier theft, and said a prayer for the Lord's forgiveness.

It was really wonderful having a God who forgave all your sins. That part of being Catholic was OK, even though to get God to do it officially you eventually had to talk to a priest about it. You could get temporary forgiveness until you went to a priest, and that's what I asked for standing there in the sixteenth pew. I figured I'd confess *all* my sins someday.

I know there's no connection, but as soon as I said my prayer, I found a long, thin piece of metal: a bobby pin.

I know everybody picks locks with a bobby pin—I think I knew it then. But I swear to God that's what I found, and that's what I used to open the poor box. It may as well have been the key. That's how easy it was. There was fourteen dollars in the box— all in change. I went out of there with my pockets full, and no one saw me. Except God, maybe.

I realized on my way back to the apartment that I still had a problem. I couldn't walk up to Mr. Wicker and say, "Here." Hand him the money as if he'd just done woodwork for me or something. He'd probably want to know where I got it, especially all in change like that. I could hear him asking me if I robbed the ice man or something. Or even worse, he'd think Etta sent me with it and try to thank her for it, and then she'd have to know where I got it. I wasn't sure if I could lie to her or not. I mean I knew I could lie to spare her feelings, but I wasn't sure if I could lie to protect myself. Although, I admit, I lied to her about the color of my soul. Still, it didn't seem like a lie then, and it certainly wasn't as bad a lie as making up a whole story to account for the money. I didn't even know what sort of story I would make up. I couldn't tell her I *found* the money—if you dropped that much money in the street you'd think somebody dropped a tire chain.

That's what I was thinking on the way back to the apartment. Even though I wasn't old enough to smoke a cigarette yet. I guess I was proud of having figured all that out about myself before I was twelve. I understood just why I was doing what I was doing, and I felt like I was right.

I decided to just put the money in his mailbox. All those coins would be impossible to trace, and he wouldn't have anything to do with them but count them anyway. Then he could spend them. Maybe pay Mrs. Proudy a little bit, and spend the rest on a new shirt so he could get a job. I figured it would take two more trips to the church to cover a month's rent for him, but I didn't mind. I was going to help him until he found work anyway. Even if it took more than a month.

When I put the coins down in his mailbox they made a sound like a derailed train. I stood there in the dim hallway, watching all the doors around me, waiting for one of them to open. I must have looked like a matador waiting for one of the bulls to come out. There were four doors around his mailbox, including his, and my eyes hit each one at least twice. But Mr. Wicker didn't come out, and neither did anyone else.

I went upstairs feeling powerful and large, like I'd done something wonderful. I knew it was going to be hard not to tell Etta what I'd done.

If I did tell her it would only be to make her stop worrying about Mr. Wicker. I didn't want to make her proud of me again —the way she was with the candles. As soon as I knew that, I remembered how guilty I felt that she thought I was a hero, and I'd committed a series of multicolored venial sins to get those candles. By the time I got to the top of the stairs, I felt as if I'd beaten up a little girl and stolen her candy or something. I knew it was a weakness in my character. The only way I could find to do good things was to commit sins and steal and lie and all the rest. I wondered if I would end up on a bunk in a cement cell one day. Smoking cigarettes and talking to Pretty Boy Floyd and the rest of the gang.

I resolved, as I opened the door to our apartment and went inside like a visitor in a hospital room, that I would try to find some way to do something good without doing something sinful and bad at the same time. But I had already embarked on my short career of crime in order to save Mr. Wicker, and, as everybody knows, you can't save a soul already lost.

•

THE TENTH INTERVIEW

1:15 P.M.

I saved the bobby pin—used it twice and sometimes three times a month. I got twenty-two dollars one night. My largest haul. Most of the time I only got ten or twelve dollars. All in change, nickels and quarters and dimes. Back then, everybody was poor, or claimed to be. It was kind of silly to have a poor box, I guess.

Mr. Wicker came to supper every now and then, carrying his black coat and wearing the tattered white shirt. He never seemed to be any better off for the money I was stealing, except he was still in the same building with us, and Etta said he came into some money and could afford his rent these days. I smiled when she said that. I really wanted to tell her then, tell her once and for all that it was I, her son, who fixed it for Mr. Wicker. But then I'd remember the sins and feel like I had a seed in my throat.

Mr. Wicker quietly took the little cache of money out of his mailbox whenever he found it. I used to see him checking it, late in the evening—long after the mail had come—and that was my signal to hit the poor box again. I must have been stealing enough for him, because Etta didn't seem to worry about him so much anymore.

He never said anything to Etta about it, although he may have suspected her of helping out—you know, giving him money secretly and all. She'd do that. She'd know a man would be too proud to take money from a woman when he needed it. Everything went as I hoped it would, to tell you the truth.

I'd been stealing from the poor box for almost a year when Father Burns yelled at the congregation one Sunday for not putting enough money in the poor boxes.

"Boxes?" I said out loud.

Etta looked at me.

"There's more than one?"

She shushed me, looked into my eyes as if they'd started to change color or something.

"There's more than one poor box?" I whispered.

She nodded, pointed to one on the wall next to the door of the sacristy.

Burns announced that both boxes were frequently found empty. "I do not understand such a thing," he said. "In these hard times." There was a long pause. He stood in one of the pie slices of light from the high ceiling of the dome, looked down on all of us as if the light had placed him there, and he was God's emissary, knowing all. He looked at me, and I felt air hiding in tiny pockets and corners of my lungs. I know my face turned as red as a glass of whiskey. I tried not to move, watched his eyes scan the room, move away from me. I felt like I was hiding in the dark, and the search light missed me.

Then he gazed over the heads of the people behind me.

He went on talking, and it began to register in the fibers of my brain that he had said "both boxes" were found empty.

I was stealing from only one.

I can't tell you how angry I was when I realized that somebody else was stealing from that other box. You'll probably find this amusing, but I actually asked myself what kind of person would steal from the poor? I also wondered what kind of person would steal from only one box and not the other one.

The thing that really got me was that Father Burns believed that people just weren't putting money in the boxes, and he yelled at the whole congregation for not being generous. I couldn't tell him the money was being stolen from the box by the sacristy, because he'd want to know how I knew that, and I'd have to tell him I knew it because I was stealing from the other one.

You see the problem I had?

I'd already spent almost a year *pretending* to go to confession, lying to Etta when she sent me on my own, and lying to the priest whenever Etta went with me and I had to actually go into a confessional. You know, lying about going into a confessional was bad enough, but to lie once you were really in there? To say "Bless me, Father," and then commit what Father Burns called "sins of omission"? To leave out the most important sins, and build up this residual of sins of omission, until it didn't seem you could ever get them all told? I just knew my soul was getting as black as a tire.

I had this overwhelming problem with confession anyway. I mean before all the lies started and everything. It's kind of personal, but I guess I need to tell it to you, so you'll understand what it's like to have to tell somebody you barely know all your sins.

About a year before I began my life of venial crimes over Etta's white candles, I had this episode with confession that made me sort of rotten for it to begin with. I found myself lying in the confessional accidentally—lying about something it was hard enough to tell the truth about, and I was trying to tell the truth the whole time. It started when I discovered masturbation.

I discovered it with a pencil.

We were doing math, near the end of the day, and I didn't understand enough of what was going on to make proper use of my pencil. So I was hitting myself, you know the way you do when you're idle and don't feel like doodling or anything. I was hitting myself with the eraser end of the pencil—sort of trying to hit the zipper on my fly. I don't know why I was trying to do that, except sometimes we set targets for ourselves and try to hit them. Anyway, I was hitting the target fairly well, and it started to feel good. At first, I thought it was a sweet yawn coming on, or that I'd found a nerve or something that felt wonderful. So I kept hitting the spot, increasing the number of hits per second as the feeling got better, and better and better, and even better. I remember thinking I'd discovered something; something everyone ought to know about. But I knew I couldn't tell anyone about it. It wasn't something you could share during show and tell. After a while, I wasn't thinking anything.

I don't even know if anyone was watching me. Near the end of it I was hitting myself as fast as an air hammer, and almost as hard. I might have closed my eyes. Suddenly, and I didn't expect it because although the feeling was building and rising and converging somewhere in the layers of my skin, it didn't seem like it was something that would stop unless *I* stopped, suddenly, all my muscles got into it and I started jerking and jolting in my seat as if I'd been hooked to an electric wire or something. I think I made this little noise in the back of my throat.

Sister Theresa looked at me. "Is anything wrong, John?"

I was suddenly real sore where I'd been hitting myself, and I felt something wet in my pants. I thought it might be blood.

"John," Sister Theresa said again. Everyone was looking at me.

"Can I have a pass to go to the bathroom?" I said.

"Are you sick?"

"I think so."

"Well, are you or aren't you?"

I hadn't started lying yet. I didn't know what to say. "I'm sore."

"Sore?" Sister Theresa put her small freckled hands on her hips, next to the black beads around her waist. She tilted her head, the white bib of her habit glaring at me.

I couldn't tell her I'd just rubbed myself until it bled. I didn't even know what I should call it if I had to tell her I'd been rubbing it. So I said, "Please, I need to go to the bathroom."

She took a pass off her desk, brought it to me.

"Are you all right?"

"Yes." I took the pass.

When I got into the bathroom, I couldn't find any blood. Also, by the time I got there the soreness was all gone, and I was already thinking about that pencil.

For a while I called it my magic pencil. I carried it with me everywhere, and it was only after I lost it—I believed somebody who knew what it was *really* for stole it from me—that I discovered I could get that feeling without a pencil, I could do it with almost anything, including my hands.

But how to do it wasn't my problem. I had to tell the priest about it. I knew it was a sin. Sister Theresa told us we shouldn't touch ourselves, and I asked her if it was OK to use something other than our hands, or if it was OK if we touched ourselves through our clothing. She said, most emphatically NO. The way she looked when she said that made me feel small and sort of wet, with steam coming off me and an odor like a swamp. I knew I'd never mention it to her again.

And I had this sin to confess.

I couldn't go in there, kneel down, and say, "Bless me, Father, for I have discovered a magic pencil."

I looked all through my missal—the little Bible Catholics use —and the only sin I could see that had anything to do with sex was the sixth commandment: "Thou shalt not commit adultery."

So that's what I came to believe. I thought it was wonderful that one single word would cover all those episodes with and without the pencil.

When I went to confession I knelt down in that dark booth, and said, "Bless me, Father, for I have sinned." Then I stopped. I looked up, saw the shadow of the old priest's head, heard him breathing behind the screen, waiting.

"I committed adultery fifteen times since my last confession." Then I remembered I was supposed to tell him how long it was since my last confession before I reported any sins. So I said, "It's been five days since my last confession." I don't know why I said five days. Etta hadn't had me down there in at least a month.

I saw the shadow dip a little, seem to shake. Then he whispered, "How old are you?"

"Ten."

"How many times did you commit adultery?"

"Fifteen." I thought he knew how good it felt, and he couldn't believe I'd only done it fifteen times. "I know it's wrong, so I try real hard not to do it at all," I said. I really did try not to do it too. Each time I'd finish, I'd feel guilty and full of self hate and wish somebody would punish me.

The priest made this sound, like a window makes sometimes when the wind hits it, then he told me my penance. "Five 'Our Fathers' and five 'Hail Marys.'"

I confessed the sin of adultery until the year I first hit the poor box. By that time, though, I'd told so many lies and all, it didn't seem right not to leave adultery out too.

And also, by that time, I knew I wasn't committing adultery. Sister Theresa gave a class in what she called "self abuse." I thought she was going to show us how to inflict pain on ourselves —you know, stick little pins in our eyes or something, and say, "See, this is abusive. It hurts." When she told us what "self abuse" was, everybody laughed. Nobody believed her but me. I knew what she was talking about. I thought it ought to be called something other than "self abuse."

So, as I said, I had this terrible problem with confession. I'd been lying *there*, too—on purpose and accidentally. I didn't see how I could ever get it all straightened out. I knew I was probably going to hell, and whenever Father Burns talked about hell— about everlasting burning, burning without blisters, without ashes; just the pain of it, the pain of it for *ever*—I'd get real sick to my stomach and my hands would sweat. Then I'd beg temporary forgiveness. I'd promise my dear God that I'd go to confession and get all of it fixed and I'd never lie again, nor would I steal. I'd promise to try not to commit self abuse anymore.

I knew the only person I could tell all this to was Etta, but I loved her so much, I loved her so completely, I didn't want to disappoint her. I knew it would hurt her that her little hero was nothing more than a liar and a thief. I didn't want to hurt her, or ever see her cry because of me again.

I figured the only thing to do was catch the other thief.

I woke up the next morning to the sound of Etta coughing in her room. I listened for a while, hoping it would stop. Then I heard someone knocking on the door so I got up to answer it. When I came into the living room I saw Etta holding her side, leaning in the light which shined through the orange curtains. She looked at me, still coughing, her mouth shaped like a little "O." She frowned, pointed to the door.

It was Mrs. Proudy. She came in and pinched my cheeks. "How are you, young man?" Her voice sounded like someone drawing the last bit of liquid out of a glass with a straw.

I nodded, let her mess up my hair.

Etta caught her breath. "Close the door, Jack."

"Another spell?" Mrs. Proudy said.

"Yes." Etta was holding her blue robe closed in the front. She had painted her toenails and they looked funny sticking out of the bottom of the robe. She wore no slippers, and Mrs. Proudy noticed that right away.

"No wonder you're coughing." Mrs. Proudy went into the kitchen, started making coffee. "You just sit yourself down, and I'll handle things this morning."

"You don't have to do that," Etta said.

Mrs. Proudy made this noise that sounded like the teapot was ready. "Nonsense."

I had to get out of there early if I was going to wait for the thief in the church. I had resolved the night before not to go to school on this Monday. I would wait all day in the church and catch my thief. I knew if I succeeded, I could confess all and still be a sort of hero. I also knew, if I waited all day in the church, and the thief didn't show up, I'd be in the position of explaining to my mother why I didn't go to school. I figured that would have to be the truth. Although, I admit, I felt like on the way to the church I could think of some other story just in case I didn't have the courage to tell Etta everything.

But Mrs. Proudy was there making breakfast, and I wasn't going to be able to sneak out early. I could have if it was just Etta because she never knew what time it was, and she was usually so busy getting herself ready for work she didn't have time to worry about me. She knew I could take care of myself, and she usually let me.

Mrs. Proudy looked at me and said, "Get dressed, John."

I went into my room. Etta started coughing again.

When I was dressed I came back out. Etta was sitting in her lounger, holding a handkerchief over her mouth. Mrs. Proudy had set cereal on the divider for me. I went over to Etta. "Are you staying home?"

She nodded. There was something in her eyes that frightened me.

"Is the doctor coming?"

"Your mother is going to see him," Mrs. Proudy said.

Etta whispered to me, "I'll be all right, dear."

I panicked. She saw my eyes grow large, and she reached for me.

"What is it?" I said.

"Nothing."

"It's just a bad cold," said Mrs. Proudy. "Now come over here and eat your bread and cereal."

"I don't want any." My stomach felt like it was full of hot water.

"It's nothing. Just a cold," Etta whispered. Then she gave this short laugh. I loved her eyes then. They reflected all the light that ever entered that room.

I felt like laughing too. I knew it was OK if she could give a laugh like that. She was laughing at how silly I was being, so I knew I was being silly and I knew for perhaps the first time, I didn't have to worry.

I went over and ate my cereal, and Etta didn't cough again the whole time. When I went out, she hugged me and then Mrs. Proudy did the same thing and I smelled the garlic on her and marveled over such an odor at eight-fifteen in the morning.

I went right to St. Michael's. I saw the old priest saying mass when I opened the door. To the right, in the front pew was the old man I'd seen the first time I went into the church to steal the white candles. He was by himself, praying in front of the tiny red candles. The door made a creaking sound, like the bleat of a calf, when it closed, but neither the priest or the old man turned around. I blessed myself (I had water left over, had to wipe it on my pants) and went silently up the aisle. I decided to sit in the second pew, behind the old man.

When I got into place, I kneeled down, crossed myself again. I could see the old man's red ears sticking out of his white hair, and it made me think of my father. He was such an old man when he died. I had seen pictures of him, a great white hedge of hair on top of his head, his neck a little twisted and sagging, his eyes looking like peach seeds trapped in the folds of a blanket. It struck me that perhaps this old man in front of me was really my father, hanging around to see what else I was capable of. But I knew it wasn't. He was just an old man, somebody else's father, wanting to pray to the little red and blue candles. Or perhaps he was the thief?

The old priest turned around, spread his hands apart, said something that sounded like, "A domino is for biscuits."

The altar boys both said, "A damn queen lay on a tiffi cot."

Then the priest put his hands back together. One of the altar boys sneezed. The priest turned back around, leaned over the altar. I wondered what a "tiffi cot" was. I always wondered that when I went to church.

Mass was always such a mystery to me. Etta just didn't take me often enough for me to understand what was going on. Not that I fault her for that. She was the best person I've ever known. But everyone else thought she was bad for not taking me to mass every Sunday.

Sister Theresa used to scream at me because I couldn't memorize the parts of the mass. I'd get to words like "canon" and think of guns and when she wanted me to name the parts of the canon I'd be lost. And I refused to take Latin. That's when Sister Theresa met Etta for the first and only time.

You see, at the beginning of the year I found out I was supposed to be studying Latin, and when I told Etta that, she turned to Mrs. Proudy—who was drinking tea with her that afternoon—and said, "Latin's a dead language. I don't know why they have to study that."

I didn't want to study a dead language. I'd just started my career as a poor-box thief, and I didn't see any point in trying to learn a language nobody in prison would ever speak. So I told Sister Theresa that Latin is a dead language and I didn't want to learn it, and she told me to come up to the front of the class. I walked up the center aisle between the desks, feeling proud of myself for knowing that Latin is a dead language, and expecting Sister Theresa to allow me to talk to the rest of the class about it, and maybe ask them how they felt and what sort of language they'd like to learn.

But Sister Theresa asked me to hold out my left hand, palm down.

I held it out, looked at it to be sure that it was my left hand and the palm was down. "Like that?" I said.

She hit me across the knuckles with a tricornered ruler.

At times like that you don't really think about what you're going to say. I said, "*Ow!*"

"Sit down," Sister Theresa said.

I sat down.

"Not there," she said. "Go to your seat."

Everybody laughed. I tried real hard not to cry, and I couldn't wait to tell Etta about it.

But when I got home, I realized I couldn't tell her. She'd only go down there and hit Sister Theresa or something, and I didn't want that. I kind of liked Sister Theresa, to tell you the truth. Also, I didn't want Etta to know Sister Theresa very well because the old nun might talk Etta into taking me to mass more often. She kept telling me about how missing mass was a mortal sin and all. Unless you couldn't help it. I figured Etta couldn't help it because her husband was dead, and she didn't have any transportation. I couldn't help it because Etta couldn't help it. Anyway, I decided getting hit with the ruler was just punishment for all my crimes.

Sister Theresa made me come to the front of the class every day. She'd ask me, "Have you studied your Latin?"

"No, Sister."

Then she'd say, "Hold out your left hand."

And I'd do it and she'd let me have it. It really hurt too. She hit every bone.

It got to be a thing with me. I'd steal from the poor box, lie in the confessional, and refuse to study my Latin. And Sister Theresa was not going to stop hitting me. I figured I was giving a little suffering to the Lord to make up for stealing His money.

One day I held up my right hand, palm down. My left hand was all swollen and had cuts in it.

"Your *left* hand," Sister Theresa said.

The class laughed.

I stood there, holding out my right hand. "It's time to give this one a few licks," I said.

"Your *left* hand." She said it in exactly the same tone of voice as before.

"You'll have to hit this one."

There was a pause. I thought she'd go ahead and hit my hand for a minute, because she looked at it, and then shook a little, as if she were trying not to burp or something. Then she screamed, "SIT DOWN!"

The whole class jumped, me included. I almost fell down because I felt the wind of it. I stood there for a minute, staring at Sister Theresa, and she dropped the ruler on the floor by her feet and started crying.

"I'll sit down," I whispered. I went to my seat. Every one in the class looked at me as if I'd just put my clothes back on. I knew I was in trouble for that one.

So Sister Theresa had a conference with Etta. About me. Etta stroked my hair the whole time they talked, and she told Sister Theresa she was shocked to see the shape my hand was in.

I have to admit I felt sort of heroic then, too. I had stood up for my rights—that's how Etta put it later—and she was proud of me. Even though I should have studied my Latin. She told Sister Theresa she would rather she fail me than break all my knuckles.

They sort of glared at each other, and Sister Theresa said, "In this school, he will do what I say, or he will be punished."

Etta didn't change her expression. She turned around, put her hand on my head and said, "If you don't want to do the Latin, then don't. But you will have to face the punishment." Then she said, "Good day," to Sister Theresa and walked out.

"You'll have a rough time in life, Jack," said Sister Theresa.

I think she was real sad.

"It's really a good thing being Etta's son," I said. I was proud of Etta too.

"You will have a rough time."

"Why?"

"Because you are stubborn and willful. So is your mother."
Sister Theresa was really a very nice lady. She just didn't understand a lot of things because they forced her to wear those black
dresses and live in the convent with all the other nuns. She never
did hit me again. She failed me. Each time she failed me she would
say she was sorry. I think she was trying to apologize for all those
times with the ruler too.

Anyway, that Monday I went after the other thief, I sat behind
the old man and watched the priest finish the mass. I didn't really
think the old man could be the thief. He was too near the end of
his life, and I figured he was transfixed with the idea of cleaning
his soul until it was at least a light beige. A man who lived that
long had to have a fairly worn out old soul. Lord knows how many
times you can clean those things before they start to fade.
   I knew I'd have to wait until the church was empty, then I could
go into one of the confessional booths and wait. As soon as I heard
anyone, I could move the door aside a little and see my thief. I
wanted to catch him in the act. Then I'd go get Father Burns and
tell him who was stealing from *both* boxes. I would turn myself
in while performing the heroic act of catching the other thief.
   When the priest was finished he left the altar. The old man in
front of me knelt there for a while. He'd gotten up and struggled
up to the railing for holy communion. The priest came down with
the gold chalice, an altar boy next to him holding a gold plate, and
the old man put his head back and received the Lord. It all only
took a few minutes, one or two quiet minutes in which the old man
might have died. No one said anything. The priest looked at the
old man's strange tongue, placed the little white wafer there, then
went back to his business on the altar. I watched the whole thing
from the second pew, realized while it was going on that if I didn't
straighten out the mess I'd made of confession, I'd never taste the
host again. I felt sort of sad, but then happy because I knew I was
there to catch the thief and once I did I'd straighten everything
out.
   The old man finally struggled to his feet. He looked at me, made

his way out to the aisle. I watched him walk toward the front doors, holding his head up high. He was proud of himself. Maybe his soul was getting whiter and whiter. He looked like his feet hurt him terribly.

When he was gone, I crept back to the confessionals. Once inside the booth, I knelt down and said a quiet prayer for the old man. I was suddenly very scared, but then I realized that was how I always felt whenever I went into one of those booths.

I was in the booth to the left of the closet where Father Burns —and on some Saturdays the old priest—had to sit in a chair and wait for everybody's whispered sins. There was really just a chair in there for him to sit on, and a little window on either side of him. The window was situated right about where his ear would be and all he'd do is reach up and slide the door back on the window and listen. He couldn't see you because there was a dark screen over the window.

Under the window, in the booths on either side of the little closet, was a wooden kneeler. When you knelt on it, it sank a few inches and made this clucking noise like a chicken. It was designed that way, so the priest would know whenever there was a sinner in the booth. Father Burns had to spend regular hours in that tiny room between the booths, and sometimes he didn't have any customers. I figured he needed the little chicken sound to wake him up in case he dozed off reading his prayer book or something. The old priest was probably hard of hearing, so I don't know what he did. I knew I'd hate to get halfway through *my* confession and find out I had to start over again because I didn't have an audience for the first fifty-two sins or so.

It was dark in the booth, but gradually my eyes got used to it and I could see my white hands on my knees. I needed to look at some part of my body and be sure I was there, and about to do what I planned.

I felt pretty courageous, to tell you the truth. Like I'd snuck into the enemy camp to catch one of my own boys and then turn him in so the enemy would make its peace with me. Except I didn't really think God or Father Burns or Etta was the enemy. I guess I was the enemy.

I put my head down, closed my eyes. I tried not to think of all the sins I'd committed in the last year and a half. But it wasn't possible. I was there. *In* the confessional. I figured I might as well have a little dress rehearsal, since I was fairly sure in less than a week I'd be in there for real. I couldn't stop thinking about it anyway.

"Bless me, Father, for I have sinned," I whispered. "Boy, have I sinned."

But when I said, "Bless me, Father," I started thinking about my father again and wondering if he was truly a good man, as Etta said. I wondered what the hell a good man was. I would have thought I was good—I never consciously hurt anyone that I knew of, and I was always trying to be good—but when I listed my sins; when I thought of the lies to Etta, who I loved completely; when I remembered telling Father Burns I wanted to be a priest, that I wanted to bring him a white candle and all the time I was stealing from him; when I pictured my hands opening the poor box so many times, stealing God's money, I didn't know how I could ever think of myself as anything but some sort of evil thing.

And I never even got to self abuse in my rehearsal. Could I tell him—by this time I was sure I wanted to get Father Burns, because I didn't want to have to repeat *any* of these sins once I'd confessed them—could I tell him that I'd been lying accidentally in the confessional too? Say I had confessed adultery for half a year, before I knew what I was doing to myself was self abuse? That once I knew *that* I'd already stopped confessing adultery?

And the worst thing: even though I'd lied and stolen God's money, I was *still* committing self abuse. I wanted to commit self abuse as soon as I found myself alone—it didn't matter where I was. (When I first went into the confessional, it crossed my mind.) *Any* time I was alone I'd get the feeling. It was like my lungs expanded and changed shape.

I didn't like the way my mind was going, so I tried to think of something else. I listened for noises outside, but it was silent in the church, and my mind got right back to self abuse.

I didn't understand why they called it self abuse. It *never* hurt, except sometimes afterward. I guess if you used a pair of pliers or something it would hurt. It was almost completely painless when I was using the pencil.

Sister Theresa told us when we did that we were only spitting in the eye of God. Wasting His miracles. And whenever I'd finish doing it, I'd think of God watching me with a real sad look on His face, His hair sort of hanging by His beard, and His eyes droopy from the sadness. And I'd plead with Him to please please please please forgive me. And I'd say I'll never never never never never do it again. As long as I live. I'd say that.

The next day I'd be pounding away.

I always thought one more time won't hurt. Just one more time. And then there'd be God looking at me that way. Sometimes I wished He'd pay attention to some other more important thing.

I sat in the booth a long time, thinking those things, when my eyes closed and sort of locked that way. I tried to open them, but couldn't. This woman seemed to alight before me, and I could see her through my eyelids. I knew I must be dreaming. It was, you know, one of those dreams where you know it's happening, and you tell yourself to wake up. You say, "Come on now, wake up." But I couldn't even say that, much less open my eyes.

"Oh, no," I said to the woman. "I'm going to sleep through the most important moment in my life. I'll miss my thief."

She smiled. "I am with you," she said. Her voice was as soothing and calm as Etta's. It wasn't Etta, though.

"I want to wake up," I said.

"Come with me," she whispered. She took my hand, led me out of the booth to a white room behind the sacristy. We didn't make any noise when we walked.

"Oh, I'm not really with you," I said. "I'm still in the booth. You can't fool me."

She smiled.

We stood in the corner of this white room, and a little door opened up beneath this gold tubular shaped thing—it was like the tabernacle—and I saw a table with a woman on it. It was a high table, like the ones in hospitals, and it rose up once it came out of the little door. The woman was dressed in red, a tight red sort of dancer's suit, with sequins and a black garter high on her leg, and lace in her hair. I think her hair was red, too.

"What's going to happen to her?" I asked my escort.

But when I turned, she wasn't there, a man was. A tall man, lean like a chimney, dressed in black. I thought it was my father for a moment, but then I realized he was too young. He said, "The woman is dead."

"What?"

"She's dead."

Then two other men came in and started dressing her, pulling black nylons up her legs, adjusting the lace in her hair. I watched her body shake like a doll's body; it didn't seem like a real thing at all. I could see she was *really* dead.

"She's dead," the man said again.

"I know," I said. "You don't have to keep saying it."

"Dead."

"I can hear." I didn't like the way her body shook.

"Why don't they stop that?"

They placed her in this silky white thing—she sank into it like a foot disappears in deep snow.

"Now she will be buried," the man said.

"Who is it?" I asked.

Then the face came up out of the white silk and I saw Etta, my Etta.

I made this scream. It may have been "No," or something like that. It was only a long sort of help me wail that scared the hell out of me.

I didn't know if I wanted anyone to hear me or not. I sat there in the dark, trembling. When my senses came swimming back, I listened as the sound of my voice finished making the rounds. Then I started crying. I still couldn't open my eyes.

I tried to cry quietly, but it only got worse. I never knew I had so much water in me. I don't know why I was crying, except I believed the dream long enough to think Etta was dead. Maybe that was it. Or maybe I was so glad it was a dream I cried for joy?

Anyway, I was sitting there, slobbering all over the red carpet, when Father Burns and the old priest came in.

They walked right to the booth and pulled back the door.

"Was that you?" Father Burns said.

I wiped my eyes. "Yes."

"What are you doing here?" He took my arm, pulled me to my feet.

"Waiting."

The old priest—I wish I could remember his name—the old priest put his hand on my back and guided me toward the sacristy. "You waiting to go to confession?" He sounded like he had a ribbon down his throat or something.

"Just waiting." I didn't know what to tell them. I was so scared my hands were cold. And I couldn't see.

Father Burns said, "Confession's on Saturday and Sunday evenings. You got a long wait."

The old priest laughed.

I went into the sacristy, sat on a little stool in there. Both of the priests pulled up chairs and sat in front of me. This was double barreled confession. Father Burns did most of the talking.

"Why aren't you in school?" he said.

"Ummm." That's all I could say. I was thinking: if you lie here, you'll never tell the truth. If you tell the truth here, you'll never catch your thief—*you* will be *it*.

"Jack."

"Yes."

"Why are you here?"

"I was praying." I figured that was true enough.

"What's so important that you have to pray now?" This was the old priest.

"Etta's sick," I said. This was also true, although I wasn't praying for *her* in the booth. I might have prayed for her if I'd had time because of the dream. Anyway, I didn't *say* I was praying for her. I just said I was praying. And then I said Etta was sick.

Father Burns sounded as if he swallowed something unpleasant. "What's wrong with your mother?" he said.

"She's not feeling well."

"Has she been to a doctor?"

"I don't know."

I tried with desperation to open my eyes. I couldn't believe neither of my confessors noticed that my eyes were frozen shut.

"Well," Father Burns said. "I don't think you really know what you're doing here."

"Yes, I do."

"You wouldn't be here for more candles, would you?" There was a half smile in Father Burns's voice. So he did know about it after all. I was right.

"Bless me, Father, for I have sinned," I said.

"Go on."

"I stole some candles."

"Look at me," Father Burns said.

"I can't."

"You don't have anything else to confess to me?"

"Is this a confession, really?"

"Yes."

The old priest coughed.

"Does there have to be a witness?"

"We are both priests."

I heard somebody's stomach growl—make a bubbling noise like something in the pipes.

"I'd rather confess in the dark." I was telling the truth.

"Why?"

"It makes me feel better."

"Because you think we don't know it's you?"

"Yes."

The old priest laughed. "Are you still committing adultery fifteen times a week?"

"It's not adultery," I said.

Now they were both laughing. They howled, slapped knees.

"It's not funny," I said. I got my eyes open a crack.

They hugged one another, their mouths open, laughing so hard it looked like crying.

"This sure doesn't look like confession to me," I said. Then I heard a noise outside. Outside. A noise.

This time I was really awake. I felt my breathing, blinked my eyes to make sure. There was someone in the church, walking quietly away from where I was. I pulled the door back, peeked through the crack. I saw a figure dressed in black, moving toward the box by the sacristy. This is it, I thought.

Now I had a problem. If this really was the thief, what was I supposed to do? I couldn't beat him up or anything, I knew that. There was no way I could hold him until somebody came. I could sneak out and go get Father Burns or the old priest and take them back to catch the thief in the act. If I was going to do that, I knew I'd have to move pretty soon. I watched to see if the figure touched the box—as soon as he touched the box I'd be out the door and headed for the rectory.

But he kept standing there, looking around. I almost said, "Hurry up."

Then he went for the box, something I didn't really expect. I thought I'd be there all day and never rally catch my thief—but he went for it. And I opened the door to the confessional and walked right toward him. I wanted to ask him, what kind of person steals from the poor? But when I was close enough that he could hear me coming, he turned and looked at me and I got something else I didn't expect. It was Mr. Wicker.

THE ELEVENTH INTERVIEW

NOVEMBER 10, 1980

9:15 A.M.

Poor Mr. Wicker looked as if he'd just crawled out from under a Ford. His white hands curled around the box and when he saw me, they trembled slightly, as if the box were cold. He didn't look directly at me.

"Mr. Wicker," I said.

"What are you doing here?" he whispered.

"Mr. Wicker."

"Aren't you Etta's boy?"

"I didn't know you were the other thief."

"What?" He took his hands off the gold box, let them drop to his side. He didn't look like he could breathe. "Shouldn't you be in school?"

"I was in the confessional."

"There a priest back there?"

"Back where?"

"You said you were in the confessional," he whispered. He still wasn't looking at me. His eyes roamed the floor around my feet.

"I was in the booth on the left."

"By yourself?"

"Yes."

He studied his hands. "I'm not even Catholic."

"You aren't?"

"I guess I better say a prayer anyway, and move along."

"I'm a thief, too."

"Nobody's a thief." He bowed his head, as if he was trying to throw water out of his hair, then moved toward the center aisle and the front doors.

"Is this the only church you steal from?" I followed behind him.

"I wasn't stealing." He kept walking in front of me.

"It's OK," I said. "I'm a thief, too."

He stopped, turned around. We were about midway between the altar and the front door. I could see the confessionals to the right of the door, and for a brief second I remembered what I had come there for. My stomach got very cold.

"I've been stealing from the other box," I said. "I was going to turn myself—"

"You have?" His brows sank in the center of his face, almost touched. "If you were my boy, I'd—"

"I've been giving it to you."

"What?" He looked at me now, right into my eyes.

"I put it in your mailbox."

"You—"

"All year."

"It was you?" He wasn't angry any more. I thought he swallowed a mouth full of air.

"I didn't know there was another box," I said.

"You?" I saw his eyes swimming.

"I'm sorry," I said. "I wanted to help."

He shook his head, looked at the floor. "You," he said again, almost whispering. Then he said, "My God," and walked slowly down the aisle. When he was near the door, he turned, looked at me again, shook his head. Then he said, "Thank you, young man. Thank you very much."

"Don't cry," I said. You should have seen his face. He looked as if he'd just lost a family in a fire.

"I thank you," he said again. "Thank you." He kept mumbling that as he stumbled out the door into the bright sun.

I stood in the aisle until the door finished its slow eclipse of the light. I knew I couldn't tell anybody who the other thief was—and knowing that, I knew I wouldn't ever be able to make it right with God and Etta and Father Burns. If I told Etta the truth, once and for all, that would ruin me and her. You see, it would hurt her, cause her pain. I might as well walk up to her and poke her eyes out. I'd never do anything like that, and I didn't see much difference between that and telling her that I was probably not going to be a good man. How could I hurt her like that? I knew it would make her cry; her husband dead and then her son turns out to be a thief and liar. She'd blame herself, and what could I do to convince her it was *me* that got into a life of crime? I made all the choices. I wasn't afraid of punishment, I swear—I was only afraid of the damage I'd do.

I figured my life was about over.

I realized it really was sort of funny: me stealing to help Mr. Wicker, and Mr. Wicker stealing from the same place to help himself.

I didn't bother to bless myself when I finally left the church. I didn't want to waste the holy water.

So now I was in real trouble. I was out of school, with nowhere to go, and it was midday. I did not have my thief, and I didn't have a reason for missing school.

I walked around the corner of the church. In front of me, waiting like a penitentiary, was the long, red brick school. I knew it was full of nuns and blue-uniformed students, all of them doing what they were supposed to do. Nonsinners.

Above me white clouds grew like plants, and I heard the leaves of the trees hissing at me. I really didn't know where I should go. I didn't want to go home because I knew Etta was there—I'd have to tell her where I'd been, and I just didn't want to lie to her any more. I knew if I walked into the school, I walked into a tricornered ruler and all sorts of questions I didn't have answers to.

I leaned against the white stone of church, stared at the school hoping somebody would pull an alarm or something and everybody would file out and form lines I could get lost in.

I swear that's how the idea came to me.

I went in and smashed the glass in front of one of those axes. It set off this bell that sounded like a bank being robbed. I didn't even hesitate before I set it off. There's a certain skill and decisiveness we thieves acquire that's not all bad. I ran out and stood under the biggest tree in the playground, thinking I'd saved myself temporarily. I watched all the blue uniforms file out of the school;

all the little blue uniforms herded by tall black nuns. When everyone was out, whirling their heads looking for black smoke, a fire or a gas leak or something—I walked casually over to the line that led to Sister Theresa.

She didn't see me. She stood so tall at the end of the blue line, I had this feeling that I was a fiber in the cloth of a long pair of pants, and Sister Theresa was the black shoe sticking out from under the cuff far far away.

There were twelve lines, one for each grade, and each line led to a nun. Some of the little children in the other lines talked, pushed one another, laughed and screamed. They didn't know yet about the tricornered ruler, or about the way a soul tends to change colors on you if you don't watch out. Sister Theresa's line was what you would call ruly.

I thought I had made it. I think I even smiled.

Then I saw the shoe move. Sister Theresa was coming toward me.

The kid in front of me—I think his name was Brian—started tucking in his shirt. I don't know if he knew I was behind him or not. But his hands moved like sand crabs when he pushed his shirt into his pants, and I remember feeling vaguely sorry for him. I saw Sister Theresa coming and realized the fear she still created in everyone. Everyone but me. I had defeated her over the Latin lesson.

"When did you get here?" she said as she approached me.

"What?" Brian said.

I blinked.

"Not you," said Sister Theresa. She brushed past him, walked up to me.

"I've been here," I said.

"No, you haven't." She put her hands on her hips, frowned as if her shoes were uncomfortable.

"Yes, I have."

"No—you haven't."

"Have."

She grabbed my ear. "Now listen."

Sister Mary Kay came over from one of the other lines. "Father Burns says it's a false alarm."

"No, it's not," Sister Theresa said, still looking at me. I tried as hard as I could not to look away. I knew, even then, that if you look away everybody knows you're lying.

"What do you mean?" Sister Mary Kay said.

"I think I know how the alarm went off."

My heart swelled up for a second. "Ask Brian," I said. I was desperate, and I figured we were all allies against the black-habited sisters. But, as I said, Brian's hands trembled when he tucked in his shirt, and there was no way he was going to risk even *one* of his knuckles for me.

"I didn't see him," said Brian.

"Do you want to tell the truth?" Sister Theresa said. By this time, a lot of the people in the lines were looking at me.

"Yes," I said. "I *want* to tell the truth." I emphasized the word "want" because I really did want to tell the truth, and it felt wonderful being able to say that since that *was* the truth. I know it sounds silly. You can't taste lies, but I have the feeling all the time—even when I plan and calculate them—that lies originate in my mouth. It's a nasty feeling. The truth is as natural as a yawn when you speak it. Since it felt so good, I don't know why I didn't speak it more often. Except I knew what sort of rotten thing the truth really was most of the time. The truth about me anyway.

"Then tell it," said Sister Theresa.

"I am." Two little words, right off my teeth.

"You weren't here this morning."

"I was too."

"You were *not*. You were *not*."

"I wasn't in the class, but I was here." The truth.

"Doing what?"

"Well, I was in the church." That was true. It felt good.

"In the church?"

"I saw Mr. Wicker, my neighbor."

"What were you doing—"

"I was in the confessional, practicing." The truth grows on you, makes you feel safe and sort of invincible. It occurred to me that if I used the right tone of voice—real fervent and full of sincerity, like Sister Theresa whenever she read us Tennyson or whatever his name was—you could actually *lie* with the truth. When I said I had been in the confessional, practicing, Sister Theresa's face looked as if somebody put an infant in her arms.

"You were praying?" she said.

"I think I may have the calling," I lied. But it was an old lie, which Father Burns had believed, so it was like the truth. I remembered it as if it were true—an advantage of old lies I guess.

Of course the rest of that day, I was Sister Theresa's hero.

I was so proud of myself, I forgot about my problems for a while. It really did seem like a rather triumphant day, even though I didn't do any of the things I'd planned to do.

It never occurred to me that *God* might get tired of my predicament and intervene.

Sister Theresa was pointing to a map of South America and talking about coffee and tin and bananas when Father Burns opened the door and motioned for her to please "come here."

I knew right away something was wrong.

"John," Sister Theresa said. "Father Burns would like to see you."

Some of the students in the class exhaled a bit loudly. Of course, being a worrier, I knew I was a goner. I felt as if my heart had air in it.

When we were outside, Father Burns said, "I've got some bad news."

"Mr. Wicker told?"

"What?"

"I was just trying to help," I said.

He put his hand on my shoulder, moved me toward the church. I followed silently behind him. I gave up. I figured he was taking me to the police, or to the rectory to beat me and then to the police. He stopped under a green tree between the church and the

school. He leaned against the bark, put his foot up behind him.
"Do you have something you want to tell *me?*"
"Is this confession?" I don't know where I got the air to talk.
"It can be."
"Is it?"
"Is that what you want?" His voice was very gentle, almost
puzzled. I didn't think he understood how frightened I was.
I looked over at the church, thought about the long crime I'd
committed there.
"What is it you want to tell me?" said Father Burns.
"It's true."
"What's true?"
"What Mr. Wicker told you."
He put his hand on my head. "John, whatever it is, you'll have
to tell me. I don't know any Mr. Wicker."
"You don't?"
He smiled, took his hand away. "No."
"Well," I said.
"Well, what?"
"I thought you knew Mr. Wicker." I tried to change the subject.
"He's real poor."
"What did you think he told me?"
"Oh, nothing," I stared at my shoes.
"If you ever want to tell me, I'm willing to listen."
I didn't say anything for a while. I knew he was dying for me
to tell him. There was no way I was going to do that. Not right
then. I figured God knew about everything anyway.
"What did you want to tell me?" I said finally.
He reached out, pulled me over next to him so he could put his
arm around me. "Your mother called me today."
"Etta?"
"Yes." He squeezed my shoulder. "She's very ill and wants you
to come home."
I felt suddenly cold. "Right now?"
"She asked me to come with you and pray."

"What's wrong with her?"

He started walking, pulling me along. "When we get to her she'll explain it to you."

That walk home, next to Father Burns, was the longest breath I ever took. I didn't see or hear anything on the way. It was like I'd gone into some sort of long black tunnel of words that said, "Etta's very ill."

When we got to the apartment, Mrs. Proudy was there, and Etta was lying down in her room. Etta's hat and scarf were piled on the divider, and the room smelled of her perfume. Mrs. Proudy wore a yellow dress, sat in the chair by the window. She put her hand up and shushed us when we came in.

"Etta's resting."

"How is she?" Father Burns said.

Mrs. Proudy frowned. I could see she had been crying. "She's afraid. Angry at times."

"What's the matter?" I asked.

"Etta wants to talk to you."

I started for the room.

"Wait," Mrs. Proudy said. "She's asleep now."

"But what's wrong?"

"She's sick," said Mrs. Proudy.

I looked at Etta's hat and scarf again, then remembered she was going to the doctor this morning. "Where did she go today?"

"She went to the doctor's."

"The doctor?"

"Yes."

I went into her room, had to pull myself away from Mrs. Proudy. "Let him go ahead in," I heard Father Burns say.

I shut the door behind me. Etta was lying on top of the covers, her dress still looking clean and unwrinkled in the dull light of the lamp by her bed. Her eyes were closed, and she breathed slowly, as if she were calculating the length of each breath and had to count while she was doing it. The light made shadows under her eyes that frightened me.

I crept toward her. I didn't try to prepare myself for anything.
I was too afraid to think, I guess. The sound of my heart beating
woke her up.

She raised her head, smiled. "You're home."

I went to her, sat on the bed. She put her arm across my lap.
She had tears in her eyes suddenly, and I realized that I did too.

"Don't cry," she said. Then she put her head against my shoulder and cried so hard I thought it would stop my heart. I never
saw her cry like that.

"What's the matter?" I kept saying through my tears.

She sat up, finally, took a Kleenex from a box on the bed next
to her. When she was finished wiping her nose, she handed me the
box.

"Blow your nose," she whispered. Her eyes looked as though
someone had poked them.

"What's wrong?" I said.

She waited while I wiped my nose. When I was done she held
out the little waste basket she kept by her bed and I threw the
tissue away. "Let's get all arranged first," she said. "We can't cry
any more after this."

"Why not?"

"Crying is what you do first. After that, you don't do it any
more." She almost smiled then. "It doesn't really do any good."

"Why are we crying?"

She hugged me, very tightly. Then she sat back, looked me
directly in the eyes and said, "Honey, I'm going into the hospital."

"You are?"

"I'm not coming out." Her chin quivered.

"What?"

"I'm going to die, Jack."

You can probably figure out what she had. Etta had cancer.
She'd been coughing and choking worse and worse all that year,
but I was so carried away with my ongoing crimes, I didn't have
time to worry about it. Besides, I didn't really understand cancer
back then. I was too young. When you're twelve years old, you

don't truly comprehend death—unless someone you know dies. Someone who is not supposed to die.

I always thought death was what happened to dogs and cats and old people like my father.

That night Etta told me she was dying, I got physically ill. I was in the bathroom most of the time I wasn't with her. I knew *why* she was going to die.

I don't remember much of anything else. Mrs. Proudy stayed around and asked me to pray some more. Father Burns said a bunch of prayers and Etta went along with it, so I didn't have time to realize what was going on until the praying stopped. Once Father Burns was gone, though, it hit me that *I* had caused Etta's illness by being a thief in the house of God. You can probably guess what sort of response I had to Mrs. Proudy's suggestion that we pray some more.

"You won't pray for your own mother?"

"It won't do any good," I said.

Mrs. Proudy lapsed into prayer. I wasn't sure if she was praying for me, or for Etta. Maybe she prayed for all of us.

•

THE TWELFTH INTERVIEW

NOVEMBER 10, 1980

1:30 P.M.

The whole world changes once somebody you know finds out they're going to die. Time moves about as fast as a tree, and all the habits you've developed, the little everyday things you do without thinking or planning, they go on, but they change. They seem to take on force—as if every thing you do has consequences, although it feels as if something in your bones has died and you're going on repeating things you're used to. But it's all somehow not real. Getting out of bed in the morning becomes an act you know you will perform, but you lie there and think about it anyway. Then you discover later that you got out of bed, but you don't remember doing it.

Etta refused to let her illness keep her in bed, so she was up with the orange light every morning. I had a hard time looking at her. I felt terrible for this, but whenever I saw her I'd remember what was going to happen, and I'd start crying and that would remind her.

"Now stop it!" she'd say. "Just stop it!"

"I'm sorry."

"We've got to carry on."

"I'm so scared."

"So am I, honey," she'd say. And then she'd hold me and I'd listen to her breathing, think of my father, and cry all the harder. She'd feel that, and tell me to stop it again.

I didn't know how to tell her it was my fault. It was me.

I guess I wanted her to die thinking I'd be a good man. But I was afraid she'd get to heaven and God would tell her.

Why would He tell her, though? I asked myself that. Heaven is supposed to be wonderful. Bliss. The last thing God ought to do is tell a good woman like Etta, who has just died, that her son is evil and probably won't be joining her.

I figured He wouldn't do that. As soon as I'd get to thinking God wouldn't do so evil a thing, I'd remember it was Him who gave Etta cancer to pay for my sins. *That* seemed really evil. A God who'd do that might do anything. Anything at all.

Etta went into the hospital in January. I know what month it was because it was right after Christmas, and she took a blue nightgown I got her—packed it right on top in her suitcase.

"I'll wear this every day," she said.

We were standing in her room, and she was all dressed, ready to go. I said I wouldn't cry, so I looked out the window while she packed. She tried to spend every minute with me, once she found out what she had, and this last day was no different. I'd watched her struggling into her dark green dress—she was much too small for it by then, and I remember being slightly embarrassed when she finally had it on and it hung on her like an adult's dress on a child.

When she had finished packing, snapping the suitcase shut as if she was going to bury it rather than carry it with her, she said, "I've made myself ready for this."

Her voice was a deep whisper. I saw a black bird fly across the window pane.

"I haven't really prepared you, son."

"I'm ready," I said. I wanted to be good for her.

"You know what I always looked forward to doing with you?" she asked. Her eyes were dry, but there was a light there that flickered, made my own eyes water.

"What?" I said. I took a deep breath, held in something that began to feel hot in my throat.

"I always looked forward to having a drink with you." She smiled.

"I wanted to too," I said. I couldn't believe I said "to too" at that moment. I felt foolish, and not real. But Etta laughed. Threw her head back and laughed, laughed until tears came to her eyes and she started to cough. I tried to laugh too, but I was really crying.

After she stopped coughing, she leaned a bit, then took my hand. "Come," she said.

I followed her into the kitchen, wiping my face so she wouldn't see that I'd been crying. She reached under the wooden shelf in the corner of the kitchen, produced a brown bottle half full. She set it on the counter, took the top off and poured two small drinks. I'll never forget the sound of that whiskey spilling into those tiny glasses she had. Then she went to the divider and lit the five white candles I'd stolen for her.

"Come sit over here," she said, pointing to the stool on the other side of the divider. "I'll stand on this side."

I went and sat down. Etta stood across from me, her head tilted toward the light of the candles so that her hair looked like it was on fire.

She lifted the glass, handed it to me. "Take a sip with me." She held her own glass up, looked at me over the brim. I couldn't tell if she was smiling or getting ready to cry.

I got a little bit of the whiskey in my mouth. It burned, and I thought I was going to cough. Right then, the most important thing in the world to me was that I not cough. I watched Etta set her glass down in front of her. She seemed to be holding the whiskey in her mouth, her eyes closed.

I drank another little bit. This time I was ready for it so it wasn't so bad.

"You know," she said, "your father and I used to sip whiskey at night when he'd get home from work."

"You did?"

"He'd come in and I'd have a little glass with him. He wasn't a heavy drinker, mind you. Just one little glass in the evening." She coughed, held her hand on her chest. "Oooh. That one hurt."

I took another sip, swallowed it fast. I wanted it to change things for me.

" 'Etta,' your father'd say, 'let's have a whiskey.' And I'd get it for him. Even though I really couldn't stand the stuff. I don't guess I like it now. But I always wanted to sip it with you. You'd be a grown man, in a dark suit with a vest, and a gold watch chain running up and down across your middle," she reached across the divider and ran her hand across my stomach. "Right here. And you'd have a high white collar, all stiff and everything. And a thin paisley tie, I think. You'd be in business. A lawyer maybe. Something wonderful, something good. And we'd have our whiskey, just like this."

She took another sip, stared at the gold fluid in the glass as if she thought it might change in front of her.

"I love you, Etta." I whispered it, raised the glass and took some more whiskey. I could see she was trying as hard as I was not to cry.

"And I love you," she said. Then she leaned across the counter and kissed me lightly on the forehead. I tried to touch her cheek but it was too late, she pulled away.

"Now," she said. "I have one more thing I want to do." She raised her glass, drank the last of the whiskey. I tried to do the same, but it was too strong.

"Easy," she said.

"I like it."

"Good."

"I just—"

"Don't ever drink too much of it."

"I won't."

"Remember your father. One drink, at night maybe."

"Yes."

"No more, no less." She smiled again, a real smile this time. "He was such a good man."

These words made an impression in my skin, I think.

"What's the other thing you want to do?" I asked.

"What?"

"You said you had one more thing—"

"Oh." She blinked, wiped her hand across her brow, blew out the candles. "Come on, I'll show you."

She put on her coat, pushed mine at me. "Hurry up now." Her voice seemed to get more and more like the old Etta, the one who wasn't going to die. It was like an outing. When we were all wrapped in coats and scarves, she opened the door and walked out into the dull light of that January afternoon—the afternoon of her last day at home—as if we'd be back within the hour. Except I was dragging her green suitcase.

It wasn't really all that heavy. She'd only packed a few things; the nightgown I'd given her for Christmas, a toothbrush, a comb, a few pairs of underwear, and some perfume. There were brown slippers—but they didn't go with the nightgown I'd gotten her, so she decided to leave them home.

"I'll probably be in the bed the whole time," she said. "I don't need these until I come home."

She always talked like that. You see, that's the thing that broke my heart—Etta talking all the time about when she got home and all, when she and I both knew the trip to the hospital was only a way of finding a bed to die in that somebody other than me would have to clean up.

Anyway, we walked down P Street, toward the river. It was cold, and the wind made noises like a cheering crowd between all the buildings. I remember the black streets, the huge cables for the streetcars overhead. The sky was white, a little gray at the edges maybe, and I remember thinking about mercy and what could have caused it to come into being.

You ever thought about that?

In the world, in nature—in all diseases, accidents, or disasters, or crimes—there is no mercy. Once cancer gets going it never lets up; the same with consumption, aging, wars, tornadoes, earthquakes, fires. A tiger gets you by the throat, you're dead. Unless it dies first. A poisonous snake? The bad ones kill you after you've had time to consider the wound, figure your chances. The good ones kill you right away.

I realized there was no mercy in anything. Mercy didn't exist in the world at all until there was man. Until man knew what to call himself, and until he knew that one day he was going to rot like everything and everyone else he knew or cared to know.

Our history is an interesting one because it is so full of what Sister Theresa called the "gory details." And it is without mercy.

Mercy was only an idea. That's what I concluded. Man invented it, probably so he could beg his captors or conquerors or torturers. But it was definitely a creation out of the mind of man —because he couldn't have gotten the idea from anything the world could show him.

That's what I thought about as Etta and I walked toward St. Michael's and the river. I still didn't know where we were going. Etta struggled alongside me. I had the most complex assortment of feelings as we trudged through the January air. I knew it was the last time she'd walk these streets, and I also knew that as long as we walked the streets, she couldn't be dying. But she was such a weak assortment of bones by that time. I marveled at her ability to continue in the same tone of voice and with the same intense interest in me while her body was gradually beginning to abandon her.

"I love this weather," she said. "It's good for all the fluids in you."

"I'm cold," I said.

"This weather is good for the flight of birds." She looked up. "The air is crisp and thin and dry." Steam came out of her as she said this. I looked away.

We walked silently for a while. I realized we were headed for Memorial Bridge and the cemetery where my father was buried. I didn't say anything, but I thought it was the wrong place to go considering our circumstances. It was too cold to walk that far carrying a green suitcase. And I didn't want to look at a tombstone just then.

The wind pushed me from behind, iced the back of my neck.

"I wish I had my gloves," I said.

"You can keep warm if you think about it," Etta said.

The suitcase got heavier and heavier. My fingers were permanently curled around the handle—I didn't see how I'd ever get them loose.

"You want me to carry that for a while?" said Etta.

"No." It was nice of her to ask, but I knew she couldn't carry anything that distance. She was working to continue walking. I wished she didn't want to go all the way to Arlington cemetery, though.

She used to walk there all the time. It's about twenty blocks to
the bridge, and then a long walk across that. I imagined the river
would be intolerably cold. I felt useless, sad, and guilty for not
wanting to take this walk with her. But I was so cold. I just wanted
to be somewhere nice and warm.

I kept switching the suitcase from hand to hand as we walked.
"Is it that heavy?" said Etta.

"No."

"I'll carry it." She reached for it.

"*No.*"

"It's like I've grown old already. Just in the last three months."

"I don't mind," I said. "That's all. I know you can carry it."

"You're such a good boy." She put her hand on my arm,
stopped me. "Let's link elbows and walk like a lady and her
gentleman." Her smile was white. The skin of her forehead was
as tight and dull colored as a fingernail.

I linked my elbow with hers, resolved to carry the suitcase in
my right hand only. I heard myself saying, "Oh, Etta, why you?
Why this?" But of course I didn't say that. I knew why. I knew
exactly why. I wanted to tell her so bad—let her know the reason
for her suffering. But I knew if I did all I'd do is make it harder
on her. She'd have to worry about me blaming myself and all, and
it wouldn't make her death any easier. I knew that. I knew she
needed to die thinking I was a good man.

When we got to the bridge, I saw the white gulls of winter
swooping down toward the icy river. I held Etta's arm and we
stood by the railing at the entrance to the bridge and studied the
blue water below. The river rushed around gathering hunks of ice.
It was colder than I thought. I saw leaves blowing along the banks,
and a little further down, toward one of the monuments, there was
a lone man with a blue ski cap, leaning over toward the water,
trying to retrieve something.

"I love this city," Etta said.

I put the suitcase down, broke the shape of my hand in the cold
wind. I watched the man in the ski cap rise up, look down the river
toward where Etta and I stood, then move along away from us.

He really had nowhere to go. Just walking by himself along the river. I think it was while I watched him get smaller and smaller along the gray bank of that river that it hit me how alone I'd be once Etta was gone.

A car went by behind us, tires squealing on the black asphalt. It was as if God wanted to remind us where we were going.

"Come," Etta said.

I picked up the suitcase, linked elbows again.

"You'll be my gentleman escort across the bridge."

The walk across the bridge was much colder. The wind seemed to want to blow us off the pavement—as if we were intruders in the ice-blue winter. Etta held to my arm tightly, and I understood that I was holding her up more and more as we approached the other side of the bridge.

By the time we were in the cemetery, Etta was breathing and coughing next to me like an old man. She held her hand over her mouth, tried to be polite about it. I didn't think it would ever stop. It was dry and deep, her cough.

I put the suitcase next to my father's tombstone, read once again the inscription etched in the stone: "With great love, we remember thee."

"He will be glad to see me," Etta said.

"I wish I knew him."

"You're just like him."

"Not *just* like him."

"Oh, yes," Etta said. "He always wanted to fix things for every-body, just like—" She started coughing again, bending over now, her hand on top of my father's stone.

It occurred to me that my father might not be in heaven, and that Etta would be disappointed when she got there. I didn't see how heaven could be bliss if the people you loved didn't make it there too. Everybody didn't go to heaven. I knew I wasn't going. And it didn't seem possible that heaven would be such a happy place, since a lot of people would have to be mourning people they loved who died at the wrong time and ended up in hell. What would make heaven so good that you'd forget a person you loved deeply?

"What if he's not there?" I said.

"What?" Etta wiped her mouth with a white handkerchief, looked at me with eyes that seemed foreign to me—trapped in her taut white face.

"Nothing."

"He'll be there. I don't know what will happen to me, or where I'm going. The only thing I'm sure of is that I'll see him." She looked at the grave.

"I wish I was going with you." The wind picked up, made my cheeks feel like ice. I knew there were tears there.

"You live a full life, son." Her voice was deep, like a man's voice. "I'll remember you."

"Yes."

"I'm asking you to live a full life for me."

"I will."

"Mrs. Proudy will take you in."

We had already arranged this. I knew I'd be safe and cared for. Mr. Wicker even volunteered to watch after me once he was working again. He said he'd welcome me into his family.

But I didn't want to go to Indiana.

Etta smiled at me, the wind blowing swirls of hair above her head. "I'm very proud of you," she said. Then she walked over to another grave, took some yellow flowers from a small pot there and placed them at the foot of my father's tombstone.

I thought about his body down there, under the earth; a body I'd never seen, or touched, and that never saw or touched me. My father was really only a photograph. But he had force in my life because of Etta.

"Thanks for being my father too," I said.

She looked at me, reached up and tried to straighten her hair. She wanted to look good when she went into the hospital. "You be a good man like your father," she said.

Then I started sobbing. I couldn't help it. She came over to me, put her arms around my neck, held me there in the cold white wind. I heard the rattle of her breathing, remembered the rising and falling of her breast when she used to hold me at night and tell me stories, and I felt like the world was certainly finished.

I had to flag a taxi to get Etta to the hospital. She was so weak when we finished crying, I sat her down on one of the low stones and went out to the street waving at every car—my eyes were so full of tears I couldn't tell a taxi from a motorcycle. When we were in the back seat of the cab, Etta held me, cried quietly on my shoulder. I looked out the window, watched the black trees go by, the green signs and white marble buildings and monuments. And I prayed the taxi would crash and kill both of us.

But we made it safely to the hospital. I followed Etta into the lobby, watched two nurses set her in a wheelchair and push her into one of the white corridors. She turned to me as she went through the door, smiled. Then she got this defiant look in her eyes, turned away from me, forever. She died in surgery. I never saw her breathing again.

And that's how Etta finally let me down. It was something she couldn't help, I know that. Even so, I was so angry when I found out she was gone already. I couldn't believe she left me so easily. I know I was selfish for thinking such things—but I thought she'd be in the hospital for a while, and I'd have a chance to visit her and see her again. I didn't know that when she held me in the taxi it was for the last time. If I'd known that, I think I might have concentrated on it a little more. I don't know. It seems like I would have tried to freeze each moment. Instead, I couldn't wait to get to the hospital because I thought she was getting weaker, and I didn't want her to die so soon.

I cried a long time. It didn't seem like anything that would ever get better. I only stopped to eat and sleep.

Mrs. Proudy gave me the option of staying home when they buried Etta. I didn't really want to go. I wanted somebody to please tell me how come Etta wasn't breathing any more. I wanted to know how come I was without parents and completely alone.

On the day of Etta's funeral, Mr. Wicker came to see me. I heard this tapping on the door and hoped for a naked minute it was Etta's soul coming for me. But when I opened the door and saw Mr. Wicker, I started crying again. I knew death was permanent.

Mr. Wicker came in, closed the door.

"You're not going to the funeral?" I said.

"No." He stood there, holding his black hat in his hands, staring at me.

I didn't know what to look at, or where I should place myself. I stood there in the middle of the room, not seeing anything, and Wicker said, "I'm sorry."

"Me too."

"Your mother was a good woman."

"I know."

"You should be thankful for the years you've had with her."

"Sure."

"That's all you can do."

"Sure." I wanted him to go away. I hated people who tried to make me feel lucky. I had twelve years with her. I should be thankful. Except I didn't know for all those twelve years that after the twelfth year I *wouldn't* have her. The way I figured it, I wasted a lot of time.

Now when I think about it, I feel sorry for Mr. Wicker. He was only trying to help me.

"You can't keep wishing for something else," he said. He put his hand on my shoulder. "There's nothing you can do to change it."

"It's not fair," I said.

"Nothing is."

"It's just not fair."

He reached into his pocket, pulled out a handful of paper money. "This is all I could scrape up." He was almost whispering.

"What?"

"It's not nearly what you stole for me. Not nearly." He held it out. "But take it."

"I don't want it."

"Take it. I owe it to you."

"No."

"You're going to need it." He stuffed it into my shirt pocket. Then he knelt down and looked into my eyes. "When I was your age, I left home."

"You did?"

"I never saw my momma again."

I started crying.

"I never went home. Now, I'm going back to my family—my wife and kids. I thank you and Etta for that."

"Etta's dead." I couldn't breathe, it hurt so bad.

He reached out, hugged me. I smelled tobacco, and a curious sweet smell, like flowers or pastries.

"You are a good boy," Wicker said. "A good boy."

"Sure."

He pulled back, put his finger on my mouth to shush me. Then he got up, whispered, "A good boy," one more time, and went out the door. He slipped out as if he was trying not to wake me. When he was gone, I went in and lay down on Etta's bed and cried myself to sleep.

•

THE THIRTEENTH INTERVIEW

NOVEMBER 12, 1980

9:00 A.M.

Everybody kept telling me I was a good boy, so maybe I was. I didn't think so, though. I used to wonder what would have happened if I had been *trying* to do evil all that time, since I caused so much misery trying to do good. I kept thinking maybe there was no such thing as goodness in the world. I knew there were good things and all—trees, and love, and rain—but just really not any goodness. I thought maybe all things were eventually evil, or caused it. If you just *survived* you were doing something evil, since you had to eat some other living thing—either plant or animal— in order not to die yourself. What could be good in a world that eats itself?

It took me years to get over Etta's death—if you can say not thinking about it all the time is getting over it. There comes a time when you get going in life, and you're busy and full of events— just living and all—there comes a time when you don't remember the things that cause you pain. I guess I got to that point with Etta, although every night before I went to sleep, for the rest of my life, I saw her face in the darkness. She always smiled, and seemed to be listening to me breathe. Some nights I even talked to her, to tell you the truth. She never answered or anything—I wasn't crazy. But I didn't mind talking to the face I saw in my dreams.

I lived with Mrs. Proudy and went on with my life, once the crying stopped. I guess that was another thing I thought was a bit evil: the fact that I *could* go on without Etta, and that some days, when I was real busy, it was just as if Etta hadn't lived at all. I remember going sleigh riding in the winter, getting all excited and out of breath and laughing with my friends, and actually having fun. Etta wasn't ever in the world then. That always made me sad, made me want to think about her more often. But like I said, once you get going in life, you don't always remember.

I guess I got used to Mrs. Proudy. She stayed fat and still smelled like a delicatessen, but she tried her best to love me. I didn't have the heart to fight too much with the old lady, because she was doing Etta a favor raising me, and I didn't want to make the job any harder than necessary. We had a few fights over the years, but she always looked me in the eye and said something like, "What would your mother think of this," and I'd pretty much give in.

I never did confess my sins. I went to see Father Burns shortly after Etta's funeral, intending to tell him all of it, but when I got there all he did was hug me and tell me how sorry he was. It was raining the day I went to see him. I walked along the street, watching the rain make tiny circles in all the puddles on the black streets, thinking that when the day was over I'd be finally free of all the evil I'd done.

Washington looked white as soap in the rain. Nearly all the buildings were white back then, with long columns and ornate statues and scrolls. I used to wonder how anyone could make stone look so much like cloth. Anyway, I walked along, watching all the buildings and the water in the puddles, and tried to rehearse what I'd say. I wanted someone other than me to know I was the one who caused Etta's disease.

This was in 1932 or '33. The streetcars were full of tattered men in long overcoats, reading newspapers and drinking something out of bottles in brown bags. I knew none of them had anywhere to go, or anything to do, so they rode the streetcars in search of work. The tracks looked like silver strips of ribbon in the road because of the rain. Every block or so one or two of the men would get off the streetcars and wander up the block in the blue rain. I felt sorry for all of them, I guess. But I had no wish to help. I didn't think I'd want to help anybody ever again.

I walked up the front walk in front of the rectory behind St. Michael's. It was a Saturday, so nothing much was going on. The rain was just letting up as I walked up the stairs and knocked on the big wooden door. I thought maybe that was God's way of letting me know he approved.

An old woman opened the door and growled something I didn't understand.

"Is Father Burns here?" I asked.

She smiled. "Come in, young fellow." Her voice was deeper than the voice of the old priest. She wasn't mean, though. Actually she was very nice. She led me into this enormous yellow kitchen, sat me in a small white chair and served me a fresh cup of hot chocolate while I waited for Father Burns to come down.

Like I said, when he saw me he hugged me and said how sorry he was.

"It's not fair," I said.

The old woman went quietly out of the room. Father Burns put his hands on my shoulders, one on each side, and tried to smile. "If you were throwing a party, wouldn't you want all the best people to come?"

"Yes," I said. Although I never threw a party; never wanted to either.

"Well," he said. He looked at me as if what he'd said about the party had changed the color of my hair or something.

"Well, what?"

"Etta's gone to God's party."

"How come she had to suffer from cancer to get there?" I really wanted to know.

"That's earth," he said. "Earth is different, separate and not like anything we can know of God."

"Why?"

"It's where we live. It's—well, don't you see?"

"No."

He went to a cupboard over the long white sink, withdrew a brown cup with the yellow word "Father B" written neatly on the side. I watched him pour coffee into the cup, return to the table, and sit across from me. He sipped the coffee, looked at me over the brim as if he expected I'd be dissolving soon. He set the cup down, sighed and said, "Earth is a creation of God, but it's ours. It is a place of man."

I didn't say anything. I just looked at my hot chocolate and tried to think of what I could say to him that would let me get into the whole story of my extended crime.

"Earth is not where God is," he said.

"He's not?"

"He's here in you, in me—in all human beings, of course. But the world is truly ours. It belongs to us. And we have a certain way of looking at it. We can only understand it from the point of view of being men since we *are* men. See?" He sipped his coffee, blinked as if the cup burned his lips.

"Etta's gone," I said.

"I know."

"She didn't do anything bad, and she's gone anyway."

"In order for her to go, she had to die. That's earth."

"I wish God didn't throw such long parties."

He laughed to himself. I'm sure he thought I was serious and that I believed him, but I really didn't. I knew there was no party, and that Etta was only dead.

"Earth leads to death," Father Burns said. He was starting to enjoy his explanation. Perhaps a sermon was beginning to take shape in his mind. He ran his hand over the top of his head, leaned forward as if he might kiss me. "It's only the death of the body."

"How can anything feel good without your body to feel it?"

"Things of the spirit," he said. I noticed a white piece of something on his lower lip, realized it was some sort of collected, used saliva and that he probably didn't even know it was there. While he talked I watched it bob up and down like one of those white dots that bounce over the words of songs in the movie show. "Things of the soul are far more important than mere feeling."

"But why did Etta have to die? She was my mother, and I thought she was so good because my father was dead. I thought —I figured God was trying to make up for that by—"

"By giving you Etta?" He nearly laughed at this, but I could tell he liked the thought. "Maybe He did. But we can't understand what God wants, or what He's going to do, or why."

"How do you know what's right or wrong, then?"

"Oh, He's told us that."

"I don't understand any of it."

"Look at it this way," he said, and the white dot bounced a little faster. He was really getting excited now. "What if you made a statue out of clay, and the statue could think and make its own choices. You know what would happen?"

I could see he was going to wait until I answered him, so I said, "What?"

He looked pleased. It occurred to me that he probably felt he was doing his job—explaining God to me. I couldn't take my eyes off the white dot. "The statue," he said, "would want to know why *you*—its creator, and so, if you created it you would be its god, see?—the statue would want to know why you created it. Would want to understand everything you did, or *didn't* do, according to what it knew about being a statue. According to statue values. From a statue's point of view."

"We're like the statue."

"Right." He was very pleased. I wanted to get out of there. I understood what he was telling me, but he was so excited about it, I was afraid by the time he was finished, he might expect me to be *glad* Etta got cancer and died. I couldn't get over how satisfied with himself he was. "You would be totally incomprehensible to the statue," he said.

"I see."

"Yes." He sipped his coffee, smiled. "So you see, Etta's dying was natural."

"I don't think God is fair," I said. The hot chocolate in front of me was beginning to smell like stale bread. I was suddenly very sick to my stomach, and found myself wondering what Father Burns would do if *he* got cancer.

"Some statues would be bitter, of course. They'd hate you for not behaving in ways they understood." He was only smiling now, looking down on me as if I was a pleasant color he admired.

"I don't think God is fair," I said, again.

"Well, maybe later—"

"If I could punch Him, I would."

"Jack," he said. He used the same tone of voice Etta always did when she said my name in two syllables and scolded me. For a brief instant, I hated him. I thought he looked like a bad reflection in a dirty mirror, and that if he said anything else to me I would probably punch *him*. I looked at his black robe, the little slot of white under the dark chin, and hated him. He reached out, touched my cheek, and said: "Try not to be bitter."

I looked at my hot chocolate.

"Just a little kindness," he said, taking his hand away.

"What?"

"That's all we have to offer."

"Who?"

"Human beings. You and me. A little kindness."

"I have to go," I said.

He nodded, smiled. "Be kind to yourself," he said.

When I went out the door, I didn't thank him for the hot chocolate. I guess you might think that was impolite, but I thought I was being kind to myself.

Like I said, it took me years to stop crying over Etta. I guess you think that's abnormal. Maybe it is. But there were so many things to remind me, you know? Summer lightning, candles, and winter evenings when the moon seemed like a thing flat and frozen. I would listen to my own breathing at night and think of her. Or I'd be walking outside and notice the steam from my own mouth and remember the flight of birds in Etta's thin winter air, and our walk across that bridge into Virginia where my father lay buried. Songs reminded me, and doors closing in bright hallways; the smell of boiling ham, or fried potatoes, or pancakes in the morning; Everywhere I breathed, there was Etta, smiling at our "small bit of good fortune" as she used to call our lives until she died. Most of all I remember the rise and fall of her breast, and her breathing late at night when I was very young and she used to hold me and explain everything she knew outside our single window. The world was a permanent and solid thing on those nights, and I've never felt such peace before or since.

I didn't try to be anything much after Etta was gone, because

I knew I was condemned, and that I'd never see her again. I was as free as anything ever is, I guess. I figured I was already punished, even for things I hadn't done yet. I guess you could say I wasn't too extremely unhappy. I was just trying to live and stay that way, since I knew that when I died my *real* punishment would begin: hell. Just the thought of all that fire made my hair come uncombed.

You know it's kind of funny, but I was even wrong about that. I thought I'd begun the worst punishment possible in life when Etta got sick. I thought it couldn't get any worse than saying goodbye to her in the hospital and not knowing that was the last time I was ever going to see her. But it did. It got much worse, once the war began; once the Japanese decided to go to war without announcing it to everyone first. I had been in the army for five months when something happened to me that made me as helpless as an infant, and I had hours—just hours and hours—to *think* about my sins and all the damage I'd done. I didn't have any luck when I was Jack Pitt, and that's the truth.

I joined the army in 1942, almost ten years after Etta's death. I graduated from St. Michael's in 1938, much to Sister Theresa's surprise. Father Burns squeezed my shoulder when he handed me the diploma, and Mrs. Proudy shed garlic tears. I spent three years working in Mrs. Proudy's establishment, sweeping floors, cleaning windows, and fixing faucet leaks in the apartments. Every time I cleaned the little apartment Etta and I shared, I did it with blurry eyes—it was part of the punishment, I thought. Then when the war came I enlisted.

I went through basic training without ever realizing I'd been through it before. Nothing seemed even vaguely familiar, but remembering it now, I can't truly identify any differences. People yell at you, tell you where to put your body and what to do with it, how to dress, eat, sleep and when to do all those things. It's hard for me to believe I didn't recognize some of that stuff, or at least have a strong sense of déjà vu. Of course, I thought about Etta a lot. To tell the truth, I was as homesick as I've ever been. I missed Mrs. Proudy and her bad breath, and that was part of it. But worse, and this is what really made me homesick, I couldn't conjure Etta before I slept in the evenings. I was usually so tired, I just lost consciousness. It was like I was away from the memory of Etta too, and I began writing long letters to Mrs. Proudy complaining about the food, and the way the army treated me generally—as if she could do anything about it.

She wrote me short little notes telling me how busy she was, and how her new tenants were as sloppy as pigs—she always had new tenants. She never once said she missed me, but I understood I was somebody else's son. She was only doing Etta a favor. It didn't bother me at all that Mrs. Proudy was too busy to write me longer letters.

I wrote one letter to Father Burns. I told him all about the army, North Carolina (where we soldiers were being manufactured), and the poor boxes. I got real emotional near the end of the letter and told him all about my life of thievery. I told him I was sorry for robbing God, and that when I got out of the army I was probably going to enter a seminary. I asked him to forgive me through the mail, but that must have been impossible, because I never heard from him. Maybe he died before my letter got to him, or perhaps he went to another parish. I know it's also possible he didn't want to forgive me.

When I wrote the letter I really *was* thinking about entering the priesthood. I only wanted to see what God would do if I became a priest. I didn't see how He could put me in hell if I did that. But then the day after I wrote the letter, I remembered how many times priests go to confession, so I dropped the idea. I never would have made it anyway. I figured the only thing worse than being in the army probably was being a priest.

When I got out of basic training, and knew to call a rifle my "piece" and not a "gun"—could walk five miles in full pack, and stab a straw bag with a bayonet faster than a fly could leave a flat surface—I stood in front of a mirror in the latrine and said goodbye to myself. The rest of my platoon whooped and hollered and celebrated leaving North Carolina by turning over bunks and upending foot lockers. We were all packed and ready to go to California, and then to the Pacific where we were losing the war. And I said goodbye to myself. I knew I would be dead soon. It didn't come to me in a vision or anything like that. I just knew it. I stood in front of that mirror, stared into my own eyes and recognized a body, my body, as a thing almost separate, almost completely independent from me— the person behind the eyes doing the staring. I wasn't really bad looking. I had Etta's eyes, and her dark hair, although there was very little of it on my head at that moment. My mouth was a little crooked, but you couldn't notice it unless I was smiling, and I didn't do much of that. I was slim, angular—and as tall as I ever was. Much taller than I am now—although I don't remember the exact figure. I'm six feet tall now, so I had to be a few inches over that. And I knew I was going to be dead.

I didn't have any friends in the platoon, but there was one man, a guy named Shucker, who followed me around everywhere as if he thought I might drop some money or something. I guess he wanted to be my friend, but he was not very smart and he was always in trouble, so I didn't want to get close to him. He was as tall as me, but much wider, with large dull brown eyes, and a rubbery mouth that was always hanging slightly open. His real name was Gage—I'm not sure about his first name, but he was from Alabama, and he didn't speak the same way the rest of the men did, so they called him Shucker.

Anyway, I was standing in front of the mirror, thinking about the end, and Shucker came in behind me and tapped me on the shoulder.

"We're shipping out, old buddy," he said.

I wanted him to go away. I looked into my eyes, tried to imagine myself in a box with my hands clasped across my breast.

Shucker stood next to me, staring at his mouth. I wondered what he was thinking, if he was capable of knowing what I felt right then. He was a man who lived each day as if it came as a surprise to him. Everything amazed him, awed him, set him to making noises through his teeth and exclaiming to anyone who would listen, "Isn't that *some*thing?" When I showed him I could tie the shoelaces of both my boots together, and throw the boots over my shoulder rather than carry one in each hand, he went and told everyone else in the platoon. He thought I was a genius.

Of course, because everything seemed new to him, and because he didn't seem to know anything at all besides his own name and which end his trousers went on, he got labeled early as stupid. He became a victim. They played every trick in the long catalog of barracks pranks, including the one where you put your hand in the shaving cream. I felt sorry for him.

Anyway, he stood behind me while I stared in the mirror, and I decided to ask him if he knew what would happen to all of us.

He looked at me as if he wasn't sure I was talking to him. "What?"

"Do you know what's going to happen?"

Somebody was playing a radio back in the halls of the barracks. Shucker looked so tired, his eyes large as poker chips and half closed.

"That's Glenn Miller," he said.

I turned back to the mirror. "We're all going to die."

"I know."

"You do?"

He blinked. "Sure."

"Aren't you afraid?"

"I'm not going to die right now."

"Come here," I said. I moved him next to me. "Look into the mirror. Look into your eyes."

"Yeah."

"You see anything?"

He opened them fully, then stepped back. "What's the deal?"

"You don't notice anything about them?"

"What?"

"Look again."

He leaned forward, stared intently into the mirror. "Have I got something in them?"

"They're fragile."

"What's that?" He looked at me. He really wanted to know.

"You're going to be dead, and those won't see anything."

"Oh." He lowered his head, as if I'd just yelled at him for something. "I don't think things like that, smacks."

He called everybody smacks. Even the men who made a fool of him, who played cruel jokes on him and then laughed along with him. (One night, while he slept—and Shucker could sleep; I had to roll him over into a pillow in the morning so he'd start to suffocate and wake up from lack of air—one night while he slept, the men tied a helmet to his penis, then laid the helmet over his groin. When he woke up he took the helmet and threw it to the floor, almost stripping himself of his equipment. Everyone laughed until their eyes watered, and Shucker came up to me and said, "Who do you s'pose did that to me, Pitt?" It was the only time he ever called me by my real name. I told him I didn't know because I was afraid he would kill one of them.)

"I don't think things like that, smacks," he said. And I realized I too was being cruel to him.

"I'm sorry, Shucker," I said. "I'm just scared."

"Let's go to the cafe and I'll buy you something to drink."

"You will?" I couldn't believe he had any money, since that too was something the other men tricked him out of.

"I didn't shoot craps this morning," he said.

"Why not?"

He pointed to himself in the mirror and said, "Because I wanted *him* to have some money for a change."

I laughed. I thought it was genuinely clever that he said that. "Come on," I said. "I'll let you buy me one drink. Then I'll buy you a bunch."

I guess I felt friendly toward him. We walked across the post to the little cafe just outside the front gate. The town of Gordon was small and clung to the side of the army post like a tumor. It wouldn't have existed if it hadn't been for the army. In fact the old people who lived in the town and ran the motels and gas stations and bars that grow up around a military base were all retired from the military and could talk about World War I—the big one, they called it—even when you made it clear you didn't have time to listen to it. The cafe never had any customers except soldiers or former soldiers. I never did see a woman in the cafe, although I'm sure they went somewhere in town to get a bite to eat. Even though there weren't ever any girls in the place, that's where we all went to drink when we finally had passes—the fifth week of basic training—because no one had a car. To tell you the truth, I liked the cafe because it had red and white checked table cloths, and nobody yelled at you in there if you weren't finished eating in seven minutes flat.

There was a great, orange tabernacle-shaped jukebox in the cafe; it lit up like a carnival ride when you put a nickel in it and pressed the button for the song of your choice—songs like "I Can't Get Started," and "In The Mood," and "Mood Indigo." I remember all the music seemed sad back then—even the fast, crazy stuff Benny Goodman used to do. It seemed sort of desperate; like the *last* music, you know? The final development before the end. I probably wasn't any different than anybody else—we *all* thought we were going to die. Maybe that's why the music seemed forlorn.

Shucker's favorite song was a Glenn Miller tune called "Pennsylvania 6–5000." When we got to the cafe, he played that one song over and over. I can still hear it: dadada*dA* dada*dA* AAda, dadada*dA* dada*dAAA* da, Pennsylvania six five oh oh oh!

We were sitting at one of the small tables next to the jukebox, which sat at the far back wall of the cafe. We could see everyone in the place; who came in and who went out.

"Don't you want to hear some other song?" I said. Shucker sat down after playing it for the sixth time.

"Isn't that lovely?" he said, tapping his fingers on the edge of the table. He'd already bought me two beers and I'd bought two of my own and was working on the third. "I love Glenn Miller."

I laughed, sipped my beer. I knew I wasn't going to break into his rapture. In a way he was happier than anyone I'd ever known —certainly happier than I was. He didn't let anything get to him; I'd seen the other men play their humiliating jokes on him,

watched them make a fool of him over and over. He just seemed
to laugh with them—and they thought he was stupid because he
never got mad and tried to kill anyone. I was beginning to wonder,
though. He seemed capable of finding joy in the most common
things.

The cafe began to fill up. Shucker turned his big head around
to watch the door. I watched his face, the way his lips hung
slightly open and looked a little wet in the light from the front
windows. He really did look stupid, as if he couldn't possibly be
thinking anything.

"What are you looking for?" I asked.

"See if any of the guys come in." He didn't look at me.

"They'll be here, probably."

"Yeah."

"They have a lot to celebrate." I raised my glass, but he didn't
turn toward me. "What are you thinking about, Shucker?"

His head came around; his face was as plain as an empty rubber
mask. "I was thinking about what you said in the latrine."

"About dying?"

"About my eyes."

I waited, watching his open mouth.

"What will happen to my eyes when I die?" he said.

"I wouldn't worry about it."

"I like my eyes." He turned back toward the door.

I drank my beer for a while, watched the benches by the counter
fill up with uniforms. Then I said, "Shucker, have you ever done
anything you hated later?"

He looked at me again. "I don't know what you mean."

"Yes, you do."

"I do?"

"You know. Something bad. Evil."

He raised his brows a bit, seemed to identify something hanging
just over my head. I figured he really didn't understand what I was
asking.

"Did you ever do anything you felt bad about?"

"Lots of times," he said.

ROBERT BAUSCH

I wanted to tell him about Etta, and my sins. It was probably because he wouldn't remember it—maybe he was as stupid as everybody thought; I knew that was possible—but I also think I wanted to find out if anyone ever had such things happen to them. I would have liked Shucker more if he'd told me he masturbated too much and confessed it as adultery for nearly a year. If he'd been the cause of similar misery as I had: the death of a person a lot of people loved and needed.

But just as I began, a man came over from the counter and put a nickel in the jukebox.

Shucker stood up, smiling. He was taller than anyone in the room, and his body seemed like an enlarged replica of the human form.

"What you going to play, smacks?" he asked.

"I was looking for Tommy Dorsey." The GI seemed nervous about something—he clasped his hands in front of his belt as if he was holding his pants up.

"Play 'Pennsylvania 6–5000.' "

"Well—I—"

"OK?" Shucker said. He put his huge right hand on the man's shoulder. "You'll like it very much."

"All right," the soldier said.

Shucker watched him press the right button, then he sat down again.

"I don't think he wanted to hear your song," I said.

"He played it," Shucker said.

I watched the man go over to the counter and talk to some friends there. They began watching us, and it didn't seem to me that they were enjoying the song. There were three of them besides the man who wanted to hear Tommy Dorsey. They were all average, even ordinary—except the one in the middle, who had red hair and a jaw that jutted too far out under his nose. He looked mean and unhappy, as if he'd just finished burying a whole family and built up an appetite doing it.

"I think you should let them play whatever they want." I almost whispered this to Shucker, watching the men at the counter all the time. The jukebox wailed, "Pennsylvania six five oh oh oh."

The man with the red hair put his cap on and walked over to the jukebox. I put both my hands on the table and wrapped them around my beer. Shucker saw the red-haired man behind him as the song finished.

"What are you going to play, smacks?" Shucker smiled.

"Whatever I want," said the red-haired man.

Shucker stood up. I saw the eyes of the red-haired man follow Shucker's head all the way to its full height. "I have a suggestion," Shucker said.

"Ha," the man said. "You sure are tall."

"Why don't you play 'Pennsylvania 6–5000'?"

"I don't want to hear that again."

"It's a beautiful song."

"I bet you think you can make me play that."

"He just likes the song," I said.

"Who are you?"

"I'm a friend."

"It's just you and him?" He pointed *up* at Shucker.

"He's really very nice. He thinks you'll like the song," I was getting irritated.

"Don't you like music?" Shucker said.

The red-haired man jutted his chin up into the air and with a snarl said, "I don't like you."

"Wait a minute," I said.

"You shut up."

"You got this all wrong. He's—"

"He's a bully!" The chin still pointed up at Shucker.

I got up. "Now wait a minute."

"You like to pick on little guys, right?"

"What?" Shucker did not know what was happening.

"Make little guys spend their money on you."

"Let's go, Shucker," I said. I realized it didn't really matter to me what happened. I wasn't trying to do anything good, or even anything I might have consciously thought of as the right thing

—I just didn't want to see the next move. I knew it would probably get violent, and somebody would get hurt. I moved toward the door, grabbed Shucker's arm.

"No, wait a minute," the red-haired man said. "Just a fucking minute."

"Look, don't do this."

I saw Shucker raise his hand, a motion he probably didn't even think about—he may have wanted to scratch his head; he was very puzzled over the attitude of the soldier with the red hair. But when he made that move the red haired man hit him with a short and powerful right hand punch under the heart. Shucker bent over as if he'd been shot. I heard the air go out of him.

The red-haired man stood back, his fists up in front of his pointed chin. I thought he was going to say something, but he only hit Shucker again: another short and powerful punch, this time on the side of the face. Then the red-haired man laughed, his mouth opening enough to reveal a cavernous jagged array of brown teeth.

"That's enough," I said.

He looked at me. "You want enough of this too?"

Shucker staggered, sat down on his chair. He still could not breathe. The first man who wanted to play the jukebox came over with his other friends.

"Guess you won't pick on a little guy again, eh?"

They all thought it was funny, and a good thing the red-haired man had done.

"He wasn't picking on anybody," I said.

"You saw it," one of them said.

"If he wanted to hurt you he would. He'd mop the place up with you."

The red-haired man laughed. "Shit," he said. Then he walked over, stood in front of Shucker, and hit him again, this time directly in the face. Shucker went over backward on his chair like a horse falling down. I saw his nose bleeding.

"Big stupid son of a bitch," the red-haired man said. Then he turned and, putting his arms around his friends, walked out with them. Everyone in the cafe cheered them as they passed.

I leaned over and helped Shucker get to his feet. He was just beginning to breathe, and I heard blood gurgling in his throat. "Goddamn, Shucker," I said. "Why didn't you fight the bastard?"

"I couldn't breathe," he gasped.

The cafe was silent, by then. The jukebox was finished, and all the troops at the tables watched Shucker and me trying to maneuver our way out. They were properly quiet for the passing of the defeated bully and his friend.

When we were outside, Shucker sighed and then he started crying. I really did feel friendly toward him then, and I regretted not helping him.

"My nose hurts," he said.

"Here," I stopped him, gave him my handkerchief. "Put your head back."

"Think it's broken?"

"Nah." I didn't know. It looked awful. "Maybe we should go to the hospital, though."

We started walking again. After a while, I said, "I'm sorry, Shucker."

"You are?"

"I should have helped you."

He didn't say anything. I wished I could know what he was thinking, find out what went on in that large head.

"Why didn't you fight?" I said, when we were back on the post.

"Is it still bleeding?" He took the handkerchief away.

It looked swollen, and there was dried blood around the nostrils, but it had stopped bleeding. "It'll be OK," I said.

He offered me the handkerchief, which looked black from the blood in it.

"Throw it away," I said.

He put it in his pocket. "I'm sorry."

We walked along the main boulevard, the only paved road on the post. Ahead of us was a playing field, and then the row upon row of barracks that made the whole area seem like an ant colony —thousands of men in green fatigues falling out in the weak light of morning, preparing for a full day's work. Beyond the barracks was the hospital, a long white building that surrounded *itself* with scrub pine and oak trees. That's really how it looked; the east and west wings of the hospital seemed to reach out and gather in the trees. It was late afternoon, in the spring, and while Shucker and I walked through the maze of barracks and headed for the hospital I had the strongest sense of regret and sadness. I felt very thin and papery—as if I might dissolve if exposed to water.

"You see, Shucker?"

"What."

"They thought you were being a bully."

"Oh."

"So you were."

"I was?"

"I guess so."

"I didn't want to hurt nobody."

"You should have fought them." I believed this. I think I still do.

"Maybe I just shouldn't talk to people at all."

"Why didn't you fight?"

"He hurt me," Shucker said. He seemed about to cry again. "I can't beat everybody up just because I'm big."

"Well, you could beat *him* up."

"He hit me hard."

"*I* could beat him up."

Shucker stopped walking, looked at me as if I'd slapped him. "I'm not tough," he said quietly. "Everybody wants me to be. But I'm not."

"I'm sorry," I said.

"Even if I was tough, I wouldn't fight as much as people always want me to."

"I couldn't beat that red-haired guy up. I just said that."

"He was tough," Shucker said, and I thought he might grin. But he shook his head and started walking again.

I followed along behind him, waited for him to settle into a rhythm, then caught up. "You OK?"

"Yes."

I realized I was following him around, now. Maybe I wanted him to be a friend by then. I don't know. I didn't want him to be alone in the army any more, and I felt like I wasn't alone any more either. But we didn't get much of a chance to find out what sort of friends we might be, because the next day we ran into the man with the red hair again, and I tried to show Shucker what he ought to do with somebody like that. In the process, my worst punishment began.

———————

The red-haired man was named Coulter. He was from New York, had apparently boxed for a living before being drafted into the army. I learned all these things the next day, when Shucker and I went to the cafe for one last beer before getting on the bus to Washington D.C., where we were going to be guarding the Potomac river for a while before traveling to California and the great war with the Japanese. I was in a good mood that morning, because the news that we were going to Washington seemed like a reprieve; I was going home, taking Shucker with me, and I wasn't going to die right away.

We should never have gone back to the cafe. I probably wanted to run into Coulter, though. I think I was vaguely excited over the idea—feeling a little vengeful for what happened the day before, and hoping Shucker would get mad and take a little revenge. I was sure my tall friend could make Coulter look like a potted plant if he got mad enough.

As soon as we walked into the cafe, it got quiet. I saw the red-haired man over by the bar with his three friends. They were in their dress uniforms, ready for travel, as Shucker and I were. The thought occurred to me that they might be on the same bus with Shucker and me; that their unit was going to Washington too.

"I'm going to play some music," Shucker said.

I walked over to the red-haired man. One of his friends said, "Hey, Coulter. You've got a visitor."

Coulter turned around, looked at me with that mean sort of "I don't care about you" grin. I heard a coin fall into the jukebox.

"My friend's going to play some music," I said. I don't know where I got my courage. I had nothing planned; I didn't think I wanted to fight, since I hadn't been in more than one or two fights in my whole life and I had no idea if I could fight or not. I just couldn't stand the idea that Coulter and his friends might think he had done something wonderful; might believe he was some sort of hero for defending the little guy who wanted to play something other than "Pennsylvania 6–5000."

Coulter stood up, took a sip of beer, looking at me the whole time over the rim of his glass. When he was finished, he set the glass down, wiped his red chin with a napkin. The jukebox started singing Shucker's song.

"Same song," Coulter said.

"That's the one he likes." I know I was loud.

"You want the same trouble?"

Then one of his friends started talking about Coulter's career in New York. I knew he was trying to impress me, but I believed all of it.

"He knocked out Mickey Spence," one of the men said.

"Who's that?" I really didn't know.

One of them said something about this Mickey Spence being a top contender; a great middleweight.

"Well, I didn't say I wanted trouble," I said.

They all laughed, even Coulter.

"I'm not backing down from anything," I said. "I didn't come in here for trouble."

"What did you and that goon come in here for?" Coulter said.

I don't know what got into me, but when Coulter said "that goon" I grabbed his tie and hit him—I tried to get his nose but he pulled back and I cut my right hand on his jagged front teeth. I still had hold of his tie, but now I was getting hit, so many times and so fast I thought they had all joined in. Then I was on the floor, watching the song on the jukebox spin above my head, listening to hundreds of voices laughing and talking in a muffled, dreamy sort of pattern—as if I was under water and there was a party going on in the seaweed.

I tried to get up, felt beer pouring over my head. I was on all fours when something hit me, fell on top of me and sent me to the floor like a broken table. I felt something give way in my spine. I couldn't breathe or see, but I heard somebody screaming. I was under this great weight, and somebody was screaming just like a woman in a fire or something. Each time the weight shifted I felt something change in my neck. I went out into darkness with the scream, until the scream died away and there was only the darkness, and then I lost that too.

I woke up in the hospital. I had been dreaming that Coulter poured beer on me and it froze—an awful, hot sort of frozen liquid that made it hard for me to breathe. I couldn't break free, and when I thought I couldn't catch my breath I opened my eyes and saw a little man dressed in white, with straight teeth, brown glasses, and a nose that traveled the length of his face and nearly covered his upper lip.

"Hello," he said. "I'm Doctor Spint."

"How's Shucker?"

"Shucker?"

"What happened to him?"

"Who?"

"Gage. His name was Gage."

"Oh. They haven't caught him yet." Spint touched his ear with a long thin white finger. "I've got some bad news."

"What do you mean they haven't caught him?"

"He escaped."

"Escaped?"

"You were nearly killed."

"What happened?"

"Luckily, we were able to save you—but there is some bad news."

"What?"

"I want to think about how good it is to have your mind—your mind is—"

"What's the news?"

He put his hand on my chest, smiled the kind of smile you always see on Jesus when he's suffering the little children to come unto him. "You must remember that your mind is the most important thing."

"OK," I said. "I've got the point."

"With consciousness," he raised his finger in front of my eyes, "one can surmont any challenge."

"Am I going to die?"

"Oh no. You're going to be fine. I mean you're not going to be—"

"What," I said, and I tried to move the covers off my neck and get my hands out to grab him by the throat. But nothing moved.

"You're paralyzed," Dr. Spint said. It was earlier than he wanted to say it, so his voice trembled slightly. "From the neck down, so far as I can tell."

I didn't say anything. He looked at me, let his eyes pass down along my body with that sad look on his face, then he said, "It may not be as bad as I think it is. There are some tests we have to run while you're awake. But the break was fairly high, and in cases like that usually total paralysis follows."

I still couldn't say anything. I lay there struggling to move, and I felt my toes fumbling under the blanket.

"I can feel my feet moving," I said.

He smiled that Jesus smile. "Nothing is moving, son."

"God," I said.

"Do you want to pray?"

"I want to die," I said. "Right away."

"You will be depressed. That's understandable. There will be a long period where you will have to get used to all this. But human beings can get used to anything, son. Even this."

"No," I said.

"I've seen it."

"No."

"Other men have dealt with this, and you will too."

"God." I didn't feel afraid, or sick or anything. I was just sort of surprised and a little angry and feeling like the most logical thing to do was to die.

"I will pray with you if you want."

"You don't understand."

"Yes, I do."

"I don't have anybody."

"What?"

"I don't have anyone to take care of me."

"Things like that get arranged, don't worry." Dr. Spint put his hand on my chest again. "You'll do fine. Be thankful you weren't killed like that other young man."

I thought about Etta, how glad I was that she didn't live after all. It would have been terrible if she'd seen me like that. I kept trying to move, but I realized everything below my adam's apple was dead. Then it hit me what Dr. Spint had said.

"What other young man?" I asked him

"The big fellow killed one of the men in the cafe."

"Shucker?"

"I don't know what his name was. You were fighting with him. At least I think—"

"Shucker killed him?"

"Snapped *his* spine too."

"Shucker didn't break my back," I said.

"They said he just went mad—started breaking people."

"I feel sick," I said.

"I'll call a nurse."

"No."

"It's no trouble." He got up, leaned over me. I could see he thought it was his job to be tender. "You can adjust to this, son."

It hit me that I couldn't get out of the bed to be sick. I turned my head to the side, and started leaking out all over the place. I felt it all warm on my neck.

Dr. Spint backed away. I felt like a festering wound that just burst in front of him. The look on his face stayed with me even after I wasn't Jack Pitt any more; even when I was only a Christmas ornament on a pillow, waiting to stop thinking about the fact that I was as helpless as an infant.

I used to wonder why you can't remember the first few years of your life. It didn't seem fair to give you consciousness and then make it impossible for you to remember all of it. Now I know why you don't remember when you were a baby. It isn't that you *can't* remember it, either; you don't *want* to remember it. Everything in your body resists even the slightest recollection of it because it's just awful.

In that hospital, I had to bawl for my food, to get my clothing cleaned when I messed myself, to get somebody to scratch an itch on my nose. I was only a ball, a round thing with a mouth, and hair and eyes connected to a long, thin, dead thing that regularly leaked all over the place. I woke up looking at the ceiling, knowing that no matter what went on outside, I'd be looking at that same ceiling all day.

But that's not the worst of it. The worst part came when I was asleep—because, in my sleep, I could still move. I dreamed I was running, leaping—I felt the wind in my hair. Then I'd wake up and feel sweat dripping down the sides of my face into my ears, and realize that I was going to have to wait for my ears to dry before they stopped tickling. Of course I'd start crying and that would add to it.

I don't want to depress you or anything, but imagine that. If you can. Imagine your head being the only thing you had—you know? Think what it would be like if your whole body was only a head resting on a pillow.

I also dreamt of wicker baskets, guillotines, and chopping blocks. I saw trails of blood dripping into baskets full of the heads of fallen kings. The heads yawned, eyes blinking, and I'd wake up in a sweat again and start crying. After a while it was a sort of ongoing struggle with myself not to dream; not to wake up in the middle of the night if I did. Not to sweat, or cry if I did that. I always lost. Always.

Dr. Spint came to visit me regularly. He'd walk in, smile and ask me how I was doing. I didn't have the heart to tell him that once I knew what happened to Shucker, I was a goner. I was going to let myself die.

It was hard to get any news of Shucker. Dr. Spint kept telling me he'd check and see if they caught him yet. But then he'd forget, or he'd come back and say, "I think he's still on the loose."

I told the MP's what really happened, and they promised to take my name off the list of Shucker's victims. They were very nice about it.

"It's very good of you to care about your friend," one of them said. He stood by the bed and looked at my legs as if he expected me to twitch or something.

"He's really sort of a hero," I said.

"Well." The MP looked at his feet. "You know he made a real mess of the fellow he killed."

"It was all my fault." I knew I was right about that. If I hadn't been so brave, Shucker and I both would have been in Washington, D.C. by then.

I had plenty of time to think lying in that white bed with my head propped up so I could watch the doctor put needles in me. I thought about Etta and about dying. I remembered Mrs. Proudy, wondered why she didn't come to see me. She sent me a card that said, "Sorry to hear of your trouble."

Sorry to hear of your trouble.

I thought about Shucker, where he might be, if he was scared. I wondered if he knew he fell on me and crippled me for life.

And at night I'd have my running battle with the dreams and the tears.

Etta came to me in broad daylight after a while. I'd be lying there, looking at the paint beginning to peel in the corners, and there she'd be—smiling like she did the night we watched the silent lightning.

"Etta," I'd say. "Look what happened to me." Then I'd start laughing. I really felt sorry for myself.

Dr. Spint began talking to me about courage.

"You've got reserves of strength," he said one day.

"I can't move."

"The nurses will move you—that way your body won't—" He stopped, looked out the window.

"Won't what?"

"You know."

"No, tell me. Won't what?"

"Won't atrophy."

"You mean 'rot,' don't you?"

"There is strength in that remark."

I turned my head to the wall.

Some days I stared out the top pane of the window, counted the clouds that passed in and out of view. One day I timed them—it was like a race. Cloud number one passed from the left pane to the right one in eight minutes. Cloud number two took twelve minutes. Then there was only a wisp of a cloud, a white soul of a cloud that didn't move across at all; it seemed to form there in the window. I dreamed it was Etta coming to get me.

"Human beings can get used to anything," Dr. Spint said.

What he didn't understand was that I didn't think of myself as a human being anymore. I was only a pair of eyes and ears, a nose, and a mouth.

I knew I'd have trouble finding a way to die. You can't kill yourself when the only thing you can move is your head. When I wasn't watching cloud races, I'd examine the possible ways I might bring about my death; I figured if I concentrated on it long enough, I might really discover something.

I knew I couldn't starve myself to death because they'd catch on that I wasn't eating and just put me on the bottle again. All the nourishment I needed would drain into my arm. Besides, I liked the nurses who fed me and fussed over me. It was the only time I had company besides Dr. Spint.

I could bury my face in the pillow whenever the nurses turned me over to wash my back—they'd take some time to notice I wasn't getting any air. But I knew if I did that they'd just blame themselves. I didn't want anybody feeling guilty for killing me; especially I didn't want any of the nurses feeling like murderers.

I thought I might bite my lip until it bled, then I could keep it bleeding long enough to die. If I bit the inside of my lip, I could keep swallowing my blood and nobody would even know I was bleeding. The only thing was, I couldn't be sure I'd succeed. I never heard of anybody dying from a cut lip—and I was afraid I'd only make a mess, alert everyone to what I was up to, and create a mouth so sore they'd have to stop giving me hot food for a while.

I considered swallowing my tongue, but when I tried to get it back far enough to see if it would do any good, I realized how impossible that was. I wondered if I could talk one of the nurses into poisoning me. Maybe I could make one of them fall in love with me first, then beg her to kill me. I laughed at that idea—I imagined myself trying to be romantic while the nurse cleaned up one of the messes I made every day.

You know, when you're paralyzed, you don't know when your body is emptying out. You can't feel it once it's happened either. I'd start to smell it, though, and that would start me crying again. The nurses tried to chart my body's functions so they could catch me before something happened; but they didn't seem able to get an accurate reading on me. They'd show up at what they charted to be the right time and nothing would happen. Then when they were gone, I'd start to smell it again.

One nurse—a round, thick-skinned woman with a black mole on the tip of her nose—got so disgusted with me that she walked in at the beginning of her shift and put a bedpan under me.

"You can't feel that," she said. "Right?"

Her name was McFee, but everybody called her "Fee." She worked the night shift, the time I was trying to sleep, so I didn't know her too well. But the other nurses told me stories about her—how she'd had a son who went to prison for molesting a little girl, and how she wouldn't allow anyone to mention her boy's name in her company. She sent money every week to the little girl's family. "Fee's got nobody but herself," one of the nurses said. "Her husband died while her boy was still in diapers."

I thought about what happens to a little boy when his father dies too soon. Fee's son in prison, and me, connected to a dead body in an army hospital.

When she put the bedpan under me, my stomach arched toward the ceiling, and I began to feel something inside—something hot —moving into my throat.

"I'm uncomfortable," I said.

"How?"

ROBERT BAUSCH

"I feel something."

She leaned over me, an excited look on her face. "Where? Tell me where?"

"Inside."

"What?"

"My stomach is leaking back toward my throat."

"Oh." She adjusted the pan. "That better?"

My stomach was lower and the feeling stopped. "I'm sorry," I said.

"If we can leave the pan there, it'll be easier on me." She smiled, the black mole seemed to enlarge. "I don't want to make you uncomfortable."

"If my stomach leaked badly enough, could I drown?"

"It's possible."

I closed my eyes.

"Why do you ask me that?" She sat down next to the bed.

"I want to die." I knew I was giving it all away; that they'd watch me closely now. But I had to tell somebody. I was so sick of Dr. Spint's encouragement.

Fee put a brown freckled hand on her fat knee, as if she was waiting for someone to offer her a cup of tea. "If you want to die, you probably will. Nobody lives for very long who really wants to die."

"I wish I'd died yesterday."

"Don't you have anyone?"

I looked at the window, searched for a cloud. It was nearly dark, and the sky was empty.

"Anyone at all?"

"I need to die," I said.

"What if we can get some of this back?" Fee said. She pointed to what I assumed was my body.

"Dr. Spint said this is for life."

"He's still running tests."

"Everybody encourages me," I said. "Some unbelievable hero had this happen to him and learned to direct traffic with a pencil in his mouth or something. So it only seems logical that I should

do OK too. It's been done before. But I can't. I just can't." I was
starting to cry again.

Fee got up and straightened out her white dress. "There, now.
You get some rest."

She left me there resting in the bedpan.

I don't know how many days went by. Fee talked to me more
frequently when she came in for her shift. She was proud of the
bedpan idea, I guess. We talked of death, and finally about her son.
She said she hated him.

"He probably didn't mean to do what he did," I said.

"It was a choice." She patted the top of her head, as if she had
a great bun of hair there, although she only wore a white hat. Her
hair hung by her face like an asparagus fern.

I told her about Shucker, the fight and all. "Shucker wasn't
really the enemy. But everybody thought he was."

"My boy is evil." She said this simply, as if she were telling me
what day it was.

"Maybe not," I said.

"No."

"I know someone who is truly evil," I said. I wanted to tell her
about me and Etta—about everything including the white candles.
But Fee suddenly started crying.

"He attacked a little girl," she said. She put her hands over her
face, made this sobbing noise that frightened me.

"Are you OK?"

She was suddenly quiet.

"Fee?"

"He's just sick," she said through her hands.

"At least he's not going to be killed in this war," I said.

"He is shame. Such a disappointment." She tried to smile,
waved her hand. "Ohh," she moaned. "Such a disappointment."

I was glad I hadn't told Etta about all my sins. I couldn't bear
to see the sadness in Fee's face, and I hardly knew her.

"My boy would be better off dead."

"What?"

"At least you've got your morality," she said. "You're not a mental cripple."

"I couldn't commit a sin if I wanted to," I said. I was almost laughing.

"I didn't mean to call you a cripple," she said.

"That's what I am."

"You *can* commit sins."

"I can curse," I said. "I've *been* doing that, but I thought I was entitled."

"The sins of the mind."

I knew what she was talking about. Father Burns talked all the time about "impure thoughts." The kind of thinking that went along with adultery fifteen times a week. I hadn't had much time for such things since Etta died. I think I had this odd idea that Etta could see me, that she watched me every day. It wasn't hard to stop masturbating once Etta was gone. Besides, I thought it was one of the sins that led to her death. That's the ironic thing about Etta's dying—even though I believed I was condemned, even though I was free to be as evil as I wanted, I was a truly good person when I thought Etta could see me.

I know that's not a good reason to be good.

"Do you dream about sex?" Fee asked.

"No." I was telling the truth.

"It would probably be understandable. But you shouldn't when you're awake."

"Are you Catholic?"

"Yes."

"I thought so."

"Why?"

"You sound like a priest I knew."

"Thank you," she said. "That's a compliment."

When Fee left that night, I wondered if Etta could know what I was thinking. I tried to think about sex, but I had no experience with it except masturbation, and somehow, when I dreamed about doing that it wasn't very pleasant. I couldn't remember what it felt like, and thinking about it couldn't bring the feeling.

While I was asleep, I dreamed it—the whole experience. I was with some faceless girl, enjoying her body, moving above her without effort. I remember thinking, "This is the cure—arousal. Put me with a woman and I can move." I cannot express the joy I felt.

Of course, waking up was awful. It was as if I had moved again. In the first weeks after my injury, I never tried to remember movement. Never saw my body doing anything, except in my dreams. I wanted sensation, feeling. Movement didn't occur to me.

I cried harder than ever. It seemed a dirty trick to let me dream my first sexual experience, then wake me up before it was over so I could truly understand my predicament. I cried out loud, wanted somebody to hear me, come to me and give me something to make me sleep. I felt my nose running and tears trickling down my cheeks, into the hair by my ears. I turned my head to the side, tried to watch out the window for something in the black pane to take my mind off the dream and its effortless motion.

The next evening, Fee came in with a priest.

I was thinking about not dreaming, about sleeping with nothing in my head, when Fee and her friend came in.

"I brought someone to see you," she whispered. I felt like I was on a deathbed, and she was afraid if she talked louder I might die on her.

"Why are you whispering?"

She looked puzzled. "It's night time."

The priest glanced at her, smiled. He held a black hat in front of him, moved toward me as if he was embarrassed to walk in front of me—as if that was the same thing as talking about sight to a blind person. He had gray hair that hung around his ears, and small black stones for eyes. I'll never forget the way he blinked when he talked, like some of the words caused him physical pain when he uttered them.

"I'm Father Drewyer," he said.

"What can I do for you?" I didn't know what to say. I was

embarrassed, and felt as if I was being stared at.

"What can *I* do for you?"

"I don't know what you mean."

"I told him you were a Catholic boy," Fee said.

"Oh."

"I will hear your confession," Father Drewyer said. "If you wish."

"My mother died when I was twelve," I said. "I never knew my father—he went to God's party before I was born. I don't have anything to confess."

"I understand how you feel."

"What kind of luck is this?" I said. "I mean—what sort of luck do you suppose I have to end up like this?"

"I'm sorry." He sounded sincere.

Fee said, "The Lord offers us consolation in our time of need."

"Amen," I said.

"Amen," Father Drewyer said.

"Amen," Fee said.

"Jesus," I said.

"Pardon?" Father Drewyer turned his hat in his hands.

"Jesus."

"In the name of the father and the son—"

"Jesus Christ!"

Father Drewyer stopped, looked at Fee. "I'm sorry, but I think—"

"Mr. Pitt," Fee said.

"I'm not a 'Mr. Pitt' or anything else. I'm just a head."

Father Drewyer came over to the edge of the bed, leaned over so I could see directly into his little black eyes. "If you want me to hear your confession, just tell Mrs. McFee here and I'll call on you again."

"Get out," I was nearly screaming.

"I understand," he said.

"I'm ashamed of you," Fee said.

"Get out."

They were both insulted, went out of my room as if they'd just wandered into somebody's private party and were being thrown out without even a brief trip to the punch bowl. Immediately I felt guilty. As angry as I was, I knew I was really only yelling at God. It wasn't Father Drewyer's fault. Everything he did was for somebody's good, I was sure of that. Or at least that's the way he intended it. In a way, he was like me: he tried to do something good for me and he made me miserable.

I was beginning to think that *I* was the only person in the world who could *not* do any more evil—since I couldn't move a single muscle below the neck.

You would not believe the sort of evil a head can do.

The day after Father Drewyer's visit, I had another guest. I had just been bathed, cleaned inside and out—they can do that in a hospital, especially when you're paralyzed and can't stop them: even when you can't feel anything, enemas are humiliating.

One of the younger nurses was combing my hair, when the door came slightly ajar, then opened.

The nurse put my head back into the pillow, turned to the door. "Who's this?"

An old man peered around the door. "I came to see Mr. Pitt." He was tall, with a square face and nose, and eyes that seemed bathed in yellow fluid. "I'm Mr. Coulter," he said.

"Who?"

He moved into the room, stepped toward the bed. "Excuse me."

The nurse put the comb on the night stand and went out.

"I'm told you knew my son," Mr. Coulter said.

"Oh," I said. I remembered then who he was. "Yes, I knew him briefly."

"He was a good boy." He seemed ready to cry. "A hero."

"Well," I started. I didn't have the heart to tell him that his son was *not* a hero; that he was a bully who thought he was taking on another bully and got killed in the process. That he had picked on the most gentle, perhaps helpless, and certainly stupid human being I had ever known: my friend Shucker.

"I heard you were there," Mr. Coulter said.

"Yes."

"I'm sorry for your condition."

"Me too."

"I would like to ask you a favor." He came over to the bed. He was wearing a white trench coat and rubber boots. He held a brown felt hat in his hands. "I have my wife here, on the post. She's very upset about all this. I would like it if you would talk to her."

"What?"

"Tell her how her son defended you."

I looked out the window. The sky was as white as a nurse's cap. I tried to find something to fix my eyes on; an object in the window I could concentrate on and forget what really happened. "Look, Mr. Coulter," I said without looking at him. "I know it's important to you for your son to be—"

"It's not important to me. I know what it probably was. But my wife, my wife—she—"

"You know what it was?"

"I need this favor."

"Why?"

"My wife is dying. She wanted to come here where her son left this earth, and try to know as much about his journey—that's what she calls it, his journey. She wants to be full of love and admiration for him before she dies."

"He was probably not such a bad guy."

"Please. If you could just tell her about it. How he defended you, saved your life."

"Is that what you heard?"

"She's talked to the others."

"Do you think it's a good idea for her to see me like this?"

"Like what?"

"I'm paralyzed."

"Oh." He lowered his head. I could see he didn't know that I couldn't move a muscle. I think the knowledge did something to him; he stiffened up, seemed to move only with great pain. "Is my son responsible for that?"

"Who knows," I said. "I was looking for trouble."

"Will you talk to my wife? I won't tell her you're—" he gestured with his hat.

"Oh, I don't know." I wanted him to go away and take his request with him.

"My wife is dying."

"Does she know it?"

"What?"

"Does she know she's dying?"

"Yes."

I thought of Etta and our little drink of bourbon. "All right. Bring her in."

"She's not here in the hospital. I'll have to bring her. Tomorrow morning I'll bring her if it's all right with you."

"OK," I said. "Bring her tomorrow."

"Oh, thank you," Mr. Coulter said. "Thank you."

When he was gone I looked for a cloud, thought about the chance to do something good again. Etta would approve of a little lie here to help a dying woman. If it *was* a lie. I couldn't tell any more. Shucker *was* making everybody play the song he liked— even if he wasn't aware of it. And Coulter was defending a person everyone thought was pushed into spending his money for something he didn't want. A victim. Poor Shucker. I wondered where he was, if he had anyone to look after him. I wondered if he knew what had happened to me.

I drifed into sleep, saw bicycles, trampolines, high wires. I felt something licking my toes, smiled down at a cat. Then my feet were in cool sand, and I could hear the ocean, could feel salt breezes brushing my legs. Then Fee was there, in a white and black bathing suit, two dimples in each fat knee. "Shame on you," she said. "Shame on you." Then she came over to me and piled the sand onto my legs, over my stomach, my shoulders. I laughed at first, then I asked her not to do that. "Don't now," I said. "It's hard to move." She laughed, piled the sand higher. Soon I was buried in it, only my head sticking through. "Very funny," I said. "You trying to remind me, get me to wake up?" Then she was gone, and I was laughing, laughing hysterically. "Somebody get me out of the sand," I screamed. "Help."

The scream awakened me. Dr. Spint was standing over the bed reading my chart.

"Did I scream?" I asked.

"Not a bit."

"I didn't make a sound?"

"You were moaning slightly."

"I thought I screamed."

"Were you dreaming?"

"Yes."

"Well, I'm glad you woke up then."

"It was a good dream at first."

He looked at me. "In your condition, a good dream is only a sort of taunting nightmare, I should think."

"I guess so."

"Sorry." He went back to the chart.

"If I can only move in my dreams, then I want to dream."

"You have to get over wanting to move."

"God," I said.

"I know it's a bitter pill. But you must get used to your condition or you'll never adapt to it." He put the chart back on the end of the bed, put his hands in the wide pockets on either side of his uniform. "I'm treating you like a man. You are not helpless unless you want to be. I will treat you with respect, and I will expect you to begin to overcome your handicap—as *soon* as you get used to it."

"You'll be with me the whole time."

"Of course not. Once you've adjusted, you will be on your way somewhere."

"God."

"Uncle Sam will see to it that you've got money. So you pick some place comfortable, and begin to adjust your life to your condition."

"You've never dealt with patients like me before, have you?"

"Of course I have. Done quite well, too."

"You or the patients?"

"Both." He smiled. "You are making the kind of progress I would have predicted. I've seen it before. Now you're mad at me, you hate me. That's a step in the right direction."

"It is?"

"Right on schedule. Six weeks and the patient has enough self-respect to hate his doctor. I wrote that in a paper on men in your condition."

"Did any of your patients ever commit suicide?"

"Of course not." He made a noise with his mouth, a clicking sound that tried to shame me.

I watched his fingers moving in the pockets, thought of my own hands, how they might be positioned at that moment.

"*All* of my patients *wanted* to commit suicide, however," he said, smiling again.

"Would you do me a favor?"

"Of course." He took his hands out, folded his arms.

"I'd like to see my hands."

"Raise your head."

He removed the cover, and I raised my head. There, along each dead thigh, rested my hands. I noticed the hair on them, the tiny wrinkles on each knuckle. I let my head fall back on the pillow.

"Thank you."

"What was that all about?"

"I just wanted to look at them."

He shrugged, put his own hands back in the white pockets.

"You don't know what it's like not to be able to do that."

He seemed uninterested, sighed as if he'd just awakened. "Well, I've got to be getting along." He moved toward the door. Just as he reached for the handle, he stopped, remembered something. "Oh, by the way, they caught up to your friend."

"Shucker?"

"Had to shoot him with a B.A.R."

"What?"

"Couldn't subdue him. He was really a strong man, apparently. Anyway, he put two MP's in the hospital, and they got him from thirty yards with a Browning automatic."

"God."

"Put twelve holes in him. One burst." He shook his head. "He was running across a cornfield. They said he ran like a crazy man."

I started to cry, remembered the terrible itch of the tears, began to choke.

Dr. Spint pulled the door open, stood there in the yellow light, looking at me as if I'd just finished screaming at him. "It's what the young man wanted. He didn't get killed, he killed himself."

"I'm tired," I said. I don't know where that came from; it was like my mouth talked without me. Dr. Spint nodded and went out.

I lay there in the dark, thinking about Shucker, trying not to cry. What did it matter to me, really? I hardly knew him. I spent all of two days even bothering to talk to him. The rest of the time he followed me around and talked to me; like a monkey with his organ grinder. So one day I feel sorry for him, decide to go have a drink with him, and I end up watching him get misunderstood as something that everybody universally agrees needs to be fought. So what? He brought it on because he wasn't very smart, and he didn't know how people were perceiving him. I got mixed up in it and got what I deserved for a life of sin. Who could tell what sort of life somebody like Shucker lived? Maybe he had things to account for too?

Still, the thought of him, running in fear across that cornfield —a place he would recognize as safe, perhaps—and getting hit from that distance by something he could not even see, made me almost as sad as I was the day Etta died.

The next morning Mr. Coulter came in with his wife. She was short, bent over like a sunflower, and when she breathed it sounded like air leaking from a tire. She had long bony fingers that clutched a little brown bag in front of her, and she wore a white coat that seemed one or two sizes too large. Her face was puffy and white, and her eyes seemed to move in tiny, exactly equal orbits while she talked. She came over to the bed as if she'd known me all her life. It hit me that when you know you're going to die, inhibitions sort of become unimportant.

"I brought this for you," she wheezed, opening the brown bag.

She pulled out a crushed and tattered chrysanthemum. "It's from my son's grave."

"God," I said.

She looked at her husband. "What did he say?"

Mr. Coulter came over to the bed, positioned himself next to his wife. "She don't hear too well."

"I can't do this," I said.

"What?" They both said this.

"You ought to know the truth before you die," I said. Mr. Coulter shook his head. "Yes," I said.

"My boy," she said.

"He was a bully. He picked on somebody—"

"NO!" Mr. Coulter screamed. His wife jumped, dropped the empty bag.

"Goodness," she said.

"Your son was a bully," I yelled. "He started the fight that put me in this bed."

Mr. Coulter took his wife's arm, started moving her toward the door.

"I'm sorry," I said. "It feels good to tell the truth."

"Did he say our boy started a fight?"

Mr. Coulter turned her around, patted her on the back. "We'll leave this young man—"

"I'm sorry," I said. "I'm real sorry."

Mrs. Coulter turned back round, avoided the hanging arm of her husband and moved back toward the bed.

"Sweetie pie," Mr. Coulter said.

She got up to me, stood close enough that her head hovered above my own. She could do that without bending over. "You are evil," she said. She really emphasized the "il" in the word. I was "evill."

"I'm real sorry," I said. "But I've told you the truth. Your boy put me here, and he's responsible for—"

"Evill!" she said again. "I hope you die."

"So do I," I said.

Mr. Coulter took her by the arm again, began moving them

both toward the door. They walked as if they were trudging through very deep mud.

When they were out the door, I yelled, "Maybe everybody's ev*ill!*"

Boy, I really wanted to die then. I wanted to die right then. But I still had my problem: how do you kill yourself when the only thing left of you is your head? Consider it, why don't you?

That night, when I told Fee what I had done, she looked at me as if I had risen from the bed. She had not talked to me since I threw her and Father Drewyer out, so I thought maybe she was surprised that I was talking to her. But then she said, "Why on earth did you do that?"

"I hated them."

"Why? What did they do to you?" She put the bedpan under me—she did this regularly now, even talked some of the other nurses into doing it on their shifts—then covered my body with a sheet.

"Shucker got killed."

"And that's *their* fault?"

"I didn't want her thinking her son was a hero. I wanted somebody to know the truth."

"Everyone *I* know says her boy tried to protect his friends. The newspaper said—"

"I was there. He was a bully." I tried to raise my head, get her attention.

"You're as bad as my son," she said.

"No, I'm not."

"Her son really didn't put you here."

"It was his fault."

"But your friend fell on you."

I closed my eyes. I was sure that's what happened, but no one told me.

"You had to tell her? A dying woman?" Fee said. She moved around the room, as if sitting still would hurt her.

"I guess I should feel bad," I said. I really couldn't tell. I was still a little angry. After the Coulters left, I stared out the windows, looked for a bird, or a windblown leaf, or a slow-moving cloud. I dreamed of being out there—out in the wind, above a cloud, free. I remembered the look on Mrs. Coulter's face and felt an odd assortment of feelings: a little sadness, but also satisfaction and a sense of power. I had actually *done* something, had an impact, even though I couldn't move. I felt sorry enough for myself that it didn't really matter how hurt Mrs. Coulter was. She's only going to die, I told myself. I believed I deserved to inflict a little punishment on somebody. I still felt that way.

Then I remembered Etta on the bridge, struggling to get to the grave of her dead husband, walking next to me like a withered stalk come to life and enjoying movement for the first time.

"What's the matter?" Fee asked.

"I just thought of my mother."

"You did?" She stopped moving, stared at me. "What does a bad boy think when he thinks of his mother?"

"She was dying," I said. "She was dying too."

"Like Mrs. Coulter."

"I shouldn't have done what I did," I said. I started to cry again. "Jesus, I am rotten."

Fee came over, put her hand on my head. "My son is rotten. He couldn't cry like this." She was crying too. "You're a good boy. You talk to the father."

"It won't do any good," I said. "You don't know how many sins I have never confessed."

"It's never too late for confession."

"My punishment's already started."

"No."

"This is part of it."

"You can always be forgiven." She smiled, touched my cheek with a chubby hand.

"Would you wipe the tears?"

She picked up a white napkin from the table by the bed and gently rubbed by my ears. "You've already started," she whispered.

"Started what?"

"Toward redemption."

"God," I said, "in His infinite wisdom, gave me these tears."

"What?"

"They torture me every night."

"Now," she said, wiping my cheeks. "Now, now."

"It's only part of the punishment."

"I will lift up mine eyes," Fee said. She had tears in her eyes now.

"That's *all* I can lift," I said.

"You'll see—"

"I'm tired of being a voice."

"You're a whole person," Fee said, her mouth trembling.

I turned my head to the wall.

"I feel close to you," Fee whispered. "You're like a son to me."

"I want to cheat God out of this part of the punishment."

"You say such things." There was a note of recovery and laughter in her voice. I realized that at that moment she probably believed she loved me.

"I want to die."

"You must live, you must go—"

"I tried everything—I mean I imagined every possible way. I can't kill myself in this condition."

"You have no right to do that," she said. She rubbed my forehead now. Her hand was warm and soft.

"I thought I would starve myself to death, but I—" Then it hit me what I had to do. I realized how I could end my life, and I got so excited, when I looked into Fee's eyes, if I could have moved I would have kissed her.

"What's wrong?" she said.

I smiled, tried to restrain my joy. "I refuse to eat any more food from this moment forward."

"What?"

"I will not eat."

"That won't work," Fee smiled. "We'll just feed you with an I.V."

"I know," I said.

THE FOURTEENTH INTERVIEW

NOVEMBER 13, 1980

9:15 A.M.

Of course, no one was more upset and hurt than Dr. Spint.

"A hunger strike," he said. "Are you trying to get attention?"

"I have all I need of that. Around the clock." This was the second day of the strike. I guess he didn't hear about it until I'd turned down three meals, and the nurses were convinced that I was serious. Anyway, there he was the second day, in the early morning, standing by my bed frowning over a plate full of scrambled eggs which steamed on a tray under my neck.

"That smell good?"

"Sure," I said.

He reached for the fork. "Have some."

I turned my head. "No, thank you."

"You can't be serious."

I smiled at the wall, but I didn't say anything.

"It's just not—" He stopped, seemed to cast in his head for the right word. "It's not on the schedule."

"I have a schedule?"

"You're not supposed to do this now." He was angry. "Turn around here and pay attention to me."

"You want some attention," I said. "Why don't you go on a hunger strike?"

"You're just going to set yourself back."

"I know what I'm doing."

"You can't kill yourself this way."

"Why?"

"Because you're—well, you're helpless. All we have to do is put you on the I.V. again."

I had to be real careful what I said here. The wrong word could spoil it all. "You can't keep me on the I.V. forever. It costs too much."

"I can keep you on it until you change your mind."

"If you think that will happen."

He turned and stomped out.

I lay there waiting for the I.V. all that day. No one offered me lunch or dinner so I expected the bottle any minute. It got dark outside, and still no bottle. I made a mess and hollered for one of the nurses to clean me up. A young and pretty black-haired, boyish looking girl came in and quietly cleaned up my mess and washed me and rolled me over several times while she changed the sheets, and the whole time she wouldn't talk to me.

"What's the matter?" I said.

She hummed this Sammy Kaye tune and ignored me.

"Is everybody mad at me or something?"

She smiled, continued her little absent-minded song. When she was done, she tucked the sheets around my feet and left the room. I waited for Fee when it was good and dark. I figured she'd talk to me, since she loved me as if I were a son. But she too, came in and put a bedpan under me, arranged some flowers on the nightstand by the bed, and went out. I didn't talk to her because I didn't want to be embarrassed again by talking to myself. So I waited and watched her go about her business, and she never even looked at me. When she was gone I said out loud, "So that's their little game."

I realized they were going to ignore me and not feed me until I got good and hungry—for both food and companionship. Then they'd have me where they wanted me.

Dr. Spint came much more frequently. He took my pulse, blood pressure, looked into my eyes with a little light, listened to my heart. I knew he was keeping an eye on me to be sure that my starvation didn't start to get to me—that he'd soon begin to feed me. I wished the signs would show up. My stomach stopped growling the third day. I only drank cold water the whole time, and by the time Spint started visiting me by the hour—about the middle of the third day—I could not even feel the water when it went down. It was like my stomach shriveled up and disappeared, and the water went right to my kidneys. It sure stopped running out of me so frequently, and that was finally what began to worry Dr. Spint.

On the morning of the fifth day, he ordered the nurses to put me on an I.V. and feed me through my veins. He said it with disgust, shaking his head.

"I don't want an I.V.," I said.

"Well, you're going to get one."

I pretended to be upset. "If I don't want to live, you shouldn't force me to."

"No patient of mine is going to kill himself," Spint said.

I smiled, looked at his hands tucking themselves into the large white pockets.

As soon as the I.V. was placed in my left arm, I gauged the distance. I needed the pole with the bottle on it to be very close to the bed, so when Fee came in on her shift, I asked her to move it. I don't know why I believed I could get her to do whatever I wanted—I mean, I didn't think she was stupid or anything. I guess I thought she'd trust me and believe whatever I told her. And you and I both know what an accomplished liar I was.

Anyway, when Fee came in, I smiled. "I'm glad to see you."

She made this grunting noise, went to the sink and filled a cup with water. Then she watered the plants by the bed.

"You can talk to me now," I said.

"I'm mad at you." She didn't look at me.

"Aw, come on, Fee."

"Nurse McFee to *you.*"

"Could you move the I.V. thing closer?"

"What?" She looked at it.

"I need it to be closer."

"It's where it belongs."

"See, the tube runs out to it and stretches the skin on my arm."

"So what? You can't feel it." She put the cup down, patted some yellow blossoms, arranged them tenderly as if she were playing with the hair of a child.

"It makes me sick to look at it."

She reached out and pushed the pole against the bed. The tube ran down along the edge of the bed and up into my arm. It still looked as if the distance was too great, though. I needed her to move the pole up toward my head.

"Now I can't see out the window."

"What?" She whined this.

"The pole runs across my view of the window. I can't watch cloud races—"

"Oh, all right," she said, moving the pole up next to my ear. I didn't have to look at it. I could see, in the corner of my eye, that the distance was perfect. Absolutely perfect.

———————

Something comes over you when you know you're going to die, and that it will be an act you perform. You will begin it and sit back and watch it happen. Something makes you feel powerful, and free, and not afraid of anything. It must be what it's like to be finally out into the air when you jump off a building. The thing has begun, and you only have to wait for the final seconds.

I said goodbye to Fee when she went out of the room. She turned and looked at me, as if I had tried to send her a signal and she were thinking about what it might mean. She looked at her feet, at the door knob and her hand resting there.

"Are you all right?" she asked.

"Sure. I'm fine."

"You sound strange."

"It must be the food pouring into my veins."

She went out, not looking back at me. I guess I shouldn't have made such a bad joke—I mean about my veins getting all that food and all——but I felt affectionate toward Fee at that moment, and I was very happy.

As soon as the door was fully closed, I began to move toward the pole. I edged my head along the pillow, arching my neck so that I was actually lifting the upper part of my body with my head, then scooting toward the edge of the bed as I let myself down. It took about an hour, and I began to fear an interruption. When I was close to the tube, when I felt my nose touching it, I reached my mouth around and clamped on the tube and began chewing. When I was through it, felt the sweet fluid run into my mouth, I took the tube full between my teeth and blew into it as hard as I could. I kept blowing into it, as if I were trying to blow up a tiny, tight balloon. I didn't feel anything in my arm. I laid my head back and waited for the end. I wasn't afraid. I thought of Etta; her breathing, the rise and fall of her breast when she held me, her soft hands, the way she smiled in the evenings when she came home. I thought of her walking across the bridge toward my father's grave. I saw her under a cold sky, preparing for her death, and so I prepared for mine. I imagined her next to me, holding my hand.

A cold sort of clammy feeling leaked into my chest. I thought I might burp or something, but then I felt my heart fold in on itself —as if it were crushed in a fist.

"Oh," I said. I tried to take in air, but I had no lungs anymore. They were gone. I turned toward the window, tried to see something of the world, and died. For the second time. I already told you what death is like and how it feels. I don't want to go over it again.

3

Our being mingles with the infinite;
Ourselves we never see, or come to know.
This world, this theatre of pride and wrong,
Swarms with sick fools who talk of happiness. . . .

—*Voltaire*

•

THE FIFTEENTH INTERVIEW

NOVEMBER 14, 1980

9:30 A.M.

I was born again in 1954—the year the Korean war ended. This time I was breathing in Chicago.

My father—his name is August Chance, but everybody including me calls him Gus—owned a laundromat on Sheere Avenue near the Loop. He met my mother when he was in the service, stationed in San Diego. (Just think, if he'd been stationed on the east coast, he might have known Jack Pitt.) My mother—you've met her; she brought me those socks and cigarettes and all—her name is Myra. Ask anybody in Champaign who Gus and Myra are and they'll tell you. My parents are the friendliest people I've ever known. In any life. I think it's because my father had his own business when he left Chicago, and he wanted to get to know as many people as possible when he moved to this city so his business would survive here too. His laundromat grew into a dry cleaners, so I guess it worked.

We moved from Chicago to Champaign two years before I entered high school. I guess if we'd stayed in Chicago, I never would have ended up in that hospital ward where I found the black woman; and I wouldn't have taken her in a taxi, wouldn't have watched her die in my arms. All this wouldn't be happening. I'd probably be wiring transistors to little epoxy boards in some factory in Hammond, Indiana. (Have you ever been to Hammond, Indiana? How do people live under those black chimneys like that?)

My father always appreciated the ironies of life. I've told you that. He used to like pointing them out to me: the little ironies and the big ones. A little irony was almost always funny. You wait all day for a particular meal, then get violently ill just before you're supposed to sit down at the table. Or you get real sick after the meal and get to look at it again. A big irony was usually tragic. Like cancer.

My father said dividing cells are the miracle that makes life possible. And so "the miracle that makes life possible" kills you when you have cancer. That's a big irony.

It's funny that the word "cancer" doesn't bother me now, but it nearly paralyzed me with fear when I was younger. Maybe that's an irony.

I'm sure my father would appreciate this situation after all I've told you. But he doesn't know any of it. I've never told him, although I've wanted to a few times. I never had the nerve. My father is a very sensible man, and I'm sure he'd probably think I was just being his "strange child" again.

That's what my mother always called me. Her "strange child." I always had problems with her. She never got used to the weather in Chicago or Champaign—it was not her beautiful San Diego— so during the winter I learned to behave myself or face the back of her hairbrush. She had almost no tolerance during the winter months. In the summers I was pretty much free to do as I pleased, since I was outdoors most of the time and could not bother her.

I had two minor problems that grew into more severe ones, however. They grew more severe because they drove my mother crazy. I already told you what they were: I was afraid of black and white photographs, and the word "cancer" made me break into an icy sweat and shake like an alcoholic. Of course, at the time I had no idea what caused these things. I didn't know I'd been here before. I just knew I had these reactions and that no one else seemed to have them, although a lot of people didn't particularly like the word "cancer." My mother thought I was sick; she thought it was a phase that hung around and festered into a mental illness. She insisted on saying the word "cancer" around me to see if I'd gotten over it, and of course, I broke into cold sweats fairly frequently.

It took me a long time to figure out my fear of black and white photographs. I still don't like them. I always thought it was the lack of color or something. But now I realize it was probably the fact that most of the black and white photographs I saw were of times and places before I was born, and that must have reminded me of my other lives and other deaths. I didn't know it was doing that, but it probably was. My reaction to the word "cancer" was, of course, because of Etta.

But, as I said, I had no idea I'd been alive before until I was in my early teens. Before that, I was just my mother's "strange child" and we went on with our lives. My mother told me when I was twelve that she never wanted children and that I was her "happy accident."

Yesterday, she told me she wasn't sure if the accident was so happy after all. I can't say I blame her. What would you do if your son dodged the draft, ended up in the back seat of a taxi with a dead black woman in his lap and no way to truly explain it? She keeps asking me why. "Why, Riley?" she says. "Why did you do this to me and your father?"

I can't tell her what I've told you. I can't. So I look at her and smile, and she remembers all the times she wanted to get professional help for me and decided against it. I know my mother believes I'm insane. Probably my father does too.

I don't remember much about my laundromat life in Chicago. To tell you the truth, much of my life before I remembered the other lives is only a blur. Something reflected in glass at night that you can't see clearly. But I do remember one episode that is important. Or at least I think it is. My next-door neighbor committed suicide, and I believe I had something to do with it. This happened the year before I remembered Ken Ezra and Jack Pitt. It may have helped me remember them, now that I think of it. I was already having some pretty terrific dreams by then, and I was having flashbacks to things I shouldn't have known about—like the smell of burning coal or kerosene, or the sound of horseshoes clanging on metal spikes.

About the time Martin Luther King decided to go to Chicago, my father decided to leave. Not that the two events were connected in any way. My father was not only sensible, he was also reasonable—and he believed that black people had just as much right to enjoy life as anyone else. But the action they took to relieve their "plight," as my father called it, too often included robbing him. So we moved to Champaign-Urbana; we moved into a neighborhood.

This was 1967. The war in Viet Nam was already fairly loud, but we didn't pay any attention to it. I went every day to a school that my mother said was "safer by far" than the school I would have attended if we had stayed in Chicago. I dreamed of football, baseball, or basketball, depending on the season. My father worked at his business, and my mother helped out.

We made friends with our next-door neighbors, the ones on both sides, because, as I said, my mother and father were establishing a business. The neighbor who killed himself was named Joe Hamm. He was about the same age as my father, although he had more hair and seemed to enjoy my company as much as anyone's. His wife's name was Frances. She was a small, round woman who laughed like a circus lady. My mother told me that their son, Matthew, was adopted.

Matthew was about six years old when we came to know him, and what we learned fairly quickly about him was that he had frequent convulsions.

"What are convulsions?" I asked my mother when I heard she and my father talking about it. We were sitting in the blue kitchen of our new house, having dinner.

"Something happens to your brain," my mother said.

Father scraped his plate with a fork, looked out the window by the kitchen sink, as if he were trying to see if anyone in the Hamm house could hear us. "The boy is sick, son. It's one of those ironies."

"Why is it ironic?"

"He's adopted, and then he turns out to have a problem with his brain."

"But what problems?" I was getting scared. I can't explain it, except that I began to think I might get it too.

"He is very touchy when he has a fever," Mother said. "Some children can't take a fever for any length of time. When they do, something happens to the brain and it goes into fits."

"Fits?"

"Convulsions," Father said. He said it with a "z" like this: "convulzions."

"Frances is worried about brain damage," Mother said, more to my father than to me.

"What happens with brain damage?" I asked.

My father crossed his eyes, let his tongue hang out of his mouth, and made this mournful sort of wailing noise in the back of his throat.

"Gus!" Mother said. "Stop that."

He laughed. "Just trying to be funny."

"It's insensitive." Mother put her plate away from her, looked at me. "Your father's not funny," she said.

My father told me later that the Hamms were a tragic family. "They waited a long time to have children, and then when they finally adopt one, he turns out like that."

At first I didn't have any idea what they were talking about. Matthew looked perfectly normal to me. He had a dark complexion, like his adoptive father, and he had huge, very dark brown eyes. They looked like pieces of coal, except they shone in a filmy bath of water. My mother said he was, quite simply, a beautiful child, although he didn't have much of a chin. I thought the worst thing that would happen to him would be that he would have buck teeth. I couldn't see any evidence that the "convulzions" were doing him any harm.

I grew to like the neighborhood almost immediately. In Chicago we lived in a row house, and cars passed all day and night —people were always walking by in high heels, or some other kind of clacking shoe, even in the early morning. I used to lie in bed and listen to the voices and the slamming car doors until late into the night, and when I woke up in the morning, I could still hear them. The new neighborhood was as peaceful as a closed shopping center. Still, there were a lot of people breathing in the houses that cluttered the hillside upon which our neighborhood was built. There were families with filthy neglected children, wild exotic pets, and fathers who drank. I remember the Foxes, who lived on the other side of us, had too many dogs and never cut their grass.

My father said once that they ought to trade those dogs in for
sheep. At least sheep would keep the yard clean. There was a
family that never went out and seemed mysteriously involved, late
at night, in some ceremony lit by neon. I remember the Hender-
sons, who were old and retired, and who worked all day in their
yard clipping, weeding, and manicuring everything. When I realized I'd been alive before, I used to watch them working on their
hedges or their lilacs, and wonder if they ever thought about
death. I wondered if either of them had ever lived before. I wish
I had had the nerve then, to ask them.

Down the street, on the same side as Joe Hamm, lived the
Webers. All of them had red hair, mother, father, two sons, and
three daughters. All of them. The children got too many toys at
Christmas, real articles advertised on television, not imitations.
On the fourth of July, every year, the Webers put on a show better
than the city. People used to come from as far away as Mattoon,
or Danville, and park their cars on our street to watch the fire-
works at the Weber house.

But I remember most Joe Hamm and his wife Frances and their
little boy. I got to know Mr. Hamm the first summer we lived in
this city—and it was the next to last summer of his life.

He came over one day shortly after we moved in and asked my
mother if he could take me out running with his dogs. Joe had the
two best hunting dogs in this county—maybe in the state of Illinois. Every fall he took them up to Wisconsin and hunted rabbit.
After I went with him a few times to let them run, he invited me
to join him in Wisconsin that fall.

"My mother won't let me," I said. We were sitting on the
bumper of his black Ford, watching the dogs running across an
open field that seemed to stretch all the way to Chicago. I'll never
forget the black dirt in that field. It made me understand why so
much of this state is farmland.

"I'll ask your mother," Joe said, after a pause. "She might let
you tag along."

"She doesn't like guns."

"Does she like hammers?"

"I don't know."

He smiled. He had very large teeth, and blue eyes. His mouth always seemed to be turned slightly down, as if he'd just finished crying.

"Why?" I said finally.

"You can kill someone with a hammer as well as a gun."

"Oh."

"A gun's a tool. That's all."

"I'm sure she's heard that before," I said.

"She's probably worried you'll get hurt or something."

"Yeah." I loved the way Joe talked to me. We sat on the bumper of that car, and I felt like a grown man—like I could say anything I wanted in front of him and I wouldn't be scolded or anything.

That night, my mother said, "Why doesn't he take his own son hunting?"

"Matt's only six," I said.

"You don't need to be riding all the way to Wisconsin."

"Please."

She stood in front of the sink washing dishes, frowning at each plate, each utensil. "Jesus," she said. "Your father needs help in the store."

My father came into the kitchen carrying a can of beer and the newspaper. He wore a white shirt open at the collar, and blue slacks, and his brown slippers. I knew he had been home for a while and that he'd been relaxing and reading the newspaper—a thing he looked forward to almost as much as I looked forward to Christmas or my birthday. I also knew he'd probably tell me I couldn't go, but he surprised me.

"Why can't he have a little vacation?" he said.

"I need a vacation. You need one. He's only twelve years old." She dropped a cup back into the sink, splashing water into her eye. "Dammit."

"What happened?" Father said.

"Both of you get out of here." She held the back of her hand over her eyes, and I looked at her thumb and suddenly I remembered Sara's thumbs the day my father hit her and she cried on the bed. I didn't know at the time it was Sara that I was remembering, so it scared me.

"Let him go," Father said.

"I just saw something," I said.

"What?"

"I saw a girl."

"Where?" My mother took her hand away.

"Just now."

My father went to the window. It was just starting to get dark outside.

"Not out there," I said.

"Where then?" He still had his hand on the curtain.

"In my memory."

"He saw a girl in his memory," Mother said. She went back to her dishes. "You're right. He does need a vacation."

My father laughed. Neither one of them wanted to know who the girl was.

Joe had this great beagle named Susan that could stay on a rabbit's trail until it had come full circle back to the place it had been jumped. Then Joe would kill it. Rabbits always run in a circle, Joe said. "You find where the dog first got him up and wait there. If the dog doesn't lose him, if the dog stays on his trail making a lot of noise, the rabbit'll come right back to that spot."

We spent many bright fall mornings, waiting in tall grass still wet with dew, listening for Susan, waiting. I never heard the rabbits. If they made any noise, it never reached me. They ran silently and well through the underbrush and the weeds. I don't believe they ever stirred a leaf. But they always came back to where they started.

Once, that fall, Joe gave me the gun and told me to shoot the rabbit when it came back. He leaned down close over my shoulder and pointed to a clump of green weeds by a bare rock near the edge of the woods, and said, "Right through there he'll come. He'll come right at us, until he sees us, and then he'll veer either right or left. When he cuts, whichever way he cuts, you've got to shoot fast because he'll really be moving. Shoot out in front of him, about five feet, and don't miss."

The air was brisk but not cold, and everything was as clear as a photograph—nothing in my view was out of focus. I looked down the barrel of the gun, to the little sight at the end, and suddenly felt as if I had aimed down the barrel of a gun before.

"I've done this before," I said.

"You have?"

"I feel like I have. But—I haven't really."

"You feel like you've been in this spot before?"

"No."

He laughed. "We were here two Saturdays ago."

"Oh," I said. The feeling went away. I tried to make it come back by looking down the barrel again and trying to remember it. But nothing happened. By then I was pretty sure something very strange was going on and I had this perverse desire to make it happen more often. You know what I mean? I knew this guy in Canada who was worried about his heart, and every time he got chest pains he went and got on his bicycle and pedaled up the steepest hills he could find. I felt sort of like him whenever I tried to make the flashbacks happen.

Anyway, the rabbit came, just as Joe said it would, and it looked so terribly small and afraid, even as it rushed toward us, I didn't want to hit it. I had seen Joe shoot rabbits before and it never bothered me, but now I had the gun.

The rabbit saw us and veered in the same instant to my left, not fifteen feet away, and I saw it going fast across the top of the rise, aimed the rifle five feet in front of it, and pulled the trigger. For a second I thought I missed, because the rabbit disappeared. I was already thinking about how I would feign disappointment, when the rabbit came down. It fell right where it had been hit without a sound. Joe patted me on the back, and I ran to pick up the dead rabbit before the dog got to it. I gave the gun back to Joe, and he looked at me kind of funny, with his head turned to the side, and said, "You bothered by this?"

"No—of course not." I didn't think I was.

He looked at the rabbit dangling from my right hand and said, "You know, that's the way it always is. You don't really have any such luck most of the time."

I didn't think it was a lucky shot and I told him so.

"I wasn't talking about you," he said. "I was talking about the rabbit."

I didn't understand him. He stared at the puzzled expression on my face, then he took the rabbit out of my hand, held it up in the fall sunlight. I saw the head dangling, the pink ears filtering the sun, blood dripping down one of them. "A good-sized rabbit, wouldn't you say?"

"Yes."

He set the rabbit down in the grass, cracked the gun open, and drew out the empty shell. "Save this so you'll remember the first time you killed anything. We're going to eat the rabbit."

The shell felt warm in my hand, almost as if it were alive. I still have it, tucked neatly away in a small wicker basket on the dresser in my room. When Joe handed me that shell and said that about the first time I killed anything, I saw a man rub the top of his head and fall into a ditch. It frightened me; I tried to convince myself I was remembering something I saw in a movie or on television. But I knew it was real. I just knew it.

I watched Joe clean the rabbit that afternoon. He said I should have the honor since I had killed it. I had never seen him do it before.

We were in the shed in his back yard, and I saw the light from the afternoon leaking in through the boards where all his tools were hung on nails. I saw Joe cut between the legs of the rabbit, and then draw the skin down off it as if he were stripping the clothing off a small child. He ripped it off, and he seemed almost furtive about it. Then he reached down into it and pulled out the smooth, gleaming, almost beautiful entrails. They came all apart in Joe's fingers. He held them in front of me, steam rising from them. "That's all it is," he said. "You and I are the same way." He threw it into a bucket at his feet. The rabbit hung now like a tiny, gray, naked fetus. "This part, we eat."

The first time Matthew had a convulsion that year, Joe wasn't home, and Frances came running across the green, late April yard and onto our white porch screaming for my father. I had never seen such terror. I thought something was chasing her.

My father raced off the porch without using the steps, and Frances went along behind him. He vaulted onto her porch and into the house, and I came fast around the hedge in front, saw him leap through the door. I was going to follow him, but when I got to the gaping front door, I stopped. Something, perhaps the silence in the house, perhaps the darkness of the hallway—something made me stop. I couldn't hear anything. It was as if my father had simply withdrawn through that door out of the world someplace. I thought I could feel air rushing past me, and an odor, a sour stench from something cold and wet.

My father was in there a long time. The ambulance came, and two men carrying great black bags, pushing a bed on wheels, rushed past me as if I were a lawn jockey or something. I stood in the yard, watching the horizon behind our house move away from me, and I heard the cries of some wild boy down the street playing, and felt, for what I thought was the first time, that I was without power and things were out of control. And I felt very small.

I wasn't outside anymore when Joe came home. I wanted to know what happened, but no one would tell me anything for sure. "Just convulsions again," my father said.

"Is he all right?"

"Who knows?"

Whatever Matthew had, I knew it was terrible and wouldn't go away.

My father said, "The boy is starting to go backward."

Of course, I was terrified. Again, I had that terrible feeling that I had no personal control over myself or what might happen to me—that there was nothing I could do that would reduce what seemed like the trembling sense of emptiness after a nightmare; a sense of the inexorable nature of things.

Twice that year my father had to save Matthew. He threw him into a tub of cold water the first time. The second time, the little guy was already in a tub of warm water and my father had to carry him to the sink. I didn't see this, but I heard about it.

Joe hardly ever talked about what was wrong with his son. I thought he must have been disappointed; I remember thinking it was a rotten deal for him, one that he would never be able to complain about. It would have broken his heart to admit he was not happy with his choice.

Later in the spring of that year—late May or early June— Matthew began to show symptoms of severe brain damage: he drooled, and an expression came into his face that was distracted and empty. I would watch him playing in front of his house, call to him, and he'd let his head loll to the side as if it was too heavy for him to hold it up. He'd tilt his head like that—like a cat or a dog trying to discover the source of some high-pitched noise— then he'd go on playing. I knew he heard me. He just didn't know what to make of the noise.

All of this had a terrible effect on Joe. Matthew was winding down, back toward birth, and Joe watched the progression, day by day. He must have gotten to know his son, before the boy began receding back into himself. Joe spent a lot of time, each day, trying to reverse the process, trying to bring back the boy he knew. Maybe he convinced himself that the boy was getting better. He was always telling me about the new things Matthew was learning: tying his shoes, putting blocks together in the right pattern. But all of Matthew's words were missing, there was nothing he could say clearly any more. Everyone could see it was only getting worse.

That was the beginning of Joe's last summer. In August, I let his boy get humiliated by a school friend of mine. It was all very spontaneous, and Joe saw the whole thing. He killed himself before I could make him understand that what happened with Matthew was not something I wanted to be involved in. It was not a choice I made.

My neighborhood friend at that time was one of the Weber boys, Jimmy, who wore thick glasses and, like the rest of his family, had dark red hair. Jimmy and I spent almost every day together that first summer we lived in Champaign—before I really got to know Joe. But during the first school year I started hanging around with Wally Harrison, who everybody seemed to like, and who never did anything without appearing to have practiced it over and over. He was what everybody called a natural athlete, although he never went out for any of the school teams. (I tried out for track—ran the mile in five minutes and fifty-five seconds, and the coach said, "Cut a minute off that time and you're on my team." I went over behind the bleachers and threw up. I knew then I'd never run a mile again.)

Wally was probably the best looking human being I've ever seen. He had a nest of blond hair that hung down just over his broad white forehead, and dark black brows which nearly touched over his eyes. He went around with his mouth open most of the time, as if he'd just finished doing a hundred push-ups or something. In a way, I hated him. But he was popular, and I was my mother's strange child. I wanted to be Wally's friend because I thought some of his practiced movements would rub off, and I thought if I was Wally's best friend, I too would be popular.

So Wally listened to Simon and Garfunkel, the Beatles, and Bob Dylan, and I followed along behind him. (He always had a pocket transistor radio, so he could hear his music. The whole time I knew him, I don't think we ever really had a conversation. He'd hold that black radio up to his ear, so I could barely hear it, and I'd agree with him that the music was "really fine.")

Jimmy, of course, followed me. His glasses were too thick for him to have many friends—everybody but me made fun of him— and I *had* spent that first summer with him wandering around all the neighborhoods. By the end of that first school year, the three of us were always together.

When summer came—that fateful summer of Joe's death—I tried very hard to continue the friendship. I was always trying to get Wally to come over to my house during that summer, and one cold August afternoon, he did. Jimmy was there and the three of us played baseball in the field that separated our street from all the other neighborhoods. We played for a long time, without stopping. As I said, it was unusually cold, and by the time we stopped the sky was beginning to turn that funny, weak, yellowish color before it gets gray and falls off into night. We came puffing up to my front porch, and sitting on the lower step, all bundled up like a toy carnival doll, was Matthew. He was smiling at me, trying to talk. His mother was in the house talking to my parents, watching Matthew through the kitchen window. The boy was just sitting there, looking at us. He was cold.

Wally said, "What's wrong with him?"

Matthew's head kept falling to the side, like a man drifting into sleep.

I was ashamed for him, and for what was wrong with him, so all I said was, "He's cold."

"Why's he got that funny look on his face?"

"He doesn't know you. He lives in the house next door."

There was this long pause, when it seemed like there was no sound anywhere in the world, while Matthew looked in that distracted way at Wally Harrison, and I stood next to both of them shivering from the cold.

Then Wally said, "Ugly fucker, ain't he?"

This made me laugh. I knew I shouldn't, but the sound of Wally's voice making such a complete statement of what I realized was the truth made me laugh hysterically. Wally laughed with me. Jimmy watched, not knowing what to do. He didn't see anything funny.

"Let's play a trick on him," Wally said, pointing at Matthew.

I wanted to stop laughing. "Nah," I said. "He's my next-door neighbor. Leave him alone." I was still laughing in the back of my throat.

I thought we would go into the house and watch TV, but Wally pulled his fly down and stepped up to Matthew.

"Know what's in here?" he said. It was really a question—as if he didn't know and wanted to find out.

I glanced to the kitchen window, but no one was there.

"Geeeee," Wally said. "Look at this—look at this—see what I found?" He was laughing at himself, trying to get as close to

Matthew as he could, and I was laughing with him, laughing wildly—and Matthew looked at both of us with absolutely no expression on his face. He may as well have been dead. "Look," Wally said. "I found a little pink piggy."

Jimmy shivered there, watching us. I wanted him to laugh too, but he didn't. I was laughing as hard as I ever have—but I really didn't want to. It wasn't a choice I made—except I didn't do anything to stop it. I didn't think Matthew knew what was happening. But then, through our laughter, I began to hear, like a siren coming from beyond the far houses, a long, slow cry that seemed to come from somewhere inside Joe's little boy.

Wally began fixing himself.

"Jesus, quiet down kid," he said, as he pulled up his fly. He was still laughing, as I was, and I glanced back to the window and saw Matthew's mother moving away toward the door, coming at us with that look of terror on her face. Before I could completely stop myself from laughing, or even check to see if Wally had finished fixing himself, I heard Jimmy say, "They did a dirty thing to Matthew."

I turned and saw Joe's huge frame behind me. He was standing over me while the echo of my laughter rang in my ears. That sound still comes to me at night in my dreams. I had been a part of it.

I looked at Matthew, saw his head leaning back toward the porch, his eyes so helpless beneath the dark brows, and I did not know how I would ever make it up to him. Or to Joe, who had been such a friend to me.

Joe leaned down and picked his son up in his arms.

"Going to take Matt home?" I said stupidly.

He withdrew, silently—carrying Matthew away as if he were rescuing him from a fire. Mrs. Hamm came out of the house and passed me on the front steps without saying anything. I felt as if I had entered some other world, and no one could see me anymore. Jimmy turned and trotted home. I think Wally said, "Shit, man. That was close," or something like that.

My father came out of the house, his hands in his pockets. He said to Wally, "You go on home, son."

ROBERT BAUSCH

I couldn't look at my father. He walked over to where I stood by the blue steps, took his hand out of his pocket and rubbed it over the top of his head.

"Tell me what happened," he said.

"Didn't you see it?"

"I want you to tell me."

"I laughed at him."

"What else?"

"Wally unzipped his fly and—"

"And you laughed." This was a statement.

I looked at my shoes.

"You laughed."

"I didn't want to."

The sky was yellow. I saw a black crow dip down over the field across from our house, and then rise up into the air again. Then I remembered silent lightning, the bright flashes ripping across a night blue sky.

"It's wrong, son." My father was not looking at me.

"I know."

"I want you to go over there and face Joe and tell him you're sorry."

I felt something rise up in my chest. "Now?"

"Right now."

I left him there and went to Joe's front porch. I went up the stairs as if I was going to break in and steal something. Just before I knocked, I looked back, saw my father leaning on the fence gate by our back door. He motioned for me to "go ahead."

I knocked on the door, felt the smooth paint there on my knuckles. I was so scared my teeth began to rattle.

I looked back again, saw my father still standing there waiting.

No one came to the door. I knocked several times, louder each time, but I never heard anything from the house. Then I saw the kitchen light go out, and I was left in the darkness on Joe's front porch. I looked at my father, and he shook his head, looked at the ground, and went through the gate. I sat outside for a long time before I went home. I watched the sky and tried to remember when it was that I saw lightning flash without sound.

Later that summer, Joe killed himself. He used the same gun I held in my hands that day when I killed my first rabbit. He left a note that explained why he was ending his life, but I never found out what it said. My father knew, and he told me it had something to do with the finality of things. That's the way he put it. He said that Joe never could get used to the ironies in life. That he couldn't accept the fact that things just happened, without any sense to them, without any logic.

"Joe was a strange fellow," my father said. "I guess he just couldn't take it."

I know that Joe didn't kill himself because he saw me laughing at his little boy. I know that. Still, I can't forget that he *did* see me, and he carried Matthew off without a sound: he had to rescue his little boy from me.

Joe didn't say anything to me after that. Twice before his death, I saw him in the yard playing with Matthew. He laughed, his voice echoing between the houses. I think he was trying to tell me something with his mirth, his joy. Trying to prove something to me. But maybe I've imagined that.

Anyway, shortly after Joe died, I was lying on the floor watching a film on the history of flight. My father was at work, and Mother sat behind me doing a crossword puzzle. We hadn't talked about Joe since he killed himself—although my mother spent a lot of time with Frances and Matthew in the first few weeks after the funeral. I think I had pretty much accepted Joe's death by then.

I always lay down on the floor to watch TV. I liked the comfort of the shag carpet, and I could get closer to the TV than any of the chairs allowed. So I was right in front of the TV, lying on my side holding my head up with my hand, watching all these early flying experiments and laughing at most of them. There were some spectacular failures, and a lot of them had to do with the fact that the inventor was more concerned with getting up into the air than with how to land once you got up there and decided you wanted to come down.

Then the narrator said, "There were some tragedies." The film

ROBERT BAUSCH

switched to a gray flat field, and a crowd of men scurrying around a single line which led to a huge dirigible. I didn't hear another thing the narrator said. I saw the ship rise, saw all the little tiny men grab onto the line and go up with it. When it went up, I felt something cold in my stomach.

"God," I said.

"What's the matter?" My mother put down her puzzle.

The ship went higher into a gray sky. The men hanging on the line looked like insects.

"What's the matter?" my mother said again.

"Look at that." I felt my hands turning cold, a crazy sort of whirling liquid in my head. "Damn."

"Riley."

The first man fell, and I jumped, sat straight up.

"What's wrong with you?"

Another man fell, this time the camera followed him to the ground.

"I've seen that before," I said.

"It's an old film," Mother said. "What's wrong with you?"

I couldn't look at her. Another man fell. Another. The narrator droned on, a voice like an animal sound you hear in your sleep.

"Riley, you're shaking."

"I'm scared," I said.

"What are you afraid of?" She sat forward in her chair, looked at the windows.

"God," I said.

"Did you hear something?" she whispered.

The second to last man fell from the line and I yelled, "Sergeant Chase!"

Mother leapt from the chair, got to the floor next to me. I couldn't take my eyes off the screen. "Who did you hear?" she asked.

There was only one man left on the line. I watched him, saw his struggle to get up the rope to safety.

"Riley, talk to me," Mother said.

"I know him," I said, pointing to the TV.

"You're not funny," she said, her voice strong and less afraid. "I do."

"Riley, don't you try to scare me." She thought I was only playing; trying to scare her because we were alone in the house. Then the last man fell. I fell. I watched myself squirming on the air, legs churning, all the way down. When I hit, I looked at my mother, thought she was suddenly very ugly and useless. Then I got up, went into the bathroom, and threw up.

It all came back in a rush after that. In a flood I remembered it all: Sara and Ogra and my father and Ben and Walker and Boone; then the long fall, the horrible dying. I remembered Etta and Mrs. Proudy; Father Burns, Sister Theresa, Shucker and Fee. I watched Etta disappear down that hospital corridor and cried all over again. I remembered lying in that hospital bed waiting for some way to die, and I realized I was in this life all over again; I was going to have to go through it all again.

I couldn't sleep for days after it all came back. I'd lie in bed all night thinking about the other lives and all—until the sun lighted the leaves outside my window—and I couldn't discover a reason for any of it. I didn't understand why I had to remember everything, and what made it all come back like that. When I was Jack Pitt, I didn't remember a single day of Ken Ezra's life. If I had, I might have saved myself a lot of grief. I might have known I could never do anything good and have it come out the way it was supposed to. I might not have caused Etta's death, or gotten involved with Shucker.

Maybe I would have had more respect for the truth, too— although I lied like a carnival barker when my father asked me what the hell got into me. This was the next morning, and he had gotten the story from my mother, who went to bed crying after I got sick. I'm sure she thought I had some fatal disease.

I ate breakfast like a man who expects to find a severed finger in his food.

"What got into you last night?" my father said. He sat across from me drinking coffee. He hunched over his cup, a blue robe hanging over his shoulders and open in the front. My mother was still asleep, probably dreaming of the coming winter months and my long illness.

"I just got sick," I said.

"From something on the TV?"

"I was thinking."

"About Joe?"

"Yes."

"It's a terrible thing."

He didn't know how terrible. I wanted to tell him. I wanted my father to know I had inhabited two other wombs, had breathed the air of this world before he was born. But I didn't. I was already "strange," and I knew he would only worry about my sanity.

"You going to help me in the store after school?"

"I guess." I always hated going to the dry cleaners after school, but I was a high school student that year, and I was expected to "do my part," as my mother put it. Before, I had only worked on Saturdays, unless there was some terrible rush or something.

My father finished his eggs and got up from the table. I still had most of mine left.

"You going to eat those?" he said.

"You want them?"

He reached over and took my plate, stood there over the table, his belly sticking out of the robe as smooth as an apple and absolutely hairless. He held the plate up, eating my eggs, and I thought of the first father I had known and of the one I never knew, and suddenly I was filled with this unbelievable rush of love for my old man.

"I love you, Dad," I whispered.

"What?" He peered over the eggs.

"I'm real glad you're my father."

He made this grunting noise he always made when he was amused, and smiled at me. "You afraid I'm going to kill myself too?"

"No."

"These eggs are cold," he said.

I put my chin in my hands, stared at the green and white table cloth.

"You know," my father said. "You didn't have anything to do with what Joe did."

"I know."

"I've seen the note, son." He put the plate down, closed the robe in front of him, his hands clamped on the material as if he was covering a wound. "Joe's death had more to do with what didn't happen to him, than with what did."

"OK," I said.

He came around the table, put his hand on my head, and rubbed my hair. "Get ready for school," he said.

I wanted to hug him, but he turned and went up to his room.

My father was the kind of man Jack Pitt wanted to be. I remember one time, when I was about ten years old and we still lived in Chicago, my mother nearly fainted when she opened the front door and stood face to face with one of the city's street people. He was an old and crooked black man with a mouth that looked like an open cave, and a shabby, worn-out flannel shirt that barely covered what looked like five layers of yellow underwear. His shoes were bent up at the toes, like one of those exaggerated cartoon figures in the Sunday papers. My mother almost slammed the door in his face, but he smiled, his face wrinkled like used aluminum foil, and stepped aside like a hotel doorman, extending his arm outward toward my father as if he were introducing him.

"Gus," my mother said. "What's this?"

"This," my father said, "is a personal friend of mine."

"Have you been drinking?"

"Not a drop," my father said, as he motioned the old man to go on in.

My mother stepped back, took in a deep breath of air, as if she planned on not breathing as long as the old man was in the house. I didn't blame her—he smelled like one of those bathrooms on the interstate. It was late February—if you remember, 1964 was one of the worst winters ever, and there was snow on the ground that had been there for over a month. I'll never forget the image of the two of them—my father and the old black man—standing on our porch letting out clouds of steam.

When they were in the house, I saw my father look at my mother nervously—a look on his face that said, "Behave yourself."

I started to go up to my room, to get away from the smell, and my father said, "Riley, I want you to meet Mr. Haslit."

I didn't want to touch him, but Mr. Haslit held out his hand.

"Nice to meet you," I said. His hand felt like some sort of shellfish.

"Yeth," he said. "Yeth." Then he turned to my father. "A nice looking kid." He sounded as if he had a mouth full of boiled potatoes.

"Come, sit down," my father said. He put his hand on the man's back, moved him toward my mother's perfect dining room. I followed along, listening to banging plates in the kitchen. I knew my mother, in her winter mood, was preparing more than snacks and coffee. She had a way of letting her anger filter into everything, without making scenes. She still does—you saw the way she threw those cigarettes at me yesterday.

"Have a seat," my father said. He took off his gray, one hundred percent wool overcoat that my mother got him for Christmas that year, and draped it across an oak credenza that rested like an altar under a huge wall mirror my mother charged at Carson Pirie Scott the first year she and my father lived in Chicago. The credenza was a gift from my grandmother—my father's mother—who never gave my father a gift without explaining the difficulty of finding it and the incredible cost to her of paying for it. Which elicited from my father enough money to buy four items exactly like it.

The old black man stared at the credenza as if it were a coffin and said, "Nice piece of furniture."

My father sat down, folded his hands in front of him and sighed. "What will you have?"

"Oh, anything," Mr. Haslit said. "I'll take anything."

I heard a cabinet slam in the kitchen.

"Cold winter," my father said. He kept folding his hands together and then taking them apart. I sat across from Mr. Haslit, tried not to look at the lines in his face, the cavernous mouth. His eyes seemed all one drab, off yellow color.

"It's cold out there," Mr. Haslit said.

"The worst winter I've ever seen," said my father.

Mr. Haslit looked at me. "You go to school?"

"Yes."

"That's nice."

"He's in fifth grade," my father said. He seemed nervous. Every time my mother banged a plate he winced, as if she had hit him with it.

"School's a good thing," Mr. Haslit said. "A real good thing."

"Did you go to school?" I said.

"A long time ago."

"Here?" my father said.

"In St. Louis."

"Ah."

My mother came in carrying two plates. She had made little sandwich squares with cheese and lunch meat. There was a little pile of mustard in the middle of each plate. She put them down in the center of the table, and went back into the kitchen.

Mr. Haslit took one of the plates and put it in his lap. His hand trembled as he put whole squares in his mouth. He rubbed each of the squares in the mustard, then swallowed it whole. There wasn't anything to chew with, anyway.

My father took little bites out of his sandwiches until he saw what Mr. Haslit was doing. Then he started swallowing them too.

"I haven't eaten for days," Mr. Haslit said.

My mother came in with two cups of coffee and a glass of milk. When she put the coffee in front of Mr. Haslit, he looked up at her and I noticed tears in his eyes.

"Thank you, Missus," he said.

Mother started to turn away, but then she stopped, tilted her head, and smiled at Mr. Haslit. I could almost see the anger go out of her.

"These sandwiches are wonderful," my father said.

Mother came around the table, letting her hand go along the top

ROBERT BAUSCH

of my father's shoulders, and I knew it would be all right. I saw my father begin to relax.

When we'd finished eating, Mr. Haslit stood up, nodded his head, and offered his hand to my father. "You're a kind man," he said. "A very kind man." He kept nodding his head, shifting his weight from one beaten foot to the other.

My father stood up, lifted his overcoat from the credenza, and placed it over Mr. Haslit's shoulders. "You take this. It's too cold out there to be without a coat."

My mother made a sipping noise with her mouth.

The old man put the coat on as if he didn't want any of it to touch his dirty clothes. I'll never forget the way he caressed that material once the coat was on him, the way he looked down at himself—as if he'd inherited a new, young, and mighty physique. "Thank you," he said. "Thank you so much."

My father took his hand. "Take good care of it."

"Oh, thank you," Mr. Haslit said. Then without looking at me or my mother, he took the two remaining sandwiches and cradled them in his left hand as it disappeared in the coat pocket. He seemed to stagger a bit, then he walked over to my mother, bent down in front of her and said, "You are a great lady."

Before he was out the door, my mother was up in her room crying. Mr. Haslit said, "Thank you" all the way out, and when he was gone, my father slapped me on the back and said, "I've got to go up and calm your mother."

"OK," I said.

"You stay here."

"Sure."

He smiled, blinked his eyes a couple of times, and went on up the stairs. I thought I would hear them yelling at each other, but it was quiet up there for a long time.

The next day, my mother went out and bought him a new overcoat.

I guess they are both good people. They just don't know what I know about life, and that makes things nearly impossible. It was

terrible when I was in high school, and all the years after. I was
always embarrassed about what they didn't know.

The old man and the overcoat is a good example, now that I
think of it. I mean it was nice for my father to do that—I'm
actually proud of him. It's one of the things I love in him—his
generosity and kindness, his care for others. But the old black man
left our house after his one meal, wearing my father's coat against
the Chicago wind, and I knew he would end up dead in some alley.
The coat would rot. I knew that even before I remembered Ken
Ezra and Jack Pitt.

How could *any* act of kindness cancel such an outcome? Even
if they decided to let Mr. Haslit live with us and fed him three
steaming plates of food a day, a thousand others like him froze to
death on the city's streets.

Sometimes I think kindness is the most useless of all human
behavior. In my worst moments, I remember Mr. Silver and his
talk of conflict, and I believe he may have been right. In my better
moments, of course, I hope with all my bones that Mr. Silver lived
more than one life too, and that one of them was the life of Mr.
Haslit.

I know you think I'm being silly—but you see? My father went
around thinking he was doing some good in the world, when really
he wasn't doing anything but offering a meal to a dying old man
on one of the last days of his life. It's like when my mother used
to dust the furniture. On sunny days you could see the little white
flecks of dust flying up into the air as her rag moved silently across
the smooth wood. But the dust only settled again, somewhere else
in the room. And when we walked around in it, breathed it, we
stirred it into the air and back onto the furniture.

One day in the spring, my father decided he had had enough
of my moping around. We had just come in from a full day at the
store—a Saturday in March or April, almost a year after I remembered the other lives. It was raining, had been raining all that
week, and I was feeling like a particle trapped in a drain. We stood
in the living room, dripping on my mother's white shag rug, and

I had said something like, "Rain makes me hate the world."

"Sit down," Father said. He took off his coat, threw it over the green easy chair he claimed was his favorite, although he almost never sat there, and went to the couch as if he thought he was going to have to catch it before he could sit on it. I was still in the middle of the room, holding my coat out away from me so it could drip on something other than me.

"What's the matter?" I said.

"Hang your coat up. I want to talk."

I put my coat on top of his, went to the couch and stood in front of him. Behind him, floor-length blue curtains covered a long picture window. The gray light from outside made the seams in the curtains visible, and created a sort of blue haze around the figure of my father.

"Sit down," he said.

I sat next to him, crossed my legs so I would appear relaxed. In truth, I was afraid of what he had to say. I just knew I had done something wrong.

"You've got to tell me what's bothering you," he said, without looking at me.

"I don't like rain."

"I'm not talking about just today."

"I don't hate the rain all the time."

He sat forward, rested his chin in his hands. He seemed to be staring at something on the far wall. We almost never had a really serious talk, so he wasn't very good at it—I think he might have been as nervous as I was. "Are you—are you, uh—" he stopped, turned on the couch and faced me. "Are you unhappy, son?"

I don't know why, but the question embarrassed me. Maybe I *do* know why. Maybe I was ashamed of my father for even talking about being happy or unhappy.

"Are you *happy*?" I asked.

"Yes." He looked at his hands, then back to me. "Yes, I am."

"Why?"

"I've got a nice home, a good business, a wife I love, and you too. I've got you too."

"In that order," I said.

"No, not in that order. Of course not."

"But that's the order that came out."

"Are you unhappy because I spend so much time at the store?"

"I didn't say I was unhappy." I leaned my head back on the top of the couch, stared at the white ceiling.

"Well, what is it, then?"

"I'm—" I tried to get the right words, the exact words that would tell him how I felt without forcing me to tell him of the other lives. "I'm just—I'm just feeling sort of tired, and unlucky, and like—like there isn't any reason for me to do anything."

"Why do you feel that way?" He sat back too.

"Because I know I don't have any luck."

"You're sixteen, for God's sake."

"That's right."

"Sixteen."

"For God's sake," I said.

"You've got your whole life ahead of you."

I wanted to say I had two whole lives behind me, but I didn't. I stared at the ceiling, listened to him breathing next to me, and waited for the conversation to end.

Finally, he sat up, leaned over close to me and said: "Tell me why you feel unlucky."

"I feel like I can never do anything—never do anything that would be completely good and would not do some damage some-where."

"You don't make any sense."

"But that's how I feel."

"Why?"

"I don't know." I was lying.

"Is it what happened to Joe?"

"I don't know."

"Well, what the hell is it?" He sat back, let his hands drop to his knees. "You seem barely alive most of the time."

I thought, "I'm a little worn down, it's my third trip through here." But I didn't say anything. I waited until he got tired of my silence, until he was off looking for something to eat in the kitchen. Then I hung my coat up and went into my bedroom to sit there in the darkness and think about Etta, and how it felt to listen to her voice and feel her breathing next to me. It was the only time I was ever happy.

I didn't get along well in school, either. I went to Champaign High School, listened to my teachers talking about the world as if it were some permanent thing with fixed values, and all we had to do was learn the values and everything would be all right. None of my teachers seemed to understand what I learned in both my other lives, and what my experience with Joe's little boy confirmed: no matter what you do, you can't really get living right. Unless you have one of those diseases that forces the doctors to keep you in a plastic, germ-free room, you are going to do *some* evil. And since the world is already overpopulated and bulging with billions of lives, it is, to put it simply, a bad place.

I spent most of my years in high school trying to convince people of that—especially my teachers. Of course, all of them thought I had an "attitude" problem, and they never failed to tell my parents that I needed "help."

My father believed it all stemmed from Joe's suicide and its affect on me. My history teacher, Mr. Hicks, thought I was a troublemaker, and it was in his class that I learned not only that I was right about the world, but that I should not involve myself in any of the world's events as long as I might live in this life.

THE SIXTEENTH INTERVIEW

NOVEMBER 14, 1980

2:00 P.M.

Mr. Hicks was the tallest man I've ever known. He had to have played basketball in college—all his students spent their time imagining big games for him, but none of us really knew if he was an athlete or not—because no coach in his right mind could pass a man as tall as Mr. Hicks without asking him if he'd ever seen a basketball. He must have been close to seven feet tall, and his body was so terribly thin he looked like a normal man somebody stretched to the breaking point. I always felt like there was something miraculous going on when he sat down, or bent his body to get something out of his bookcase. It didn't seem normal for a body that long to make any sort of angle without breaking at the bend. He always wore a suit—dark blue or gray—and his nose came to such a point it was hard to see his upper lip.

The one gift Mr. Hicks had, if it wasn't basketball, was his voice and his eloquence. He could make "pass the butter" sound good. So his class in American History became the sort of class you never expect to find in high school: interesting and important. Everybody loved Mr. Hicks, and he seemed to feel the same way about everybody.

The first time I saw him, I almost laughed. He ducked down to get into the room, and when he walked over to his desk he looked like one of those electrical towers moving out of its corridor of land and tearing wires in the process. I was a junior by then, and Joe was dead, and I already knew I'd been dead before too.

"As most of you know," Mr. Hicks said, "my name is Hicks. You can say it right if you have indigestion."

Everybody laughed, seemed to relax. He talked about what we would be studying—America since the great war; the one Ken Ezra enlisted for—and about "our place" in the "long catalog of human crime which is history."

When he said that, I thought I would really like him. But when the class was over, he asked me to wait—a polite request, in front of the whole class, which embarrassed me. I felt as if my ears had moved and everybody saw it.

I stayed at my desk, and after the room emptied, he came over to the desk in front of me, bent his long leg at the knee so that his foot rested on top of the desk (I kept waiting for the desk to topple over but it never did) and said, "I'm told you're a troublemaker."

"I am?"

"I'm told you won't work, and you complain about everything."

"I do?"

He frowned. He had brown hair that came to a point just above the frame of his glasses. Outside the room I could hear all the rushing feet and laughing voices of students changing classes. He stood there, up there near the neon lights, and seemed to stare at my forehead.

I cleared my throat, looked at the little pouch in my notebook where I'd collected a compass, two pencils (number 2) and a little red ruler.

"What do you say to that?" he said finally.

"Who told you that?" I didn't really want to know who told him, I wanted to know if that was what I should say.

"You probably know," he said.

I felt picked on. Every high school has its share of criminals, and the two most violent henchmen in Champaign High sat next to me in Mr. Hicks's class: Evelyn Weston and Ralph Eisely. They went together—Evelyn was a thick seventeen-year-old gangster who could beat up every boy in the school except her boyfriend, Ralph. Ralph already had a beard, hands that were puffy and dirty like a construction worker's, and a little tiny mouth that made me wonder if he could eat with anything larger than a fondue fork. And yet *I* am the one Mr. Hicks keeps after class in order to forestall trouble. I asked him about Evelyn and Ralph, and his mouth formed like he was going to kiss me or something, then he put his foot on the floor and gave out this long sigh.

"That's what I've been told," he said.

"What?"

"You've always got some answer."

"No, I don't."

"Evelyn and Ralph don't disrupt classes."

"Yes, they do. I've seen them."

"They don't disrupt this class."

"We've only had one."

"They were in my class—" he stopped, put his foot up again. "See? Now you're arguing with me."

"I'm sorry." I closed my notebook, started gathering my things.

"Look," he said. "I know you've had some trouble. I know your friend killed himself and you've had a hard—"

"How do you know that?"

"I had a long talk with your father." He looked at his foot on the chair, brushed something off his shoe.

It was quiet for a moment—even outside in the halls—and I wondered if Mr. Hicks would believe me if I told him the real problem. He was a history teacher, I thought. Surely he'll at least be interested. I almost told him, almost said, "This is my third life." But he looked at me and said, "I don't care if you disagree with me—in class or not—but I won't have you asking everybody what's the point."

"OK."

"I won't have you announcing to the whole class that they're only going to die so why—"

"I never did that." I really didn't.

"You know what I'm talking about."

"OK."

"Some things *are* true, young man."

"Oh, I know," I said. "You wouldn't believe what I know."

"Tell me."

"I can't."

"Why?"

"You wouldn't believe me."

"I believe there's a whole lot you don't know."

"Sure." I wanted to say, "About events, maybe." But I figured he'd think I was arguing with him. Besides, I really didn't know a lot of things. What I did know was what it's like to die, and how impossible it is to live without injuring lots of people. I didn't think anybody knew that but me.

"So why don't you resolve to keep your comments about the uselessness of everything to yourself, and try to learn something from me?"

"OK," I said. I would have agreed to letting him adopt me if he wanted. I needed to get out of there.

"Good," he said, letting his mouth appear from under the nose in a sort of bent smile. His left brow rose above his glasses and he said, "Run along."

In the second week of school, Evelyn Weston got bored with Mr. Hicks's lecture on the cruelty of the Germans during the great wars, so she got Ralph's attention and pointed to the boy sitting in front of her. The guy in front of her was named Dean something, I don't remember. He was one of those kids that nobody goes near—like my neighbor Larry—only Dean's problem was that his nostrils were too large and his body was the only body in the school thinner than Mr. Hicks's. Even his parents must have thought him ugly, since he wore clothes too small for him and shoes that somebody stole from a telephone repairman. His hair was thin and white and rose in points off his head like shampoo —although it was never washed or combed.

Ralph smiled when Evelyn pointed at Dean, and so I watched her to see if I could discover what she had noticed about him. Mr. Hicks wanted us to see a film on the Holocaust (we got to the second great war fairly quickly), and we were all waiting for him to turn off the lights.

Dean sat upright in his chair as he always did—a position that never failed to remind me how hard and uncomfortable the desks at Champaign High were. But I didn't see anything unusual about him, so I looked back to Evelyn. She sat forward, leaning down so Mr. Hicks wouldn't call on her, and her hands gripped the front edge of the desk, a few inches behind Dean's back. Still I could see nothing unusual. I looked at Ralph, who sat in front of me, and next to Dean on that day, but I could see nothing interesting there because he had turned back to face Mr. Hicks. Then the lights went out, and the projector came on. Mr. Hicks stood by the projector, surveying the class, and on the screen bulldozers shoved thousands of bodies into piles that looked like nothing but white bones, white rubbery bones. I heard a dull, heavy thud of a noise next to me. Then what sounded like someone holding his breath. Ralph leaned over in front of me and whispered something to Dean.

When my eyes were more used to the dim light, I realized that Evelyn was giving Dean her most powerful punches right in the middle of his back. And while he sat there, upright in the chair, losing his breath, Ralph leaned over and threatened to kill him if he made a sound. I saw Ralph's huge, dirty fist held out so Dean could see it. Evelyn just kept hitting him, and he held it in, although he began to lean in the chair a bit.

I turned and saw Mr. Hicks engrossed in the film, and realized that he wasn't going to notice the pounding noises—he did have the film turned up fairly loud.

I remembered Jack Pitt and Shucker, and the whole terrible idea of trying to do something good, something wonderful, and decided at first that I couldn't do anything. But when she kept hitting him, when I saw him dip his head from trying to cry so silently, I couldn't take it anymore. I got up and walked over to Mr. Hicks, intending to tell him what was going on.

"Sit down!" he yelled. He screamed it at me.

"I have to tell you something," I whispered.

"Either sit down or get out!"

"Someone is hitting Dean!" I yelled.

Mr. Hicks turned the projector off, went to the lights, and lit everything up like he was setting fires. Then he went to the door, opened it, and motioned with his hand for me to go through in front of him.

"What about Dean?" I said.

Mr. Hicks seemed to slump, his head tilted, and he said with a sigh, "Dean, is anybody hitting you?"

"No," Dean said. His voice was so shaky and unnecessarily loud, I thought for sure Mr. Hicks would see that he was lying. But he didn't.

"Let's go," he said.

"I don't—you haven't—" I could not make a sentence.

"*Now!*" Hicks yelled.

So I became the first student in the history of Champaign High School to get kicked out of Mr. Hicks's history class.

I didn't have a single conversation that week without somebody saying, "YOU got kicked out of *Hicks*'s class?" After a while, I was fairly proud of it—except that my father had to come to school and talk with Mr. Hicks before I could get back into the class.

"I can't go over there right away," my father said. "Couldn't I just talk to him on the telephone?"

"He insists on seeing you personally."

"You've told me the truth about this?"

"Yes."

"And Hicks won't listen to you?"

"Dean was afraid to tell him what happened."

"So you stick your neck into it."

"I guess."

"Now I got to go over there and talk to this Mr. Hicks, or you'll fail history." He shook his head. We were sitting at the breakfast table, my father fully dressed and ready for work, me still in my green pajamas. My mother stirred scrambled eggs in a pan, striking the bottom of the pan with a fork every time I said anything about what happened. She told me I should just mind my own business.

"I can't get back into the class," I said.

"Why do they do things like that?" Father said to my mother.

"I don't have time to be going over—"

"I'll go," she said.

"Mr. Hicks said he wanted to talk to Dad."

"Why?" Mother said.

"I've talked to him before," Father said. "Maybe he feels like he knows me."

"I'm a parent too." I thought my mother was going to stir the eggs out of the pan. They clung to the fork, a rubbery yellow piece of cloth.

"I'll go talk to him on Friday."

"He'll miss the whole week," Mother said. She put a yellow puff of egg on my plate, moved behind me holding the steaming pan over the table. The sleeve of her red robe went across my head.

"That's the best I can do."

"I don't mind missing the week," I said. I didn't want my father to go to the school at all, but if he had to go, I wanted it to be as far away in time as possible.

"Sure," Father said. "You get out of the class."

"I have to sit in the library," I said. Mother sat across from me. "I have to see the assistant principal and he gives me a card for the librarian to sign that says I've been there for the whole hour."

"I wouldn't mind having the time to sit in a library," Mother said.

"I'd rather do something else," I said.

"What?"

"Anything." I tried to think of something in any of my lives that I truly enjoyed—something I wanted to do every day for an hour. And I couldn't remember anything. My face must have showed the disappointment, because my mother said, "What's wrong with you?"

"Nothing."

"Eat your eggs."

Then I remembered Etta, and the conversations we had late at night, after the city got quiet, and I felt suddenly warm and even slightly happy. I realized my time in the library wouldn't be so terrible after all.

On Friday, while I was getting my lunch box out of the floor-length locker I shared with Larry, Evelyn walked up behind me and gave me one of the punches I had prevented her from giving Dean. I almost went into the locker. She turned and walked down the hall, touching a little bun of hair on the back of her head. I remembered Walker Adams, saw him pitch over into the gully, and it occurred to me that Evelyn had hit a murderer—that she had now stumbled into what my father would have called "the big leagues."

Before she got around the corner, I was on her. She went to the floor easier than a coat rack, and I landed on top of her, reached down and put my arms under her chin—she landed on her stomach, her hands out in front of her like the antennae of an insect —and I sat back as far as I could. I bent her the wrong way, and I heard the breath squeeze out of her. I let out this loud, angry grunt—I really felt like some sort of animal—and then I let go. She caught her face on the back of her hands, but still it bloodied her nose.

She lay there crying, and I stood over her, breathing as if I had just made love to her or something. When I looked up, I saw Mr. Hicks down the hall, staring at me with little, red eyes that looked like blisters.

I couldn't believe the way Evelyn cried. When my father came to the school that afternoon to talk to Hicks, he was greeted by two Champaign County police officers, and the principal of the school—a man named Bernard C. Mooth.

Mr. Mooth never went into the halls where the students could tease him about his name—"What has four legs and goes 'mooth, mooth, mooth?' A cow with a lisp"—so when Mr. Hicks dragged me into his office, I was seeing him for the first time. He looked like a real estate salesman; his hair was puffy and jet black, and he wore dark rimmed glasses a gray, three-piece suit, and a gold ring with a blue stone in the middle of it. Evelyn stood next to me crying, and I listened to her instead of Mr. Mooth. She seemed so helpless, so sad and everything. I really was beginning to feel bad for what I had done.

By the time my father arrived, I knew something about Evelyn that made me just want to hold her—and I wished I had died before I ever leaped on her like that.

Mr. Hicks told me about it. Evelyn couldn't stop crying, and Mr. Mooth took her to the nurse's office to get cleaned up. Hicks went around the desk and pulled a file out of the drawer there. The police had not arrived yet, so we were alone in the office. The only sound was probably my heart beating.

"I want you to see something," Hicks said. He paged through the file.

"I'm sorry," I said. "She hit me."

"I believe you."

"You do?"

He looked over the file. "Evelyn has had a lot of trouble here."

"Why didn't you believe me about Dean?"

"I did."

"But—"

"Dean has to learn to take care of himself." Hicks's voice was louder, although he was still almost whispering. "Dean wanted to take that punishment, or he wouldn't—"

"Eisely said he'd kill him if he made a sound," I said.

"I don't care." He seemed to find something in the file, marked his place and closed it, looking at me as if he was afraid I might steal the folder out of his hands. "It's very good of you to stand up for your friends—"

"Dean's not my friend." I couldn't brook the idea that he thought *Dean* was my friend.

"But—" he said, stopping me. "But, in my class everything that goes on is something I want to go on."

"What?"

"What goes on, goes on because I let it, and because I think it should go on."

"Even somebody beating up—"

"Right." His voice was normal, now. In fact, I thought if I went on he would yell at me. "Dean has to learn *somewhere* to fight his own battles. I won't protect him, and I won't allow you to protect him."

"What about Evelyn?"

"What about her?"

"Aren't you protecting her?"

He opened the folder, took out a piece of paper. "Here," he said, holding it out. "I want you to read this."

"What is it?"

"Just read it."

It was an essay Evelyn had written about death for one of her English classes. What I read there, on the clean white page, stunned me. I can't remember it word for word, but she said she was riding in a car with her father when she was seven years old, and she and her sister had been playing ghosts and trying to scare each other. She had been making ghostlike sounds, saying things like "Bewaarrre," and "Begoonnne." At just the right moment, while Evelyn was moaning to her father, "Begoonne, begoonne," he suddenly closed his eyes and slumped over the wheel. The car went off the road and slammed into an embankment. I remember these two sentences from her essay: "My sister and me were in the car a long while before it hit anything, but when it stopped, my father was no longer alive. My sister and me weren't hurt."

I gave the paper back to Hicks.

"Pretty horrible, isn't it?" he said. He put the folder back.

I couldn't believe I had been so mean to Evelyn. "I guess I deserve whatever you guys do to me," I said.

"It looked like you were going to kill her," Hicks said, and I thought I noticed a trace of emotion in his voice—as if he too were about to cry.

"I'll never attack anyone again," I said. And I made up my mind at that moment that I'd never involve myself in the world's events again as long—or as often—as I might live.

Of course, my father was appalled that I had beaten up a little girl.

"She's not little," I said. We were riding home from the big conference, where we learned that I was not only suspended from

Mr. Hicks's history class, but that I would not be allowed on the school grounds for at least a week.

"Suspended from school," father said. He gripped the steering wheel as if he were trying to make it squeal in pain. "I don't believe it."

"I'm sorry."

"You've spent your whole life saying that."

"More than one," I said. He didn't understand it. He looked at me, then back to the road. When we got to the stop sign at the end of our street, he said, "Are you ever going to do something good?"

"What?"

"Something to make me proud of you?"

"Gee, I hope so," I said. He didn't know I was not going to be involved in anything, anything at all. I couldn't tell him that it was very nearly impossible to do anything really good in the world. It would have crushed him to know that. I rode next to him, crying just like a child, because I knew it.

I don't know, maybe Evelyn hated her father. Maybe it was the best thing that ever happened to her when he keeled over. I can't believe she was ever a helpless seven-year-old girl. She probably beat up all the little boys in the neighborhood when she was seven. And if her father'd lived, by the time she was seventeen, when I ran into her, she could probably have licked him. She was built like a huge fire extinguisher.

And yet.

Her hair was so light brown it was almost blond, and she had this funny, vulnerable sort of voice, you know? It's embarrassing to think about now, but after Mr. Hicks let me read her essay, I felt very close to her. I'm not overly passionate or anything—and I never have had a truly lasting relationship with a woman—but I think I was a little bit in love with Evelyn after that episode in Mr. Mooth's office. You might know I'd get attached to a girl that looked like Dick Butkus—what with my luck and all. But to tell you the truth, when Evelyn and Ralph let the word out that they were going to kill me, it was real hard for me to dodge her in the halls and after history class.

I was allowed to return to Mr. Hicks's class, even though everybody knew Evelyn and Ralph were in there and they were going to get me.

I went to every class expecting her to sit behind me and give me a little of Dean's treatment. But she didn't. She sat in her regular seat and just stared at me. Ralph hunched in front of me like the boulder in front of the tomb, and I sat back and basked in Evelyn's eyes. I thought if I was calm and sort of disinterested, she'd begin to like me a little bit.

I don't think I was trying to save myself or anything. Near the end of the year—my last year in high school—I sent her a note telling her what I knew.

"I heard about your father," I wrote. "I was very sad. I think I know how you feel, since I once saw my father die. If you'd like to talk to me about it, I'd sure like to listen. Please destroy this note."

I signed it, "Trying to be your friend."

She unraveled it, read it as if it was the directions on a cereal box or something. Then she rolled it up into a little white ball and threw it to Ralph. I tried to intercept it, but he got it, sat up in front of me so I could admire the broadness of his back. I know my face was as red as a Christmas ribbon. I sat there, looking at Evelyn, and she stared at her hands, seemed to marvel at the way they moved.

Ralph put the note back on my desk. At the bottom, he had written, "Fuck you."

I got another piece of paper, wrote, "Your boyfriend is real bright," and passed it to her.

She laughed, put her hand over her mouth to hold it in. Ralph squirmed in his seat, signaled for her to let him see it, but she folded it up and put it in her purse.

I thought I had won. I got so excited, I wrote her another note. It was the only time I ever tried to tell somebody else about all this. I wrote, "I've lived two other lives. Trust me. I'll tell you about it when we talk."

She laughed even harder at that. Then she got out a pencil and wrote something at the bottom of my note. I waited for her to give it to me, but she watched Mr. Hicks, listened to everything he said as if she was the only other person in the room with him. I couldn't make myself exist for her during the rest of the class. When the bell rang, she took her books and her purse and got out of her chair as if the seat was hot. I usually hung around Mr. Hicks's desk at the end of class, until I was sure she and Ralph were safely in another class, before I left the room. But this time, I sat in my chair and waited.

Evelyn looked at me, then at Ralph. He stood up, put his hands in his pockets and stepped on my left foot, leaning into it like a man trying to break something small.

"Get off my foot!" I yelled.

"Shuttup."

Mr. Hicks shuffled some papers on his desk, watched us with those little red eyes.

I pulled my foot out, and Evelyn came around her desk, put the note in front of me with a smile on her face.

"Come on, Ralphie," she said, taking his arm. He smiled, hooked his thumb in my belt buckle and pulled me up out of the chair.

"You got to be alone sometime," he said. Then they both turned and went out. I picked up the note, feeling really stupid for telling her about my other lives.

The note said, "You're going to *need* more than one life, you little turd."

It went on like that. I never gave up, completely—and Evelyn and Ralph never did get hold of me. There was something in Evelyn that made me believe she'd understand if I could only talk to her. If I could only get rid of Ralph.

I swear to you that I am not a murderer—at least not in this life—but I have killed a man, and knowing that, it was easy for me to consider doing the same thing to Ralph. I didn't think about it too seriously, because I remembered the guilt I felt for Walker Adams. I remembered the way his eyes looked when he fell over into the ditch. But I wanted to talk to Evelyn so badly—I think I really needed to tell somebody about Ken Ezra and Jack Pitt.

Anyway, I decided if I told Evelyn, she'd probably only think I was crazy. When I graduated—534th in a class of 537—I watched her skip over to her mother carrying a little white diploma, saw them get into a yellow Buick and drive off, and I never saw her again. I thought my secret would stay just that until the day I died; until I went down for the third time.

But then I got drafted—I was one of the last people that happened to. They had a lottery, and guess whose birthday came out of the tumbler first?—and I left home to escape military service. And because of that, because of my refusal to fight in Viet Nam, I ended up in that hospital where I found the black woman, and where I made the fatal choice that brought me here before you, an accused man.

•

THE SEVENTEENTH INTERVIEW

NOVEMBER 15, 1980

9:30 A.M.

It should be pretty easy to figure out why I didn't want to serve. Aside from the fact that I'd already decided I wasn't going to get involved in any of the world's events, I also knew I had been in the army twice before and didn't do too well either time.

My father couldn't believe what I was telling him.

"You mean you're going to be one of those?"

"One of what?"

"You know what I mean."

"I'm just not going, Dad."

"Your mother will be heartbroken." He lowered his head, seemed to lose air. "Just heartbroken."

We were standing in his bedroom, where he always went to change clothes when he got home from work. My mother was downstairs watching "The Dinah Shore Show."

"I'm sorry, Dad."

He pulled the tie from around his neck, threw it on the bed, and then sat down next to it. He seemed tired, as if it hurt him to carry his head around. "My God," he said.

"I wish I could tell you why."

"You don't know?"

"I know, but I can't tell you."

"Why can't you tell me?"

"You wouldn't believe it."

"Try me."

I never even considered it. At that moment, if I had told him what I've told you, he would have put me out the window. I could see his frustration, could even understand it a little bit. I had never done anything to make him proud of me. I had only caused him one headache after another since the day I first opened my eyes.

"You wouldn't understand," I said.

"It's not politics, is it?"

"No."

"You're not against the war or anything?"

"Everybody is against the war."

"What am I going to tell your mother?" He unbuttoned his shirt, staring at the wall behind me as if there was a movie projected there.

"You think she *wants* me to get killed?"

He looked at me. "That wasn't fair."

"I know."

"If you say that to her, I'll never forgive you." He had his shirt off, and without taking his eyes off me, he placed it neatly over the tie. Behind him, I could see through the window—it was dark outside, fall, and the trees in our front yard were orange and red and yellow even in the dark. They looked as if they were lit up by something other than the moon.

"Where will you go?"

"Canada."

He got up, took his shirt and tie and threw them into the closet. Then he went into the bathroom. When he passed me, he said, "It will break your mother's heart."

"I'm sorry," I said.

Later, downstairs, I told my mother. Dad was upstairs doing something—I think he didn't want to be there when I told her.

"It will break your father's heart," she said.

"I already told him."

"Oh, my God."

"Dad said the same thing."

"Why?"

"He was shocked, I guess."

"Now stop it." Her face got that winter look on it. I didn't feel like her son anymore. I felt sort of like her nephew. "You know what I mean."

"I can't tell you why."

"You have a reason?"

"Yes."

"What is it?"

"I already served," I said. She blinked, put her long fingers in her hair.

"You're not funny."

"I can't really tell you," I said. "I don't feel right about this war."

"It's not your choice."

"I know, but it should be."

"You have a duty—"

"It isn't anything like that," I said, and I realized my voice had gotten loud. "I'm not doing this because I'm a pacifist, or anything else. I have a very good reason that I can't tell you."

"And that's it."

"Yes."

"You just announce you're not going, and that's it."

"Right."

"Your father will be heartbroken."

"I'm sorry," I said.

I was drafted in September, 1972. I had two weeks before I was supposed to report to the induction center in Chicago. We were getting out of the war by then, you may remember, but people were still getting sent home in silver caskets. I hated myself for hurting my parents so, and they walked around the house being heartbroken until the day I left for Canada: my mother threw my breakfast at me in the morning, and she didn't speak a word to me until the time came for her to throw my lunch at me. My father didn't want me to work in the store, and when he came home for dinner the three of us sat at the table chewing like a small pride of lions. I felt like one of the derelicts my father brought home those cold days in Chicago.

The last night I was home, my father came into my room carrying his best suitcase.

"You'll need this," he said.

"Thank you." I set it on the bed, began throwing some of my shirts into it.

"You going by bus or what?"

"I'm taking the train to Chicago, and then a bus from there."

"Will you write?"

"I'll call," I said.

He sat on the bed. "I considered turning you in."

"Why didn't you?"

"I guess I hoped you'd change your mind."

"Is this war important to you?"

He folded his hands in his lap, watched the fingers seem to play with each other. "It's important that my son do the right thing." He just didn't know. "Dad," I said. "There isn't any such thing as rightness."

"Yes, there is." He believed it so firmly he seemed shocked that I could say such a thing. I felt like I owed him at least one of the reasons I was fleeing to Canada.

"Do you believe there's goodness in the world, Dad?"

"Of course."

"Do you believe this war is good?"

"No."

"It's not good."

"Well, it's for a good—" he looked up at me. "I know what you're getting at. You're not going to get me to say the war is bad and you're good and therefore—"

"I don't want you to say that."

"The war's for a purpose."

"A purpose."

"Right."

"Dad, you just don't know," I said. I felt like I was going to cry. I knew I couldn't tell him—that he'd only be further disappointed in his only son. He would probably think either that I was disturbed, or that I had nothing but contempt for him and could tell him anything and expect him to believe it. I knew I was doing the right thing not to tell him, and so I guess I really did believe there were things that you could call right and things you could say were wrong.

"You aren't in trouble, are you?" He seemed so concerned when he asked me that, I wanted to hug him. Just kiss him on the cheek and tell him to trust me. But I stood there staring at him.

"I can't tell you."

He shook his head.

"I'm not in any trouble, Dad." I went to the closet, pretended to look for something in there. I was trying to hide the fact that I was beginning to cry.

"Are you ever coming back, son?" His voice shook.

"Yes," I said to the closet.

He got up, stood behind me. "Make sure you tell your mother that," he said. Then he walked silently out of the room. I stood there, staring at my coats, and slacks, and jackets, and boots, thinking of my first father—the life in that cabin, the gin, and the fights with Ogra, and the way his eyes looked when he died—and I didn't think I could get enough air to let my weeping out. To this day I can't think of that time without getting tears in my eyes.

If my father hadn't been so sensible all the time, if he'd dreamed out loud once in a while, I might have believed I could tell him. I knew he loved me—I think he still loves me—but I didn't know much else about him. He either wouldn't let me, or he couldn't let me. Or maybe after I knew who I was, I pulled away from him. I don't know. It wasn't much different with my mother. When I went out the door, my last day home, she hugged me as if she was dangling in space. I cried into her ear, said I was sorry. She never said a word. She hugged me like that until I thought she wouldn't let go, and then she took her arms away and stood there in front of me as if I'd just hit her.

"Goodbye," I said.

She nodded, put her hands behind her back.

When I closed the door, she was still standing there like that, her eyes filled to the brim with tears.

"God damn," I said to myself as I went on up the street. "God damn."

———

I stayed in Canada until the war ended. I lived alone, in an upstairs apartment on Silva Street in a little town called Barstow, near Toronto. There were a lot of Americans in that area, but I kept pretty much to myself. I had no interest in anything but living day to day and trying to remember every detail of my other lives. I was fortunate enough to get a job in a library—I stacked, shelved, and checked out books all day—so I could take the time to do research on the times of Ken Ezra and Jack Pitt. I got involved in family histories—tried to trace what happened to Sara and Ogra—but Canadian libraries have almost nothing in the way of American books. Mostly I read old newspapers. They had plenty of those.

I scanned the obituaries of all the Baltimore and Pittsburgh papers, from 1905 until 1950—I figured Sara would have had a hard time living much longer than that. I never found any mention of her, although there were a few Saras who died during that time. None of them sounded like my Sara, though, so I still don't know what happened to her. I knew I wouldn't find anybody named "Ogra" since I only made that name up.

I found the story of Ken Ezra's death, although the name wasn't mentioned. It was a big story—thirty-one people injured and fourteen dead. There was a photograph of the last man to let go. I wanted to grab somebody and tell them it was me. It was me.

I found no obituary for Jack Pitt in the Washington papers. I guess nobody let Mrs. Proudy know about it, and no one else in the city even knew who I was. Except for Father Burns, and nobody had any reason to tell him.

When I could find no further information, I started reading books on reincarnation. None of them were very convincing. Everybody seemed to think there is some mystery that only gets partially unraveled, if at all. One of the books said, "The subject is nearly always tormented."

So I was a subject. I wondered who I could ever tell all this to.

My father wrote to me regularly. He tried to be cheerful, but underneath all the chattery sentences I could hear his voice trembling. He signed all his letters, "Your father, no matter what."

I never got a letter from my mother. Every now and then, my father would say, "Your mother says to say hello." And when I wrote back to him, I always asked how she was and all. I knew she was so completely disappointed in me that she'd probably never be able to forgive me. After all, when she met my father he was in the army, doing his duty. For all she knew, it was some gene in her that made me a traitor to my country. I was her son the coward. Her strange child grew up and became a strange man.

The funny thing is, I was very homesick the whole time I was in Canada. I remembered how many times in the other lives I'd been alone and afraid and without comfort or warmth or affection. I had a nice apartment and all, but I wanted the room in my father's house. At least until I met a woman I could tell my story to, and who would believe me.

Maybe there isn't a woman like that in the world.

Also, I had a terrible time staying out of events. I ignored everybody and everything, but once in a while I would see something and act before I had time to think.

I remember once I was in the park near the center of Barstow, feeding the ducks out of a small bag of yellow popcorn. There were hundreds of ducks in that park, and they were used to eating such things as popcorn or cheese curls or Doritos. I didn't go there to feed them very often, but on this day I was bored and had nothing to do and wanted to think. I like to watch ducks eat when I'm thinking, I guess because they can't think and it's fun to watch them trying to eat more than I can give them. I used to think each kernel of corn was a new thought, and when my brain gave me an idea or something I was trying to remember, I'd give away another bit of corn.

One of the ducks, a small mallard with a knot in the middle of his head, wasn't getting anything because the other ducks were too large or too fast, and he wasn't very aggressive. I watched him for a time, saw him fail every attempt, and felt suddenly that it wasn't fair. I pushed the other ducks aside—they flapped their wings and squawked as if I had wounded them—and tried to give the little one all my corn. He ate as excitedly as the others had, defended his corn just as meanly, and it occurred to me that I had again involved myself in one of the world's events—even if it was a very small one. I let the other ducks back into the action and watched as the little one got shoved back to the edge of the pond.

I was in Canada, living the life of a recluse, for six years. I made no friends, and except for the thousands of patrons who checked out and returned books, and the few people I worked with, I had more contact with the ducks than I did with human beings. I believe I was happy.

My father kept me aware of the events in "our country," as he called it. He was very happy when the program for pardoning draft dodgers was approved. He thought I would come home right away, but I hesitated.

I knew going home would mean involvement with other human beings—if only because I would have to live, for a time at least, with my mother and father, and I knew that in spite of what I'd done, they loved me. And I suppose I loved them. In fact I still do. I hope I can make them believe that, once this is over. I never realized before all this how important their love is to me.

I stayed in Canada, even though my father said "our country" was ready to welcome me back. "You have been pardoned," he wrote. "All you have to do is come back here, turn yourself in, and serve two years in some sort of charitable service to the public. Is that too much to ask?"

I wrote back that I was not interested in doing any sort of work for the government or any other agency if I could help it. I couldn't explain to him that it was because I didn't want to have any contact with other human beings or any of the world's troubles—after all, he was the one who brought a derelict into our dining room, fed him, then gave him a brand-new overcoat. So I told my father I didn't think it was fair that I had to be "drafted" into service anyway—even if that service was peaceful. I told him I wanted to be free to go to school, or work any job I pleased.

I didn't hear from him for three months. I went about my solitary business, thinking it didn't matter if I ever heard from him again—I might have felt slightly bitter because of the pressure I

was getting from his silence. Finally I called him. I hadn't talked
to him in over a year—we didn't use the telephone very often while
I was in Canada, because it was expensive, and probably because
when we did talk we both spent a lot of time listening to the static
in the lines.

It was after eleven when I called, and my mother answered with
a rickety voice that told me she'd been sleeping.

"It's me," I said. "Sorry I woke you."

"Riley," she said. It was the only thing she ever managed to say
to me when I called. "Riley." Then she'd start crying.

"Mother."

"Oh, Riley."

"Mother, don't start crying."

"Riley."

"Is Dad around?"

"Riley, Riley," she sobbed.

"Is Dad—" I heard him take the phone from her.

"Is everything all right?"

"Yes," I said. "Tell her to stop crying."

"What's the matter?"

"I just wanted to talk."

"OK."

I listened to some distant ringing—some other long distance
conversation.

"Well?"

"I haven't heard from you," I said.

"I don't have anything more to say."

"So that's it?" I was beginning to think I was having the last
talk with my father; that if I said goodbye and hung up, I'd never
hear his voice again. Even after six years, I was still homesick.

"What do you want, son?"

"I don't know."

"You're there, and we're here."

"I know."

"The war's over. Nobody but your mother and I give a damn
that you missed it."

"I know."

"You could come home any time, if you wanted to."

"I don't know if I can do it, Dad."

"What's stopping you?"

"It's hard to explain."

"Are you in love with someone up there?"

"No."

"Look," he said. "I'm getting old. So is your mother. We're not going to be alive much longer—"

"Dad—"

"You're all we have." His voice trailed off. I could hear my mother crying in the background, and I was fairly certain that my father had joined her.

"I guess part of me wants to come home, or I wouldn't be so homesick all the time."

"We've done everything we could," he said, in a voice I didn't recognize. "I've talked to the draft registrar here—he's a personal friend of mine—"

"Everybody in that town is a personal friend of yours," I said.

He laughed, nervously, seemed to get his voice back. "Son, it's all arranged. You only have to come home."

"Maybe I will," I said.

"Well, don't take too long to think about it."

"OK," I said, but he was already gone.

So I came home. I packed my bags—I had only books and clothing—and boarded a bus for Chicago feeling like the only human being in the world.

I don't really know why I came home, except that my father seemed to want it so much, and I had spent the better part of three lives disappointing people. If I had stayed in Canada, none of this would have happened. I'd be a free man right now, and maybe that black woman would still be alive—although I doubt it. She looked so old for a woman under fifty. I still can't imagine what sort of life she must have had to end up in that hospital, a thin collection of brittle bones. All I know is, when I saw her it took all the air out of me, and left me sitting at the end of her bed, crying like a helpless infant. I knew I was going to be involved in one of the world's little dramas again, and it was because of my overwhelming desire to save her that I foolishly helped her to the end of her life.

•

THE EIGHTEENTH INTERVIEW

NOVEMBER 15, 1980

12:00 noon

One of the things I'll always regret about coming home—besides this mess—is the reaction I had to my father's greeting. When the taxi pulled up in front of the house, it was already dark. This was in October, last year. The sky was absolutely clear, and there was no moon. My father's house looked solid and warm in the darkness, and I remember thinking, "Yes, this is where I belong."

My father must have seen the lights of the cab, because before I could get my bags from the trunk, he was out of the house and coming down the driveway toward me with his arms open. He came right up to me, put his arms around my neck, and held me as if I was leaving and he was trying to stop me.

After I reached a certain age—somewhere in my teens—my father almost never hugged me. So when he put his arms around me like that, I was surprised and I think it must have shown in my face. Before I could reach up and hug him, he pulled back.

"Welcome home, Son," he said. He had tears in his eyes.

I was already wishing I had hugged him back. "I'm glad to be home," I said.

"Are those your things?" He didn't look at me.

"That's everything," I said. He shuffled his feet, stepped beside me to take my bags, and it hit me that I could grab him right then; just put my arms around him and hold him. So few people in the world had ever loved me.

But the moment was so awkward; he seemed so nervous and embarrassed, I only put my hand on his shoulder and said, "I can get those."

"Today," he said, "I carry the weight."

I followed him into the house, watching the back of his head with tears in my eyes. I knew I could never let him *really* know me.

My mother came over to me when I was inside the door, put her hand on the back of my neck, bent me over, and kissed me on the cheek. I felt as if I had kept an appointment or something.

"How was the trip?"

"Fine."

She seemed ready to cry. "I'm glad you decided to come home."

"Me too."

"God knows, I cried myself to sleep every night all these—"

"Myra," my father said.

"Every night," she said. She took her hand away, walked back to the center of the room, took a deep breath. "Well, why don't you take your bags to your room and then we'll talk."

"I'm very tired," I said.

"We can talk tomorrow," my father said.

I took my bags to the small bedroom off the den where I had spent most of my time in that house. My father came right behind me, smiling, his hands in his pockets now. He was much more relaxed, seemed genuinely happy.

"We painted it," he said.

"It looks nice."

He stood there in the door frame, watched me unpacking my things. When I had all my books out, he said, "You got a lot of those."

"Yes."

"You read them all?"

"Most of them."

I started on the clothing. Still, he watched me, as if he thought I might dissolve.

After a while, he said, "Your mother has had a hard time."

"She has?"

"She loves you, you know that."

"Sure."

"It's just that, well, she can't get used to the idea that you—"

"Refused to fight?"

ROBERT BAUSCH

"That you left your home and all."

"Everybody leaves home, eventually."

"I know that."

"You left home, so did she—"

"I'm not trying to pick a fight."

"Oh, I know," I said. I was telling the truth. I thought I might hug him then, let him know I was glad to see him. But he crossed his arms in front of his chest, leaned on the door frame.

"You get everything straightened out with the draft board tomorrow. I'll go with you. She'll feel better after you've begun your service."

"OK," I said.

"She only wants to be proud of you."

"I never made anybody proud," I said. "In this life or any other."

"I'm proud of you," he said, his voice trembling. I knew he really wasn't.

"I fished for that," I said.

"Well," he said. "You caught something."

I laughed, and he went back into the living room.

My father told me the truth when he said he had everything arranged. The day after I got home, he took me to the draft board on Neill Street, and introduced me to Mr. Pratt, the registrar. I filled out seven forms, signed all of them with my father as witness, and then Mr. Pratt gave me a referral form that introduced me to the doctors and nurses at the Crowell Clinic, Champaign's alcoholic rehabilitation center.

"You will work there for no less than two years," Pratt said, as if he were pronouncing a sentence. He grinned at my father as if I were a truant and he had caught me out of school.

"What if they don't hire me?"

"They'll hire you. We've worked it out so they take all our deserters."

"I'm not a deserter," I said.

"Well," he said. "Whatever."

"Is that all?" my father asked.

"That's it. You take that form over there and present yourself," he said to me, "and they'll put you to work."

"OK."

"Go anytime in the next two weeks. Your term starts from the first day of employment."

"Thank you," my father said. He seemed sort of sad, as if he'd just bailed me out of jail or something.

When we were outside, my father put his hand in his hair and said, "That was embarrassing."

"Why?"

"His son was killed over there."

"You'd feel better talking to him if that happened to me?"

"I'd feel better if you'd fought."

"But lived through it."

"I know," he smiled. "It's silly."

"The whole world is silly, Dad," I said.

We went and had lunch after we left the draft board. We sat in a McDonald's restaurant and ate cheeseburgers and french fries. We didn't talk much. Then near the end of our lunch, I looked at him and said, "They've got these restaurants in Canada."

He put his cheeseburger down and started crying.

"What's the matter?"

He waved his hand, stared out the window. The sun was bright outside and made clear avenues of dark and light in the room. The tears collecting in his eyes seemed lit up by the sun.

"Come on, Dad." I was embarrassed. Two dirty construction workers sat across from us, watched my father silently—as if they were in an audience and my father and I were on the stage.

"I'm sorry," my father said, wiping his face.

"I'm sorry too."

"It's just that—it's just—" He went off again, this time he sobbed loud enough for the people behind the counter to hear.

"You're going to have me crying," I said.

"I don't know what happened to you, Son."

"What?"

He wiped his eyes again. "You changed so much, since the—since—"

"Since when?"

"Since Joe killed himself."

"Oh," I said. I knew then that he was crying because he was ashamed of me. "I understand, Dad."

"Understand?"

"It wasn't Joe's death."

"What was it then?"

"Something happened after he died."

"What?"

"Joe's death made me think about a lot of things," I said. I thought I might tell him, might just blurt it out and see what happened. But the look on his face was so expectant I knew he thought he'd hear something that made sense; something logical and clear that would make him feel better. "Maybe Joe's death did have something to do with it."

"I thought so," he said. His face seemed to recover something. He wasn't crying any more.

"You didn't have anything to do with it, if that's what you're feeling bad about."

"I did the best I could."

"I know."

"Your mother, too."

"It was just something in my own head," I told him.

"Maybe we should have gotten help for you."

"Nothing anybody could have done," I said.

He tilted his head, sat back staring at me. I thought he was going to start crying again. Then he said, "Well, we can start over."

"Sure," I said.

"You can work hard at the clinic, and we'll get this behind us." He picked up his cheeseburger, took a small bite out of it. "This is cold now."

I watched him for a moment. Then I said, "You remember you

once told me that Joe couldn't get used to the idea that things just happened?"

He nodded, took another bite of his burger.

"Maybe that's my problem," I said. "Maybe I can't get used to the idea that I have no control over what happens to me."

"Nobody does, Son."

"That doesn't make it feel any better."

"You just have to go on with your life," he said. "There are some things you *can* control."

"I know." I cleaned up the papers in front of me.

"We'll get over this," my father said as we were getting up to leave. "We'll get over this. I know we will."

I wish he had been right. Now, he thinks I'm a murderer, and so does everybody else.

Things went well at the Crowell Clinic, for the first two years anyway. Up until last month. I worked there the same way I worked in the library when I was in Canada: I kept to myself, and went home when I got off work.

I thought the Crowell Clinic would be a hospital. It does have clean walls, rooms with beds and aluminum sinks, even doctors and nurses with thermometers and clipboards—but it isn't really a hospital. There's no emergency room, no surgery, no obstetrics unit. It's really a sort of rest home for people who've lost something in the head.

When I first reported there, I was met by a man named Carlton. He wore a white shirt and pants, but I wasn't sure if he was a doctor or not. He had thin brown hair, a short little nose that looked like an avocado seed, and wire-framed glasses that drooped down his cheeks. He took my papers out of the envelope I handed him, and told me to sit down.

"Another one from Pratt," he said.

"Yes, sir."

He sat behind a little table that was piled so high with papers

I could barely see his face. When he was finished looking at my referral form, he moved a stack of papers aside and looked at me.

"You know what we do here?"

"No, sir."

"We're trustees, here. Nothing more. People come here, the disease has already been diagnosed. We're caretakers."

"OK."

"The state pays for all this. The state thinks alcoholics are victims of disease the same as any other. So we've got all kinds here."

I didn't think he was a doctor, and as it turned out I was right. Mr. Carlton was the chief administrator of the Crowell Clinic. And he, like almost everyone else who worked there, hated his job.

He told me I was responsible for keeping rooms, beds, and when the nurses needed help, even patients, clean. I was to follow orders explicitly—and since my service was obligatory, I had no avenues for complaint or grievance.

"Of course," he said, "we will treat you fairly. Your shift will not change—barring any unforeseen emergency—without at least a week's notice."

"What is my shift?"

"You will start during the day—until you're fully trained— eight to five-thirty. When you've got the hang of things, it'll probably be seven to midnight, or midnight to seven in the morning."

"OK," I said.

Everybody ought to spend an hour or so at the Crowell Clinic. The walls are light green and the paint is cracking around all the edges and corners—as if people have been bumping furniture into them. The light switches are covered with aluminum plates, all the cabinets and sinks are aluminum. The floor is white tile, the beds are gray, and the sheets are yellow—a drab, urine-looking yellow. Above each bed is a square-shaped metal device with oxygen outlets, a water spigot, and an odd-looking pointed outlet that looks like one of those tools doctors use to look into ears or down throats. I never found out what that device is for—although I saw them pull the metal thing down and give people oxygen almost every day. The rooms are cluttered with metal chairs, moving tables, and I.V. stands. In each room, usually within reach of both beds, is a little yellow machine that makes beeping noises, even when it is not in use. I think it keeps track of heart rate and respiration.

All of the patients at the Crowell Clinic are technically alcoholic, although a lot of them have emphysema, Alzheimer's disease, uremia, and all sorts of liver diseases. Most of them are old. Not real old, like somebody's great grandfather or anything. Some of them have been under fifty. But all of them look as if they could be somebody's great grandfather.

"They're all just drunks," Carlton said that first day. "The guy who donated the money to build this place—Walter C. Crowell the third—donated the money in 1935 because his young wife died in an alcoholic stupor before she could bestow on him a Walter C. Crowell the fourth."

Carlton took me around, showed me the staff break area—the walls were green in there too, and so were the ashtrays—the lounge where patients could play cards or read magazines or stare out the window at the trees, buildings, parking lots, and signs that surrounded the hospital. He showed me the green room—I don't know why it was called that, since the walls in there were the same drab green color as the walls in all the other rooms. The green room is important, though.

"When you have an expired patient, you bring him here," Carlton said. There was a curious glint in his eye—I thought he might begin to laugh.

"An expired patient."

"Right. That's one of your duties." He winked.

"OK," I said.

"You ever seen a stiff?"

I wanted to say, "I've made a man into one of those, and I've been one myself—twice." I reached up, pulled on my collar, though, and only said, "I know about death."

He opened the door, motioned for me to follow him in. There were two tables in the room, with huge gray light fixtures over them. The only nongreen wall was lined with great aluminum drawers. I knew what those were for.

"Looks like a morgue, doesn't it?" Carlton said.

"A lot of people must die here."

"No—not really," he said. "It's just that a lot of them stay here a long time before anybody claims them—so we need some way to keep them fresh."

I stared at one of the lights, tried to keep my memory from giving me death. I was beginning to think I should have let the army take me.

"We get a lot of derelicts in here," said Carlton. "People completely alone in the world, it seems. Takes a long time to be sure there aren't any relatives around."

"What happens to them if they're alone?"

"The state buries them."

"Oh."

"Just like taking out the trash. No ceremony. No prayers. No nothing."

"That's real sad."

"We try to find out about family and all, when they first come to the hospital. But a lot of them can't talk any more. And those that can—" He shook his head. "Hell, you can't believe what an alkie says to you."

"Guess not."

"You drink?"

"No." I did drink a beer every now and then, but I didn't want to tell him that. He looked as if he was going to lecture me.

"Me neither. I worked here one day, the first day, and haven't had a drop since." He moved toward the door. "We don't have a body in here now, so there's nothing more to see."

I was very happy to hear that.

I hated the little yellow machine that monitored the heart and respiration. I couldn't find a place in the hospital where I didn't hear the incessant beeping of those little machines. And the oxygen supply was always on, so it sounded like somebody left a water spigot wide open. I still hear those sounds in my dreams. It was the only thing I couldn't get used to.

I was standing in the lobby, where the sound of the heart monitor and the oxygen supply was the thinnest, when they brought the black woman in. I was leaning on a broom, and two men in gray suits wheeled her in as if they had just plucked her out of the city's sanitary landfill—a tragic discovery in among the beaten couches, worn out kitchen cabinets, and broken TV sets. I watched them bump her cart into the admitting desk, saw her tiny, thin body shake. She looked like something that ought to rattle.

"Is she alive?" the admitting nurse said.

"Just barely."

The nurse was a short, muscular woman called Beth. She almost never spoke to me, except to give orders. I thought she hated me because her brother was killed in Viet Nam, and she knew what sort of "soldier" I was. But when I asked Carlton about it, he told me she never talked to anybody.

"She's all business," he said. "That's why I like her."

"I guess I wouldn't blame her for hating me."

"Just do what she tells you. Around here, anybody dressed in white is your boss."

On that night they brought the black woman in, Beth tried to talk to her—tried to fill out the proper forms by leaning over the top of the desk to talk to the pile of bones on the high bed with wheels.

"I can't understand what you're saying," Beth whispered. She looked at one of the men in gray, a bald man with a full brown beard.

"Found her in front of the bowling alley," he said.

"How old would you say she is?"

"Eighty."

Beth laughed. "Seriously."

"Late forties, early fifties."

"Hard to tell." Beth leaned closer to the bed. "Can you hear me, honey?"

The bones moved slightly.

"How old are you?" Beth pulled the cart around so that it was parallel to the desk, then leaned down and stared into the small face on the pillow. "Do we have permission to treat you?"

There was a slight sound that seemed to come from a place high in the room.

"I don't want to repeat what I think she said," Beth laughed. Then she looked at me. "Third floor. Leave her in the hall until I assign her a room."

I moved the bed back away from the desk, started to push it down the hall to the elevators, when the black woman raised her head and opened her eyes.

"What?" she said. Her tongue was thick and white, seemed to stick to her lips. I looked at her face, watched her eyes roll back into her head. Then she let her head back slowly onto the pillow —as if she expected it to explode.

"She's gone," Beth said. "Take her up."

"What's her name?" I asked.

"Who knows? She's a Jane Doe."

"I wonder how people get like that."

"They drink," Beth said. "Take her up."

While I was on the elevator with Jane Doe, she woke up again. This time her eyes moved around and fixed on me.

"Hello," I said.

She blinked, and I thought I saw something in her irises—a movement, or a point of light—that froze my blood. It was a thing my mind wanted to remember.

"Damn," I said out loud. Things like that were always happening to me. I stared at the signs on the elevator wall that said "Inspection certificates in Engineer's office," and "In case of fire do not use elevators, use stairwells." I felt her eyes on me, but I was afraid to look at her.

When we reached the third floor, I pushed her bed out into the hall, moved it over against the wall, and was turning to leave when Jane Doe said, in a deep, thick, lost voice, "Jack."

I couldn't breathe or move. I saw her looking at me, felt my heart swell up like a thin balloon. I stood there, at the foot of the bed, and listened to her breathing. I tried not to think. I don't know how long I waited there.

Then I found myself moving around the bed. I leaned down, close to her face, tried to see into her half-closed eyes.

"Etta," I said. "Is that you?"

•

THE LAST INTERVIEW

NOVEMBER 16, 1980

9:00 A.M.

You can imagine how I felt. I waited there by her side, telling myself that I really was crazy. I didn't quite believe it yet. When I spoke to her, she smiled slightly, then closed her eyes completely, and I sat there at the foot of her bed and cried like a man discovering tears for the first time.

Beth came up behind me. "What's the matter?"

"Nothing." I wiped my nose, stood up as if Beth were a sergeant and she'd just called me to attention.

"Take her to room 317," Beth said.

I pushed the bed down the hall, my hands trembling so badly I thought I could see the black woman's body register each tremor. When I had her in a stationary bed, Beth came up behind me.

"Take the stretcher back."

I just stood there, staring at Jane Doe.

"Go on," Beth said.

"I know her."

"You do?"

"Her name is Etta. I mean it *was* Etta."

"She changed it?"

"I don't know what her name is now."

"Get out of here, Riley."

"She spoke to me," I said.

"She didn't give you permission to treat her, did she?"

"You can't treat her?"

"All we can do is dry her out."

"Do you have—can you tell what's wrong with her?"

"From the looks of her, just about everything."

"God," I said.

"Where do you know her from?" There were windows on the

other side of Jane Doe's bed, and Beth stood in front of them, only a shadow above the body under the yellow sheets.

"A long time ago," I said.

"What happened to her?"

I didn't know what to say. I shrugged my shoulders. "She didn't have any luck."

"Well, take that cart back," Beth said.

I went home that night feeling strangely happy.

It's hard to describe the mixture of emotions I felt when I got home. There was my mother, in the living room, her brown hair in curlers, standing over a washbasket full of freshly dried clothes (she folded everything, including underwear).

"What are you doing up so late?" I said.

"Couldn't sleep."

I had worked the seven to midnight shift for nearly the entire year, and I don't think my mother was awake when I got home more than once or twice the whole time. I thought it was an extraordinary coincidence that the day Etta came back to me—if Jane Doe really *was* Etta; I still had trouble letting myself believe that—my mother decided to wait up for me.

"Did you want to talk?" I asked.

"No—I really couldn't sleep."

My mother tried, for that whole year, to "get over" what I had done. She told her friends she was trying to help me "get back to normal." She thought she could smooth out the terrible problems of my life as if they were only wrinkles in a bedspread. Most of the time I felt sorry for her. But on this night, I felt as close to her as I ever did. I can't say why—except that I believed if the black woman really *was* Etta, I would finally be able to explain everything to my parents. They would finally understand why I had no friends, and why I ignored everything the world had to offer except my job and food and sleep. They would know why I had been such a strange child. I even thought they might be proud of me when they learned that I had already served my country—twice.

I went into the kitchen and got a beer.

"Want something to eat?" my mother said.

"I feel like I want to celebrate."

"Why?"

"Something happened tonight."

She put down a towel, looked at me with a half smile on her face. "Did you meet someone?"

"No." I took a long sip of the beer.

"Well, what?"

"I can't tell you, yet."

She sat on the couch, let out a breath of air. "Why did you bring it up then?"

"I'm feeling very good."

"You don't look too good."

"Where's Dad?"

"Making pig noises upstairs."

"Is that why you can't sleep?"

"No." She looked at the floor, her face so sad she might have been viewing the body of a loved one there. "Not really."

"Why then?"

"I've been worried about you."

"I'm going to be all right." I took another gulp of beer.

"I'm so afraid you're going to end up on drugs, or an old man like those bums your father used to drag in here."

"I'm not even twenty-five yet."

"You don't—your whole life is—empty." I thought she was going to cry.

"I never wanted to be involved in anything."

"That's the trouble—you—"

"Maybe soon I'll be able to explain it all to you."

She threw her hands up, let them slap onto her knees. "Maybe soon," she said.

"Sooner than you think." I finished my beer, threw the can into the basket of clothes.

"Hey!" She picked it out and threw it back to me.

"See," I laughed. "I can surprise you, sometimes."

"Go to bed," she said.

I knelt on the floor in front of her. "I will explain it to you soon."

"Soon."

"Believe me, Mom," I said. I thought I was going to cry again. "Soon you'll know all of it."

I can't explain the elation building in me. I just knew something would happen that, once and for all, would free me from having to be *only* Riley Chance. I just knew I would be allowed, finally, to explain to my mother and father why I had been such a disappointment to them. And I wanted so much to talk to Etta.

I had no idea I'd end up telling you about it in a jail cell.

———————

The next night I went right to Jane Doe's room. She was asleep, lying on her back as if she was already dead. Her thin, black arms were outside the covers, resting next to her body like dead branches. Her hair was stiff and gray, and she looked like a prisoner of war all trussed up in that yellow bed. The room was warm and smelled of pine.

I approached the bed, almost afraid she would wake up.

"Etta," I whispered. She didn't move. "Etta, it's me."

The streetlights outside made shadows on the wall above her bed; one of the shadows looked like a great hand pointing down at her. She moved her head slightly, opened her eyes. She was already crying.

"I don't want to die in a hospital again," she said.

"Etta, look. It's Jack."

She looked at me, smiled. There were still tears in her eyes, but now light seemed to play around the irises. "Save me, Jack."

"How?"

"I want to see something good, something growing, outside."

"It's dark."

"I want to see something growing." Her voice seemed to come from a great distance.

I sat on the bed, placed my hand on her forehead. She looked right through me. I started crying again, felt her touch me with a bony hand.

"It's all so terrible," I said.

She frowned, then blinked slowly, a smile returning to her face. I saw the skin on her face give way—as if something palpable had dissolved. "It's all we have, Jack."

"I hate it."

"Jack," she said.

Then I put my head on her breast, felt her hand on the back of my neck. I listened to her breathing, and remembered all those gray nights in Washington, D. C., when Etta held me and loved me and made my life something fine. Something wonderful.

When I felt her hand on the back of my neck, heard her breathing, I stopped thinking. It was like I was on that rope again, suspended above the world. Here was Etta, asking me to save her.

So that's why I picked her up and carried her out of there. I was going to take her someplace where she could look at a tree, or a hedge, or maybe even a child. In the back of my mind I thought I might even take her home, tell my parents about her. Save her from this death.

But Etta couldn't make it. She was light, only a handful of sticks. When I had her in my arms, she looked into my eyes, a slight frown on her face—as if she couldn't believe it was really me. Then she smiled again; a peaceful smile with slowly blinking eyes.

I walked down the corridor with her, thinking at last I was doing something good. She looked at me the whole way with those eyes. We were in the taxi, and I didn't know where to take her. We went down Neill Street, and the lights of the city invaded the cab in rapid intervals, so I could see Etta's eyes, then I couldn't see them, then I could see them again. She tried to hold the smile.

I held her hand, felt the bones.

"You're going to have to make up your mind, Mac," the cabbie said.

"I want to go where there are some trees."

"Trees?"

"Not just any trees. I want evergreens."

"You crazy?"

"Do you know where some pine trees are?"

"They got them all around the assembly hall," he said. "I don't know why you—"

"Take us there."

I heard Etta make a gurgling noise, and I knew death was beginning. "Hurry up," I said.

The cabbie shook his head, but the cab speeded up, and I watched Etta's face appearing and disappearing in the passing lights. Finally I saw the assembly hall, looming like a huge flying saucer in the distance. The place was all lit up, and the field in front of it was crowded with tiny pine trees.

"Must be something going on tonight," the cabbie said.

"Stop the cab up there," I said, pointing to the entrance where the trees seemed larger and healthier.

"Etta," I said. "We're here. We're here."

She tried to sit up, but her arms wouldn't hold her. I put my hands under her head, lifted her up gently, and she turned her face to the window.

"Pine trees," she said.

I couldn't stop crying. "I love pine trees, Etta."

"Always green," she whispered.

"I love you, too, Etta. I love you."

I don't know if she heard me. She died without saying anything. I sat there, held her head in my arms, and tried to stop crying while the cab driver drove to the police station. We were such a strange and quiet hearse. I had no idea he thought I'd choked her to death. When the police came out to arrest me, I was just holding her, rocking back and forth, whispering her name.

Maybe you can't get living right. Maybe it's only a little love you need to keep you from fever and fret. I don't know. Etta said it's all we have. Maybe there's no use expecting anything more.

Etta came back to me. She touched me with her hand. I listened to her breathing once again, held her against me. I got her out of that hospital and helped her see something she loved before she died. I have that. I have that.

Nobody loses all the time.